D0051898

As if she'd stepped from a dream ...

Raising a hand, she touched her fingers to her lips, gently, wonderingly. She could still feel the lingering warmth, the knowing pressure.

Who was he? She wished she'd been bold enough to ask. Then again, perhaps it was better she didn't know. Nothing, after all, could come of such a meeting—from the intangible promise in a kiss ...

STEPHANIE LAURENS

The Promise In A Kiss

AVON BOOKS

An Imprint of HarperCollinsPublishers

This is a work of fiction. Names, characters, places, and incidents are products of the author's imagination or are used fictitiously and are not to be construed as real. Any resemblance to actual events, locales, organizations, or persons, living or dead, is entirely coincidental.

AVON BOOKS
An Imprint of HarperCollins*Publishers*
10 East 53rd Street
New York, New York 10022-5299

First Avon Books paperback printing: November 2002
First William Morrow hardcover printing: December 2001

Avon Trademark Reg. U.S. Pat. Off. and in Other Countries, Marca Registrada, Hecho en U.S.A.
HarperCollins ® is a trademark of HarperCollins Publishers Inc.

Printed in the U.S.A.

10 9 8 7 6 5 4 3 2 1

To
Keith, Stefanie, and Lauren
&
Nancy, Lucia, and Carrie
&
"The Lunch Mob"

for the past, the present, and the future

The Promise
In A Kiss

The Bar Cynster

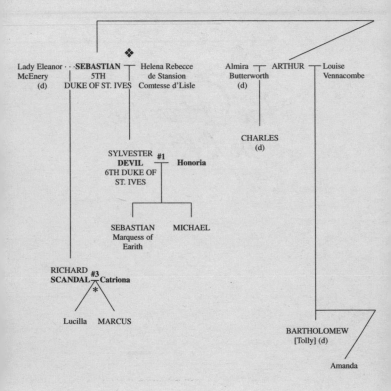

Lady Eleanor··· **SEBASTIAN** ┬ Helena Rebecce   Almira ┬ ARTHUR ┬ Louise
McEnery   5TH   de Stansion   Butterworth   Vennacombe
   (d)   DUKE OF ST. IVES   Comtesse d'Lisle   (d)

                                                CHARLES
                                                  (d)

          SYLVESTER
           DEVIL #1 **Honoria**
          6TH DUKE OF
            ST. IVES

          SEBASTIAN   MICHAEL
          Marquess of
            Earith

RICHARD
SCANDAL #3 **Catriona**
         *

Lucilla   MARCUS

                                                BARTHOLOMEW
                                                 [Tolly] (d)

                                                        Amanda

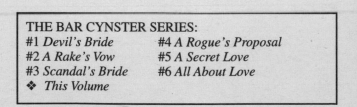

Family Tree

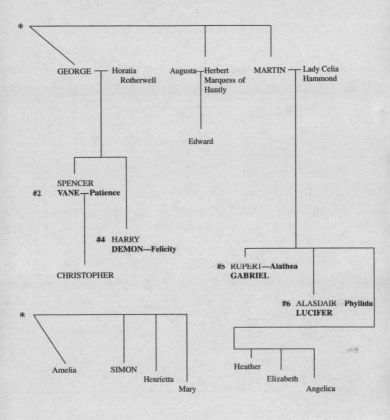

MALE Cynsters in capitals   * denotes twins

Prologue

Midnight had come and gone. Helena heard the small bell of the church chime as she paused in the doorway of the infirmary. Three o'clock. Ariele, her younger sister, was at last sleeping deeply; her fever had broken—she would be safe enough in Sister Artemis's care. Reassured, relieved, Helena could again seek her own bed in the dormitory beyond the cloisters.

Drawing her woolen shawl about her shoulders, she stepped out from the shadows of the infirmary wing. Her wooden pattens clacked softly on the stone flags as she crossed through the gardens filling the convent's grounds. The night was icy, clear. She was wearing only her nightgown and robe—she'd been asleep when the night sister had summoned her to help with Ariele. Common sense urged her to hurry—her shawl was not that warm—yet she walked slowly, comfortable in the moon-drenched gardens, confident in this place where she'd spent most of the last nine years.

Soon, as soon as Ariele was well enough to travel, she would leave forever. She'd celebrated her sixteenth birthday three months ago; her future lay before her— an introduction into society followed by marriage, an arranged union with some wealthy aristocrat. That was the way of her class. As the comtesse d'Lisle, with extensive estates in the Camargue and connected to the powerful de Mordaunts among others, her hand would be a sought-after prize.

The branches of a huge linden threw deep shadows across the path. Passing through them, stepping once again into the silvery light, she stopped, lifted her face to the infinite sky. Drank in the peace. So close to the Lord's fete day, the convent was empty, the daughters of the wealthy already at home for the season's celebrations. She and Ariele were still here only because of Ariele's weak chest; she'd refused to leave until her sister could travel with her. Ariele and most of the others would return again in February, and their lessons would recommence. Until then . . .

Peace lay heavy on the silver-tipped bushes, shimmered in the moonlight pouring from the cloudless sky. Stars twinkled overhead, diamonds strewn across night's velvet shroud. The stone cloisters stood before her, a familiar, comforting sight.

She wasn't sure what awaited her outside the convent's walls. Helena breathed deeply, ignoring the chill, savoring the sweetness of the last days of her girlhood. *The last days of freedom.*

Dry leaves rustled in the night. She looked to where she knew an old creeper, gnarled and ancient, hugged the high wall of the dormitory, just ahead to her left. The wall was in shadow, dark and impenetrable. She narrowed her eyes, trying to pierce the gloom, unafraid, even at this hour; the convent had a zealously guarded reputation for security, which was why so many noble families sent their daughters there.

She heard a muted thud, then another, then, in a flurry of thumps, a body slid and tumbled from high on the wall, missing the edge of the cloister roof to land, sprawled, at her feet.

Helena stared. It didn't occur to her to shriek. Why shriek? The man—a very tall, broad-shouldered man—was unquestionably a gentleman. Even in the uncertain moonlight she could make out the sheen of his silk coat, the gleam of a jewel in the lace at his throat. Another, bigger gleam adorned one finger of the hand he slowly raised to push back the locks that had pulled free of his queue to fall across his chiseled features.

He lay as he'd landed, half propped on his elbows. The position displayed his chest to advantage. His hips were narrow, his legs long, with well-muscled thighs clearly delineated under satin knee breeches. He was lean and large—his feet were, too, encased in black pumps with gold buckles. The heels were not high, confirming her guess he had no need to add to his height.

Although he'd landed on the stone path, he'd managed to slow his fall. Other than a few bruises, she doubted he'd hurt himself. He didn't look hurt—he looked aggravated, disenchanted. But wary, too.

He was watching her intently. Doubtless waiting for her to scream.

He could wait. She hadn't finished looking.

Sebastian felt as if he'd fallen into a fairy tale. Fallen at the feet of an enchanted princess. It was her fault he'd fallen—he'd looked down, searching for his next foothold, and seen her step from the shadows. She'd lifted her face to the moonlight, he'd stared, forgotten what he was doing, and slipped.

His coat had fallen open; beneath the thrown-back flap, he shifted his hand, fingers searching the folds. He located the earring he'd come there to get, still safe in his pocket.

Fabien de Mordaunt's family dagger was now his.

Another wild wager, another crazy exploit to add to his tally—another victory.

And an unexpected encounter.

Some deeply buried instinct, long dormant, raised its head—recognized the moment, paid it due heed. The girl—she was surely no more than that—stood watching him calmly, studying him with an assurance that shouted her station more surely than the fine lace at the neck of her demure night rail. She had to be one of the convent's highborn charges, still here for some reason.

Slowly, as smoothly as he could, he got to his feet. *"Mille pardons, mademoiselle."*

He saw one dark, finely arched brow quirk; her lips, full but unfashionably wide, relaxed fractionally. Her hair, unrestrained, cascaded about her shoulders, wavy locks dead black in the moonlight.

"I didn't mean to frighten you."

She didn't look frightened; she looked like the princess he'd thought her, supremely assured, faintly amused. He straightened to his full height, but slowly. She was a small woman; he towered over her—her head didn't reach his chin.

She looked up at him. The moon lit her face. There was no trace of concern in her pale eyes, large under their hooded lids. Her long lashes laid a faint tracery of shadows over her cheeks. Her nose was straight, patrician; her features confirmed her birth, her likely station.

Her attitude was one of calm expectation. He should, he supposed, introduce himself.

"Diable! Le fou—"

He whirled. A clamor of voices spilled into the night, shattering the stillness. Flares sprang to life at the end of the cloister.

He stepped off the path, sliding into the shadow of a large bush. The princess could still see him, but he was hidden from the noisy crowd hurrying up the path. She could point him out in an instant, direct the guards his way . . .

Helena watched a bevy of nuns approach at a run, habits flapping wildly. Two gardeners were with them, both brandishing pitchforks.

They saw her.

"M'amzelle—have you seen him?" Sister Agatha skidded to a halt at the end of the cloisters.

"Seen a man." Mother Superior, already out of breath, struggled to preserve her dignity. "The comte de Vichesse sent a warning about a madman intent on meeting with Mlle Marchand . . . and that silly, *stupid* girl—" Even in the dark, the Mother Superior's eyes flashed. "The man's been here—I'm sure of it! He must have climbed down the wall. Did he pass you? Did you glimpse him?"

Eyes wide, Helena turned her head to the right, away from the figure concealed by the bush. She looked toward the main gates, raised a hand . . .

"The gates! Quick—if we hurry, we'll have him!"

The group charged off through the cloisters and plunged into the gardens beyond, fanning out, calling, beating the borders lining the drive, searching frantically—more like the mythical madman they sought than the man who had fallen at her feet.

Silence returned; the shouts and yells faded into the night. Rewrapping her shawl, refolding her arms, she turned to see the gentleman step from the shadows.

"My thanks, mademoiselle. I am not, needless to say, a madman."

His deep voice, his cultured diction reassured her more than his words. Helena glanced at the wall from which he'd fallen. Collette Marchand had left the convent the year before but had been returned to its safety two days ago by her incensed relatives, there to await her brother who would come to fetch her away to the country. Collette's behavior in the Paris salons had, it was rumored, caused quite a stir. Helena looked at the stranger, prowling nearer. "What manner of man are you, then?"

His lips, long, somewhat thin, fascinatingly mobile, quirked as he halted before her. "An Englishman."

She would never have guessed from his speech—he spoke with no discernible accent. The revelation did, however, explain much. She'd heard that the English were often large, and quite mad, wild beyond even Parisians' lax standards.

She'd never met one before.

The fact was clearly written in her expression, in those hauntingly lovely pale eyes. In the silvery light, Sebastian couldn't tell if they were blue, gray or green. And regretted that he couldn't dally to find out. Raising a hand, with the back of one finger he traced the upward line of her cheek. "Again, mademoiselle, my thanks."

He tensed to step away, told himself he should, that he must. Yet still he hesitated.

Something shimmered in the gloom—he glanced up. Just behind her, a clump of mistletoe hung from one of the linden's branches.

It was almost Christmas.

She looked up, following his gaze. Considered the trailing mistletoe. Then her gaze slowly lowered, to his eyes, to his lips.

Her face was that of a French madonna—not Parisian but more dramatic, more vital. Sebastian felt a tug more primal than any he'd felt before. He lowered his head.

Slowly. He gave her plenty of time to step back if she would.

She didn't. She tipped up her face.

His lips touched hers, then settled in the most chaste kiss of his life. He felt her lips quiver under his, sensed her innocence in his bones.

Thank you. That was all the kiss said, all he allowed it to say.

He lifted his head yet still didn't draw back. Couldn't bring himself to do it. Their gazes met, their breaths mingled . . .

He bent his head again.

Her lips met his this time, soft, generous, hesitant. The urge to devour was strong, but he reined it in, took only what she innocently offered, and returned no more than that. An exchange—a promise—even though he recognized the impossibility, and was sure she did, too.

Ending the kiss took effort and left him slightly dazed. He could feel her warmth along his body even though he hadn't touched her. He forced himself to step back, to look up, draw breath.

His gaze touched the mistletoe. On impulse, he reached up and snapped one trailing tendril—the feel of the twig between his fingers gave him something real, something of this world, to cling to.

He took another step back before letting his gaze meet hers. Then he saluted her with the twig, inclined his head. *"Joyeux Noël."*

He kept moving back, forcing his gaze past her to the main gates over which he'd entered.

"Go that way."

Her blood pounding in her ears, her head oddly dizzy, Helena waved him farther back, in the opposite direction to the main gates. "When you reach the wall, follow it away from the convent. You'll find a wooden gate. I don't know if it's unlocked or . . ." She shrugged. "It's the way girls go when they sneak outside. It gives onto a lane."

The Englishman looked at her, studied her, then again inclined his head; his hand had shifted to his pocket, slipping the twig into its depths. His gaze remained on her as he stated, *"Au revoir, mademoiselle."*

Then he turned and melted into the darkness.

In less than a minute she could no longer see or hear him. Hugging her shawl more tightly about her, Helena drew in a breath, held it—tried to hold in the magic that had embraced them—then, reluctantly, walked on.

As if she'd stepped from a dream, the cold she hadn't noticed cut through her gown; she shivered and walked faster. Raising a hand, she touched her fingers to her lips, gently, wonderingly. She could still feel the lingering warmth, the knowing pressure.

Who was he? She wished she'd been bold enough to ask. Then again, perhaps it was better she didn't know. Nothing, after all, could come of such a meeting—from the intangible promise in a kiss.

Why had he been here? No doubt she would learn from Collette in the morning. But a madman?

She smiled cynically. She would never trust anything the comte de Vichesse might say. And if the Englishman was in some way engaged in tweaking her guardian's nose, she was only too happy to have helped.

Chapter One

Collette had refused to divulge his name, her mad Englishman, yet there he stood, long, lean, and as handsome as ever, albeit seven years older. Surrounded by fashionable conversation, on her way from one group to the next, Helena halted, transfixed.

About her, Lady Morpleth's soirée was in full spate. It was mid-November, and the ton had turned their collective mind to the festive season. Holly abounded; the scent from evergreen boughs filled the air. In France, the approach to *la nuit de Noël* had long been another excuse for extravagance. Although the ties between London and Paris were slackening, in this, London still concurred; for glitter, for glamour, for richness and splendor, the ton's entertainments rivaled those of the French court. In terms of honest cheer, they excelled, for here there was no threat of social unrest, no *canaille* gathering in the shadows beyond the walls.

Here, those wellborn and wealthy enough to belong to the elite could laugh, smile, and freely enjoy the whirl of activities filling the weeks leading to the celebration of the Nativity.

The smaller room into which Helena had ventured was crowded; as she stood staring into the main salon, the incessant chatter faded from her mind.

Framed by a connecting archway, he—the wild Englishman who had been the first ever to kiss her—paused to chat to some lady. A subtle smile curved his lips, still thin, still indolently mobile. Helena remembered how they'd felt on hers.

Seven years.

Her gaze raced over him. She hadn't seen him well enough in the gardens of the convent to catalog any changes, yet he still moved with the prowling grace she remembered, surprising in one so large. Devoid of powder and patches, the planes of his pale face seemed harder, more austere. His hair, now she could see its color, was a honey-toned brown, wavy locks drawn back in a queue secured with a black ribbon.

He was dressed with understated richness. Every garment bore the subtle stamp of a master, from the froth of expensive Mechlin lace at his throat, the abundant fall of the same lace over his long hands, to the exquisite cut of his silver-gray coat and darker gray breeches. Others would have had the coat trimmed with lace or braid. He had left it unadorned but for its big silver buttons. His waistcoat, darker gray heavily embroidered with silver, glimpsed as he moved, combined with the coat to create the impression of sleekly luxurious packaging concealing a prize even more sinfully rich.

In the salon crammed with lace, feathers, braids, and jewels, he dominated, and not just because of his height.

If the last seven years had left any mark at all, it was in his presence—that indefinable aura that clung to powerful men. He'd grown more powerful, more arrogant, more ruthless. The same seven years had made her an expert; power was, to her, as blatant as the color of skin.

Fabien de Mordaunt, comte de Vichesse, the aristocrat who'd exploited various family connections to have himself declared her guardian, exuded the same aura. The last seven years had left her both weary and wary of powerful men.

"*Eh, bien*. How goes it, *ma cousine*?"

Helena turned; she nodded coldly. "*Bon soir*, Louis." He wasn't her cousin, not even distantly related; she refrained from haughtily reminding him of the fact. Louis was less than nothing; he was her keeper, no more than an extension of his uncle and master, Fabien de Mordaunt.

She could ignore Louis. Fabien she'd learned never to forget.

Louis's dark eyes were roving the room. "There are some likely prospects here." He leaned his powdered head closer to murmur, "I've heard there's an English duke present. Unmarried. St. Ives. You would do well to garner an introduction."

Helena raised her brows faintly and glanced about

the salon. A duke? Louis did have his uses. He was devoted to his uncle's schemes, and in this instance she and Fabien were pursuing the same agenda, albeit for different reasons.

For the past seven years—almost from the time the Englishman had kissed her—Fabien had used her as a pawn in his games. Her hand was a prize much sought after by the powerful and wealthy families of France; she'd been *almost* betrothed more times than she could recall. But the volatility of the French state and the vicissitudes in the fortunes of the aristocratic families, so dependent on the king's whims, had meant cementing an alliance through her marriage had never been an option sufficiently attractive to Fabien. More attractive had been the game of dangling her fortune and person as a lure to draw those with influence into his net. Once he'd gained from them all he wanted, he would cast them out and again send her into the Paris salons to catch the attention of his next conquest.

How long the game would have gone on she dreaded to think—until she was too gray to be a lure? Luckily, at least for her, the increasing disaffection in France, the groundswell of discontent, had given Fabien pause. A natural predator, his instincts were sound—he didn't like the scent on the wind. She'd been certain he was considering a shift in his tactics even before the attempt to kidnap her.

That had been frightening. Even now, standing beside Louis in the middle of a fashionable salon in a different country, she had to fight to quell a shiver. She'd been walking in the orchards of Le Roc, Fabien's fortress in the Loire, when three men had ridden up and tried to take her.

They must have been watching, biding their time. She'd fought, struggled—to no avail. They would have kidnapped her if it hadn't been for Fabien. He'd been riding past, had heard her screams and come galloping to her aid.

She might rail against Fabien's hold over her, but he protected what he regarded as his. At thirty-nine, he was still in his prime. One man had died; the other two had fled. Fabien had chased them, but they'd escaped.

That evening she and Fabien had discussed her future. Every minute of that private interview was engraved in her memory. Fabien had informed her the men had been hirelings of the Rouchefoulds. Like Fabien, the most powerful intrigants knew that a storm was coming; each family, each powerful man, was intent on seizing all estates, titles, and alliances they could. The more they built their power, the more likely they would be to weather the storm.

She'd become a target. Not just for the Rouchefoulds. *"I have received strongly worded requests for your hand from all four of the major families. All four."* Fabien had fixed his dark eyes on her. *"As you perceive, I am not* aux anges. *All four constitutes an unwelcome problem."*

A problem indeed, one fraught with risk. Fabien did not want to choose, to commit her fortune and by inference his support to any of the four. Favor one and the other three would slit his throat at the first opportunity. Metaphorically, definitely; possibly literally. All that, she'd understood; the observation that Fabien's manipulative schemes had come home to roost with a vengeance she had kept to herself.

"It is no longer an option to approve an alliance for you inside France, yet the pressure to bestow your hand will only increase." Fabien had eyed her thoughtfully, then continued in his silken purr, *"I am therefore of a mind to leave this now-unsatisfactory arena and move to potentially more productive fields."*

She'd blinked at him. He'd smiled, more to himself than her.

"In these troubling times it would, I feel, be in the best interests of the family to develop stronger connections with our distant relatives across the Channel."

"You wish me to marry an émigré?" She'd been shocked. Émigrés were generally of low social standing, those with no estates.

A frown had flitted through Fabien's eyes. *"No. I meant that if you were to attract the attentions of an English nobleman, one of station and estates equal to your own, it would provide not only a solution to our present dilemma but also a valuable connection against the uncertain future."*

She'd continued to stare, stunned, surprised, her mind racing.

Misinterpreting her silence, Fabien had drawled, *"Pray recall that the English nobility is largely if not exclusively composed of families descended from William. You might be forced to learn their ghastly language, but all of any consequence speak French and ape our ways. It would not be so uncivilized as to be insupportable."*

"I already know the language." It had been all she could

think of to say, as a vista she'd never thought to see had opened before her. Escape. *Freedom*.

Seven years of dealing with Fabien had taught her well. She had held her excitement in, kept it from her expression, her eyes. She'd refocused on him. *"You are saying you wish me to go to London and seek an alliance with an Englishman?"*

"Not any Englishman—one of station and estates at least equal to your own. In their terms, an earl, marquess, or duke, with considerable wealth. I need hardly remind you of your worth."

All her life she'd never been allowed to forget that. She'd frowned at Fabien, letting him believe it was because she didn't wish to go to England and consort with the English, while she'd assembled her plan. There'd been one very large hurdle in her path. She'd let disillusionment and disgruntlement color her face, her voice. *"So I go to London and glide about their salons, being oh-so-nice to the English milords, and then what? You decide you do not after all wish me to marry this one. And then later, maybe not that one, either."*

She'd given a dismissive humph, folded her arms and looked away. *"There is no point. I would rather go home to Cameralle."*

She hadn't dared peek to see how Fabien responded to her performance, yet she'd felt his dark gaze on her, intent as always.

After a long moment, to her considerable surprise, he had laughed. *"Very well. I will give you a letter. A declaration."* He had sat at his desk, drawn forth a piece of parchment, then picked up his pen. He spoke as he wrote. *"I hereby confirm that as your legal guardian I agree to your marrying a member of the English nobility of station equal to your own, of estates more extensive than your own, and with income greater than your own."*

She'd watched him sign and hadn't been able to believe her luck. He'd sanded the paper, then rolled it and held it out to her; she'd managed not to snatch it. She'd accepted the document with a resigned air and agreed to come to London and search for an English husband.

The document was secreted in her trunk, sewn into the lining. It was her passport to freedom and the rest of her life.

"The Earl of Withersay is an amiable man." Louis's dark eyes had fixed on the portly earl in the group she had recently left. "Did you speak with him?"

"He's old enough to be my father." And not the right sort of man. Helena searched the crowd. "I will find Marjorie and learn about this duke. There is no one else here suitable."

Louis snorted. "For a week you've been surrounded by the flower of the English nobility—I think you're becoming too nice in your requirements. Given Uncle's wishes, I believe I can find any number of candidates for your hand."

Helena shifted her gaze to Louis's face. "Fabien and I have discussed his wishes. I do not need you to—how do they say it?—scupper my plans." Her voice had grown cold. Holding Louis's stubborn gaze, she haughtily inclined her head. "I will return to Green Street with Marjorie. There is no reason you need feel obliged to accompany us."

She stepped around him. Allowing her lips to relax into an easy smile, she glided through the throng. Marjorie, Mme Thierry, wife of the Chevalier Thierry, a distant kinsman, was her nominal chaperone. Helena had glimpsed her across the room. She headed in that direction, conscious of the male eyes that tracked her progress. Relieved that, in this season with society caught up in a frantic whirl, her entrance upon it had been much less noticeable than it would otherwise have been. Clusters of tittering ladies and garrulous gentlemen filled the room, spirits soaring, flown on the combination of her ladyship's mulled wine and the goodwill of the season; it was easy to slip past with a nod and a smile.

Fabien had arranged for Helena and Louis to stay with the Thierrys in lodgings in the best part of town. There was never any lack of funds where Fabien, or indeed, Helena, was concerned. The Thierrys, however, were not affluent and were exceedingly grateful to monsieur le comte de Vichesse for providing lodgings and board, servants, and an allowance permitting them to entertain the numerous friends and acquaintances they had made in their single, regrettably expensive year in London.

The Thierrys were well aware of the influence Fabien de Mordaunt wielded, even in England. Helena's guardian had a notoriously long arm. They were eager to provide whatever services monsieur le comte required, perfectly happy to introduce his ward to the ton and assist her in securing an acceptable offer.

Helena had carefully nurtured the Thierrys' gratitude. Despite the fact that Marjorie had a tendency to defer to Louis, she was nevertheless a fount of information on the eligibles within the English ton.

There had to be one who would suit.

She found Marjorie, a thin but elegant blonde of thirty, chatting animatedly with a lady and gentleman. She joined them. Later, they parted, and she drew Marjorie aside.

"Withersay?"

Helena shook her head. "Too old." Too rigid, too demanding. "Louis said there was a duke present—St. Ives. What of him?"

"*St. Ives?* Oh, no, no, *no.*" Eyes wide, Marjorie waggled her head and shook her hands for good measure. She glanced around, then leaned closer to whisper, "*Not* St. Ives, *ma petite.* He is not for you—indeed, he is not for *any* gently reared mademoiselle."

Helena raised her brows, inviting further details.

Marjorie fluffed her shawl, then leaned closer still. "His reputation is of the most shocking. For years and years, so it has been. He is a duke, yes, and rich and possessed of estates the most extensive, but he has declared he will not marry." Marjorie's brief gesture indicated her incomprehension of such things. "This, the society accepts—they say he has three brothers, and the eldest of them is now married with a son . . ." Another Gallic shrug. "So the duke is not at all an eligible, and indeed, he is . . ." She paused, searching for the right word, then breathed, "*Dangereux.*"

Before Helena could speak, Marjorie glanced up,

then closed her fingers about Helena's wrist and hissed, "See!"

Helena followed Marjorie's gaze to the gentleman who had just stepped through the archway from the main salon.

"Monsieur le duc de St. Ives."

Her wild Englishman, he of the cool, forceful lips gentle in the moonlight.

A picture of elegance, of arrogance, of power, he stood on the threshold and surveyed the room. Before his gaze reached them, Marjorie drew Helena around to stroll in the opposite direction.

"Now you see. *Dangereux.*"

Helena could indeed see, yet . . . she still remembered that kiss and the promise inherent within it, the sense that if she gave herself she would be forever cherished. Elementally seductive—more potent than any lover's entreaties. He was a rake; he'd perfected his art, she had not a doubt. Dangerous—that she would admit and wisely leave him be.

She would never be fool enough to escape one powerful man only to put herself in the hands of another. Freedom had become far too precious to her.

Luckily, monsieur le duc had declared himself out of her race.

"Are there any others here I should consider?"

"You've met monsieur le marquess?"

"Tanqueray? Yes. I do not believe he would meet monsieur le comte's stipulations. From what he let fall, he is in debt."

"Very possibly. But he is a proud one, that, so I have not heard. Let us see . . ." Passing through a doorway into another salon, Marjorie paused and looked about. "I can see none here, but it's too early for us to leave. It would give offense. We must circulate for another half hour at least."

"Another half hour, then. No more." Helena allowed Marjorie to lead her to a lively group. The conversation was entertaining, but as a newcomer she watched, observed, and remained for the most part silent. None knew her well enough to know that self-effacement was not her customary tack; tonight she was happy to hold her tongue and leave her mind free to wander.

She'd had more than enough of being Fabien's pawn, yet the law and society consigned her to his control, leaving her powerless. This trip to London was her best and perhaps only chance to escape—a chance fate had thrown her, one she'd used her wits to enhance, one she was determined to seize. With Fabien's declaration, in writing, signed and sealed, she could marry any English nobleman she chose, provided he met Fabien's stipulations regarding station, estate, and income. To her mind the stipulations were reasonable; there were English noblemen who might fit her bill.

They had to be titled, established and rich—and manageable. The fourth criterion she'd added to Fabien's three to define the perfect husband for her. She would not allow herself to continue as a puppet with any man pulling her strings. Henceforth, if any strings were to be pulled, *she* would do the pulling.

She would not marry only to become another man's

chattel, a thing with no feelings of consequence. Fabien cared nothing for others' emotions beyond how they affected his schemes. He was a despot, a tyrant, ruthless in crushing any who resisted him. She'd had his measure from the first, and she had survived in his care with her spirit undaunted only because she understood him, his motives, and had learned to mute her independence.

She had never been foolish enough to embark on a crusade she could not win. This time, however, luck was on her side. Winning free of Fabien, free of all powerful men, was an attainable goal.

"Well met, my dear comtesse."

Gaston Thierry appeared beside her. In deference to her rank he bowed low, smiling genially as he straightened. "If you are free, I have received a number of requests for introductions."

The twinkle in his eye made Helena smile. The chevalier was a spendthrift, but an engaging one. She readily gave him her hand. "If madame your wife will excuse me . . ."

With gracious nods to Marjorie and the others of their group, she let Gaston lead her away.

As she'd suspected, the requests had come from a number of gentlemen, but if she had to spend time in Lady Morpleth's rooms, then she might as well be entertained. They all did their best to accommodate her, putting themselves out to engage her, relating the latest *on-dits*, describing the most recent Christmas extravaganza planned by some inventive hostess.

Inquiring as to her plans.

On that subject she remained vague, which only increased their interest, as she well knew.

"Ah, Thierry—do introduce me."

The languid drawl came from behind her. Helena didn't recognize his voice, yet she knew who it was. She had to fight not to whirl and face him. Slowly, smoothly, she turned, polite distance infusing her expression.

Sebastian looked down into the madonnalike countenance he had not forgotten despite the passage of seven long years. Her expression was as aloof, as self-contained as he remembered, a blatant challenge for such as he, although he doubted she knew it. Her eyes . . . he waited until her lids lifted and her gaze rose to his face.

Green. Palest green. Peridot eyes utterly startling in their crystal clarity. Eyes that tempted, that would allow a man to see into her soul.

If she permitted it.

He'd waited seven years to see those eyes. Not the slightest trace of recognition showed in them, or in her expression. He let his lips curve appreciatively; he'd seen her watching him, knew she'd recognized him. Just as surely as he'd recognized her.

It was her hair that had caught his attention. Black as night, a froth of thick locks framing her face, brushing her shoulders. His gaze had roved, taking in her figure, provocatively displayed in a sea green silk gown with brocade overskirt and petticoat. His mind had been assessing, considering . . . Then he'd seen her face.

The silence had grown strained. He glanced at

Thierry and raised a brow fractionally, well aware of the reason for the man's reticence. The chevalier shifted his weight like a cat on hot coals.

Then the lady threw Thierry a glance and raised a commanding, rather more pointed brow of her own.

"Ahem." Thierry waved. "Monsieur le duc de St. Ives. Mademoiselle la comtesse d'Lisle."

He held out his hand; she laid her fingers on his and sank into a deep curtsy.

"Monsieur le duc."

"Comtesse." He bowed, then raised her. Quelled an urge to close his hand about her slender fingers. "You have lately come from Paris?"

"A sennight since." She glanced around, as assured as he remembered her. "It is my first visit to these shores." Her glance touched his face. "To London."

Helena assumed he'd recognized her, but there was nothing to confirm it in his face. His angular, chiseled features resembled a stony mask, eradicating all telltale expression; his eyes were the blue of a summer sky, impossibly innocent, yet framed by lashes so long and lush they dispelled any thought of innocence. His lips held a similar contradiction, long and thin, embodying more than a hint of ruthless will, yet, relaxed as they presently were, they suggested a subtle sense of humor, a dryly appreciative wit.

He was not young. Of those currently about her, he was unquestionably the most senior, definitely the most mature. Yet he exuded a vibrant, masculine vitality that threw the rest into the shade, made them fade into the wallpaper.

Dominant. She was accustomed to being in the presence of such a man, used to holding her own against a powerful will. She lifted her chin and regarded him calmly. "Have you visited Paris recently, my lord?"

Eyes and lips gave him away, but only because she was watching so closely. A gleam, a faint quirk, that was all.

"Not in recent years. There was a time when I spent part of every year there, some years ago."

He placed subtle emphasis on the last three words; he had definitely recognized her. A frisson of awareness raced over Helena's skin. As if he sensed it, his gaze left her eyes, lowered to brush her shoulders.

"I confess I'm surprised we haven't met before."

She waited until his gaze returned to her eyes. "I visit Paris infrequently. My estates lie in the South of France."

The ends of his lips lifted; his gaze rose to her hair, then returned to her eyes, then lowered again. "So I had surmised."

The comment was innocent enough—her coloring was indeed more indicative of the south rather than the north of France. His tone, however . . . it was deep enough, murmurous enough, to slide through her, striking some chord within, leaving it resonating.

She flicked a glance at Gaston, still nervously standing by. "Your pardon, Your Grace, but I believe it is time we left. Is it not so, monsieur?"

"Indeed, indeed." Gaston bobbed like a jack-in-the-box. "If monsieur le duc will excuse us?"

"Of course." Amusement lurked in the blue eyes as

they returned to Helena's face. She ignored it and curtsied. He bowed, raised her; before she could retrieve her hand, he murmured, "I take it you will be remaining in London, comtesse—at least for the present."

She hesitated, then inclined her head. "For the present."

"Then we will no doubt have the opportunity to further our acquaintance." He raised her hand; his eyes on hers, he brushed his lips across her knuckles. Releasing her smoothly, he inclined his head. "Once again, mademoiselle, au revoir."

To Helena's relief, Gaston did not pick up that "once again." He and Marjorie were so exercised over her meeting St. Ives at all—at his requesting an introduction—that they also failed to notice her abstraction. Failed to notice her fingers trailing over her knuckles where his lips had pressed. By the time they reached Green Street and entered the tiled hall, she had her reactions under control.

"Another evening gone." She sighed as her maid hurried forward to take her cloak. "Perhaps tomorrow we will meet with more success."

Marjorie glanced at her face. "It's Lady Montgomery's drum—it will be packed to the rafters. Everyone who is anyone will be there."

"*Bon.*" Helena turned to the stairs. "It will be a good venue to go hunting, I think."

She bade Gaston good night. Marjorie joined her as she climbed the stairs.

"My dear . . . monsieur le duc—he is not a suitable

parti. It would not do to encourage him to dally by your side. I am sure you understand."

"Monsieur le duc de St. Ives?" When Marjorie nodded, Helena waved dismissively. "He was merely amusing himself—and I think he enjoyed discomfiting Thierry."

"*Eh, bien*—that is possible, I grant you. Such as he . . . well, you are forewarned and thus forearmed."

"Indeed." Helena paused by her door. "Do not trouble yourself, madame. I am not such a fool as to waste my time on a man such as His Grace of St. Ives."

"Finally—they have met!" Louis dragged his cravat from about his throat, threw it to his waiting valet, then loosened his collar. "I was starting to worry that I would have to make the introduction myself, but she finally crossed his path. It went as Uncle Fabien predicted—he came to her."

"Indeed, m'sieur. Your uncle is uncannily prescient in such matters." Villard came to help Louis out of his coat.

"I will write to him tomorrow—he will want to hear the good news."

"Rest assured, m'sieur, that I will make certain your missive is dispatched with all speed."

"Remind me of it tomorrow." Unbuttoning his waistcoat, Louis murmured, "Now for the next stage."

Helena met monsieur le duc de St. Ives at Lady Montgomery's drum, at Lady Furness's rout-party, and at the Rawleighs' ball. When she went walking in the park, by sheer chance he was there, strolling with two friends.

Indeed, wherever she went in the next four days, it seemed he was present.

She was, consequently, not the least bit surprised when he joined the group with whom she was conversing in the Duchess of Richmond's ballroom. He loomed on her right, and the other gentlemen spinelessly gave way, as if he had some claim to the position. Hiding her irritation—at them as well as him—Helena smiled serenely and gave him her hand. And steeled herself against the reaction that streaked from her fingers to her toes when, his eyes on hers, he pressed his lips to her knuckles.

"*Bon soir*, my dear."

How such simple, innocent words could be made to sound so wicked was a mystery. Was it the light in his blue eyes, the seductive tenor of his voice, or the reined strength in his touch? Helena didn't know, but she did not approve of having her sensual strings so skillfully plucked.

But she continued to smile, and let him stand by her side and join them. When the group dispersed to mingle, she dallied. She knew he was watching, always alert. When, after a fractional hesitation, he offered his hand, she laid her fingers across his with a genuine smile.

They strolled; they had gone only a few yards when she murmured, "I wish to talk with you."

She didn't look at his face but was quite sure his lips would have quirked.

"So I had supposed."

"Is there some place here—in this room—in view of all but where no one will hear?"

"There are open alcoves along one side."

He led her to one containing an S-shaped love seat, currently empty. He handed her to the seat facing the room, then lounged in the other.

"You perceive me all ears, *mignonne*."

Helena narrowed her eyes at him. "What are you about?"

His finely arched brows rose. "About?"

"Precisely what do you hope to gain by hounding me in this fashion?"

His eyes held hers, gaze-to-gaze direct, but his lips were not straight. He raised a hand, languidly laid it across his heart. "*Mignonne,* you wound me deeply."

"Would that I could." Helena held on to her temper—just. "And I am not your *mignonne*!"

Not his pet, not his darling.

He merely smiled—patronizingly—as if he knew so much more than she.

Helena clenched her fingers about her fan and fought the urge to hit him with it. She'd anticipated such a response—a nonresponse—and had come prepared. She was, however, surprised by the depth of her irritation, by how easily he could make her temper soar. She was not normally so quick to prickle, to react.

"As you will no doubt have guessed, omniscient as you are, I am searching for a husband. I am not, however, searching for a lover. I wish to have this clearly understood between us, Your Grace. Regardless of your intent, regardless of your expertise, there is no likelihood whatever that I shall succumb to your legendary charms."

She'd heard enough about these from a worried Marjorie and surmised even more from the whispers and wondering looks. Even talking in public as they were—if it weren't for the fact she was twenty-three and highly born, she would have courted the danger of being labeled "fast."

Her gaze locked on his, she waited for some flippant response—some taunt, some crossing of swords. Instead, he regarded her thoughtfully, consideringly, letting the moment stretch before fractionally raising his brows. "You think not?"

"I know not." It was a relief to grab the conversational reins again. "There is nothing for you here—no hope at all—so there is no reason for you to cling to my side."

His lips relaxed into a definite smile. "I . . . er, cling to your side, *mignonne*, because you amuse me." He looked down, resetting the lace spilling over one white hand. "There are few in the ton who can accomplish that."

Helena suppressed a snort. "There are many only too ready to try."

"Alas, they lack the ability."

"Perhaps your standards are set too high?"

He lifted his head and looked at her. "My standards might be exacting. They are demonstrably not unachievable."

Helena narrowed her eyes to slits. "You are a *pest*!"

He smiled, genuinely amused. "That is not my intention, *mignonne*."

She gritted her teeth against the urge to scream—she was definitely *not* his *mignonne*! But she'd planned for even this—his intransigence. Getting a habituated tyrant to accept defeat and go away—she hadn't expected to succeed at first tilt. She drew in a breath, reined in her temper. "Very well." She nodded, head high. "If you insist on clinging to my skirts, you may as well be useful. You know all the gentlemen of the ton—know more, I daresay, than most regarding their estates and circumstances. You may help me select a suitable husband."

For one instant Sebastian didn't know what to say. The fact proved his thesis that she and she alone possessed the ability to honestly astound him—and, yes, make him laugh. The impulse, even if he didn't give way to it, felt unexpectedly good. Refreshing.

He hadn't, however, gained his reputation by being slow to see—and seize—opportunity. "It will be entirely my pleasure, *mignonne*."

The look she shot him was suspicious; he kept his intent from his eyes. Hand over heart, he bowed. "I will be honored to assist you in looking over the field."

"*Vraiment?*"

"*Vraiment.*" He smiled, prefectly ready to indulge her. What better way to ensure she met no one of any note? And she would now permit him to remain close beside her while he considered . . .

He reached out and closed his hand over hers. "Come. Dance with me."

He rose, rounded the love seat and drew her to her feet; Helena found herself acquiescing despite the command, no request. Despite the fact that she had until now avoided dancing purely so she could avoid having to cope with the sensation of his long fingers locked about hers.

A set was forming close by; they joined it. The first chord sounded, and she curtsied. He bowed. Then they linked hands, and the measure began.

It was worse than she'd imagined. She couldn't drag her gaze from his, from him, even though she knew it would be prudent to do so, to pretend her attention was general and not fixed on him. Prudence stood no chance against his magnetism. Like some sensual lodestone, he drew and captured her awareness, until the dancers around them, the crowd, the room itself, faded from her mind.

He moved with the grace of a god, impossibly assured, impossibly controlled. She would have taken an oath he barely registered the music—he was expert enough, experienced enough, not to need to. She had danced the minuet from the age of twelve, but it had never been like this, as if she now danced in a dream where every movement, every gesture, every clash of eyes held power. A power she'd never before felt, never before seen wielded with such consummate skill.

It was a net he cast over her. She knew what it was, what he was doing, knew in some corner of her bemused brain that at the end of the dance she could, and would, step free. But while they revolved and paced through the stately figures, she was caught, enthralled.

Fascinated.

She was aware of breathing more rapidly, of the sensitization of her skin. Aware of her body, her breasts, arms, hips, legs, as she never had been before. Aware that the fascination was mutual.

A heady experience, one that left her slightly dizzy when the music finally died. He raised her from her curtsy; she half turned from him. "I wish to return to Mme Thierry."

From the corner of her eye she saw his lips lift; she looked, met his gaze, and realized that his expression was not one of triumph but of indulgent understanding.

Dangereux.

The word whispered through her brain. She shivered.

"Come." He held out his hand. "I'll take you to her."

Laying her fingers in his, she let him lead her across the room. Delivering her most correctly to Marjorie's side, he exchanged bows with Louis, posing beside Marjorie, then bowed formally to her and withdrew.

"*Mon Dieu*! Helena—"

She raised her hand, cutting off Marjorie's words. "I know—but we have come to an agreement of sorts. He accepts I will not be his lover, but—as he finds me amusing and there is no way I can see to dismiss him if he does not wish to be dismissed—he has consented to help me in finding a suitable gentleman to wed."

Marjorie stared at her. "He has agreed . . . ?" After a moment she shook her head. "The English—they are mad."

Louis straightened. "Mad or not, he could be a valuable ally, a most useful source of information. If he is inclined to be indulgent, and he is so much older, after all—"

Marjorie snorted. "He is thirty-seven, and if half I have heard is true, those of *twenty*-seven would be hard put to keep pace with him."

"Be that as it may"— Louis tugged at his waistcoat; *he* was twenty-seven—"if Helena has made it clear she will not be his latest conquest and he is yet of a mind to be helpful, it would be foolish indeed not to avail ourselves of his aid. I am certain my uncle, monsieur le comte, would encourage us to accept monsieur le duc's offer."

Helena inclined her head. "On that, I would agree." Fabien was ever one to use any tool that came to hand.

Marjorie looked uncertain but sighed. "If you are sure that is what monsieur le comte would expect . . . *eh, bien*, we will follow that road."

Chapter Two

*Marjorie might have acquiesced to their scheme, but she remained unconvinced; every time Helena returned to her escorted by St. Ives, Marjorie behaved as if he were a wolf in temporarily amiable mood, but certain, when hunger struck, to revert to type.

"There is nothing to fear, I assure you." Beside Marjorie, Helena squeezed her arm. They were standing in Lady Harrington's ballroom surrounded by holly and ivy; trailing leaves swirled about the ornate columns while red berries winked from garlands gracing the walls.

St. Ives had just arrived. Announced, he paused at the top of the steps leading down to the ballroom's floor, scanning the crowd, noting their hostess, then searching further . . . until he saw her.

Helena's heart leaped; she told herself not to be silly. But as he descended, languidly elegant as always, she couldn't deny the excitement flaring in her veins.

"He's just helping me decide on a suitable husband."

She repeated the phrase to calm Marjorie, even if she'd never believed the "just." She might have told him she would not be his lover, but he'd never agreed or accepted that. He had, however, said he would help her find a husband—she believed he was sincere. It wasn't hard to see his reasoning. Once she was safely married to a suitably complaisant lord, he, St. Ives, would be first in line to be her lover.

And in such a position he'd be doubly hard to resist.

A thrill of awareness—a presentiment of danger—flashed through her. Once he'd helped her to a marriage such as the one she sought, he'd be even more dangerous to her.

Then he was there, bowing over her hand, speaking politely to Marjorie, then asking her to stroll. She agreed; danger or not, she was already committed and could not easily draw back.

Easily escape his net.

The realization opened her eyes, had her attending more closely. He sensed it; she felt it in his glance, the brush of his blue eyes over her face.

"I have no intention of biting, *mignonne*—not yet."

She slanted him a glance, saw the amusement in his beautiful eyes, and humphed. "Marjorie is worried."

"Why? I have said I'll help you find a husband. What is there to concern her in that?"

Helena narrowed her eyes at him. "You would be wise not to attempt ingenuousness, Your Grace. It does not become you."

Sebastian laughed. She continued to delight him, continued, at some level few had ever touched, to engage him. He steered her through the crowd, stopping to chat here and there, to point out this one or that, to admire the ice sculpture of an angel standing in a bower of holly on the terrace, the pièce de résistance of her ladyship's decor.

He wished he could increase the pace, curtail this phase and hurry on to the stage where he could touch her, caress her, kiss her again, but given his intent, that wouldn't be wise. He was a past master at playing society's games, and the outcome of this particular game was of far greater moment than that of any previous dalliance.

Once they'd circled the room, he steered her to one side. "Tell me, *mignonne,* why were you still at the convent all those years ago?"

"My sister was ill, so I stayed behind to help nurse her." She hesitated, then added, "We're close, and I didn't want to leave her."

"How much younger is she?"

"Eight years. She was only eight then."

"So she is now fifteen. Is she here in London with you?"

She shook her head. "Ariele was sickly as a child. Although her chest is much improved and grows better with the years, it seemed foolish to risk bringing her to England in winter. Our winters are much milder at home."

"And where is home?"

"Cameralle is our major estate. It's in the Camargue."

"Ariele. A pretty name. Is she pretty, too?"

Two ladies rose from a nearby chaise, leaving it empty. Sebastian guided Helena to it, waited until she settled her amber skirts, then sat beside her. Given the difference in their heights, if she became pensive and looked down, he couldn't catch her expression. Couldn't follow her thoughts.

"Ariele is fairer than I."

"Fairer in coloring. She could not be fairer of face or form."

Her lips twitched. "You seem very certain of that, Your Grace."

"My name is Sebastian, and, given my reputation, I'm amazed you dare question my judgment."

She laughed, then looked around them. "Now you may tell me, why is it that, given your reputation, they— the mesdames, the hostesses—are not . . ." She gestured.

"Overreacting to my interest in you?"

"*Exactement.*"

Because they couldn't imagine what he was about and had given up trying to guess. Sebastian leaned back, studying her profile. "They're still watching, but thus far there's been nothing worthy of an *on-dit* to be seen."

The softly drawled words sank into Helena's brain. Another premonition of danger skittered over her skin. Slowly, smoothly, she turned her head and looked into his blue eyes. "Because you've ensured that that's so."

He returned her regard with an enigmatic gaze, steady, direct, but unreadable.

"You're lulling them, waiting them out, until they grow bored and stop watching."

It could have been a question, yet even in her mind there was no doubt. Her chest felt suddenly tight. It was difficult to breathe, difficult to say, "You are playing a game with me."

A hint of what that meant to her must have colored her tone; something flickered in his eyes. His face grew harder. "No, *mignonne*—this is no game."

She hated and abhorred the games of powerful men, yet here she was, having escaped one such man, entangled in a game with another. How had it happened—so quickly, so totally against her will?

Although he remained relaxed, elegantly at ease, a frown had darkened his eyes. They searched hers, but she'd learned long ago to keep her secrets.

His gaze sharpened; he reached for her hand. *"Mignonne—"*

"There you are, Sebastian."

He looked up; Helena did, too. She felt his fingers close about her hand—he didn't let go as a lady, a large English lady with a round face framed by brown ringlets, swept forward. She was so weighted down by jewelry one barely noticed the odd shade of her gown. Helena thought she heard Sebastian sigh.

The lady halted before the chaise. Slowly, his very slowness an indication of his displeasure, Sebastian uncrossed his long legs and rose. Helena rose with him.

"Good evening, Almira." He waited. Somewhat belatedly, Almira bobbed him a curtsy. Inclining his head in reply, he glanced at Helena. "My dear comtesse, allow me to present Lady Almira Cynster. My sister-in-law."

Helena met his gaze, read his irritation very clearly, then looked to the lady.

"Almira—the comtesse d'Lisle."

Again Sebastian waited; so did Helena. With ill-concealed annoyance and little grace, Almira curtsied again. Her temper prodded, Helena smiled sweetly and showed her how the curtsy should have been performed.

Straightening, she caught an appreciative gleam in Sebastian's eyes.

"I understand St. Ives has been introducing you around." Her gaze flat and cold, Lady Almira surveyed her—blatantly, rudely.

"Monsieur le duc has been most kind."

Lady Almira's lips tightened. "Indeed. I don't believe I've had the pleasure of meeting monsieur le comte d'Lisle."

Helena smiled serenely. "I am not married."

"Oh. I thought—" Lady Almira broke off, genuinely puzzled.

"Under French law, in the absence of male heirs, the comtesse inherited the title from her father."

"Ah." If anything, Almira looked even more puzzled. "So you're not married?"

Helena shook her head.

Almira's face darkened; she turned to Sebastian. "Lady Orcott is asking after you."

Sebastian raised one brow. "Indeed?"

His retort made it clear he was totally uninterested.

"She's been searching for you."

"Dear me. If you come across her, do point her this way."

Helena bit her tongue. Sebastian's caustic retort had no discernible effect on his sister-in-law.

Almira shifted, facing Sebastian fully, giving Helena

her shoulder. "I wanted to tell you—Charles has started climbing stairs. He's growing sturdier by the day. You must call and see him."

"How fascinating." Sebastian shifted his hold on Helena's fingers; raising her hand, he glanced her way. "I believe, my dear, that Lady March is signaling us." He flicked a glance at Almira. "You must excuse us, Almira."

It was a command not even Almira could miss. Disgruntlement clear in her face, she bobbed a curtsy to them both and stepped back. "I'll expect you in the next few days."

With that piece of impertinence, she turned on her heel and swept away.

Along with Sebastian, Helena watched her go. "Is Lady March—whom I have never met—truly signaling us?"

"No. Come, let's go this way."

They strolled again; Helena glanced at his face, at his politely bored mask. "Lady Almira's son—is he the one who will eventually inherit your title?"

Not a flicker of emotion showed in his face. He glanced down at her, then looked ahead. And said nothing.

Helena raised her brows faintly and asked no more.

They merged with the throng, then another large, lean, darkly elegant gentleman spied them and moved to intercept them. Or rather, he spied Sebastian. Only when he stepped free of the crowd did he see her.

The gentleman's eyes lit; he smiled and swept her a leg almost as graceful as Sebastian's.

Sebastian sighed. "My dear comtesse, allow me to present my brother, Lord Martin Cynster."

"*Enchanté*, mademoiselle." Martin took the hand she offered and raised it to his lips. "Little wonder my brother's been so hard to find."

His smile was open, amused, and devil-may-care. Helena smiled back. "It's a pleasure to meet you, my lord."

Martin was considerably younger than Sebastian, yet from his manner it was clear he stood in no awe of one whom all others she'd thus far met approached with a degree of circumspection.

"I had meant to ask," Sebastian drawled, drawing Martin's gaze from her, "whether you had recovered from your night at Fanny's."

Martin flushed. "How the dev—deuce—did you hear about that?"

Sebastian merely smiled.

"If you must know," Martin continued, "I ended the night ahead. Dashed woman marks the cards, though—take my word for it."

"She always has."

Martin blinked. "Well, you might have warned me."

"And spoil your fun? I'm not such a curmudgeon and am no longer, thank God, your keeper."

Martin grinned. "It was fun, I must admit. Took me awhile to see through her tricks."

"Indeed." Sebastian glanced at Helena. "But I fear we're boring Mlle d'Lisle."

"Well, this isn't exactly a scintillating venue." Martin turned to Helena. "It's a pity you've arrived so late in the year, too late for Vauxhall or Ranelagh. Mind you,

there's old Lady Lowy's masquerade coming up—
that's always a night to remember."

"Ah, yes, I believe we have a card. The costumes will
be intriguing."

"What character will you be masquerading as?"
Martin asked.

Helena laughed. "Oh, no, I've been warned not to
tell."

Martin took a step back, eyeing her as if committing
her physical characteristics to memory.

"You needn't bother," Sebastian informed him.

"How else am I to find her?"

"Simple. Find me."

Martin blinked twice. His lips formed an "Oh."

"Ah, there you are, *ma petite*." Marjorie came up,
smiling but, as always, wary in Sebastian's presence.
She smiled more easily at Martin and gave him her
hand, then turned again to Helena. "We must go."

Reluctantly, Helena made her adieus. Sebastian
bowed over her hand. "Until tomorrow night, *mignonne*."

His murmur was too low for the others to hear; the
look in his eyes was likewise for her alone.

Helena rose from her curtsy, inclined her head, then
turned and, wondering, left him. Joining Marjorie, she
glided into the crowd.

Martin stepped to Sebastian's side. "I'm glad I found
you." All levity had flown. "I don't know how much
more of Almira's nonsense you can stomach, but
George and I have had enough. Her behavior's insupportable! The way she's carrying on, you're already un-

derground, and Arthur, too, come to that. God knows why he ever married her."

"We know why." Sebastian looked down, straightening the lace at one cuff.

Martin snorted. "But the why never eventuated, did it? She never was pregnant—"

"Look on the bright side. We do therefore know that Charles is indeed Arthur's son."

"He may be Arthur's get, but it's Almira who has him in hand. Good God—the lad's been hearing nothing but Almira's rantings from the moment of his birth. You know how she hates us."

"She doesn't hate us."

"She hates all we are. She's the most bigoted person I've ever met. If you and Arthur go, and Charles inherits as a minor . . ." Martin blew out a breath and looked away. "Let's just say that neither George nor I sleep all that well o'nights."

Sebastian looked up, studied his brother's face. "I didn't realize . . ." He hesitated, then said, "Neither you nor George need worry." He grimaced. "Nor Arthur, come to that."

Martin frowned. "What . . . ?" Then his face cleared; light returned to his eyes. "You're going to do something about it?"

"Disabuse your mind of the notion that I approve of Almira as the next Duchess of St. Ives."

Martin's jaw dropped; his eyes widened. "I don't believe it. You're truly serious?"

"I used to believe I had an iron constitution—Almira proved me wrong. I had hoped that motherhood would improve her." Sebastian shrugged. "It appears I was overly optimistic there, too."

His mouth still open, Martin looked in the direction in which Helena had gone. "You're looking for a wife."

The glance Sebastian shot him could have cut glass. "I would greatly appreciate it if you could refrain from letting such words pass your lips. To anyone."

Martin stared at him for a moment; then understanding dawned. "Hell's bells, yes!" His grin returned. He glanced around at the glamorous throng, at the eyes, the smiles that even now were surreptitiously cast their way. "If that little tidbit ever gets out—"

"You'll be even sorrier than I. Come." Sebastian started for the door. "There's a new hell opened in Pall Mall—I've an invitation, if you're interested."

Martin fell in by his side, grinning even more widely than before.

"To my mind, *mignonne*, you could do much worse than Lord Montacute."

Helena threw Sebastian a glance as they strolled beneath the trees. She and Marjorie had come to walk among the ton on what seemed likely to be the last fine afternoon of the year. Sebastian had joined them and offered her his arm. They'd left Marjorie chatting with friends to enjoy the Serpentine Walk. Along the way, Sebastian had introduced her to a number of potential husbands.

"I do not believe," she said, "that I could stomach a gentleman who wears virulent pink coats and compounds the sin by adding pink lace."

Her gaze swept Sebastian's dark blue coat with its restrained use of gold at cuffs and pockets. His lace, as always, was pristine white and finely made.

"Besides"—she looked ahead—"there is the matter of his title."

She felt Sebastian's gaze touch her face. "He's a baron."

"Indeed. But my guardian has stipulated that any man I choose must be of a station at least the equal of mine."

She glanced at Sebastian—he caught her gaze. "Earl or above." He sighed, raised his head, looked around. "*Mignonne*, it would have been helpful if you had told me this before. There are not so many earls or marquesses, let alone dukes, languishing unwed among the ton."

"There must be some—there *are* some."

"But we have other criteria to satisfy, do we not?"

Her criteria weren't the same as his, but unfortunately, satisfying her criteria would also satisfy his. An acquiescent husband who would allow her to rule their marriage would not raise a fuss should she decide to take a lover. Indeed, who knew? She might. But any lover she took would be of the same ilk—a man who pandered to her wishes rather than expecting her to pander to his.

In other words, not the man walking by her side.

"Let us start with the title first. It will narrow the field."

"It will indeed." He considered the knots of people scattered over the lawns as they strolled slowly along.

"Will your guardian's stipulations stretch to viscounts? In most cases they will, after all, eventually be earls."

"Hmm—it is possible, I suppose. If all other criteria were met."

"In that case let me introduce you to Viscount Digby. He's the heir to the Earl of Quantock, who has considerable estates in the west of the country. An estimable man, so I hear."

He led her to a group of gentlemen and ladies, introducing her generally, then, as only he could, "arranged" for her to stand beside the young viscount. After ten minutes coping with the viscount's tongue-tied adoration, Helena caught Sebastian's eye.

"Well?" he asked as they strolled away.

"He's too young."

That got her a stony glance. "I was not aware there was an age minimum."

"There isn't. He's just too young."

"Viscount Digby is twenty-six—older than you."

Helena waved dismissively. She looked around. "Who else is here?"

After a moment Sebastian sighed. "*Mignonne*, you are not making a difficult task any easier."

Nor was he. It occurred to Helena that spending so much time with him, with his often too-perceptive understanding and his accumulated experience in all manner of social intercourse, was not conducive to showing other men—younger, less experienced men—in any favorable light.

If one was accustomed to gold, one was unlikely to be dazzled by tin.

He introduced her to another viscount, a hedonistic youth almost too taken with his own beauty to notice hers. After listening to her opinion on that encounter with a resigned, somewhat paternal air, he led her to another group.

"Allow me to present Lord Were." Sebastian waited until they'd exchanged bows, then asked Were, "Any news from Lincolnshire?"

Were was, Helena judged, close to Sebastian's age. He was dressed well but soberly and had a pleasant countenance and a lively smile.

He grimaced. "Nothing yet, but the leeches tell me it'll be any day."

Sebastian turned to Helena. "Lord Were is heir to his uncle, the Marquess of Catterly."

"Old devil's about to pop off," Were informed her.

"I see." Helena spent the next ten minutes chatting on general subjects with his lordship. Beside her, she was conscious of Sebastian's growing impatience. Eventually he drew her away.

She went reluctantly. "He seems a kind man."

"He is."

She glanced at Sebastian, unsure how to interpret the hard note in his voice. As usual, his face told her nothing.

He was looking ahead. "I'd better return you to Mme Thierry before she starts imagining I've kidnapped you."

Helena nodded, willing enough to return; they'd been strolling for about an hour.

Despite knowing his ulterior motive in finding her a

complaisant husband, she had, on reflection, concluded that there was no point refusing his aid. Once she'd found the right candidate to fulfill Fabien's stipulations and hers and married him, any subsequent relationship between herself and Sebastian would, after all, still be at her discretion.

She would still be able to say no.

She was far too wise to say yes.

Over the past week she'd spent enough time with him, seen how others reacted to him, to be confident that, regardless of all else, he would ultimately accept her refusal. Despite his reputation, he was not the type of man to force or even pressure a woman to his bed.

She glanced briefly his way, then looked down to hide her smile. The idea was laughable; he had too much pride and too much arrogant self-assurance to need always to win.

The thought reminded her of Fabien. Sebastian and he were much alike, yet there were indeed differences.

A bevy of ladies resplendent in elegant walking gowns hailed them. They stopped to chat. Helena was amused that as the last week had progressed, her acceptance by the female half of the ton had steadily increased. She was still viewed as a too-beautiful outsider by some—primarily the mamas with marriageable daughters to establish—yet many others had proved eager to welcome her into their circles. Contrary to Marjorie's oft-stated opinion, St. Ives's squiring of her had helped rather than hindered.

She chatted with the Ladies Elliot and Frome, then turned to Lady Hitchcock. The group formed and re-formed several times. Eventually Helena turned to find the Countess of Menteith turning her way.

The countess smiled; Helena had already accepted an invitation for a morning visit. The countess glanced across the group to where Sebastian stood talking with Mrs. Abigail Frith. "I'll lay odds St. Ives will be driving out to Twickenham tomorrow. You don't have any engagements planned with him, I hope?"

Helena blinked. *"Pardon?"*

Still smiling at Sebastian, Lady Menteith lowered her voice. "Abigail's on the board of an orphanage, and the local squire's threatening to force the magistrate to shut it. The squire claims the boys run wild and thieve. Of course, it isn't so—he wants to buy the property. And, of course, the vile man has chosen this week to make his push, no doubt hoping to turn the orphans out into the snow while no one's about to see. St. Ives is Abigail's—and the orphans'—last hope."

Helena followed her gaze to where Sebastian was clearly questioning Mrs. Frith. "Does he often help with things outside his own interests?"

Lady Menteith laughed softly. "I wouldn't say it's outside his interests." Her hand on Helena's arm, she lowered her voice still further. "In case you haven't yet guessed, while he might be the devil in disguise in some respects, St. Ives is a soft touch for any female needing help."

Helena looked her puzzlement.

"Well, he's helping you by introducing you around, lending you his consequence. In a similar vein, half of us here owe him gratitude if not more. He's been rescu-

ing damsels in distress ever since he came on the town.
I should know—I was one of the first."

Helena couldn't resist. "He rescued you?"

"In a manner of speaking. I fear I was silly and
naive in those days—I'd recently married and thought
myself well up to snuff. I played deep and thought it
fashionable, as indeed it was. But I've no head for
cards—I ended losing the Menteith diamonds. God
only knows what Menteith would have said, and
done, had he heard. Luckily, he didn't—not until I told
him years later. At the time, I was deep in despair. St.
Ives noticed. He dragged the story out of me, then, the
next day, the diamonds were delivered to me with his
compliments."

"He bought them back for you?"

"No, he won them back for me, which, considering
the blackguard who'd taken them from me, was far, far
better." Lady Menteith squeezed Helena's arm. "He
rarely gives money, unless that's the only way. To many
of us, he's our white knight. He'll drive to Twickenham
tomorrow and have a chat with the magistrate, and
that's the last we'll hear of the orphanage closing."

The countess paused, then added, "I wouldn't want
you to think ladies run to him with every concern. Far
from it. But when there's no other way, it's immeasur-
ably comforting to know there's one last person who, if
the thing's possible at all, will help. And with the ut-
most discretion. Even if you ask him outright about the
Menteith diamonds, even after so many years, he
won't say a word. And by tomorrow evening he'll have
forgotten all about Twickenham."

Helena was fascinated. "Does he do the same for gentlemen in distress?"

The countess caught her eye. "Not that I've ever heard."

Helena laughed. Sebastian crossed to her side, one brow arching. She shook her head.

"We had best get on. Mme Thierry will be anxious."

An understatement; Helena nodded. They made their adieus, then walked quickly back to the carriage drive. Their appearance together, Helena noted, drew little attention, even from the most rabid scandalmongers perched in their carriages swapping the latest *on-dits*.

They reached the carriage, and Sebastian handed her in. Although relieved to see her return, even Marjorie seemed less concerned than previously. Sebastian bowed, then left them, strolling languidly to where his own carriage waited farther along the avenue.

Helena watched him go. She couldn't imagine Fabien helping anyone for no reason.

Now that her eyes had been opened, Helena saw a great deal more. At Lady Crockford's soirée that evening, she watched Sebastian make his way toward her, watched as he was stopped again and again, by this lady, then that. Before, she had assumed that it was he who stopped to speak—now she saw it was they who spoke first, who caught his eye with a smile.

Gentle words, grateful smiles.

The ladies were not, in the main, the sort one might imagine would catch his roving eye. Many were older than he, others too awkward or plain ever to have been likely candidates for his less-acceptable attentions.

He'd cut a swath through the London salons with a double-edged sword. Sheer arrogant masculinity on the one hand, unexpected kindness on the other.

He neared, and his gaze met hers. She fought to quell a shiver.

Joining them, he exchanged bows, spoke a few words with Marjorie and Louis, then turned to her. One brow arched.

She smiled and gave him her hand. "Shall we promenade?"

His expression was indulgent. "If you wish."

Sebastian guided Helena through the throng and tried to ignore her nearness—the subtle warmth of her slender figure, the light touch of her fingers on his. Tried to block out the French perfume she wore, that wreathed about her and none too subtly beckoned the beast, urged him to seize and devour.

Spending so much time with her was fraying his reins, raising expectations yet leaving them unfulfilled. Only his supreme dislike of conducting his affairs in the full glare of the ton's attention held him back from pursuing her overtly. The news he was to wed would cause a sensation, but if he waited just a few weeks more until Christmas drew close and the ton quit the capital, then the necessary formalities of his offer and her acceptance could be played out in private.

Infinitely preferable, given he was not entirely sure of her.

A surprise and a challenge—she continued to be both.

Taking advantage of his height, he scanned the guests, noting any gentlemen potentially useful for passing the time—for distracting her. Carefully avoiding Were. That had been a misjudgment; Were was a friend. He had never been one to fashion rods for his own back. Helena would not get another chance to consider Were, not if he could help it.

They were leaving a group of ladies who'd waylaid them when George emerged from the throng. One glance at his brother's face was enough to tell him Martin had opened his lips to one person at least.

George's delight was unfeigned; he beamed at Helena and didn't wait for an introduction. "Lord George Cynster, comtesse." He bowed extravagantly over the hand she extended. "I'm enchanted to meet you, quite enchanted." The light in his eye declared that no lie.

"And I am equally glad to make your acquaintance, my lord." Amused, Helena shot Sebastian a glance. "How many brothers do you have, Your Grace?"

"For my sins, three. Arthur, Almira's husband, you've yet to meet. Arthur and George are twins. Martin's the youngest."

"No sisters?" Helena shifted her gaze to George. He was not quite as tall as Sebastian but of similar build. He had darker hair but the same blue eyes. The same somewhat dangerous aura hung about him. In Martin that had been less pronounced; in Sebastian it was more powerful, more blatant. Helena concluded that the characteristic developed with age and experience—she judged George to be in his early thirties.

"One."

The answer came from Sebastian. Helena glanced up to find his gaze fixed on the crowd behind her.

"And unless I miss my guess—"

He stepped sideways, reaching through the crowd to close his fingers about the elbow of a lady flitting past.

Tall, elegantly dressed, with her brown hair piled high, the lady turned, brows rising haughtily, ready to annihilate whoever possessed the temerity to lay hands on her. Then she saw who it was. Her expression changed in a blink to one of joy.

"Sebastian!" The lady clasped his hand in both of hers and stepped free of the crowd. "I hadn't expected to find you still in town."

"That, my dear Augusta, is patently obvious."

Augusta wrinkled her nose at him, at his censorious tone, and let him draw her to join them. She grinned at George. "George, too—how goes it, brother dear?"

"So-so." George grinned back. "Where's Huntly?"

Augusta waved behind her. "Somewhere here." Her gaze had come to rest on Helena. She glanced briefly at Sebastian.

"Augusta, Marchioness de Huntly—Helena, comtesse d'Lisle." Sebastian waited while they exchanged curtsies, then added to Helena, "As you've no doubt gathered, Augusta is our sister. However"—his gaze shifted to Augusta and sharpened—"what I fail to understand, Augusta, is why you're gadding about London given your present state."

"Don't fuss. I'm completely all right."

"You said that last time."

"And despite the panic, it turned out perfectly well in the end. Edward's thriving. If you must know—and I suppose you'll demand to—I was quite moped in Northamptonshire. Huntly agreed just a little socializing would do no harm."

"So you travel to London to attend balls and routs."

"Well, what would you? It's not as if there's any socializing in Northamptonshire."

"It's hardly the far end of the world."

"In terms of entertainment it might as well be. And anyway, if Huntly doesn't mind, why should you?"

"Because you wound Herbert around your finger before you were wed and have yet to set him loose."

Far from denying it, Augusta replied, "It's the only way to keep a husband, dear Sebastian, as I think you well know."

He caught her gaze, held it. Augusta tilted her chin at him but shifted, then glanced away.

Helena stepped into the breach; she caught Augusta's gaze. "You have a child?"

Augusta beamed at her. "A son—Edward. He's at home at Huntly Hall, and I do miss him."

"A situation easily rectified," Sebastian put in.

Helena and Augusta ignored him.

"Edward's just two. He's a scamp."

"He takes after his mother." When Augusta pulled a face at him, Sebastian's lips curved; he tugged a lock of her hair. "Better that than prose on like Herbert, I suppose."

Augusta pouted. "If you've a mind to be disagreeable over dearest Herbert—"

"I was merely stating a fact, my dear. You must admit that Huntly is singularly lacking in, er . . . devilment, while our family is, if anything, overendowed."

Augusta laughed. "You can talk."

"Indeed. Who better?"

Helena listened as, between them, Sebastian and George extracted a list of Augusta's likely engagements and the date she planned to return to Northamptonshire.

"Then we'll see you at Christmas at Somersham." Augusta glanced at Sebastian. "Do you want me to bring Edward?"

Both her brothers looked at her as if she'd grown two heads.

"Of *course* you'll bring him!" George said. "We'll want to see our nephew, won't we?"

"Quite," Sebastian said. "But I apprehend you've been talking to Almira. Pray discount anything she may have said regarding my wishes over Christmas or anything else. I'll naturally be expecting Edward at Somersham—aside from all else, Colby's been searching out a present for him and would be disappointed if he didn't appear to claim it."

Helena watched Augusta's expression change from guarded to relieved to happy, but at the mention of Colby's name she frowned at her brother. "*Not* a horse—he's too young. I've already forbidden Huntly even to think about it."

Sebastian flicked a speck of lint from his sleeve. "Herbert did mention your restriction, so I've instructed Colby to look for a pony—one small enough for Edward to sit on and be led. He's old enough for that."

Helena hid a smile as Sebastian pretended not to notice Augusta's struggle between maternal delight and maternal disapprobation. Then he slanted her a sidelong glance. "You may thank me at Christmastime."

Augusta threw up her hands. "You're impossible." Leaning on his arm, she stretched up to plant a kiss on his cheek. "Utterly."

Sebastian patted her shoulder. "No, I'm merely your very much older brother. Take care," he said as she pulled away and drew back, nodding to Helena and George, "and do bear in mind that, should I hear you've been overdoing things, I'm quite capable of packing you off willy-nilly to Huntly Hall." Augusta met his gaze, and he added, "I'm not Herbert, my dear."

Augusta wrinkled her nose at him, but all she said was, "I guarantee I won't put you to such inconvenience, Your Grace."

As she turned away, she murmured sotto voce to Helena, "He's a tyrant—beware!" But she was smiling.

"All very well," George grumbled watching Augusta disappear into the crowd, "but I'll keep an eye on her just in case."

"No need," Sebastian said. "Herbert might feel unable to rein Augusta in, but he's well aware I suffer from no such constraint. If he wishes her to retire from the capital early and she proves difficult, I'm sure he'll let me know."

George grinned. "He might be a prosy sort, but old Herbert does have his head screwed on straight."

"Indeed. Which is why I approved of Augusta's choice." Sebastian caught Helena's gaze. "You've been very patient, my dear. Shall we dance?"

She'd been perfectly happy listening, learning, drinking in their interaction and all it told her of him, but she smiled and gave him her hand, exchanged nods with George, then let Sebastian lead her into the nearest set.

As usual, dancing with him was a distraction—a distraction so complete she lost touch with the world and there existed only the two of them, circling, bowing, gliding through the figures, hands linked, gazes locked. At the end of the dance when he raised her, her heart was beating just a little faster, her breathing just a little shallower.

Her awareness as she met his gaze was more acute.

Acute enough to sense the thoughts behind the innocent blue of his eyes, behind the heavy-lidded gaze that dropped from her eyes to her lips.

Her lips throbbed; she looked at his, long, lean . . . and remembered, too clearly, what they'd felt like against hers.

The tension between them drew tight, quivered, then his lips curved. He turned her from the floor, glancing about them once more.

Helena barely had time to draw breath before another lady—this one black-haired and black-eyed—swept up.

"Good evening, St. Ives."

Sebastian nodded. "Therese."

The lady was in her early thirties, striking rather than beautiful, and dressed to take advantage of her unusual looks. As Augusta had, she stretched up and kissed Sebastian's cheek. "Do introduce me."

Helena sensed rather than heard Sebastian's sigh.

"Mademoiselle la comtesse d'Lisle—Lady Osbaldestone."

Her ladyship curtsied prettily; Helena curtsied back, conscious of her ladyship's sharp black gaze.

"Therese is a cousin of sorts," Sebastian added.

"A distant connection I take shameless advantage of," Lady Osbaldestone corrected, speaking directly to Helena. "Which is why, having heard that St. Ives's latest start was to introduce a comtesse into society, I had, of course, to meet you." She slanted a glance at Sebastian; Helena couldn't interpret the look in her black eyes. "So interesting."

Looking back at Helena, Lady Osbaldestone smiled. "One never knows what Sebastian will be at next, but—"

"Therese."

The softly spoken word held enough menace to halt the flow of Lady Osbaldestone's not-quite-artless discourse. She grimaced and turned to him. "Spoilsport. But you can hardly expect me to be blind."

"More's the pity."

"Anyway"—much of her ladyship's sharpness evaporated—"I wanted to thank you for your help in that small matter of mine."

"It's been settled satisfactorily, I take it?"

"Eminently satisfactorily, thank you."

"And would I be correct in assuming Osbaldestone remains in blissful ignorance?"

"Don't be daft, of course he doesn't know. He's a man. He'd never understand."

Sebastian's brows rose. "Indeed? And I am . . . ?"

"St. Ives," her ladyship promptly retorted. "You're unshockable."

A faint smile curled Sebastian's lips. Lady Osbaldestone turned to Helena. "The mind boggles at the number of ladies' secrets he keeps."

Helena's mind boggled at the fact they trusted him with such secrets at all. The notion of any lady willingly trusting Fabien was beyond ludicrous.

She chatted with Lady Osbaldestone, who had recently visited Paris. It transpired they had acquaintances in common; despite her sharp tongue, her ladyship was both interesting and entertaining. Helena enjoyed the short interlude but was conscious that Sebastian was alert, his blue eyes beneath their heavy lids fixed on her ladyship.

Lady Osbaldestone proved equally aware; she eventually turned to him. "All right, all right, I'm going. But I take leave to tell you you're becoming transparent."

She bobbed a curtsy to him, bowed to Helena, then swept away.

Helena glanced at Sebastian as he retook her hand. Did she dare ask what about him was becoming transparent? "She seems very well informed."

"Unfortunately. I don't know why I bear with her—she's the most enervatingly astute woman I know."

Helena debated whether to ask for an explanation, then realized she'd spent most of her evening thus far with him, learning more about him, becoming more fascinated—which was not necessary at all. She lifted her head, looked around. "Is Lord Were here, do you know?"

An instant's hiatus ensued; she could have sworn Sebastian tensed. But then he murmured, "I haven't seen him."

Was she imagining it, or was there steel beneath his smooth tones? "Perhaps if we stroll . . ."

He steered her along the side of the room, skirting the crowd congregating at its center about a monstrous decorative piece formed of gilded, star-shaped lanterns surrounding and supporting a gilt and porcelain setting of the Nativity. Viewing the closely gathered ladies, Helena noticed that, presumably in celebration of the season, many had taken to wearing bright red or forest green.

Among the throng she spied Louis, keeping an eye on her. Dressed as usual in black, emulating his uncle Fabien, he stood out against the multihued crowd. He was usually hovering somewhere in sight. Despite Sebastian's reputation, Louis hadn't overtly interfered in his squiring of her.

They were nearing the end of the room. She couldn't see past the outer ranks of the crowd; she knew that Sebastian could. "Can you see—"

"I can't see anyone you would wish to meet in furthering your goals."

To her surprise, he drew her on and then to the side, to where an alcove partially screened by potted palms looked out over gardens. The alcove was deserted.

The day had been fine; the night was, too, cold and frosty. Beyond the glass, the shrubs and walks were bathed in silver-white moonlight, the barest touch of snow crystallizing like diamond frosting on each leaf, on each blade of grass. Helena drank in the view; it shimmered, touched by a natural brilliance infinitely more powerful, more evocative of the season, than the effort of mere mortals at her back. The scene, so reminiscent, whisked her back to that moment seven years before—the moment they'd first met.

Quelling a shiver, she turned to find Sebastian regarding her, his expression indolent, his gaze intent.

"It occurs to me, *mignonne*, that you have not yet favored me with a complete list of your guardian's stipulations concerning the nobleman he will accept as your husband. You've told me this paragon must bear a title the equal of yours. What else?"

She raised her brows, not at the question—one she was ready enough to answer—but at his tone, for him unusually clipped and definite, quite different from his customary social drawl. Much more like the voice in which he spoke to his sister.

His lips quirked, more grimace than smile. "It would help in determining your most suitable suitor."

He'd softened his tone. Inwardly shrugging, she turned back to the windows. "Title I've mentioned. The other two stipulations my guardian made concerned the size of my suitor's estate and his income."

From the corner of her eye, she saw Sebastian nod. "Eminently sensible conditions."

Hardly surprising he thought so; he and Fabien could be brothers in some respects—witness his despotic attitude to his sister, even if he was moved by caring rather than some colder reason. "Then, of course, there are my own inclinations." She stopped. There was no need to tell him exactly in which direction her inclinations lay.

A wolfish smile touched his lips. "Naturally." He bowed his head. "Your inclinations should not be forgotten."

"Which is why," she said, turning from the windows, "I wish to seek out Lord Were."

She intended to return to the room and do so.

Sebastian stood in her way.

Silence stretched, suddenly tense, unexpectedly fraught. Lifting her chin, she met his gaze. His eyes were hooded, so blue they seemed to burn. Her nerves flickered, senses older than time screaming that she was baiting something wild, unpredictable—something well beyond her control.

Dangereux.

Marjorie's warning whispered through her mind.

"Were."

A statement uttered in a flat tone she had not before heard. He held her with his gaze; she couldn't break free.

Raising a hand, he slid one long finger beneath her chin and tipped her face to his. He studied her expression; his gaze fastened on her lips, then rose once more to her eyes. "Has it not yet occurred to you, *mignonne,*" he murmured, "that you could do a great deal better than a mere marquess?"

Helena felt her eyes flare, in shock, in reaction to what she sensed rather than knew. His fingertip was cool beneath her chin; his blue eyes were hot, his gaze heated.

Her heart thudded, racing—then a commotion behind him drew her gaze.

At the edge of the crowd, Marjorie shook free of Louis's restraining grip; from her frown and the quick word she threw him, he'd been holding her back. Twitching her shawl into place, Marjorie swept forward.

Sebastian had turned his head and looked; his hand fell from her face.

"*Ma petite*, it is time we left." Marjorie shot him a censorious look, then turned to Helena, her expression determined. "Come."

With barely a nod to Sebastian, Marjorie swept away.

Puzzled, Helena curtsied, then, with one last glance at Sebastian and a murmured adieu, she followed Marjorie.

As she glided past him, Louis was scowling.

✨

*H*e was the only unmarried duke she'd met. Helena tried to make sense of his last comment; it kept her awake half the night. But he couldn't mean himself. He'd declared years ago he would not wed. She couldn't see why he would change his mind. He might want her—she accepted that, although she didn't, truth be told, entirely understand such predatory desire— but to his mind, to his way of thinking—to *society's* way of thinking—he could have all he wanted without marrying her.

Not that she had any intention of allowing that to come to pass, but he didn't know that.

He must have meant something else, yet no matter how she twisted his words, no matter how much she discounted the effect he had on her and any consequent misconstruction, she still couldn't explain the intensity that had flared—that had echoed in his tone and burned in his eyes.

She was relieved that his appointment in Twickenham meant she'd be free of him for the day.

It didn't help. Evening arrived and she was still confused, still wary. Still feeling like a doe in a hunter's sights.

The argument between Louis and Marjorie on the way to Lady Hunterston's ball was an added distraction.

"You're making too much of it." Louis sat back, arms folded, and stared blackly at Marjorie. "If you meddle needlessly, you will damage her chance of making a proper match."

Marjorie sniffed and pointedly looked out the carriage window.

Helena inwardly sighed. She was no longer so sure Majorie wasn't right, despite what logic told her. Logic couldn't explain the power she'd felt last night.

On entering Lady Hunterston's ballroom, Helena kept Marjorie with her and determinedly quartered the room. She found Lord Were by the card room; the group about him parted readily to allow them to join.

The topic under discussion was the imminent demise of Lord Were's uncle, the Marquess of Catterly.

"I'll have to head north tomorrow," Were told them. "The old reprobate's been asking after me. Seems the least I can do."

He grimaced as he said it; Helena considered his attitude as a black mark against him—then realized whom she was comparing him with. She thrust the comparison aside. However, to her satisfaction, as they chatted and the topic shifted to Christmas and the entertainments planned, she found herself much more in tune with Were's views. He was an amiable if unexciting soul, solid and somewhat doggedly unassuming. That, she told herself, was a welcome relief from others who were too well aware of their worth.

Catching Marjorie's eyes, she let an unspoken question infuse hers. Marjorie smiled meaningfully and inclined her head. She, too, approved of Lord Were.

Sebastian entered Lady Hunterston's ballroom to be met by the sight of Helena smiling delightedly up at Were. He noted it, paused to sweep an elegant bow to her ladyship, then, for once ignoring the smiles directed his way, made straight for the group outside the card room.

He walked through the crowd, his attention riveted on Helena; inwardly, he canvassed his options. He could tell her he wished to marry her, deliberately dazzle her and draw her to his side, *but . . .*

That "but" held considerable weight. Any hint to the ton that he'd changed his mind and decided to make her his duchess would cause a sensation and focus all eyes, every last one, on them. And the thoughts going through the minds behind the eyes, and the consequent whispers, would not all be felicitious. Some, indeed, would choose to be blind and speculate that his intention wasn't honorable at all. Such rumors would not be to his liking—nor hers, and even less her guardian's.

He'd received a report from his Parisian agent; her maternal uncle, Geoffre Daurent, had become her guardian on her father's death. Thierry presumably stood in Daurent's shoes, but calling formally in Green Street was impossible. Impossible to keep such a meeting secret, not in the heart of the ton.

A discreet invitation to visit his principal estate,

Somersham Place, when the ton dispersed from the capital in just under two weeks was his preferred way forward. No one beyond the Thierrys and Louis de Sèvres would need to know; he himself would tell only his aunt Clara, who acted as his hostess at his ancestral home. In privacy he could speak—and persuade if need be.

That last grated. Helena enjoyed his company but did not, so her peridot eyes declared, consider him a potential husband.

Yet.

The fault might be his, with his antipathy to marriage so publicly declared; that didn't prevent him from viewing her dismissal as a challenge.

"Comtesse." He halted by her side. She'd seen him approach but had feigned ignorance. Now she turned and, with a cool smile, held out her hand. He took it, bowed over it. Before she could retrieve her fingers, he locked his about them. "Madame." He acknowledged Mme Thierry's curtsy with a nod, then inclined his head to Were. "If you'll excuse us, there's a matter of some import I wish to convey to mademoiselle la comtesse."

Skepticism flared in Mme Thierry's eyes, but none dared gainsay him—not even Helena. Her expression studiously serene, she allowed him to lead her away, down the long room.

"And what is it you wish to tell me?"

Her voice held a haughty chill. She glided beside him, her gaze fixed ahead, her expression betraying not the slightest perturbation.

"That Were is not for you."

"Indeed? And why is that?"

He could not lie about a friend. "Suffice to say I believe your guardian would not approve."

"How odd. From all I have learned, the estates Lord Were will shortly inherit are extensive and the income sound."

Not as extensive nor as sound as his own.

"His lordship is all things amiable," she continued. "I foresee no problem at all."

Sebastian bit back a retort to the effect that she didn't foresee the half of it. Her dismissal of his caveat had been delivered with a regal air—an air few would attempt with him.

The fact that she had done so did not surprise him; his agent's report had confirmed his supposition. She and her sister were the last of the de Stansions, a very old aristocratic French family. Her mother had been a Daurent, another senior house of the French nobility. Helena's birth was as good as his; she'd been reared, as had he, to know her worth. Their arrogance was a part of them, bred into them—she had her own brand, as did he.

Unfortunately for her, such feminine arrogance brought out the conqueror in him.

"You would do well to consider, *mignonne*, that there might be more to a gentleman than meets the eye."

"I am not a child, Your Grace—I am well aware that most men mask their true natures."

"Sebastian—and permit me to point out, *mignonne*, that not all women are as open as you."

How had they got onto that point? Helena barely had time for the thought before Sebastian whisked her through a pair of curtains she'd imagined were merely wall hangings. Instead, they'd concealed an archway leading into a small, luxuriously appointed salon.

Finding herself in the middle of the room, cut off from the ballroom now that the curtains had fallen shut, she dropped her own mask and frowned—openly.

"This is not, I am sure"—she gestured—"*comme il faut.*"

She all but glared at Sebastian as he came to stand before her. The infuriating man did nothing more than raise one brow. Why she was so irritated with him she could not say, but she'd had a strong suspicion even before he'd arrived that he'd been deliberately steering her away from Lord Were.

To her mind, Lord Were was looking more and more like the perfect avenue for her escape to freedom.

"I appreciate your help in introducing me to the ton, Your Grace, but I am—how do you English say it?— more than eight, so I will be my own judge. And your veiled aspersions on Lord Were's character I do not credit at all."

She capped her dismissal of his arguments with a contemptuous wave; she would have preferred to sweep back to the ballroom on that note, but he was standing directly in her way. She held his blue gaze belligerently.

The aggravating man had the temerity to sigh.

"I fear you will have to readjust your thinking,

mignonne. The gentleman to whom I referred was not Were."

Helena frowned. It took her a moment to replay his statement: . . . *there might be more to a gentleman than meets the eye*. She looked at him, blinked.

His lips quirked. "Indeed. The gentleman I referred to was me."

"You." She couldn't credit it—couldn't believe what logic was telling her, nor what she could see in his eyes.

She felt his hand at her waist, sliding, felt a quiver run the length of her spine.

He drew her closer. "You remember that night in the moonlight in the gardens of the Convent des Jardinières de Marie."

His voice had taken on a mesmerizing cadence; the blue of his eyes was even more hypnotic.

"I kissed you. Once, to thank you."

Trapped in his web, she was incapable of pulling back. Her hands rose to rest on the silk of his sleeves as he urged her nearer. And she went, lids falling as he bent his head.

"Why?" she whispered as his lips neared hers. She moistened her own. "Why did you kiss me a second time?"

The question to which she'd always wanted an answer.

"The second time?" His breath brushed her lips. "I kissed you a second time . . . to savor you."

He did so again. His lips closed over hers, cool, firm, knowing. She knew she should resist, hold back; instead, she teetered on some invisible brink, then something inside her unlocked, gave. He sensed it. His hands locked about her waist, and he drew her to her toes. His lips hardened, firmed, became more demanding.

And she was tumbling, falling . . .

Why she would want to appease his arrogant demands she could not fathom, yet she did. Clinging to his strength, giving herself up to the thrill of the kiss was akin to madness, yet she did that, too.

When his lips urged hers open, she complied; he swallowed her gasp as he surged in and took her mouth, took her breath, then gave her his. He was bold—blatantly, sensually evocative; her senses reeled as she struggled to absorb the sensations, to follow his lead. To satisfy one demand so they could progress to the next.

Madness indeed. Her skin heated, her bodice grew tight, her breathing fractured. Her whole body felt alive, different, awake as it never had been before.

She wanted more. Her fingers closed on his silk sleeves, holding him. His grip tightened; his head angled, and he deepened the kiss.

Never had the urge to seize, to take, raged so powerfully. Sebastian fought to rein it in, yet he was hungry, so greedy, and she was luscious, so generous, so very much to his taste.

Never before had he coveted the taste of innocence, but she was different, not entirely untutored but naively and naturally sensual—he was caught, enthralled, addicted. He'd sensed her worth seven years before and had never forgotten it—the promise in her kiss.

Only experience, long steeped, hard won, allowed him to dam the welling tide, turn it back, let it subside.

The time was not right; he'd already gone further than he'd intended, lured by her lips, by the surprise of his need. Her lips would be bruised as it was.

He broke the kiss and shook with the effort of stopping himself from going back, from taking her mouth again. Touching his forehead to hers, he waited, listening to her breathing slow in time with the pounding in his blood.

He forced his arms to function, to set her back on her feet.

Her lids fluttered, then lifted. He drew back so he could see, watch puzzlement flow across her features, confusion invest her green eyes.

"There are other criteria you should consider in your search for a husband."

He murmured the words, watched her brow furrow, then realized she might not even now correctly divine his meaning.

Easing his grip about her waist, he held her lightly with one hand, then raised the other. He looked down, knowing she would follow his gaze, then watched as he lifted his hand, trailing his fingertips from her throat, over her collarbone to the silken skin just above her scooped neckline.

She caught her breath; one brief glance confirmed she was watching, fascinated more than horrified. He let his fingers trace over the silk, felt her flesh firm in response. Then he cupped her breast lightly.

The quiver that raced through her made him ache. Deliberately slow, he circled her nipple with his thumb and watched it peak and pebble.

"You want me, *mignonne*."

"No." A sound of desperation. She didn't want to want him; Helena was sure about that. On all else— what was happening between them, what he intended, what he wanted of her—she was confounded, utterly and completely at sea.

His fingers touched her, traced, and she couldn't think. She pulled back, pushed away. He let her go, but she sensed the brief clash between his desire and his will. Even if will won, she had to wonder if it would the next time.

Dangereux.

"No." She sounded more definite the second time. "This will do us no good."

"On the contrary, *mignonne*, it will be very good indeed."

Pretending ignorance would be futile, disingenuousness worse. Lifting her chin, she fixed him with a stubborn look and went to take another step back— only to feel his fingers tighten about her waist.

"No. You cannot run from me. We need to talk, you and I, but before we go further, there's something I want of you."

Searching his eyes, blue on blue, Helena was certain she didn't need to hear what it was. "You have read my intentions wrongly, Your Grace."

"Sebastian."

"Very well—Sebastian. You misunderstand. If you think—"

"No, *mignonne*. It is you who fail to realize—"

The curtain over the archway rattled. They both looked. Sebastian's hand fell from her waist as Were, smiling genially, looked in.

"There you are, m'dear. It's time for our dance."

They could hear music wafting from behind him. One glance at his open expression was enough to tell them both that he suspected nothing scandalous. Helena stepped around Sebastian and swept forward. "Indeed, my lord. My apologies for keeping you." She paused as she reached Were's side and looked back at Sebastian. "Your Grace." She curtsied deeply, then rose, placed her fingers on Were's hand, and let him lead her out.

Were grinned at Sebastian over her head. Despite all, Sebastian smiled and nodded back. He and Helena had not been apart, alone, for long enough to give the gossips sufficient cause to speculate, and Were had, intentionally or otherwise, covered the lapse.

The curtain fell closed; Sebastian stared at its folds.

And frowned.

She was resisting—more than he'd anticipated. He wasn't sure he understood why. But he was certain he didn't approve. And he definitely did not appreciate her quick-wittedness in avoiding him.

Society had grown used to seeing them together— they were now growing used to seeing them apart. That was not part of *his* plan.

From the shadows of his carriage drawn up by the verge in the park, Sebastian watched his future duchess animatedly holding court. She'd grown more confident, even more assured; she controlled the gentlemen around her, with a laugh, with a grimace, with one look from those wonderful eyes.

He couldn't help but smile, watching her listen to some anecdote, watching her manipulate the strings that made her would-be cavaliers extend themselves to entertain her. It was a skill he recognized and appreciated.

But he'd seen enough.

Raising his cane, he rapped on the door. A footman appeared and opened it, then let down the steps. Sebastian descended to the ground. The carriage he'd used was not his town carriage; this one was plain black and bore no crest on its panels. His coachman and footman were also in black, not his livery.

Which explained why he'd been able to sit and watch Helena without her noting him and taking flight.

She saw him now, but too late to take evasive action, to discreetly avoid him. Social constraint was, for once, working to his advantage—she was too proud to create a public scene.

So she had to smile and offer him her hand. She curtsied deeply, and he bowed, raised her. Then raised her hand and brushed a kiss across her knuckles.

Temper flared briefly in her eyes. She fought to quell her reaction, but he felt it. Increasingly haughty, she inclined her head. "Good afternoon, Your Grace. Have you come to take the air?"

"No, my dear comtesse, I came for the pleasure of your company."

"Indeed?" She was waiting for him to release her hand, too wise, after their recent meetings, to tug.

He looked around the circle of gentlemen, all younger, far less powerful than he. "Indeed." He glanced at Helena, met her gaze. "I believe these gentlemen will excuse us, my dear. I have a wish to view the Serpentine in your fair company."

He saw her breasts swell—with indignation and a hot-bloodedness he found unexpectedly alluring. Glancing around the circle again, he nodded generally, confident none would be game to cross swords with him.

Then he saw Mme Thierry. She'd been part of the group but until then blocked from his sight. To his surprise, she smiled at him, then turned to Helena. "Indeed, *ma petite*, we have stood here in the breeze long enough. I'm sure monsieur le duc will escort you back to our carriage. I'll wait for you there."

Sebastian could not have said who was the more surprised—he or Helena. He glanced at her, but she'd masked her reaction to the unexpected defection. However, her lovely lips set in a rather grim line as, after making her adieus to her cavaliers, she let him turn her down the walk to the water.

"Smile, *mignonne*, or those interested will believe we have had a falling-out."

"We have. I am not pleased with you."

"Alas, alack. What can I do to make you smile at me once more?"

"You can stop pursuing me."

"I would be happy to do so, *mignonne*. I confess, I find pursuing you increasingly tedious."

She looked at him, surprise in her eyes. "You will stop . . ." She gestured with one hand.

"Seducing you?" Sebastian met her gaze. "Of course." He smiled. "Once you're mine."

The French word she muttered was not at all polite. "I will *never* be yours, Your Grace."

"*Mignonne*, we have been over this many times— you will, one day, most definitely be mine. If you were honest, you would admit you know it."

Her eyes spat fire. She bit back a retort, flung him a furious glare, then looked haughtily ahead.

If they'd been in a room with a vase to hand, would she have thrown it? Sebastian found himself wondering— and then wondered at that fact. He had never before encouraged tantrums in his paramours, yet in Helena . . . her temper was so much an intrinsic part of her, so indicative of her fire, he found himself drawn to it—wanting to provoke all that energy so he could plunge into it, then deflect it into passion.

He was aware that his imperviousness, his calm reaction to her outbursts, was irritating her even more.

"There are not so many others around. Is it wise for us to be thus alone?"

The walks along both banks of the Serpentine were nearly deserted.

"It's the end of the year, *mignonne*. Plans are being made, the last-minute whirl all-consuming. And the day is hardly encouraging."

It was gray, cloudy, with a definite breeze carrying the first chill of encroaching winter. His gaze sliding approvingly over Helena's warm cloak, he murmured, "However, as to propriety, the gossipmongers have grown tired of watching us, grown weary of expecting a scandal. They've turned their eyes elsewhere."

She threw him an uncertain look, as if wondering just what he might risk in a nearly deserted public place.

He had to smile. "No—I will not press you here."

He thought she humphed, but her eyes said she accepted the assurance. After a moment she said, "I am not a horse to be walked so I don't chill."

Obligingly, he turned her up the next path, taking them back toward the carriage drive. "Mme Thierry's words invoked an unfortunate allusion."

"Her words were ill judged." Helena threw him a frowning look. "She has changed her opinion of you. Did you speak with her?"

"If you mean did I buy her cooperation, no. I haven't spoken with her except in your presence."

"Hmm."

They walked on in silence; the carriage drive lay not far ahead when he murmured, "I have enjoyed our walk, *mignonne*, but I want something more from you."

The glance she shot him was sharp—and furiously stubborn. "No."

He smiled. "Not that. All I wish for today is the promise of two dances at Lady Hennessy's ball tonight."

"*Two* dances? Is that not frowned on?"

"At this time of year no one will think anything of it." He looked ahead. "Besides, you deliberately denied me any dances last night. Two tonight is fair recompense."

Her head rose haughtily. "You were late."

"I am always late. If I arrived early, my hostess would faint."

"It is not my fault there are so many gentlemen eager to partner me that there were no dances left for you."

"*Mignonne*, I am neither gullible nor young. You deliberately gave all your dances away. Which is why you will promise me two for tonight."

"You forgot the 'or else.' "

He let his tone lower. "I thought to leave that to your imagination." He caught her eye. "How much do you dare, *mignonne*?"

She hesitated, then, exceedingly haughtily, inclined her head. "Very well, you may have your two dances, Your Grace."

"Sebastian."

"I now wish to return to Mme Thierry."

He said no more but led her to the Thierrys' carriage, then made his adieus. He stood back, and the coachman flicked the reins; he watched the carriage roll away down the avenue.

For four days they'd been sparring—he tempting her to him, she trenchantly resisting. A gentleman would have spoken, told her he meant marriage. As things stood . . .

He was a nobleman, no gentleman—the blood of conquerors flowed in his veins. And often, as now, dictated his actions.

It was impossible even to contemplate simply offering for her hand, not knowing she was so coolly appraising candidates and that he, more than any other currently in the ton, fitted her bill.

Face hardening, he turned and walked to his carriage.

Her resistance—unexpectedly strong—had only raised the stakes, focused his predatory senses more acutely, made it even more imperative that he win. Her.

He wanted her to accept him on his own terms, because of who he was and who she was underneath the glamour, stripped of their rank, man and woman, an equation as old as time. Wanted her to want him—the man, not the duke. Not because his rank exceeded hers and his estates and income were considerable.

Because she wanted him as he wanted her.

He wanted some hint of surrender, some sign of submission. Some sign that she knew she was his.

Only that would do. Only that would appease his need.

Once she'd acknowledged what lay between them, then he would speak of marriage.

The footman stood waiting, holding the carriage door. Sebastian called an order to return to Grosvenor Square, then climbed in. The door shut behind him.

Steeling herself, Helena curtsied to Sebastian, then rose and linked hands, twirling into the first figure of her first dance with him. *Think!* she ordered herself. *Of something other than him. Don't meet his eyes. Don't let his nearness swamp your senses.*

When, in the carriage on the way to the ball, she'd complained of his arrogance in demanding two dances, Marjorie had smiled and nodded, patronizingly encouraging, for all the world as if St. Ives were not one of the ton's leading rakes. As if he weren't the one Marjorie herself had labeled *dangereux*.

More surprising still had been Louis's complacency. He was supposed to be her protector. Helena stifled a snort. She suspected that Louis was not entirely aware of monsieur le duc's reputation, nor of his determination to avoid matrimony. When St. Ives had come to claim this dance, Louis had looked stupidly smug.

Aggravation, she'd discovered, was her best defense against Sebastian. Emboldened, she met his eyes. "I assume you'll be leaving London shortly?"

His long lips curved. "Indeed, *mignonne*. After next week, along with the rest of the ton, I'll quit London for the country."

"And where will you spend the festive season?"

"At Somersham Place, my principal estate. It's in Cambridgeshire." They circled, then he asked, "To where do you plan to retire, *mignonne*?"

"The Thierrys have not yet decided." As she crossed him in the dance, Helena noted the quality of Sebastian's smile. Everyone, it seemed, was smug tonight.

The devil prompted her to ask, "Has Lord Were returned to London?"

She glanced up.

His features hard, Sebastian trapped her gaze. "No. Nor is he expected in the near future."

They circled once more; she couldn't drag her gaze

from his—didn't dare. The movements of the dance seemed to mirror their interaction, hands touching, parting, she twirling away only to have to return to him.

She did, her skirts swishing as she turned before him, then paused, held up her hands. He stepped close behind her; his fingers locked about hers, and they stepped out in concert with the other dancers.

"Tempt me not, *mignonne*. Lord Were is not here to save you tonight."

The softly murmured words were threat and promise; they feathered over her exposed shoulder—goose bumps spread over her bare skin.

She turned her head slightly and murmured back, "I have told you, I am not for you, Your Grace."

He was silent for one instant, then whispered, "You will be mine, *mignonne*—never doubt it."

He released her and they separated, flowing with the dance—as she moved away, his fingers touched her nape, then trailed down and away.

She felt the touch in the tips of her breasts, as a wash of heat flaring beneath her skin. She forced her expression to an easy smile, forced her eyes to meet his directly.

At the end of the dance, he raised her, then carried her hand to his lips. "Soon, *mignonne*—soon."

Never! she vowed, but it wouldn't be easy to gainsay him.

She couldn't break her promise to grant him another dance, but if he couldn't find her . . .

She chatted, laughed, smiled, and silently plotted.

Louis, as always, hovered; on impulse she claimed his arm. "Stroll with me, cousin."

With a light shrug, he complied. Helena steered him toward the far end of the room where the dragonlike dowagers sat, sharp eyes scanning the throng, tongues wagging incessantly, brows poised to rise at the slightest sign of scandal.

"I've been thinking," she said, "that Lord Were might suit me as a husband. Have you an opinion on his lordship and whether Fabien would welcome an offer from him?"

"Were?" Louis frowned. "Is he the large, dark-haired, somewhat corpulent gentleman who favors brown coats?"

She wouldn't have called him corpulent. "He's about to step into a marquess's shoes, which will satisfy Fabien as to title. As for the rest, to me he seems eminently suitable."

"Hmm . . . from what I have heard, he is not highly regarded, this Were. He is quiet, retiring—self-effacing." That last, Louis said with a sneer. "I do not believe Uncle Fabien would think it wise for you to ally yourself with a weak man."

"Weak"—to her the word was the highest seal of approval. But, *"Bien sûr,"* she said. "I must think more on that."

In the corner of the room beyond the dowagers, a door stood ajar.

"Where are we going?" Louis asked as she led him to it.

"I want to see what lies beyond here. The air in this room is so stale." She stepped past him and through the door as the first strains of a minuet—her second dance with Sebastian—drifted over the crowd's head.

Louis followed her into a gallery. Three couples, summoned by the music, passed them, returning to the ballroom, leaving the gallery with its long windows overlooking the gardens deserted save for them.

"*Bon!*" Helena smiled. "It is much more peaceful in here."

Louis frowned but was distracted by a sideboard. He went to investigate the decanter and glasses sitting atop it. Helena drifted down the narrow room, drawn to the windows.

She was standing, gazing out at the stars, when a faint sound reached her.

A second later a deep voice drawled, "De Sèvres."

She turned to see Louis bowing deeply. Sebastian strolled out of the shadows shrouding the door.

He spoke to Louis. "Mademoiselle la comtesse is engaged to me for this dance, but as she feels the need for a few moments in quieter surrounds, I will remain with her here. No doubt you have engagements of your own in the ballroom."

Even through the gloom, Helena saw the sharp look Louis directed her way.

"Indeed, Your Grace." Louis hesitated for an instant, glancing once more at Helena. She couldn't believe he would leave her.

"You may rest assured," Sebastian drawled, "that

mademoiselle la comtesse will be safe with me. I will return her to Mme Thierry at the conclusion of the dance. Until then, I believe, her time is mine."

"As you say, Your Grace." Louis bowed again, then turned on his heel and left. He closed the door behind him.

Dumbfounded, Helena stared at the door. Louis couldn't be so witless as to believe she'd be safe alone with a man of Sebastian's reputation.

"I do not know the answer, *mignonne*, but he has indeed left us alone."

The faint amusement in Sebastian's voice fanned her anger. She clung to it and faced him as he crossed the room toward her. She lifted her chin, ignoring the skittering panic chasing over her skin. "This is not wise."

"I must agree, but it was your choice, *mignonne*." He halted before her; she saw he was smiling—a distinctly predatory smile. "If the minuet is not to your liking, there's another dance we might try."

She studied his eyes, found them impossible to read in the poor light. "No." She moved to cross her arms; he reached out and caught her hands, holding them lightly in his. She frowned at him. "I do not at all understand why you are doing this."

His lips quirked. "*Mignonne*, I assure it is I who do not understand why you are behaving as you are."

"*Me?* I would think the reason for my behavior was obvious. I have told you more than once that I will not be your mistress."

One brown brow arched. "Have I asked you to be my mistress?"

She frowned. "No, but—"

"*Bon*, we have that much clear."

"We have *nothing* clear, Your Grace—Sebastian," she amended as he opened his lips. "You admit to pursuing me, to wishing to seduce me—"

"Stop."

She did, puzzled by his tone, neither drawling nor cynical—straightforward.

He considered her, then sighed. "Would it help, *mignonne*, if I gave you my word I will not complete your seduction at any function we might attend, such as this ball?"

His word—she knew without asking that he would honor that to the death. Yet . . . "You said before that you are not playing a game with me. Is that true?"

His lips twisted, half wry smile, half grimace. "If you are a pawn, *mignonne*, so am I, and it is some higher power that moves us on this earthly board."

Helena considered for one minute more, then drew breath and nodded. "Very well. But if you are not to seduce me *en effet*, then what . . . ?"

She raised her hands, palms up, ignoring the light grasp of his. He changed his grip, took her hands in his. She saw his smile dawn again, still predatory, still too fascinating for her peace of mind.

"The music will end soon. In lieu of my dance, I would claim a favor."

She let her suspicion show. "And what is this favor?"

His smile deepened. "A kiss."

She considered again. "You have already kissed me twice—no, three times."

"Ah, but this time, I wish you to kiss me."

She tilted her head, considered him. If it was she doing the kissing . . . "Very well." She shook off his hands, and he let her.

Boldly, she stepped closer. Because of the difference in their heights, she had to slide her hands up over his chest, over his shoulders, and lock them about his neck—stretching herself against him.

He stood, passive, watching her from under hooded lids.

Praying that the sudden shock of the contact—breast to chest, hips to thighs—didn't show, valiantly ignoring the fascinating contrast between the silken softness of his coat and the hard body it covered, she drew his head down, stretched up on her toes, and set her lips to his.

She kissed him, and he kissed her back, but only in response, in equal measure. Reassured, pleasantly distracted, she repeated the caress, a little firmer, a little longer. His lips returned the pleasure, then parted slightly. She couldn't resist the temptation.

He tasted . . . male. Different, enticing. His tongue met hers, retreated, returned. Another dance, another play, the ebb and flow of a physical touch, one rather more intimate than the meeting of hands.

It was novel, exciting. She wanted to know more, learn more. Feel more.

Ten minutes later—ten totally enthralling, fascinating minutes of complete and utter abandon—she surfaced on a gasp. Lips parted, her heart thudding in her ears, she stared into his eyes, gleaming from beneath his heavy lids. Then she stared at his lips. Long, lean, lightly curved—so mobile.

So satisfying.

She swallowed. "The music's stopped."

"As you say."

Sometime while her wits had been distracted, his arms had closed around her, supporting her against him. She was caged by muscles that felt like steel, yet she'd never felt so comfortable, so secure. So uninterested in safety.

She dragged in a breath and kissed him again—just one last time to imprint the sensation on her memories. To let the feel of him, hard as rock beneath his finery, sink to her bones, to revel in the way her softer flesh sank against him.

He drew her deep but didn't try to hold her. When she pulled away, he let her.

She looked into his eyes. "You may set me down now."

"If you're quite sure you've finished?"

He didn't smile as he said it.

"Quite sure," she replied.

He let her slide down, set her on her feet; his arms fell from her, but reluctantly.

"My compliments, *mignonne*." Capturing her hand, he raised it, kissed it. "You play fair."

"*Certainement.*" She lifted her head, fighting down her dizziness. "I believe we should return to the ballroom."

She turned for the door; he stopped her with a hand

on her arm. "No—not that way. We've been here, alone, too long. It would be best to go by another route so the dowagers don't see us return."

She hesitated, then inclined her head. He had given his word; if the last ten minutes had proved anything, it was that she could place her trust in that.

Sebastian led her through a maze of corridors; they reentered the ballroom at the opposite end. He returned her to Madame Thierry's side, wondered fleetingly at that lady's clear encouragement, then, well satisfied, retired.

If Helena Rebecce de Stansion could resist the temptation to enjoy all he offered without risk, he'd eat his chapeau. And once she'd enjoyed, if he couldn't convince her to declare herself his . . .

He couldn't think of a suitable punishment, but no matter. He wasn't about to fail.

"It is all going well—fabulously well. Uncle Fabien's plan, under my guidance, is unfolding just as it ought." Louis stripped off his waistcoat and flung it in Villard's direction.

Stooping to pick up the garment, Villard murmured, "So she has caught his eye?"

"He has her in his sights, no doubt of that. He is hunting in earnest now. Until tonight"—Louis waggled his hand—"it could have been mere idle interest. But he is not idle now. And she, the prey, she is running. The chase is on!"

"Perhaps—if I might suggest—a note to your uncle to apprise him of your good news?"

Louis nodded vigorously. "Yes, yes, you are right. Uncle Fabien likes positive results. No sense in missing a chance to claim his notice." He waved at Villard. "Remind me to write first thing in the morning."

"If I might be so bold, m'sieur, the fast packet leaves early in the day. If you were to write this evening and a rider left tonight, monsieur le comte would have your good news days earlier."

Louis plopped down on the bed and stared at Villard.

Villard calmly added, "And monsieur le comte does like to have the most up-to-date news."

Louis continued to stare, then he grimaced and waved at Villard. "Bring me my writing case. I will write my communiqué now, and you may see it off immediately."

Villard bowed. "At once, m'sieur."

Chapter Four

⚜

The next morning Helena paced her bedchamber; eyes narrowed, she considered the night before.

Considered the unexpected tack Sebastian had taken.

Remembered her dreams.

Wondered again what it would have felt like to spread her hands over his chest, beneath the silk and satin of his coat, to feel the width and weight of his muscles . . .

"Non, non, non, et non!"

Furious, she whirled, kicking her skirts before her. *"That* is why he did it!"

To make her dream, yearn, desire . . . want. To make her come to him, surrender like some witless lovelorn maid.

A sneaky, underhanded conquest.

Safe and alone in her bedchamber, she could admit it might have worked.

"But not now." Not now that she'd realized his true goal. She was twenty-three—no starry-eyed innocent when it came to the games men played. A seduction could be achieved by more than one route; monsieur le duc assuredly knew every road.

"Every *twist* in every road. Hah!"

He would not catch her.

There was only just over a week to go before the ton left London; she could assuredly hold him at bay until then.

"*Mignonne*, it is customary to pay some attention to the gentleman who partners you in the dance."

Helena shifted her gaze to Sebastian and widened her eyes. "I was merely taking note of the ladies' jewels."

"Why?"

"Why?" She stepped around him, circled, then returned to face him, her gaze straying once more to the ladies nearby. "Because the quality here is quite remarkable."

"Given your heritage, you must possess a king's ransom in jewelry."

"*Oui*, but I left most of it in the vault at Cameralle." She gestured at the simple sapphire necklace she was wearing. "I did not bring the heavier pieces—I did not realize the need."

"Your beauty, *mignonne*, outshines any jewels."

She smiled, but not at him. "You have a very quick tongue, Your Grace."

Helena was at the breakfast table the next morning when a package was delivered.

"It's for you." Louis dropped it beside her plate as he joined her.

Marjorie peered up the table. "Who is it from?"

Helena turned the package in her hands. "It doesn't say."

"Open it." Marjorie set down her cup. "There will be a card inside."

Helena tore open the wrappings and reached in. Her fingers touched the plush cover of a jeweler's case—a frisson of presentiment raced over her skin. She stared at the open package, almost afraid to draw out the contents. Then she steeled herself and pulled.

A green leather case. She set aside the paper, opened the case. Inside, on a bed of deep green velvet, nestled a very long double strand of the purest pearls. The strands were interrupted at three points by single stones, each a perfect rectangle, cut very simply to showcase their color. At first she guessed peridot, but as she lifted the necklace and draped it between her hands, the stones flashed and the light caught them; their depth of color was revealed. Emeralds. Three large pure emeralds more vividly green than her eyes.

Earrings, each with a smaller emerald set above pearls, and a matching pair of bracelets—miniature versions of the necklace—completed the set.

Of the king's ransom she already owned, no piece appealed to her half as much.

Helena dropped the necklace as if it had burned her. "We must send it back." She pushed the case away from her.

Louis had been examining the packaging; now he glanced at the case. "There is no card. Do you know who sent it?"

"St. Ives! It must be from him." Helena pushed back her chair; some impulse was urging her to run, to flee from the necklace—from her wish to touch it, to run her fingers along the smooth strands. To imagine how it would feel around her throat, how it would look.

Damn Sebastian!

She stood. "Please arrange to have it returned to His Grace."

"But, *ma petite*." Marjorie had searched the packaging for herself. "If there is no card, then we cannot be sure who sent it. What if it wasn't monsieur le duc?"

Helena looked down at Marjorie; she could almost see Sebastian's smug smile. "You are right," she eventually said. She sat again. After a moment of staring at the pearls lying like temptation on their velvet bed, she drew the case closer. "I will have to think what is best to be done."

"*You* sent me these, did you not?"

The fingers of one hand caressing the pearls encircling her throat, Helena turned to face Sebastian. The silk of her pale green skirts swished sensuously; she let her fingers trail lovingly over the pearls, following the strands over her breasts.

Lips lightly curved, Sebastian watched every move. She could tell nothing from his face or his eyes.

"They look very well on you, *mignonne*."

She refused to think how well, how they made her feel.

As if she were *dangereuse*, too.

Only he could have delivered the ultimate temptation to play his game. Never before had she felt so powerful—powerful enough to engage with a man such as he.

A thrill of excitement, of insidious attraction flared; she turned, paced, unable to keep still.

When he'd appeared by her side in Lady Carlyle's ballroom, his eyes had gone straight to the necklace, then he'd quickly noted the other pieces she'd also donned. She'd acquiesced readily to his invitation to stroll the room. Sure enough, he had, as only he could, found an anteroom giving off the ballroom. An empty room, poorly lit by wall lamps, with a tiled floor and a small fountain splashing at its center.

Her heels clicked on the tiles as she paced before the fountain; she threw him an openly considering glance. "If not you . . . perhaps it was Were? Perhaps he is missing me."

Sebastian said nothing, but even in the weak light she saw his face harden.

"No," she said. "It was not Were—it was you. What do you expect to gain by it?"

He watched her—whether considering his answer or merely stretching her nerves tight, she could not tell—then said, "*If* I had sent such a gift, I would expect to receive . . . whatever response you would naturally give to one who had so indulged you."

She let her eyes flash, let her temper show. She'd grown accustomed, over the weeks, to letting him see it. Even now there seemed no reason to hide her feelings from him. With a swish of her skirts, she swung to face him and lifted her chin. "The thanks I would give to whoever had so indulged me . . . that I could give only if I knew who that gentleman was."

He smiled. With his usual prowling gait, he closed the distance between them. "*Mignonne*, I care not, in truth, whether you judge me the one deserving of your gratitude."

Halting before her, he raised one hand and tangled his long fingers in the strands below her throat. He lifted the pearls; fingers sliding, he gathered the lengthy strands in his hand until the slack was locked in his fist, poised above her neckline.

"I would much rather be assured," he murmured, voice deepening to its most dangerous purr, "that every time you wore this piece, you thought of me."

He opened his fist, let the pearls fall.

Weighted by the largest emerald, the strands dropped down her cleavage, slithered between her breasts.

She gasped at the heat—the heat of his hand held trapped in the pearls.

"I would much rather know that every time you wore this, you thought of us. Of what will be."

He hadn't completely released the necklace; one long finger remained hooked in the strands. Watching the strands, he raised them, then let them slide and slither down, around, caressing her bare breasts in defiance of her gown and chemise—her completely clothed state. Deliberately, he made the pearls rise and fall to a slow, sensuous rhythm, one she could all too readily imagine his fingers themselves following.

Her lungs had locked; she dragged in a shuddering breath, briefly closed her eyes. Felt her breasts rise, swell, heat.

He shifted closer—she sensed rather than saw or heard it, felt him like a flame on her skin. She opened her eyes—and fell into the blue of his.

"Every time you wear these, *mignonne*, think of . . . this."

She hadn't meant to let him get so close. Hadn't meant to tip up her face and let him kiss her. But with the intoxicating warmth of him so near, the murmurous sound of his deep voice in her ear, the sense-stealing sensation of the pearls, still warm, still shifting provocatively between her breasts, she was lost.

His lips closed over hers. At the first hint of pressure, the first demand, she opened to him, not submissively but defiantly, refusing, even now, to surrender.

She could kiss him and survive, let him kiss her and still not be his. If he thought otherwise, he would learn. Reaching up, she slid her fingers into his hair and boldly kissed him back. Surprised him for a second, but only that.

His response was unexpected—no suffocating rush of passion, of overwhelming desire. Instead, he matched her, gave her all she wanted, hinted at more. Lured her on.

She knew it, but resistance was impossible. The only way she could hold on to her self, retain some semblance of awareness and self-will, was to immerse herself in the kiss, give herself over to it and follow his lead, noting each step along the way, knowingly taking each one.

Within seconds he had taken her from this world. Only he could lead her back.

Sebastian released the pearls, left them to lie, a faint memory between her bare breasts. Closing his arms about her, he drew her to him, until her soft flesh was once again pressed against his much harder frame. Desire swelled, gnashed like some ravenous beast, wanting more—much more.

Wanting her beneath him, sheathing him.

He knew it couldn't be—not yet. Not tonight. Not tomorrow. He didn't even dare caress her more definitely, his rake's instincts warning not yet, not yet.

She was driving him slowly, steadily, mad. If he didn't have her soon . . .

Never had he waited so long; no other woman—none he had desired—had ever denied him. Had ever refused to take the journey with him.

Yet despite the fact that her body was his, despite the fact that her pulse leaped when he neared, her pupils dilated and her skin warmed the instant he touched her, her mind refused to yield—her will stubbornly stood in his way.

Every night he went without her only increased his desire, that primitive urge to seize, slake his lust . . . possess.

Her hands touched his cheeks, framed his face, held it steady as she pressed a flagrantly passionate kiss on him in return for his most recent foray. He felt his control shake, quake, as she teased and taunted him to reply . . .

He did, for one instant let his shield slip, let her glimpse what waited for her—the heat, the unbridled passion behind his suave mask.

All resistance fled before his onslaught; her spine, until then infused with her stubborn will, softened. Melted.

He drew back, quickly, before desire and rampant passion ran away with him—with them. Chest laboring, he lifted his head. Felt her drag in a long breath, felt her breasts press against his chest.

Then her lids fluttered; from beneath the lace of her long lashes, he saw her eyes gleam. They were more jewel-toned than his emeralds about her throat, hanging at her ears, circling her wrists.

Despite his frustration, satisfaction welled and warmed him. He eased his hold on her; she opened her eyes, blinked, stepped back.

Glanced at him warily.

He managed not to smile. "Come, *mignonne*—we must return to the ballroom."

She gave him her hand and let him lead her to the door. He paused as they reached it. Raising one hand, he hooked a finger in the pearl strands and lifted them from beneath her bodice, then draped them over the silk once more.

"Remember, *mignonne*." He caught her wide gaze. "Whenever you wear them, think of what will be."

* * *

When Helena awoke the next morning, the first thing she saw was his pearls cascading out of the green leather case. They sat on her dresser where she had left them—and mocked her.

"Je suis folle."

With a groan, she turned her shoulder on them, but she could, like phantoms, feel them as if they were still about her throat, at her ears, on her wrists.

She'd been mad indeed to think that, in that arena, she could hope to stand against him and prevail.

Her eyes narrowed as she thought back over the entire episode. Turning, she looked at the pearls again. Her first impulse had been to bury them at the bottom of her trunk. Pride dictated that she wear them every night. He'd comprehensively won that round, but she couldn't let him know it.

Which meant . . . that she would indeed remember every touch of the pearls, warm from his hand, against her bare breasts. Would indeed wonder . . .

She was getting very close to being out of her depth. She couldn't let him win the next round.

And she couldn't call a halt to the game.

She was doing it again—pulling back, tumbling obstacles into his path.

Across Lady Cottlesford's ballroom, Sebastian watched Helena with something very like aggravation simmering behind his façade.

Time was running out. He hadn't imagined, when he'd set out to make her admit she wanted him, that it would take this long. There were only five days left to

Lady Lowy's masquerade, the event that in recent years had heralded the ton's exodus from London.

He had five more days—five nights, more accurately—to gain her capitulation. To gain some indication that she would welcome his advances quite aside from a formal proposal of marriage. That was the minimum he would accept.

Five nights. Plenty of time normally. Except, with her, he'd already been laying siege for seven nights. Although he'd dented her walls, he hadn't yet set them crumbling, hadn't yet convinced her to lower her drawbridge and welcome him in.

"How's the wife hunting going?"

Martin. Sebastian turned as his youngest brother clapped him on the shoulder.

One glance at his face and Martin took a step back, held up his hands. "No one heard, I swear."

"Pray that that's true." Yet another irritation.

"Well? Do you still have your eye on the comtesse? Fetching piece, I admit, but sharp, don't you think?"

"Let her hear you speak of her like that and she's liable to demand I string you up by your thumbs. Or worse."

"Fire-eater, is she?"

"Her temper is marginally better than mine."

"Oh, all right, all right, I'll stop teasing. But you can't deny the issue has a certain personal relevance. You can hardly expect me to be uninterested."

"Uninterested, no. *Less* interested, certainly."

Martin ignored that and looked around. "Have you seen Augusta?"

"I believe," Sebastian said, studying the lace at his cuff, "that our dear sister has quit the capital. Huntly sent word this morning."

Martin glanced sharply at him. "She's all right?"

"Oh, entirely. But she and I agreed she'd had enough of the ton for the nonce, and as I've asked her to organize the festivities at Somersham, she had plenty to distract her."

"Ah!" Martin nodded. "Excellent strategy."

"Thank you," Sebastian murmured. "I do my poor best." Would that he could do better with a certain comtesse.

"There's Arnold. I must have a word." Martin clapped him on the back. "Good luck, not that you need it, but for God's sake don't fail."

With that injunction, he took himself off.

Sebastian resisted the urge to frown; instead, he looked across the room again—and realized he'd lost Helena.

"Damn!"

She must have been watching him, a good sign in itself. But . . .

He visually quartered the room but couldn't see her. Lips setting, he stepped away from the shadows and into the crowd.

It took him a good ten minutes of smiles, greetings, and sliding out of conversations before he came in sight of Mme Thierry, seated on a chaise. She was engaged in an animated conversation with Lady Lucas; Helena was nowhere in sight.

Sebastian swept the gathering again. His gaze fell on Louis de Sèvres. The man was Helena's nominal escort, but everyone assumed he was the protector sent by her family to keep a watchful eye on her. De Sèvres was ogling one of the Britten sisters. Sebastian strolled to his side.

His shadow alerted de Sèvres; he looked up—to Sebastian's surprise, he smiled and bowed obsequiously. "Ah—Your Grace. You are looking for my fair cousin? She has adjourned to hold court in the refreshment salon, I believe."

Sebastian considered de Sèvres and suppressed the urge to shake his head. The man was supposed to be protecting her . . . Mme Thierry, too, had changed her tune. If none within the ton had yet fathomed his true motive—and he would certainly know if they had— then it was inconceivable that the Thierrys and de Sèvres had seen through his mask.

De Sèvres shifted under his scrutiny; Sebastian decided to accept the unlooked-for assistance until he had Helena in hand. *Then* he would investigate what was behind de Sèvres's encouragement.

He looked over de Sèvres's head to the archway into the smaller salon. "Indeed? If you'll excuse me?"

He didn't wait for any answer, but strolled on.

One glance through the archway and he saw what she'd done—fortified her defenses. She'd surrounded herself with, not gentlemen of the ilk of Were and the others she'd been assessing, but with the latest crop of bucks and bloods looking to make their mark.

They were he twelve years ago, drawn like moths to her flame and brash and bold enough to consider any madness, even the madness of challenging him.

Especially over her. They were not in his league, but would never admit it, certainly not in her presence, something he understood.

He pondered that, considered the sight of them gathered around her, considered the pearls lying about her throat, at her ears, encircling her wrists. He turned away and beckoned a footman.

Helena breathed an inward sigh of relief when Sebastian quit the archway. She was rarely unaware of his gaze; over the last week it had become almost familiar, like a warm breath feathering her skin.

She quelled a shiver at the thought and doggedly focused her attention on young Lord Marlborough; although he was at least five years her senior, she still thought of him as young. Not experienced. Not . . . fascinating. At all.

But bored though she might be, at least she was safe. So she smiled and encouraged them to expand on their exploits. Their latest curricle races, the latest hell with its Captain Sharps, the latest outing of the fancy. They were so like little boys.

She'd relaxed, relaxed her guard, when a footman materialized at her elbow, a silver salver in his hand. He presented the salver to her; upon it resided a simple note. She considered it, picked it up. With a smile for the footman, who bowed and withdrew, then a swift smile around her protective circle, she stepped a little to the side and opened the note.

Which one will it be, mignonne? Pick one, and I will arrange that it will be he who will meet me. For when I come to fetch you from their midst, nothing is surer than that one of their number will be unable to resist and will challenge me. Of course, if you would prefer none meet his fate on some green field with tomorrow's dawn, then leave them and join me in the anteroom that gives off the front hall.

But if that is to be your choice, do not dally, mignonne, for I am not a patient man. If you do not appear shortly, I will come to fetch you.

Helena read the last words through a scarlet haze. Her hands shook as she refolded the note, then crammed it into the tiny pocket in her gown. She had to pause for an instant, draw breath, fight down her fury. Hold it in until she could let it loose on he who had provoked it.

"You must excuse me." To her ears, her voice sounded strained, but none of her self-engrossed cavaliers seemed to notice. "I must return to Madame Thierry."

"We'll escort you there," Lord Marsh proclaimed.

"No—I beg you, do not put yourselves to the trouble. Madame is only just inside the ballroom." Her tone commanding, Helena swept them with an assured glance.

They fell in with her wishes, murmuring their adieus, bowing over her hand—and forgetting her the minute she left them, she had not a doubt.

She reached the front hall without drawing undue attention. A footman directed her to the anteroom, down a short corridor away from the noise. She paused in the shadows of the corridor; eyes fixed on the door, she tweaked the note from her pocket, flicked it open, then she drew in a breath, gathered her fury about her, opened the door, and swept in.

The small room was dimly lit; a lamp burning low on a side table and the crackling fire were the only sources of light. Two armchairs flanked the fire; Sebastian rose from one, languidly, moving with his customary commanding grace.

"Good evening, *mignonne*." The smile on his lips as he straightened was mildly, paternalistically, triumphant.

Helena shut the door behind her, heard the lock fall with a click. *"How dare you?"*

She stepped forward, saw the smile fade from Sebastian's face as the light reached hers. "How *dare* you send me this?" She thrust the hand holding the note at him. Her voice quavered with sheer fury. "You think to entertain yourself by pursuing me, yet I have told you from the first that I will not be yours, my lord." She let her eyes flash, let her tone lash, let her polite mask fall entirely. She stalked forward. "As you find it so difficult to accept my decision, my steadfast rejection of you, let me tell you why I am here in London, and why you will *never* advance your cause with me."

With every word she felt stronger; her temper coalesced, hardened, infused her tone as she stopped two yards from him.

"I was sent to England to seek a husband—that you know. The reason I agreed to do so was to escape the clutches of my guardian, a powerful man of wealth, breeding, inflexible will, and unceasing ambition. Tell me, Your Grace, does that description sound familiar?"

She arched a brow at him, her expression contemptuous, coldly furious. "I am determined to use this opportunity to escape men such as my guardian, men such as yourself, men who think nothing—*nothing!*—of using a woman's emotions to manipulate her into doing as they wish."

His expression had lost all hint of animation. *"Mignonne—"*

"Do not call me that!" She flung the injunction at him, flung her hands in the air. "I am not *yours*! Not yours to command, not yours to play with like a pawn on some chessboard!" She flourished his note again. "Without thinking, without in any way considering my feelings, on discovering yourself thwarted you reached for a pen and invoked guilt and fear so I would do as you wished. So that you would triumph."

Sebastian tried to speak, but she cut him off with a violent slash of her hand.

"No! This time you will hear me out—and this time you will listen. Men like you—you are elegant, wealthy, powerful, and the reason you are so is because you are so adept at bending all around you to your will. And how do you accomplish that? By manipulation! It is second nature to you. You turn to manipulation with the same degree of thought you give to breathing. You cannot help yourself. Just look at how you 'manage' your sister—and I'm quite sure you tell yourself it's for her own good, just as my guardian doubtless tells himself that all his machinations are indeed ultimately for my good, too."

Sebastian held his tongue. Her anger burned, an almost visible flame. She reined it in, drew herself up. Her gaze remained steady on his.

"I have had half a lifetime of such managing, such manipulation—I will not suffer more. In your case, like my guardian, manipulating others—especially women—is part of your nature. It is part of who you are. You are helpless to change it. And the last man on earth I would consider as my consort is a man so steeped in the very characteristic I wish to flee."

She flung his note at him; reflexively, he caught it.

"Never dare send me such a summons again."

Her voice vibrated with fury and contempt; her eyes blazed with the same emotions.

"I do not wish to hear from you nor see you ever again, Your Grace."

She swung on her heel and swept to the door. Sebastian watched as she opened it, went out; the door shut behind her.

He looked down at the note in his hand. With two fingers, he opened it, smoothed it. Reread it.

Then he crumpled it. With one flick, he sent it flying into the fire. The flames flared for an instant, then subsided.

Sebastian considered them, then turned and strode for the door.

Chapter Five

*I*t started raining during the night and continued through the dawn, a steady, relentless downpour that left the streets awash and the skies a leaden gray.

Sebastian spent the morning at home attending to estate business, then essayed forth to White's for lunch—for distraction. But the conversation was as desultory as the weather; he returned to Grosvenor Square in midafternoon.

"Do you wish for anything, my lord?" Webster, his butler, shook water from his cloak, then handed it to a waiting footman.

"No." Sebastian considered the library door; he started toward it. "If anyone should call, I don't wish to be disturbed."

"Indeed, Your Grace."

A footman opened the door; Sebastian crossed the threshold, then paused. The door closed behind him. He grimaced, and headed for the sideboard.

Two minutes later, a brandy balloon liberally supplied with amber liquid in one hand, he sank into the leather armchair before the fire and stretched his damp shoes toward the blaze. He sipped, let the brandy and the fire warm him and chase away the chill that was only partly due to the weather.

Helena—what *was* he to do about her?

He'd understood very well all she'd accused him of; the unfortunate fact was that all she'd said was true. He couldn't deny it. There seemed little point in pretending that skillful manipulation wasn't, at base, a large part of his power, a large part of the arsenal men such as he—ex-warrior conquerors—used in these more civilized times. If given a choice, most people would rather accept his manipulation than face him over a battlefield.

"Most people," most unfortunately, did not include females reared to be the wives and queens of warrior conquerors.

She, in fact, was too much like him.

And, very clearly—very obviously to his highly attuned senses—she'd been subjected to her guardian's manipulations for too long, too consistently, too much against her unexpectedly strong will.

He could understand far better than most that enforced submission to another's will, especially coupled with awareness of the means of ensuring such submission—an awareness of the manipulation practiced on her—would have grated on Helena's proud and stubborn soul. Would ultimately have become unbearable. Her will was a tangible thing, not to be underestimated—as he'd discovered last night.

Spoiled by ladies who would at the most have pouted at his strategy, then allowed him to cheer them up, he'd been completely unprepared for Helena's fury. Her revelations, however, were what had given him pause.

They were what had him here, taking refuge in brandy and silence, hoping some solution would spontaneously emerge. As things stood . . .

He could hardly pretend he was not what he was, and if she'd set her stubborn mind against all liaisons with men such as he, if she could not bear to be the wife of a man such as he . . . what, indeed, could he do?

Other than brood. The occupation was unfamiliar. He didn't appreciate the hold she had on his mind, on his senses, on his thoughts, let alone his dreams.

Somewhere along the line, simple pursuit had transmuted to obsession, a state with which he'd had until now no serious acquaintance. His previous conquests, predatory though they might have been, had never really mattered.

Despite her eminently clearly stated position, he couldn't turn away and let Helena go. Simply let her disappear from his life.

Accept defeat.

Allow her to go through life never knowing what it would be like to scale the heights with him.

He watched her through the crowd at Lady Devonshire's drum and inwardly shook his head. At himself. If Helena heard his last thought, she'd have his entrails for garters, yet . . . it was, underneath all else, how he felt.

Her life would be so much less if she didn't live it to

the full—and she would never do that other than at the side of, in her terms, a powerful man. If he didn't make some push to rescript her thinking—to introduce the notion of compromise into her disdainfully dismissive mind, the idea that compromise with him might have bonuses beyond what she'd yet experienced—then she looked set to throw her scintillating self away on some mild and unsuspecting nobleman.

Her interest in Were and his ilk was now explained, the reason for her uninterest in him patently clear. She was as adept at manipulation as he was; she'd have Were, or any like him, in the palm of her small hand. She was determined no longer to be a puppet; to ensure that, she intended being the one who pulled the strings.

With him, that would never work.

With Lord Chomley, who she was currently charming, it might.

Keeping his expression impassive while gritting his teeth was not easy. Engaging in the usual social discourse while his attention remained riveted six yards away was, however, well within his abilities. Lady Carstairs had not yet realized he'd heard not one word of her story.

Helena touched Lord Chomley's sleeve and spoke to him; his lordship flushed, bowed extravagantly, then turned toward the refreshment room.

Sebastian refocused on Lady Carstairs. "I've just seen my brother. I must catch him. Do excuse me."

He bowed; her ladyship, thrilled that he'd remained listening for so long, released him with a smile.

Merging with the crowd, he circled to come up behind Helena, who was standing, waiting, by the side of the room. *"Mignonne,"* he murmured, taking her hand as he stepped around her, "I would like a word with you."

She'd jumped, stiffened. Now she looked haughtily at him as he bowed, then she bobbed a curtsy and tugged. He hesitated but let her fingers go without kissing them. She straightened and looked past him, head high.

"I have no wish whatever to speak with you, Your Grace."

Sebastian sighed. "You cannot avoid me forever, *mignonne*."

"Luckily, you will repair to your estates shortly and be gone from my life."

He couldn't stop his voice from hardening. "While you may believe you've had the last word, there's more that must be said between us, and of some of that you are as yet unaware."

She considered, then shifted her gaze to meet his eyes. "I do not trust you, my lord."

He inclined his head. "That I understand."

She narrowed her eyes. "Of what nature are these things of which I am 'as yet unaware'?"

"They're not the sort of things it would be wise to discuss in a crowded ballroom, *mignonne*."

"I see." She nodded, her gaze going beyond him. "In that case, I do not believe we *have* anything to discuss, Your Grace. I will not, not for any reason, go apart with you."

On the words, her brilliant smile lit her face. "Ah,

my lord—what perfect timing. His Grace was about to retreat."

Swallowing that word—retreat be damned—ruthlessly suppressing his reaction to the flash of fire in her green eyes, Sebastian exchanged bows with Chomley, returning with a glass of orgeat, then turned back to Helena and reached for her hand. She was forced to extend it.

"Mademoiselle la comtesse." With exquisite grace, he bowed and pressed his lips to her knuckles. He caught her gaze as he straightened. "Until later, *mignonne*."

With a calm nod, he strolled away, leaving Lord Chomley staring after him, mouth opening and closing like a fish.

His lordship turned to Helena. "Later?"

She smiled serenely, quashing the impulse to scream. "His Grace has an odd sense of humor."

A dry, rather caustic wit that, despite all her intentions, all her self-admonitions, Helena missed. Increasingly missed. She used the fact that she'd come, unwittingly, to rely on his company to leaven her evening entertainments as a prod to stiffen her resolve. To ensure she did not weaken. None knew better than she how foolish it was to become dependent in even the smallest way on a powerful man.

He'd exploit her weakness if he knew.

She concentrated on ignoring him, despite the fact that she was, as always, aware of his presence, his gaze—forced herself to give her attention to the increasingly urgent task of choosing a suitable nobleman to marry.

About her, Lady Castlereagh's ball was in full swing. The ton, it appeared, flung itself into this last week's entertainments with an energy to rival Parisian society at its most frenetic. Tonight, a troupe of Morris dancers had opened the ball, decked out in festive colors, twirling ribbons of green and red. In addition, a concoction derived from mead, claimed to be a modern equivalent of the ancient wassail, was being freely served; its effect on the guests was already evident. Helena smiled and declined to imbibe—she needed to keep her wits about her.

Two nights had passed since Lord Chomley had failed to discern the humor in St. Ives's "later"; his lordship had clearly not been for her. Since then she'd been doggedly paring her list—thanks to the weather, she could accomplish little else through the days. Other than Were, currently out of town, there were three others who might do. She didn't doubt her ability to dazzle them, to successfully encourage them to offer for her hand, but which one should she choose?

As far as she'd been able to learn through all manner of discreet inquiries, in title, estates, and income there was little difference between them. Each possessed, it appeared, an easygoing nature; any of the four should be easy to manage. With all her criteria met, she'd had to add another—a deciding factor.

She'd spent seven years being paraded before the most exacting connoisseurs of the French nobility; she had long ago realized that, for her, physical touch was a most useful means of categorizing men. There were those whose touch made her flesh creep—she'd met too many of that group for her liking. Not one had been kind or trustworthy. Then there were those whose touch might have been that of a friend or a maid. Such men were generally decent, upright souls, but not necessarily of strong will or strong mind.

There had ever been only one whose touch had made her glow.

To her, he was the most dangerous of all.

So . . . it was time to assess the three candidates now in London for how their touch affected her. She'd already danced with Were, strolled with him. His touch did not warm her, excite her, but neither did it make her flesh creep. Were had passed the test. If the others did not make her flesh creep, or glow, they would remain on her list, too.

Lord Athlebright, heir to the Duke of Higtham, was at this moment dancing attendance on his mother, but Viscount Markham, an amiable gentleman of some thirty-odd years, heir to the Earl of Cork, was approaching.

"My dear comtesse." Markham bowed gracefully. "You must have only recently arrived. I could not have remained in ignorance of your fair presence for long."

Helena smiled. "We have just arrived." She extended her hand. "I would like to stroll, if you're agreeable?"

His lordship took her hand, smiling easily. "It would indeed be my pleasure."

The touch of hands, more precisely of fingertips, was not enough to judge. Helena glanced around but couldn't see any musicians. "Will the dancing start soon?"

"I doubt it." Markham looked at her. Was she imagining the calculating gleam in his eye? "Lady Castlereagh calls her evenings balls, but in reality, dancing is the last thing on her mind. Consequently, there'll be but a few dances, and those most likely late."

"Ah, I see." Helena bided her time as they stopped and chatted, then moved on through the crowd. "I have to confess"—she leaned closer to Markham and lowered her voice—"that I find the English penchant for such crowded rooms somewhat . . . enervating." She glanced up and met his eyes. "Dancing, that gives one a little space for a time, but . . . *tiens*, how is one to breathe?"

She made the question a laughing one, but Markham had already raised his head, looking over the crowd to scan the room. Then he looked down at her, his gaze unreadable. "If you would like to stroll in less crowded surrounds, there's a conservatory just off the music room. We could repair there if you wish."

There was an eagerness in his tone that alerted her, but she needed her list narrowed to one name by the end of tomorrow night—the night of Lady Lowy's masquerade, the last night the ton would grace the capital. "You know the house well?" she asked, temporizing.

"Yes." Markham smiled ingenuously. "My grandmother and Lady Castlereagh were bosom-bows. I was often dragged here to be shown off when I was young."

"Ah." Helena smiled back, feeling rather more comfortable. "Where is this music room?"

He led her into a side corridor, then down an intersecting corridor. The music room lay at its end; beyond, through glass-paneled doors, stood a room with walls and roof primarily composed of glass. Built out into the gardens, it was lit by weak moonlight.

Markham opened the door and ushered her in. Helena was entranced by the plethora of shadows, the odd shapes cast upon the green tiles. The air was cool but not chilly, the gentle splash of raindrops on the glass a curiously soothing sound.

She sighed. "It is very pleasant here." She did find the crowds trying, the sense of being hemmed in with nothing but hot, heavily perfumed air all about her suffocating. But here . . . gratefully, she drew in a deep, deep breath. As she turned to Markham, she was surprised to find his gaze somewhat lower than her face.

He recovered swiftly and smiled. "There's a pond—this way, from memory."

His memory was good. The conservatory was bigger than she'd guessed; within a minute of leaving the area before the door and plunging down a series of narrow paths, she wasn't sure which way led back.

"Ah—here it is."

The pond, quite a large one, was set into the floor, its raised lip and the inside surface covered in bright blue tiles. It was filled to the level of the floor; against the tiles, Helena could see shapes drifting in the water.

"Fish!" Looking down, she leaned over the pool.

Markham leaned beside her. "There's a fat one—look!"

Helena edged farther; Markham shifted. His shoulder bumped hers.

"Oh!"

She grabbed for Markham—he grabbed her.

"Helena! My dear, dear comtesse."

He tried to kiss her.

Abruptly bracing her arms, Helena struggled to hold him off.

"Don't fight me, sweet, or you'll fall in the water." Markham's tone was warm and far too knowing, too amused.

Helena inwardly cursed. She'd been too trusting.

His hands shifted on her back and her nerves leaped—not pleasurably. He'd yet to touch her bare skin, but every sense she possessed was rebelling at the mere thought.

"Stop this!" She put all the command she could muster into her tone.

Markham chuckled. "Oh, I will—eventually."

He tried again to draw her to him. She resisted. Struggled. *"No!"*

"Markham."

He started so much he nearly dropped her. The single word—and its tone—sent relief pouring down Helena's veins. She didn't even care what the fact portended—she just wanted to get out of Markham's arms.

They'd gone slack. She got her balance, then, with a wrench, pulled back. Stepped back, glanced around.

Markham shot her a frowning glance but immediately returned his gaze to her savior.

Sebastian stood half obscured by the shadows, yet no shadow could dim the menace he projected. It was there in his stance; it hung in the tense silence. Helena had experience aplenty of being in the presence of displeased powerful men. Sebastian's displeasure rolled past her like a wave and broke over Markham.

Involuntarily, Markham stepped back, putting more space between himself and her.

"I believe you were about to apologize?"

Sebastian's voice held the chill of hell, the promise of damnation.

Markham swallowed. Without taking his gaze from Sebastian, he bowed to Helena. "Pray accept my apologies, comtesse."

She did nothing, said nothing, regarding him as coldly as Sebastian.

"As mademoiselle has grown weary of your company, I suggest you leave." Sebastian, ever graceful, walked forward; Markham backed, glanced around wildly, then edged toward one path. "One thing—I take it I don't need to explain how . . . unhappy I would be if any mention of this incident or, indeed, of mademoiselle la comtesse at all were to be traced to you?"

"No need at all." His face set, Markham looked at them both, then nodded curtly. "Good night."

He left; they heard his footsteps striding along, faster and faster, then they paused; the door opened, shut, and he was gone.

Helena let out a shuddering sigh of relief; crossing her arms, she shivered.

Sebastian had halted two feet away; he turned his

head and his gaze to her. "I think, *mignonne,* that you had better tell me just what you are about."

The evenness of his tone did not deceive her; behind his mask he was angry. She lifted her chin. "I do not like such crowds. I thought to walk in less stifling surrounds."

"Perfectly understandable. What is somewhat less understandable is why you chose Markham as your escort."

She threw a frowning glance in the direction the viscount had gone. "I thought he was trustworthy."

"As you have discovered, he is not."

When she didn't respond but continued to frown distantly, Sebastian ventured, "Do I take it you've struck him off your list?"

That got her attention; she turned her frown on him. "Of course! I do not like to be mauled."

He inclined his head. "Which brings me back to my original question—what are you about?"

She considered him, then drew herself up. "My actions are no concern of yours, Your Grace."

"Except that I choose to be concerned. I repeat, what game are you playing with your prospective suitors?"

Her chin rose another notch; her eyes flashed. "It is none of your business!"

He merely arched a bored brow and waited.

"You cannot"—she gestured at him with both hands as she searched for the word—"*compel* me to tell you just because you wish to know!"

He said nothing, simply looked at her—let his intent reach her without words.

She met his gaze, read his eyes, then flung her hands in the air. "No! I am not some weak-willed pawn in some game. I am not part of any game of yours. This is not some battle you must win."

His lips curved, his smile wry. "*Mignonne*, you know what I am—precisely what I am. If you insist on standing against me, then . . ." He shrugged.

The sound she made was one of muted fury. "I will not tell you, and you cannot make me." She folded her arms and glared at him. "I doubt you carry thumbscrews in your pockets, Your Grace, so perhaps we should adjourn this discussion until you have had time to find some."

He laughed. "No thumbscrews, *mignonne*." He caught her irate gaze. "Nothing but time."

Her thoughts flitted through her eyes, which then widened. "That's preposterous. You cannot mean to keep me here . . ."

She glanced at the nearest path.

"There is no possibility whatever that you will leave this clearing until you tell me what I wish to know."

She glared at him, belligerently furious. "You are a *bully*."

"You know very well what I am. Equally, you know that you have no choice, in this instance, but to concede."

Her breasts rose; her eyes sparked. "You are worse than even he!"

"He who? Your guardian?"

"*Vraiment!* He is a bully, too, but he would never admit it."

"I regret that my lack of duplicity offends you, *mignonne*. However, unless you wish to feature in a scandal, even at this last gasp of the year, you would do well to start explaining. You have been absent from the ballroom for twenty minutes."

Helena shot him a furious look but knew she had no choice. "Very well. I wish to narrow my list to one by tomorrow night, before the ton leave for their estates. There were four gentlemen to consider—now there are only three."

Sebastian nodded. "Were, Athlebright, and Mortingdale."

She stared at him. "How did you know?"

"Acquit me of ignorance, *mignonne*—you told me your guardian's criteria, and I guessed yours some nights ago."

"*Eh, bien!*" She put her nose in the air. "Then you know all, so we may return to the ballroom."

"Not quite."

She glanced at Sebastian; he caught her eye.

"I know why those three and Markham were on your list. I know why Markham no longer is. I do not know what other quality you have chosen to assess, only that you've chosen something and that is what brought you here."

She looked toward the path. "I merely wished for a moment's peace."

Sebastian's long fingers slid around her chin and firmed; he turned her face to his. "It's pointless to lie to me, *mignonne*. Despite all you say, you are much like those you run from—powerful men. You are enough like me that I can see at least part of what is in your mind. You are coolly and calmly assessing these men as your suitors. You care nothing for those three, only that they meet your needs. I am . . . concerned, if you wish, over what the final need you've focused on is."

Her temper unfurled—she felt it spread its wings; she lunged and tried to drag it back, but it shrugged aside her will and flew free.

It wasn't simply the fact that he did indeed understand her well—as well as Fabien had always seemed so effortlessly to do; while she might, in some cool part of her mind, admit that he was right in comparing her to them, she did not like the notion at all, did not like hearing it so calmly stated as truth. But it wasn't that that loosed her fury.

It wasn't even that, this close to him, she was acutely aware of the weight of his will, a tangible entity pressing her to submit.

It was her reaction to his touch, to the heat of his fingers cradling her chin—the instantaneous leaping of her heart, the tightening of her breathing, the sudden focus on him, the wash of heat within. The flare of recognition, the flash of a fire as old as time.

Her suitors were as nothing to her. Fabien's touch did not set her heart racing. But this man—his touch—did.

Madness.

"Since you are so boorish as to insist, I will tell you." Madness to do so; impossible to resist. "I have decided to test that each gentleman's touch does not repel me." She lifted her chin from his fingers, her eyes locked challengingly on his. "That is, after all, a most pertinent consideration."

His face hardened, but she could read nothing in his eyes, blue on blue, oddly shadowed. He lowered his hand.

"Were—does his touch repel you?"

His tone had deepened; a lick of caution skittered up her spine. "I have danced with him, walked with him—I feel nothing when he touches me."

Satisfaction glimmered briefly in Sebastian's eyes; she deliberately added, "So Lord Were, at present, is the only one who has attained my final list."

He blinked; his focus remained on her as he thought, weighed, considered . . .

"You will not attempt to test Athlebright or Mortingdale."

Those who knew him not might have assumed the comment to be a question; Helena recognized it as a decree, an order not to be disobeyed. Supremely assured—flown on temper—she lifted her head. "But of course I shall test them. How else am I to decide?"

With that eminently rational response, she turned to the path leading back the way she'd come. "And now, as I have told you all, you will hold by your word and allow me to return to the ballroom."

Buoyed by even so mild a triumph, she stepped out.

"Helena!"

A growl—a clear warning. She didn't stop. "Mme Thierry will be growing worried."

"Damn it!" He broke from his stance by the pool and stalked after her. "You can't be so witless—"

"I am not witless!"

"—as to imagine, after your *success* with Markham, that encouraging men to take you in their arms is a good idea!"

He was speaking through his teeth—a most wonderful sound. "I did not encourage Markham to be so . . . *outré*. He engineered the incident and grabbed me. I did not know he was no true gentleman."

"There are many things you don't know." She only just caught Sebastian's mutter, although he was following close behind her. The next instant he said, "I want you to promise me you won't plot to get Athlebright or Mortingdale alone—that any *testing* you do will be done in the middle of a damn ballroom in sight of the entire ton."

She pretended to consider, then shook her head. The glass-paned doors lay before her. "I do not think I can promise that. I am running out of time." She shrugged. "Who knows what I may need to—"

She had no chance to gasp, to scream. Sebastian's hand closed about hers; he swung her to face him, backed her toward the wall beside the door. A narrow ledge ringed the room, running around the base of the wall; she stumbled as, eyes wide, fixed on his, she backed into it.

He caught her other hand, lifted both, steadying her as, instinctively, she stepped up, back—her shoulders and hips hit the wall.

She caught her breath, opened her lips—

He raised her hands on either side until they were

level with her head, then pressed them to the wall—
and deliberately stepped nearer.

Leaned nearer.

Caged her.

Trapped her.

She could barely breathe, didn't know if she dared.
His strength surrounded her, held her—imprinted itself on her senses. No more than an inch separated
their bodies; she could feel his heat the length of hers.

Because of the step, all he needed to do was lower his
head to look her in the eye. He did; his gaze locked
with hers. His features could have been hewn from
granite. "You will promise me you will do no more
testing—not unless it's in public."

Her temper returned with a vengeance. She let it
burn in her eyes as she tested his grip, more out of instinct than expectation. His fingers tightened, just
enough for her to feel their steely strength, to know she
couldn't break free, but he wasn't gripping tightly
she couldn't claim he was hurting her. She didn't dare
shift her body away from the wall. If she did, she'd
move into him.

"Men!" She spat the word like an epithet into his
face. "You are all alike! Not to be trusted!"

By sheer luck, she hit a nerve—touched tinder to his
temper; she saw it spark in his eyes, saw his lips thin.

"We are *not* all alike."

Every word was gritted out.

She raised a haughty brow. "Do you mean I can trust
you?" She widened her eyes, daring him to lie.

His eyes remained on hers; she caught a glimpse, un-expected, of sudden turmoil.

"Yes!" He flung the word at her; it struck her, left her reeling. She immediately sensed him soften, rein in his temper. "In your case . . . yes."

Her heart had leaped to her throat. Shocked, she searched his eyes. He wasn't lying, even though his temper still prowled, as did hers. But she knew truth when she heard it; he had no reason to lie. But what reason could he have? . . .

"Why?" She searched his hard features, hoping to catch some hint.

Sebastian knew the answer—could feel the power rise through his anger, shading it, controlling it.

She'd refused to go apart with him—to let him talk with her privately, feel his way with her—even though his intentions were, this time, of the most honorable. Instead, she'd tapped Markham on the shoulder and slipped away with him.

He'd been coldly furious. Why? Because she meant more to him than any other woman ever had.

He'd been watching when she and Markham had left the ballroom. He'd followed to ensure nothing came of the incident. Only to learn . . .

The idea that she might willingly put herself in the way of the type of insult Markham had offered was not to be borne.

Why? Because he cared.

The realization left him shaken—left him, for once, without any glib words, any drawling phrase to turn her mind away from what he'd only just realized and didn't yet want her to see.

Her eyes were wide green pools, easy to read, easy to drown in. She was caught, tempted . . . fascinated.

So was he.

He breathed deeply, trying to clear his mind, trying to think.

Her skin had heated, courtesy of his nearness; her perfume, French, elementally exotic, rose and wreathed his senses.

Their faces were close, as were their bodies—close enough for her to sense the change in his intent. Her eyes widened fractionally, then her lids fell as her gaze shifted from his eyes to his lips.

He closed the distance between them, slowly, un-threateningly.

She lifted her face, tipped back her head.

Their lips brushed. Touched.

Met.

Fused.

The power flared—like a spark set to dry grass, it flamed, then raced, taking them both, drawing them in, sucking them into its heat.

It was like nothing he knew. No kiss he'd ever experienced had caught him as this did, held his attention so completely, so effortlessly, so focused on her, on her lips, on her mouth, on the dark thrill of sliding deep, caressing her intimately, on the sensual mating of their tongues.

She followed his lead, matching him step for step,

fearless in her innocence. He'd kissed her deeply before, but this time she wanted more, lured him on.

Unknowingly—or knowingly? He couldn't tell.

He couldn't think. Couldn't reason. Couldn't draw back from the conflagration.

His senses were reveling, in her, in the honeyed taste of her, the warm haven of her mouth, the supple softness of her breasts firm against his chest, the flagrant promise in the body arching lightly to meet his.

He could do nothing more than take all she offered and return all she demanded. Fall more deeply under her spell.

Helena had stopped thinking some instants before their lips had met. The knowledge that he was going to kiss her was enough, of itself, to focus her mind on one thing and that alone.

Him.

She wished it weren't so, but it was. Her mind, her senses—her very heartbeat—seemed to be his to claim. And no matter how much she might lecture herself when apart from him, she couldn't hold back from this part of his game.

Dangereux.

The word whispered through her mind but she no longer believed it, at least not in the physical sense. He would not harm her—he'd told her she could trust him. In truth, she already did.

He might prey on her mind and lay waste to the defenses she'd erected against powerful men, but while in his arms with his lips on hers, she knew, and understood, only one thing.

He was hers.

Hers to command at least in this arena—hers to claim if she wished. He was in control, but it was she he sought to please—a conundrum perhaps, but the thought of having a powerful man at her feet was too tantalizing, too tempting, too elementally enthralling to forgo.

His pleasure was hers. She sensed it through his kiss, through his immediate response to any demand she chose to make. Any hint of trepidation and he would ease back, soothe her, wait for her sign he could take her mouth again, that she was ready again to sink deep into the kiss, let his tongue probe, caress, slide about hers, seductively tangling.

He hadn't released her hands; instead, his fingers had locked, not painfully, but his grip was unbreakable, his forearms outside hers against the wall, holding his weight from her. She wanted his weight on her. Her whole body had come alive, heated, nerves afire. She wanted him against her, chest to breast, thighs to hips. Wanted him.

She arched, touched him. For one glorious instant, she let her body caress him.

Sensed his immediate response—sensed the depth of the fire she hadn't yet walked through. Felt his control quake.

They broke the kiss.

Both of them. They needed to breathe, needed to think. Had to pull back from the brink.

They were both breathing rapidly, each one's gaze locked on the other's lips.

Simultaneously, they lifted their eyes; their gazes met, held.

They searched each other's eyes; her thoughts were reflected in his—she felt as if he could see into her soul.

This was not the right place, not the right time.

Whether there would ever be a right place, a right time, neither knew, but they could not go further tonight.

They both knew it. Recognized the fact.

When the pounding in her ears eased enough for her to hear, Helena drew in a deep breath and softly said, "Let me go."

Not an order, but a simple direction.

He hesitated. Then his grip eased, bit by bit. As his touch left her skin, she eased her hands from under his, lowered her arms. She ducked under his arm, stepped away from the wall, out of the cage of his arms.

He turned his head but didn't otherwise move.

She took another step away, already missing—regretting the loss of—his heat. Then she lifted her head; without turning around, she said, "For your help with Markham—thank you."

She hesitated for an instant, then walked to the door.

Her hand was on the knob when she heard him murmur, soft and low, "Until later, *mignonne*."

Sebastian let himself into his house in Grosvenor Square in the small hours. After leaving Lady Castlereagh's, he'd repaired to his club, then gone with friends to a hell. No game of chance had been able to distract him from his thoughts; the hours had served only to crystallize his resolution.

Leaving his cloak and cane in the front hall, he went into the library. After lighting a lamp, he settled behind his desk—settled to the letter he'd decided to write.

He addressed it to Thierry. Helena was staying under Thierry's roof, nominally in his care; his wife had introduced her to society. De Sèvres's relationship to Helena he was less sure of, and when all was said and done, he didn't trust the man. Thierry, despite being a Frenchman, was a straightforward soul.

The scritch-scratch of his pen across the page was the only sound discernible; the silence of the huge house, his home from birth, lay like a comfortable blanket about him.

He paused, looking down, considering what he'd written, what he had yet to say. Then he bent and wrote again, until he reached the end and closed with his flourishing signature: St. Ives.

Sanding the letter, he sat back. Looked across the room to where the embers of the fire glowed in the grate.

He didn't know if he could do it—if he could make the concessions she'd demand, the concessions she might indeed need in order to become his duchess. But he would try. He had accepted that he must, that he had to do everything within his considerable power to ensure she became his.

His wife.

The equation was a simple one. He had to marry.

And at the last moment, he'd met her, the only woman he'd ever wished to possess for all time.

It was she or no one.

He'd wanted, waited for, some sign that she wanted him, that she recognized the fact that she did. Tonight . . . tonight they'd come very close to stepping over that invisible line, taking what had thus far been an acceptable interaction into another arena, an illicit one.

They'd drawn back, but only just, and she'd known it, realized the truth as well as he.

It was enough—sign enough. Confirmation enough, if he'd needed any reassurance.

She wanted him in precisely the same way he wanted her.

He glanced at the letter, let his eyes run over his careful phrases inviting the Thierrys, mademoiselle la comtesse d'Lisle and M. de Sèvres to spend the next week at Somersham Place. He had made it clear that this was to be a private visit, that the only others at his principal estate would be Cynster family members.

That last should make his direction patently clear; such a summons, couched in such terms, could mean only one thing. But with that "thing" unstated, it could not be taken for granted.

He smiled as he considered how Helena might react— he couldn't, even now, predict it. But he would see her tomorrow night, at Lady Lowy's masquerade. Whatever her reaction, he was sure he'd learn of it then.

Tipping the sand aside, he folded the parchment, lit the candle, and melted a stub of wax, then set his seal to the letter. Rising, he turned down the lamp, then crossed to the door.

In the front hall, he dropped the letter on the salver on the side table.

Done.

He paused, then headed for the stairs and his bed.

Chapter Six

⁂

The following morning at nine o'clock, Villard pulled back the curtains about his master's bed. Louis started awake, then scowled.

Villard hurried into speech. "M'sieur, I knew you would wish to have these immediately." He deposited a package on the bed beside Louis.

Louis frowned at the package, then his face cleared. "*Bon, Villard. Très bon.*" Louis struggled free of the covers. "Bring me my chocolate, and I will read my uncle's dispatches."

Settling against the pillows, Louis ripped open the package addressed in Fabien's distinctive hand. Three letters wrapped in a single sheet of parchment spilled onto the sheets. There was writing on the parchment, an order: *Read my letter to you before you do anything else. F.*

Louis studied the three letters. One was for him; another, also from Fabien, was addressed to Helena. The third was also for Helena, but addressed in a girlish hand. After a moment of pondering, Louis decided it must be from Ariele. He set aside Helena's letters and opened his.

There were two sheets closely covered in Fabien's forceful black script. Smiling in anticipation, Louis smoothed them out—he looked up as Villard reappeared with his chocolate on a tray. He nodded, picked up the cup, took a sip, then held up the letter and started to read.

Villard saw the smile fade from his master's face, saw it pale. Louis's hand shook. Chocolate spattered the sheets, and he swore. Villard jumped to mop the spill. Scowling, Louis set the cup back on the tray. He returned to his letter.

Under pretext of readying Louis's clothes, Villard watched. When Louis set down the letter and stared blankly across the room, he deferentially murmured, "Monsieur le comte was not pleased?"

"Eh?" Louis blinked, then waved the letter. "No, no—he was pleased with the progress. Thus far. *But.*" Louis looked at the letter again, then carefully folded it. Villard said nothing; he would read it later.

Some minutes passed, then Louis ruminated, "There is, it seems, more to my uncle's plans than meets the eye, Villard."

"It has ever been so, m'sieur."

"He says we have done well but we must move faster. I was not aware—it seems the English nobility invariably adjourn to their estates in but a few days. I was anticipating another week."

"The Thierrys have not mentioned this."

"No, indeed. I will take it up with Thierry when he returns. But for now there is a great challenge facing us, Villard. We must somehow ensure that St. Ives is sufficiently taken with Helena to invite her to visit at his country house. The dagger Uncle Fabien seeks to reclaim is apparently kept there."

Shaking out a coat, Villard frowned. "Do you think monsieur le duc is liable to issue such an invitation?"

Louis snorted. "He's been hot after Helena since we arrived, just as Uncle predicted. Don't forget, these English ape our ways, so yes, as Helena has successfully held him at bay, then the natural course would be for him, a powerful nobleman, to invite her and the Thierrys and myself to stay, with a few others to generate the necessary camouflage, then seduce Helena into his bed. It is the way things are done at home—it will be the same here."

"Is there not a certain danger there?"

Reaching for his chocolate, Louis smirked. "That is what is most entertaining. It is Helena against St. Ives, and my money is on Helena. She is a prude, that one." Louis shrugged. "Twenty-three and a virgin yet—what would you do? She isn't likely to succumb to St. Ives's blandishments, and you and I, Villard, will be there to ensure he has no chance to force her."

"I see." Villard turned to the wardrobe. "So the plan now is . . . ?"

Louis drained his chocolate, then frowned. "The first thing will be to secure this invitation, and that *must* be done tonight." He glanced at the folded letter. "Uncle Fabien makes it very clear we are to do everything needful—*everything*—to ensure that Helena is invited to St. Ives's estate."

"And once the invitation is in our hands?"

"We ensure Helena accepts, and goes."

"But will she?"

Louis's gaze went to the two letters addressed to Helena. "Uncle instructs that I use my best endeavors, but if she proves stubborn ... I am to give her these letters."

"Do we know what they contain?"

"No—only that once she reads them, Helena will do as he has ordered." Louis drew in a breath and dragged his gaze from the fascinating letters. "However, Uncle strongly advises that I wait until we are at St. Ives's estate before giving the letters to Helena. He says I should not show his hand too soon, not unless she balks entirely at the first fence."

Louis stared unseeing across the room. "So! We must secure this invitation tonight. I will need to make sure that Helena plays the game hard with St. Ives—that she inflames him and leaves him no choice but to act as we wish. That is the first thing." Louis glanced at the letters. "For the rest, we will see."

Villard laid a waistcoat on the dressing tree. "And what of m'sieur's own plans?"

Louis grinned as he threw back the covers. "Those have not changed. Helena should have been wed long ago. The matter of her marriage is now a difficulty for Uncle Fabien—a liability. The solution I propose is one I'm sure he will support, once he sees its brilliance. It would be nonsensical to lose the de Stansion wealth to another family when we can keep it for ourselves."

Standing, Louis allowed Villard to help him into his dressing robe. His gaze was distant as he recited what was clearly an oft-rehearsed plan. "When we have Uncle's dagger safe in our possession and have crossed once more to France, I will marry Helena—by force, if necessary. In Calais there is a notary who will do as I ask for a price. Once our marriage is a reality, we will travel to Le Roc. Uncle Fabien is too much the strategist not to appreciate the beauty of my plan. As soon as he grasps that there is no longer any desirable marriage for the factions to squabble over and that thus I have freed him from their threats, he will fall on my neck and thank me."

Behind Louis, Villard's expression betrayed his contempt, yet he quietly murmured, "As you say, m'sieur."

If Helena had had her way, she would not have attended that morning's gathering at the Duchess of Richmond's house. Unfortunately, so Marjorie informed her, it was a tradition as venerated as the masquerade to be held that evening and, therefore, impossible to miss. Helena had had half a mind to appeal to Thierry, more easygoing than his lady, but her host had been absent for the past day.

"He has gone to Bristol," Marjorie confessed as the carriage rattled toward Richmond.

"Bristol?" Helena looked her surprise.

Marjorie's lips thinned; she looked out the window. "He has gone to look into some business opportunity."

"Business? He—" Helena broke off, sensitive to the connotations.

Marjorie shrugged. "What would you do? We are

currently monsieur le comte's pensioners—what is to become of us when you marry and leave?"

Helena hadn't thought, didn't know, but thereafter she held her tongue and carped at Marjorie no more.

"*Eh, bien*," Marjorie murmured when the carriage eventually drew to a halt and they descended. "Thierry will return later. He will escort us to Lady Lowy's tonight. Then we will see."

Helena held to Marjorie's side as they entered and greeted their hostess. An unexpected tension, an apprehension, stretched her nerves taut. Moving into the considerable crowd, awash with laughter and good cheer, she searched with her eyes, with her senses, and breathed a tight, small sigh of relief when she could detect no glimmer of Sebastian's presence.

After some minutes of chatting, then moving on, she parted from Marjorie and ventured on alone. She was assured enough, now well known enough, to make her way with confidence. Although unmarried, she was so much older, so much more experienced than girls in their first or even second season, that she was accorded a different status, one permitting her greater social freedom. Speaking to this one, then that, she worked her way through the crowd.

She still had three names on her list, but only Were was confirmed. Were Athlebright and Mortingdale present? Quite how she might engage with them to assess the effect of their touch in the middle of a crowded salon where talk and not dancing, certainly not touching, was the principal aim was a problem—one at which her mind boggled and failed.

Turned too readily aside. After last night, her mind had more troubling thoughts to ponder.

Damn Sebastian! She had constantly, throughout the night, through the silent hours in which she'd tossed and turned and tried to forget, tried to wipe from her mind the sensation of his lips on hers, the warmth of his nearness, the allure of his touch.

Impossible.

She'd spent hours lecturing herself, pointing out how directly against her careful plans falling victim to such a man would be—only to wake from lustful dreams of doing precisely that.

Shocked, she'd sat up, risen from her bed, washed her face and hands in cold water, then stood before her window staring out at the black night until the cold had forced her back to her quilts.

Madness. He had sworn never to marry. What was she thinking of?

It was impossible, more than impossible, for a woman such as herself—an unmarried noblewoman of old family—to become his mistress. Yet to marry a complaisant husband knowing herself driven by a need to be free to engage in an illicit but socially acceptable liaison with another—that, too, was unthinkable. At least to her.

Sebastian, she was sure, had thought of it, but that had never been part of her plans.

Still wasn't.

Which left her with one very large problem—he surprised her by appearing in the doorway to an adjoining salon just as she approached it.

"Mignonne." He took the hand she instinctively raised to ward him off, bowed, and raised it to his lips.

Her eyes met his over her knuckles as she belatedly bobbed a curtsy; what she saw in the blue depths made her lungs seize.

"Your Grace." Cursing her breathlessness, she struggled to marshal her wits as, still holding her hand, he urged her back from the doorway toward the side of the room. Forced to comply, she reminded herself of how dangerous he was—only to have another part of her mind airily point out that with him, she knew she was safe.

Dangereux on the one hand, knight-protector on the other. Was it any wonder she was confused?

"Indeed, I am very glad I met you." Attack suited her more than defense. She faced him, head high. "I wished to say good-bye and to thank you for your assistance through these past weeks."

She could tell nothing from his expression—the polite mask he so often wore—but she saw his eyes widen a fraction. At least she'd surprised him. "I understand that the masquerade tonight will be very crowded, so it's possible we will not meet again."

She stopped there, bit her tongue against a nervous urge to babble on. If what she'd already said didn't put him in his place—didn't tell him how she'd decided to react after last night—nothing would.

He was silent for some minutes, his unnerving blue gaze locked on her eyes, then his lips curved, just enough to tell her that the smile was indeed genuine.

"Mignonne, you never fail to surprise me."

Briefly, she glared. "I am honored that I amuse you, Your Grace."

His smile only deepened. "You should be. There's so little these days that amuses such a jaded soul as I."

There was sufficient self-deprecation in his tone to make it difficult to take offense. Helena contented herself with another glare—then felt heat shoot up her arm as his fingers shifted and one stroked her palm. He'd lowered their hands but hadn't released hers; his fingers curled protectively around hers, their linked hands hidden from all by her wide skirts.

"But there's no reason to bid me farewell. I'll be by your side tonight."

She narrowed her eyes at him. "You will have to find me in all that crowd, and then be sure it is me."

"I will know you, *mignonne*—in exactly the same way you will know me."

His confidence grated. "I will not tell you my costume."

"No need." He continued to smile. "I can guess."

He'd guess wrong, along with all the others. She'd been to masquerades before. Supremely confident, she looked about at the crowd. *"Eh, bien*—we shall see."

After a moment she glanced at him. He was studying her face. He hesitated, then asked, "Have you spoken with Thierry this morning?"

She blinked. "No. He is out of town but should return this evening."

"Ah. I see." That, Sebastian realized, explained why she didn't know of his invitation. Relieved his concern that she might indeed know but had decided to resist, to play even more difficult to win. Hard to imagine, but . . .

"Why such an interest in Thierry?"

He refocused to find Helena regarding him suspiciously. He smiled. "Merely an interest I have that concerns him. I will no doubt see him tonight."

The suspicious light didn't leave her eyes, but her gaze suddenly moved past him.

"There's Lord Athlebright!"

"No."

She looked at him. "*No? No what?*"

"No, you cannot try to ascertain how his lordship's touch affects you." Lifting her hand, he turned her in the opposite direction. "Believe me, *mignonne,* you do not need to work on your list of prospective husbands any further."

She heard the steely note in his voice. Puzzled, she searched his face. "You are not making any sense—no, you are making even *less* sense than usual."

"Acquit me of any wish to confuse you, *mignonne,* but am I right in assuming you will not agree to leaving this uncomfortably overcrowded salon with me to seek a quieter place where we might talk?"

She'd instantly stiffened. "You assume correctly, Your Grace."

Sebastian sighed. "You are the devil's own daughter to seduce, *mignonne.*"

The smile that curved her lips suggested she approved of the epithet.

"For all that, you'll still be mine."

The smile vanished. She flashed him a look of righteous fury; if he hadn't still held her hand, she would have whirled, curtsied, and flounced off. But the instant she started to move away, he drew her back. "No—don't leave me." He covered the simple, far-too-heartfelt plea with an easy smile. "You're safer with me than with any other—and together we're better entertained than we otherwise would be." He caught her eye. "A truce, *mignonne*—until tonight."

He'd intended to speak with her of his intentions, the purpose behind his invitation. He'd counted on Thierry's having received his letter and having told her of his request—she would have agreed readily to a private discussion after that. But . . . not knowing of his invitation, she would not go apart with him—and it was impossible for him to mention the word "marriage" in such a crowded place; he would bring all conversation to a halt.

She was searching his eyes, well aware of the caveat—that when he said "until tonight," he meant just that. That tonight he would come for her, and *then* they would see.

She tilted her head, then nodded. "As you wish, Your Grace—a truce."

Sebastian smiled, raised her hand to his lips. "Until tonight."

Her cloak already wrapped about her, her mask already in place, Helena left her room and headed for the stairs, summoned by Marjorie's call.

"We will be late, *ma petite*! Such a wait we will have!"

"I'm coming."

Helena started down the stairs just as the front door opened. Thierry, still in his morning coat, tired and weary, came in.

Marjorie had whirled; now she rushed to her husband. *"Mon Dieu!* Thank God you are come—we must go *immédiatement!"*

Thierry summoned a smile for her and for Helena. "You will have to permit me to change, *chérie.* Go ahead, and I will follow."

"But, Gaston—"

"Madame, I cannot grace the masquerade in all my dirt. Let me get my costume"—Thierry's glance took in the mail stacked on the side table—"and glance over these letters. Then I will follow *tout de suite, chérie*—that I promise."

Marjorie pouted, but accepted the assurance. She kissed Thierry's cheek. *"Tout de suite, oui?"*

Thierry returned the kiss. *"Oui."*

He beamed at Helena and kissed his fingers to her. "You look ravishing, *ma petite.* Have fun."

Scooping up his letters, he strode quickly for the stairs, passing Louis with a reassuring word.

Louis helped Marjorie and Helena into the carriage, then joined them. The coach lurched and rumbled off toward Berkeley Square. As Marjorie had prophesied, there was a long line of carriages waiting to set their passengers down before Lowy House.

The night was clear and bitingly cold, yet the sight of wave after wave of fantastically garbed guests arriving in costumes both outrageous and rich had drawn a large knot of onlookers. A plush red carpet laid from front door to pavement's edge was flanked by banks of holly and ivy. Flares burned brightly, illuminating the arriving guests for all to see.

When Helena was handed down from the carriage, there were no oohs and aahs. She appeared a gray mouse, draped in rich velvet, true enough, but hardly outstanding. Then she lifted her head and put back the hood of her cloak. Every eye fixed on her. The light from the flares caught the gold circlet of laurel leaves set amid her black curls, danced over the solid gold mask, also stamped with laurel leaves, that hid her face. Even though the cloak still concealed the rest of her costume, mouths dropped open as the onlookers stared.

With every indication of proprietorial pride, Louis led both Helena and Marjorie up the sweep of red and on through the open front door. The moment they were inside, Helena retrieved her hand and tugged at the gold cloak strings at her throat.

She'd worn the costume before, was well aware of its effect on susceptible males; as she handed the heavy cloak to a waiting footman, his eyes nearly started from his head. In the slim sheath of pale blue silk fashioned in a Roman toga, with telltale laurel leaves worked in gold thread at the neckline, hem, and along the fluttering border, she was every man's fantasy of a Roman empress. Which was who she'd elected to be: St. Helena, mother of the Emperor Constantine. Seduced by the dramatic tone that pervaded masquerades, everyone who knew her always assumed she would come as Helen of Troy.

The silk sheath was anchored by a gold clasp on her

right shoulder; the costume left most of her shoulders and arms bare. She wore gold amulets on both arms, gold bracelets on both wrists. There was gold dangling from her lobes and a heavy gold necklace encircling her throat. Her skin was whitest ivory, her hair blacker than black in contrast. With the gold and pale blue as a foil, she looked stunning and knew it. Drew confidence from the fact.

Extremely high heels concealed beneath the long skirts added to her mystery—fully masked, her lack of height was the characteristic most searched for.

Expecting to enjoy her evening thoroughly, spiced with the anticipation of a seminal and final victory over St. Ives, she walked beside Marjorie into the ballroom, head high, looking around boldly—as an empress, she could do as she pleased.

She'd triumphed at masquerades at the French court in this costume—the flowers of the English nobility gathered tonight were to be her next conquests. Separating from Marjorie, who was rather too easy to spot with her auburn hair imperfectly concealed by her shepherdess's hat, Helena moved into the crowd.

The room was bedecked as a magical grotto with the symbols of yuletide the theme. Midnight blue silk scattered with gold and silver stars was draped across the ceiling; the walls were decorated with swags of green and brown velvet against which evergreen boughs, holly, and ivy had been fixed. Huge logs burned in the hearths, adding to the considerable heat; spiced champagne was being continuously served by footmen dressed as elves.

Against this backdrop, the elite of the ton formed a rich tapestry of shifting colors and costumes, of fantastic wigs and amazing hats. At this early stage the revelers were looking about, weaving and reweaving through the crowd, some in groups but most moving independently, recognizing and noting others, searching for those they hoped to meet but had yet to identify.

Helena spotted her first Paris within minutes. He stood tall, eyes narrowed, scanning the crowd, examining all the women in sight. His gaze rested on her for one instant, then moved on. Helena smiled behind her mask and turned away. Paris One was Lord Mortingdale. A good sign perhaps? Or did his choice of costume show a sad lack of appreciation of her wit?

Continuing around the room, she found three more Parises; they all saw her—one looked interested but did not pursue her when she moved away. One of the three was Mr. Coke, a gentleman who had tried to pay her considerable attention. The other two she could not identify, but neither of them was Sebastian—of that she was sure.

There were a number of Roman senators in the crowd. As was usually the case, they were gentlemen for whom the toga meant freedom from their corsets. To Helena's relief, none had thought to array himself as an emperor. One of the portly crew, on spying her, came rustling up to suggest they were a pair. One glance and a cool word disabused him of the idea.

"Oh, well, had to try, you know!" With a grin, the gentleman bowed and left her.

Gaining the side of the room, Helena paused and

turned to scan the throng. Even with her high heels, she couldn't see far; the huge wigs and elaborate head-dresses so many wore blocked her view. She'd covered nearly half the long room. Farther ahead she glimpsed an archway leading to another salon. She craned her neck, peering between bodies . . .

And felt Sebastian's presence materialize like a flame at her back.

As she registered the fact and turned to face him, his fingers closed about her hand.

"*Mignonne*, you are exquisite."

She felt the usual jolt as his lips brushed the backs of her fingers, was momentarily lost, adrift in the blue of his eyes, in the warmth that shone there, real appreciation tinged with desire, edging into . . .

She blinked, and her conscious view expanded—to take in his gold half-mask, like her own embossed with laurel leaves. She blinked again, lifted her gaze—took in the gold wreath set amid the burnished brown of his hair. Sucking in a breath, eyes wide, she swept her gaze down—over the white toga edged with gold-embroidered laurel, topped with the purple robe of an emperor.

"Who—" She had to stop to moisten her lips. "Who are you supposed to be?"

He smiled. "Constantius Chlorus." He raised her hand again, held her gaze as he turned it and pressed his lips to her palm. "Helena's lover." He changed his hold, touched his lips to her wrist, to where her pulse raced beneath her skin. "Ultimately her husband, the father of her son."

Breathing was increasingly difficult; Helena tried to find her temper—she couldn't even summon a frown. "How did you know?"

The curve of his lips was triumphant. "You do not like being taken for granted, *mignonne*."

He was right, so right she wanted to scream—or weep, she wasn't sure which. Being with someone who knew her—could read her—so well was unnerving— and so appealing.

She finally managed a slight frown. "You are an extremely difficult man to deal with, Your Grace."

He sighed, his fingers shifting over hers as he lowered her hand. "So I have often been told, *mignonne*, but you don't truly find me so difficult, do you?"

Her frown grew more definite. "I'm not sure."

There was so much about which she was unsure when it came to him.

He'd been studying her face; now he said, "I take it Thierry has yet to return?"

"He arrived home just as we were starting out. He will no doubt be here shortly."

"Good."

She tried to read Sebastian's face. "You wish to talk with him?"

"In a manner of speaking. Come." Sebastian took her hand and drew her on down the room. "Stroll with me."

She threw him a puzzled, slightly suspicious glance but consented to stroll by his side. Others had similarly found mates; they were stopped frequently as other guests tried to guess their identities.

"That Neptune is magnificent—and the Sun King, too."

"Mme de Pompadour is Therese Osbaldestone, which is something of a surprise."

"Did she recognize us, do you think?"

"I expect so. Very little misses those black eyes."

They were nearly at the end of the room when Sebastian tightened his hold on her hand. He glanced down as she looked up questioningly. "*Mignonne*, I need to speak with you privately."

Helena stopped walking. Started to frown. "I cannot—will not—be private with you. Not again."

He exhaled through his teeth, glanced around, noted how close others were. "I cannot discuss what I wish to discuss in such surrounds—and it's not possible to arrange to meet with you privately by any other means." Not without tipping the wink to the gabble-mongers.

She didn't say anything. The stubborn set of her lips gave him her answer.

Sebastian knew he was close to losing his temper. It had been a very long time since anyone—let alone a slip of a woman—had dared deny him so stubbornly. And for once in his life, his intentions were honorable.

"*Mignonne*—" He instantly knew he'd chosen the wrong tone; her spine stiffened like a poker. He exhaled, then stated, "I give you my word that you will be safe with me. I do need to speak with you."

The stubborn set of her chin eased; her lips shifted, twisted, grimaced lightly. But . . .

Briefly she returned the clasp of his fingers, then shook her beautiful head. "*Non.* I cannot . . ." She drew breath, lifted her chin. "I dare not go apart with you, Your Grace."

Helena watched his eyes darken, although his face changed not at all.

"Do you question my word, *mignonne*?"

The words were soft, steely.

She shook her head. "No—"

"You don't trust me?"

"That is not it at all!" It wasn't *him* she didn't trust— but she couldn't tell him that. Too revealing, too much an acknowledgment of her susceptibility, her vulnerability—her weakness over him. "It is just that . . . No. I cannot go apart with you, Your Grace." She tugged. "Sebastian, let me go!"

"Helena—"

"No!"

Their altercation, albeit conducted in hissed whispers and low growls, was starting to attract attention. Gritting his teeth, Sebastian forced himself to release her. "We are not finished with this discussion."

Her eyes blazed. "*We* are finished entirely, Your Grace."

She turned and stormed off—an imperial termagant leaving a conqueror, dismissed, in her wake.

Sebastian stood perfectly still for three minutes before he got his temper back under control. Even then he had to stop himself from snapping when some unfortunate lady thought to offer him solace. Then he glimpsed Martin, a corsair, through the crowd. He started to prowl, his mind fixed on one object—and on how to achieve his goal.

He hadn't prowled far when he was approached by a pirate.

"Monsieur le duc, I do hope my cousin is not"—a vague gesture punctuated the pirate's words—"being difficult?"

De Sèvres. Biting back the urge to articulate just how difficult his cousin was indeed being, Sebastian drawled, "Mademoiselle is an extremely stubborn woman."

"*Vraiment.*"

De Sèvres was wearing a half-mask; Sebastian could see his worried frown.

"If I could help in any way . . . perhaps be of some assistance . . . ?"

Sebastian fought to keep his expression impassive. What was going on? He was tempted to pursue the matter—why a man supposedly sent to protect Helena was offering instead to assist in what, for all he knew, was to be her seduction—but at that precise moment, he had a more imperative goal.

"I wish to speak privately with mademoiselle la comtesse, but she is proving elusive."

"I see, I see." De Sèvres nodded, frowned harder.

"Perhaps if I were to set a location and wait there, you might endeavor to persuade her to join me?"

Looking into the crowd, de Sèvres considered, calculated; eyes narrowed, he chewed his lower lip. Sebastian would have taken an oath he wasn't worrying over the propriety of his actions but rather how to persuade Helena to comply. Then de Sèvres nodded. "What location?"

Not why did he wish to speak with her—for how long, how privately . . . Sebastian made a mental note to investigate de Sèvres a great deal more closely once he'd secured Helena's hand.

"The library." A sufficiently formal setting, which would likely make Helena less suspicious; Sebastian had little faith in de Sèvres's powers of obfuscation. He nodded to a doorway across the ballroom. "Go through there, turn right, then follow the hall to a long gallery. The library is the main room giving off that. If you wish to assist me, bring mademoiselle there in twenty minutes."

At this hour the library should be empty, although as the evening progressed, others, too, would seek out its amenities.

De Sèvres tugged on his waistcoat. "I will bring her." With a nod, he moved off in the direction Helena had gone.

Sebastian watched him go and inwardly shook his head. Later . . .

He turned—and found himself facing Martin.

One look into his eyes and his brother grinned. "It *is* you! Now, where is she?" He glanced around. "You wouldn't believe it, but I've found three Helen of Troys so far, and none of them is she."

"If you're referring to mademoiselle la comtesse, she's here, but not as Helen of Troy."

"Oh?" Martin frowned. "Then who . . . ?"

He cocked a brow at Sebastian—who considered

him, then shook his head. "I know for a fact that you received a classical education. I wouldn't want to inhibit the exercising of your intellect." He clapped Martin on the shoulder. "Think hard, and the answer will come to you."

With that, Sebastian strolled on, leaving Martin scowling good-naturedly after him.

The library was indeed deserted when he reached it. He surveyed the long room, then strolled to the large desk set out from one corner. Beyond it, in the corner of the room, sat a commodious armchair. Sebastian sat, stretched out his legs, folded his hands, and waited for his duchess-to-be to appear.

Helena didn't notice Louis hovering until she turned from chatting to Therese Osbaldestone and saw him step toward her. She inclined her head, expecting to pass him by.

Instead, he put a hand on her arm. "You must come with me—quickly."

Louis's manner was agitated. He was glancing around.

"Why? What is it?"

"There is someone Uncle Fabien requires you to meet."

"*Fabien?* What is this?" Thrown off balance, Helena allowed Louis to draw her to the side of the room. "Who does Fabien know here?"

"That is not important. I will explain all later. But I can tell you this—Fabien wishes you to meet with this gentleman and hear him out."

"Hear him out?"

"*Oui.*" Louis continued tugging, surreptitiously dragging her to a doorway. "This man will have a request to make—an invitation. You are to listen, then accept! *Comprends?*"

"I don't understand anything," Helena complained. "Stop pulling." She wrenched her arm free, stopped Louis with a glare, then straightened her gown. "I do not know whom Fabien wishes me to meet, but I will not meet anyone *en déshabillé!*"

Louis gritted his teeth. "*Vite, vite!* He will not wait forever."

Helena heaved a resigned sigh. "Very well, where am I to meet him?" She followed Louis through the doorway into a corridor.

"In the library."

"*Allons!*" Helena waved Louis on. She had little confidence in Louis, but set much more store in Fabien's good sense. Her guardian was not a man to put at risk anything that was of value to him. If Fabien wished her to meet some gentleman, there would be some sane explanation. Although she railed against Fabien's hold on her, she was too wise not to humor his wishes until she was free of him.

Louis led her to a long gallery, then somewhat hesitantly opened a door and peered in. He stood back. "*Bon*—this is it. The library." He waved her in.

Helena glided forward.

Louis lowered his voice. "I will leave you together, but I will not be far, so I can conduct you back to the ballroom if you wish."

Helena frowned, grateful for her mask as she stepped over the threshold. What *was* Louis about? If she wished? Why . . . ?

The library door shut softly behind her. She scanned the room, expecting to see some gentleman waiting for her, but there was no one there. No one rose from the large armchairs before the hearth, no one sat behind the desk.

Pirouetting, she scanned the long room. Bookcases lined the walls. The tall windows were uncurtained, but it was dark outside. There were lamps, lit but turned low, set on side tables and credenzas around the room, shedding a gentle glow, revealing the fact that the room was empty save for her. She could see the entire room from where she stood, all except . . .

The huge desk cut off a corner of the room. Beyond it, set in the wall beside the corner, was a door leading to the next room. It was shut. Some way before it stood an armchair; she could see its high back, but otherwise the desk hid it from view. On a side table to the left of the chair sat a lamp, like the others burning low.

She started toward the desk; she may as well check the chair before returning to Louis and telling him that Fabien's friend had not appeared. Thick Aubusson carpets muffled the click of her heels. She rounded the desk—and saw a hand, relaxed on the arm of the chair. A very white hand, with very long fingers . . .

Premonition washed over her; a tingling awareness told her who it was who waited so patiently. Slowly, disbelievingly, she came around to stand before the chair and looked down at the occupant.

He'd taken off his mask—it lay hanging from the other arm of the chair, glinting dully.

Sebastian sat, effortlessly elegant, watching her from beneath hooded lids. She saw blue flash, then he murmured, "*Bon, mignonne.* At last."

Outside in the corridor, Louis chewed his nails. In a fever of uncertainty, he glanced this way, then that, then eased open the library door. As before, it opened noiselessly; he peeked but could see nothing, put his ear to the crack but could hear nothing.

Biting back a curse, he was about to shut the door when he noticed the sliver of a crack that had opened on the hinged side. He put his eye to it—and saw Helena, standing in the far corner of the room, staring down at an armchair. St. Ives must be in it, speaking, but Louis could hear not a word, could not even distinguish the tone. He stared—then saw the door in the wall beyond the chair.

Carefully, he shut the library door.

"This *must* work." He whispered the words through gritted teeth. "He *must* ask her tonight!"

He hurried to the next room. It proved to be an office—empty, unlit, clearly not intended for the use of guests. Thanking the saints, Louis entered, shut the door silently behind him, then tiptoed to the door giving access to the library.

There was no lock on the door—just a knob. Holding his breath, he turned the knob. The door eased open a fraction.

Chapter Seven

*H*elena stared at Sebastian. *"You?"*

He raised his brows. "You were expecting someone else?"

"Louis told me I was to meet an acquaintance of my guardian's."

"Ah. I did wonder how de Sèvres would persuade you to hear me out. However, I regret I have not had the pleasure of your guardian's acquaintance."

"Bien!" Temper erupting, she started to turn, to sweep to the door and leave—

Sebastian held up a languid hand—caught her attention. And she saw she'd walked into his trap.

To return to the door she had to pass him. If she tried . . .

She swung back to face him. Folding her arms beneath her breasts, she regarded him stonily. "I don't understand." An understatement.

"For that I fear I must apologize, *mignonne,* yet before we leave here, I intend that all will be plain between us."

He studied her for a moment, then leaned forward,

slowly reached up and tugged one of her hands free. He sat back, drawing her to the chair. She frowned but consented to move closer.

"Sit with me."

She assumed he meant on the arm of the chair, but when she realized he meant on his lap, she pulled back.

He sighed. "*Mignonne*, do not be missish. I wish to speak with you, yet if I stand close, I cannot always see your face. Likewise if you sit beside me. If you sit on my lap, it will be easier."

There was sufficient irritation in his voice to dispel the idea that he was intent on ravishment—at least, not yet. Helena allowed herself a small "humph!" then, suppressing all reaction to the skittering thrill that raced up her spine, she smoothed her skirts and sat.

Beneath the folds of his toga, under the satin breeches he wore beneath it, his thighs were rock hard, but warm.

He closed his hands about her waist and lifted her, resettled her so they were indeed essentially face to face. Then he raised his hands and tugged on the ribbons that secured her mask; the two small bows unraveled. He drew the mask free, then set it on the floor beside the chair.

"*Bon.*"

Sebastian heard the reined temper in his tone and knew she heard it, too. He hoped it made her wary.

Step by step. That seemed the only way to accomplish the task with her. Every inch had been a battle thus far.

He looked into her peridot eyes.

She stared haughtily back.

I intend to offer for your hand would have done the job with most women, but with her, instinct prodded him to be rather more definite.

I'm going to make you my duchess had a more forceful ring to it—left less leeway for her to cavil.

Unfortunately, given her prejudice against powerful men, neither approach was likely to lead to quick success. She'd immediately dig in her heels, and he'd be reduced to pleading his case from a very weak position.

Mining her walls—undercutting her arguments before she had a chance to make them—was undoubtedly the road to victory. Once he'd weakened her defenses, then he could speak of marriage.

"You've told me you don't like being the pawn of a powerful man. All you've said has led me to believe that your guardian is such a man—am I right?"

"Indeed. I know of what I speak."

"And am I also correct in stating that your reason for seeking a meek and mild-mannered husband was that such a man could never rule you?"

She narrowed her eyes. "So that he would never manipulate me, use me as a pawn."

He inclined his head. "Has it not yet occurred to you, *mignonne*, that marrying a man who knows little of, as you have put it before, 'the games men such as I play,' will leave you still in the power of the very man you seek to escape?"

She frowned. "Once I am married . . ."

When she didn't continue, he hesitated, then quietly said, "My sister is married. Yet if I decide, for her own good, that she should return to the country . . . she returns to the country."

She searched his eyes. "Her husband . . . ?"

"Huntly is a good-natured man who never pretended to be able to manage Augusta. He does, however, have extremely good sense and so knows when she needs to be managed. He then summons me."

"My husband—the one I choose—will not summon my guardian."

"But if your guardian doesn't wait to be summoned . . . what then?"

He gave her time to think, to venture on her own down the lane of thought he'd pointed out. To see the possibilities, to come of her own volition to the realization he desired.

Even now he was too much the consummate manipulator to speak too soon, to push too hard.

Especially not with her.

Helena frowned—at him, at his hard face, the pale, austere features limned but not softened by the lamplight. Reluctantly, already sensing what she would see, she let her mind turn—almost as if she were mentally turning around and looking at something behind her, something she'd failed to see.

He was right. Fabien would not be deterred from using her by the protestations of a weak husband. Look what he'd done with Geoffre Daurent, her uncle, her initial and natural guardian. Although not a particularly weak man, Geoffre was weaker than Fabien. Because controlling her fortune and marriage conferred considerable political power, Fabien had "discussed" matters with Geoffre, a distant kinsmen, and an agreement had been reached that had seen Fabien legally installed as her guardian.

How Fabien might use her once she was married she did not know, but his intrigues were manifold—power flowed from many sources, from the control of myriad subjects, in their world. And power was Fabien's drug.

"You are right." The words fell from her lips as she refocused; she frowned. "I will need to think again."

"There are not that many options to consider, *mignonne*. Indeed, as one of the ilk against whom you struggle, I can tell you there is only one."

She met his eyes, narrowed her own. "I will not—" She broke off, an image of Fabien rising in her mind. In truth, there was very little she wouldn't do to escape his web.

Sebastian searched her eyes; then his gaze steadied, holding hers. "How alike are we, your guardian and I?"

His words were soft, wondering, inviting her to make the comparison. She recognized the ploy, enough to acknowledge it as a bold and brave stroke. He didn't, after all, know Fabien.

"In nature you are much alike." Honesty forced her to added, "In some respects."

He was infinitely kinder. Indeed, many of his actions, albeit executed with typical arrogance and high-handedness, were prompted by a detached, quite selfless wish to help, something she found immensely endearing. Kindness was not a quality Fabien possessed; it was her considered opinion that in all his years Fabien had never once thought of anyone but himself.

Where St. Ives arranged for his sister to return to the country for her own good, Fabien would do the same for his own purposes, irrespective of whether that benefited or indeed even harmed his pawn.

She continued to study Sebastian's face. He raised one brown brow. "Which would you rather, if you could choose—your guardian, or me?"

And that, she knew, was the question he'd sought this interview to ask. A single, simple question that, as he'd correctly seen, was the central, crucial issue in deciding what she did next.

"Neither would be my first choice."

His lips lifted lightly. He inclined his head. "That I accept. However, as you've now realized, that choice will not free you of powerful men. If not your guardian, if not me, then it will be some other like us."

He hesitated, then lifted a hand and traced her face, his fingertips lightly touching. "You are extremely beautiful, *mignonne*, extremely wealthy and of the highest echelons of the nobility. You are a prize and a woman— that combination will always determine your fate."

"That combination is not something I can change." She stated it flatly, knowing it as a truth—one she disliked but had long ago accepted.

"No." His gaze held hers. "All you can do is choose the best of the options it leaves you."

Which would she rather?

She blinked, drew in a breath, allowed herself to

imagine, to speculate. "You are saying that if I accept you, you will become my champion, that you will protect me from others, even my guardian."

His eyes were very blue. "*Mignonne*, if you were mine, I would protect you with my life."

That was no idle statement, not from him.

She studied him, aware that all he'd said was true. And wondering, now that she'd been brought to face the choice, whether there truly were no other options.

"The only freedom you will ever know, *mignonne*, will be under the protection of a powerful man."

He had, once again, read her mind, her eyes, her soul. "How do I know that you won't seek to use me as he has—to play with my future, my life, as if they are your possessions to dispose of as it suits your whim?"

Her words had flowed without thought or hesitation; his answer was just as swift.

"I can promise that I won't—and I do. But you can never know absolutely; you can only trust, and trust that your trust will be honored. But on that matter there's little point denying that, at some level at least, you already trust me." He held her gaze. "You wouldn't be here now if you didn't."

That also was true. She trusted him, while she trusted Fabien not at all. Perched on his knees, face-to-face, gaze to gaze, Helena knew she was being managed by a master. Every minute of their interaction thus far had been staged and played to foster not just her trust but her belief in his sincerity.

And beneath all else was her awareness of him, of

the blatantly sexual connection that had from the first moment they'd met each other all those years ago flared between them.

He hadn't sought to hide it, to pretend it didn't exist, to draw a veil over that part of their interaction.

"If I agreed to . . ." She paused, searched his eyes, then lifted her chin. "Accept your protection, what would you ask in return?"

His gaze didn't waver. "You know what I would ask—what I wish."

"Tell me."

He studied her eyes, her face, then murmured, "I think, *mignonne*, that we have had enough words. I think it's time I showed you."

A shiver skittered up her spine, but when he arched a brow at her, she haughtily arched one back. She had to know if she could do this—if becoming his, placing herself under his protection, was an option for her. If she could withstand the fire of his touch, if she could become his and still be herself.

She said nothing, simply waited, coolly expectant. He read the determination in her eyes, then his gaze lowered. Washed over her bare shoulders, drifted lower, rose again—she felt it like a physical sensation, the brush of an ephemeral touch. Then his gaze fixed on the gold clasp at her shoulder.

With his habitual languor, he raised one hand; extending one finger, he nudged, then pushed the clasp sideways until it and the gathered silk it held slipped over the arc of her shoulder. His finger followed the upper curve of her arm, trailing down the smooth skin. Just a few inches.

She couldn't breathe. Couldn't move. Couldn't shift as he slowly leaned forward, bent his head and set his lips like a brand to her shoulder.

To the very spot he'd uncovered—the only spot on her shoulders that had been concealed, the only place where she felt vulnerable, now it had been exposed. Bared. To him. By him.

She closed her eyes, concentrated, caught by the shift of his lips on her skin, seduced by the hot sweep of his tongue. Opening her eyes, she watched, fascinated, as he pressed his lips again to the sensitized spot; she felt her spine shake, quake, felt his hand close about her waist, fingers pressing in response.

Driven by an inner force she didn't recognize, she lifted her hand to his nape, slid and spread her fingers into his silky hair. His lips firmed on her skin. She turned her head as he lifted his. Their lips met.

That balancing power she'd experienced before still operated between them. As they kissed—taking, giving, pausing to savor, to entice, to indulge—she felt it like a constraint, some limit on a tipping scale that prevented him, or her, from taking too much without giving, from conquering without first surrendering.

Again and again that power tipped the scales. He took her mouth in a hot, heated rush, a primitive ravishment that left her senses reeling. Then she gathered herself and boldly pressed her own demands, and he was the one giving way, laying himself open to her conquest. Shuddering when she pressed deep. Following when she retreated.

The wave washed back and forth; the hot tide steadily rose between them.

They broke for an instant to breathe. She lifted her lids, met his blue eyes, only inches distant. One hard hand framed her jaw; the other was locked at her waist, fingers burning through layers of silk. Her own hand cradled his skull, holding him to her; her other arm circled him, hand splayed on his back.

Her lids fell; their lips met again, and the tide rose higher.

Ten yards away, on the other side of the connecting door, Louis frowned. Lifting his ear from the crack of the open door, he stared at the panels.

He could see nothing more than a sliver of bookcase, but he didn't dare push the door farther open. Unable to see, he'd listened. He'd heard Helena and St. Ives talking but hadn't been able to catch many words. Nevertheless, he'd heard enough to know that matters were proceeding in the direction Fabien had predicted. Wanted.

But he'd yet to hear St. Ives issue the invitation that was so critical to their plan's success.

And now they'd stopped talking.

If it had been any woman but Helena, he'd have known what to think, but he'd been her shadow for years—she was cold, remote. As far as Louis knew, she'd never allowed men to maul her.

But if not that, then what was going on in the all-but-silent library?

Perhaps some haughty standoff—that he could imagine. And the English, they were unpredictable at best. So much more laissez-faire than the French over some things, yet such high sticklers on other matters—and there seemed no logical distinction over which matter would be what.

The English were confusing, but Helena was much more reliable, at least in her temper.

A low murmur reached him; Louis quickly put his ear to the crack again and waited for them to resume talking.

Helena felt sure she was on fire, that flames were licking her skin. Head back, fingers sinking into Sebastian's shoulders, she gasped, felt his lips slide from her jaw to her throat.

Gasped again as they pressed heat into her veins, then slid lower. Found the pulse at the base of her throat and pressed there, too. Then he licked, laved; a fierce shiver rushed over her skin.

A low sound of satisfaction rumbled from him. His hands had shifted to her waist; they tightened, letting her feel their strength, then both slid upward, brushed, then closed about her breasts.

Her body arched, eager for his touch, eager for more. She turned wildly and caught his lips as he raised his head—tasted his satisfaction, his triumph as his thumbs cruised over the silk, over and about her nipples, tight and hard as pebbles. He teased, squeezed, kneaded; she squirmed, gasped—then kissed him desperately.

"Ssshh." He drew back from the kiss and looked down.

She did, too; a tremor of elemental sensation racked her as she watched his long fingers stroke, caress, fondle.

She felt him glance at her face, then his hands eased. His fingers shifted, reached for her neckline, slipped beneath.

Her breath strangled in her throat. One tiny part of her brain screamed for her to protest; she shut it out, locked it out—she wasn't interested in stopping him. He'd said he would show her. She wanted to see, know, feel it all—all that he would demonstrate.

She needed to know, needed to be certain just how difficult it would be, how dangerous. Before she agreed to be his.

Once she was . . .

Her breasts had swollen; the gown was now tight.

She helped him ease down the silk, lifting her arm free of the gown's shoulder, breathing out as he held the material away from her breasts, then edged it lower bit by bit until her breasts were free. That freedom was a relief; she drew in a quick breath as he released the gown and pressed it down about her waist. She was conscious of his gaze again touching her face as he reached for the bow securing the drawstring of her chemise. One tug and the bow slithered free.

He hesitated, his hand falling from the dangling ribbon. She looked up, caught his gaze, burning blue under heavy lids. She read the challenge in his eyes, dragged in a breath, looked down. Eased open the neckline of the chemise, then drew it down.

She glanced up, but he'd already looked down. She saw the concentration in his face as he raised one hand and trailed his fingers over her breast.

Over and around, between, but never touching the tightly ruched peaks. Until she was panting, aching, so hot she was burning.

"Touch me." She shifted one hand and closed it over the back of one of his, pressing it to her heated flesh.

He complied, filling his hands, closing his fingers about her nipples, gently at first, then tighter, tighter, until she gasped.

He kissed her then, deeply, deeper than before, or so it seemed. As if he would devour her, as if their earlier kisses had been a mere prelude to this deeper, richer intimacy.

When he drew back, her head was reeling. She reached to draw him back, but he swooped on the instant. His hand cupped her breast, his lips closed about her nipple.

Her gasp filled the room, then shattered.

Spine rigid, head back, she struggled to breathe, struggled to hold on to her whirling senses—her wits she'd lost long ago.

He feasted; her hand tight on his skull, she urged him on. Urged him, when sensation at that breast became too great to bear, to turn his attention to the other.

Then he suckled, and she could have sworn she lost consciousness, just for one second, for that moment when sensation overwhelmed her and swept her into some black void. But he drew her back again, into the world of the living, the sensate, where feeling—exquisite and enthralling—ruled.

She'd wanted to see, and he'd opened her eyes; she was grateful, very ready to let him kiss, caress, lick, and fondle to their mutual satisfaction. Untried she might be, but she was no man's fool. He was demanding, commanding, but generous, too, more than willing— indeed, insisting—that they share. He didn't leave her behind, overwhelmed, buffeted by sensation, as he certainly could have done. He was patient, encouraging, ready to give her the time to brace her hands on his chest, spread her fingers, flex them, sink her fingertips into the heavy muscles, then trace them. The silk of his toga muted her touch; his gown was caught at both shoulders—there was little bare skin for her to stroke. Much to her dissatisfaction.

Before she could press any further demands, he kissed her hard, then drew back and shifted her, drawing one knee up and over his thighs. His hands were on her breasts, his lips on hers again, before she could think.

Then she couldn't think at all.

Their kisses had been hot before; now they turned incendiary. They burned—with desire, passion, with all the primitive emotions she'd never before felt, never had a chance to feel, to experience, to lose herself in. He gave them to her, pressed them on her, and she drank them in.

Gloried in the moment.

Wondered, in the instant she heard his soft murmur, felt his hand slide from her breast to her bare stomach, pressing aside the silk folds, felt his fingers reach deeper, why.

Why she did nothing but cling, eyes closed, as she reveled in his touch, as his fingers brushed her curls, then pressed farther and touched her. Parted her, stroked, caressed, gently probed.

She'd stopped breathing. Stopped thinking long ago. Nevertheless, even now, she was sure. As she shivered, shuddered, let him slide one finger into her body, felt him catch his breath, hold it, too, she knew.

With him, in this arena, it was her wishes that prevailed, his will that drove them. He was dominant, she submissive, but it wasn't as simple as that. Her surrender could only be bought with his devotion.

Fair exchange.

She shuddered again as he stroked, touching her so intimately her mind couldn't quite complete the thought, envision the reality. She gulped in air, turned her head, found his lips.

Sensed his need.

Power—elemental, primitive, passionate—flowed between them freely. She felt it swirl around them; she could call on it as easily as he. It was that that kept the balance.

She kissed him hungrily, fed his need, fed the power.

Felt it rise.

Who held it, commanded it? Him? Her?

Neither.

It was intangible, forged between them, brought into this world, then set free.

She could feel it building, rising inside her as he

rhythmically stroked, his tongue mimicking the play of his fingers. A cry built in her throat; she pulled away from the kiss—

He pulled her back, drank her cry as she broke, shattered. The power imploded, then surged through her, through her veins, along her nerves. It dazzled her senses, then engulfed her in brilliance, in heat, in exquisite pleasure.

Louis stood staring at the connecting door, his hand over his mouth, horror in his eyes. He couldn't believe what his ears were telling him. Couldn't believe . . .

If St. Ives gained all he wished tonight, would he bother inviting Helena to his country house?

Did he, Louis, dare take the chance?

How would he explain . . . ?

Swallowing a yelp of sheer panic, he whirled, raced for the gallery and yanked open the door.

And came face-to-face with two couples—one a merman and mermaid, the other a Dresden milkmaid and an improbable Tyrolean shepherd.

He'd surprised them; they blinked at him bemusedly, then the milkmaid giggled.

Louis dragged in a breath, closed the door behind him, tugged down his waistcoat, and gestured to the door along the gallery. "The library is through there."

The milkmaid giggled; the mermaid gave him a sly look. Both men smiled their thanks—man to man—and steered their partners on.

Louis watched them go, watched the merman open the door, watched them all disappear inside.

Better they than he. He could barely think.

He breathed deeply, then again.

It suddenly occurred to him that this way things might fall out even better. If St. Ives were prevented—and surely he would be—then he would only be more determined, more insistent that Helena journey to his country home.

But why, after all these years of glacial frigidity, had Helena suddenly melted? He hadn't heard a single gasp of outrage, let alone a protest. She'd *permitted* St. Ives to take liberties.

Frowning, wondering how that unexpected and unwelcome development would affect his plans, Louis headed for the ballroom.

"Oh, *look*! It's such a large room. And a *desk*! Darling, do let's."

Sebastian jerked to attention—jerked out of the state of deep desire and reined lust that had overwhelmed his senses, tried to shake his wits free from their drugging coils.

Felt the jolt of alarm that flashed through Helena as she lay slumped on his chest, until then boneless in repletion.

His hand was still between her thighs. Before he could retrieve it and grab her, she did exactly what she shouldn't.

She bobbed up, looked over the chair back, then gasped and ducked down.

Too late.

"*Ooh!*" The woman who had entered gave a little

scream, cut off—Sebastian could imagine her hand clapped over her lips, her eyes like saucers.

Grasping Helena, still naked to the waist, he did the only thing he could; he stood, letting her slide down until her feet touched the floor, then he turned his head, keeping his body, his broad shoulders, between her and the new arrivals.

All four of them. As he glanced at their faces, already unmasked, and saw their eyes widen, he inwardly cursed. He was unmasked—and Helena was, too.

"St. Ives." The merman recovered first; shock held the others silent. "We . . . ah . . ." He suddenly seemed to realize the full magnitude of the situation. "We'll leave . . ." He tried to urge his mermaid to the door, but the woman didn't move, her saucerlike eyes trained disbelievingly on Sebastian.

"St. Ives," she said. Then her gaze shifted past him. "And mademoiselle la comtesse . . ."

Mademoiselle la comtesse was muttering French curses he hadn't imagined she would know. Luckily, only he could hear. Reaching blindly, he found her arm, slid his fingers down to lock about her wrist, holding her, anchoring her, where she couldn't be seen.

With his other hand, he waved languidly. "Mademoiselle la comtesse has just done me the honor of consenting to be my duchess." Beneath his fingers he felt Helena's pulse leap, then race wildly. "We were . . . celebrating."

"You're to *marry*?" The Dresden milkmaid, until then struck dumb, recovered her voice. Her avid expression

stated she had an excellent grasp of the social implications. She clapped her hands. "Oh, *wonderful*! And
we've learned it first!"

"Felicitations," murmured the Tyrolean shepherd,
one of the young lordlings who had at one time joined
Helena's court. He grasped the milkmaid's arm.
"Come on, Vicky."

Eyes still huge, the milkmaid turned with alacrity.
"Oh, yes. Do let's hurry back . . ."

The four piled out of the room faster than they'd entered it. Their whispers hung in the air even after the
door shut behind them.

As Sebastian released her and turned to her, Helena
hit him on the arm. "*Now* what are we going to do?"
She lapsed into French as she hitched her gown up,
dragging the shoulder back into place. Shaking out the
skirts, she looked down. "*Sacre dieu!*"

Sebastian looked and saw her chemise tangled in her
high-heeled shoes.

She swore some more, bent and swiped up the tell-
tale garment, scrunching the silk in her hand—then realized she had nowhere to hide it.

"Give it to me." He held out a hand.

She slapped the chemise into it. He shook out the
garment, then folded it and tucked it into his breeches
pocket, taking the opportunity to rearrange a few other
things at the same time. Glancing at Helena, he noted
that her nipples, no longer screened by the chemise,
stood proudly erect under the silk sheath of her toga.
Looking at her face, he decided not to mention it.

She already looked . . . distraught.

"My apologies, *mignonne*. That is not how I planned to ask you to be my wife."

Her head rose. She blinked at him, her expression blanked. "Wh-what?"

"I had, strangely enough, imagined making some reasonable attempt at a proposal." When she simply stared at him, clearly stunned, Sebastian frowned. "It's customary, you know."

"No! I mean . . ." Helena clapped a hand to her forehead in a vain attempt to halt her whirling wits. "We were not discussing *marriage*! We were discussing me accepting your protection."

It was his turn to blink, then his features hardened. "And precisely what sort of protection did you imagine I would extend to an *unmarried noblewoman*?"

She knew the answer to that. "You—we—were talking of me marrying some complaisant gentleman and *then*—"

"No. That was not what I was talking about. *I* was talking of marrying you."

She narrowed her eyes. "Not until those foolish people came in—I have told you before I am more than eight."

"Seven."

She frowned. "*Comment?*"

He shook his head. "Never mind. But contrary to your misguided notions, I was *always* thinking of marrying you."

"Pull my other arm, Your Grace." Putting her nose in the air, she went to sweep past him.

He caught her arm and swung her back to face him. "No. We are settling this here and now."

The look in his face, in his eyes—the tension that emanated from him—warned her not even to attempt to gainsay him.

"I had already decided that I would have to marry before I met you again. Years ago I made it plain that I would not—I have three brothers who were quite willing to see to the succession, and I did not, in my estimation, possess the most amenable temperament for marriage. However . . ." He hesitated, then said, "You have met my sister-in-law."

Helena nodded. "Lady Almira."

"Indeed. If I tell you that she does not improve on further acquaintance, you will understand that the thought of her as the next Duchess of St. Ives has been seriously agitating many members of the family."

She frowned. "I do not understand. Was her marriage to your brother not . . ." She gestured. "Vetted and approved?"

"No, it was not. Arthur, who's next in line for the title, is the mildest of the four of us. Almira trapped him into marriage with the oldest trick known."

"She claimed she was pregnant?"

Sebastian nodded. "She wasn't, as it turned out, but by the time Arthur realized, the wedding had been announced." He sighed. "What's done cannot be undone." He refocused on her. "Which brings me to my point. You understand what it is to be the holder of a title, what responsibilities—whether one wishes them or not—lie on one's shoulders. I waited to see how Almira would develop, whether she had it in her to become more . . . gracious, more tolerant. But she has not. And now she has a son who would ultimately inherit and whom she is clearly intent on ruling—ultimately ruling through."

He shook his head. "I cannot in all conscience permit that. And so I decided I must marry and sire a son of my own."

His gaze rested on her. "I had never forgotten you. I recognized you the instant I set eyes on you in Lady Morpleth's salon. I'd been looking for a suitable wife and had found none—then, suddenly, you were there."

She narrowed her eyes at him. "You seem very certain I am suitable."

He smiled, a sincere and, for him, oddly gentle smile. "You will never bore me to tears. Your temper is as bad as mine, and you are not, to my annoyance, the least in awe of me."

She fought against a smile, frowned instead. "I am not in awe of you, yet I am not fool enough to underestimate you. You are very adept at twisting the truth to suit yourself. You have *not* been thinking of marriage."

"Acquit me, *mignonne*—I assure you, in regard to you, I have thought of nothing else. I did not make my intentions plain for a very good reason."

"Which was?"

"That any hint of my change of heart would have caused a sensation—any suggestion I had decided on you as my duchess would have turned the ton rabid. Every single lady with a marriageable daughter would have stood in line to attempt to change my mind. I saw no reason to invite such interest. Instead, I thought to bide my time until now. Tomorrow I will leave London, and so will you. We will not be subjected to the full glare of society's interest."

"How do you know I will be leaving London?"

"Because I have issued an invitation to the Thierrys and to you to visit at Somersham Place—hence my interest in Thierry's return." He raised a hand, touched her cheek. "I thought that there, I could . . . persuade you that marriage to me would be your wisest choice."

She arched a brow at him. "Persuade?" Sweeping around, she gestured to the door through which the four others had gone. "You have *declared* we are to wed!" The recollection sparked her temper; she let her eyes flash as she swung back to face him. "And now you are going to behave as if the matter is signed and sealed." She folded her arms and glared at him. "When it is not!"

He studied her, his features impassive. Then he said, his tone even, low—and steely, "Am I to understand, *mignonne,* that you were at the point of accepting me as your lover but that you are now balking at becoming my duchess?"

She looked him in the eye, then nodded. "*Vraiment!* There is no point taking that tone with me. It is a very different thing, being your wife compared with being your lover. I know the laws. A wife has no say in things—"

"Unless her husband is willing to indulge her."

She narrowed her eyes, studied his—guilelessly

blue. "Are you saying you would indulge me?"

He looked down at her. A long moment passed before he said, "*Mignonne*, I will indulge you in anything, with two caveats. One—I will never permit you to expose yourself to danger of any kind. Two—I will never allow you to develop any interest in any man other than myself."

She raised her brows. "Not even your sons?"

"With the sole exception of our sons."

She felt as if she were swaying, even though the ground felt firm beneath her feet. His offer was beyond tempting, yet . . . To trust him to that degree—especially him, who understood her too well, who could slide around her temper, inflame her senses, who already held too much power over her.

As usual, he seemed to know what she was thinking—he seemed to track her thoughts through her eyes. His gaze was sharp, shrewd. Before she realized what he intended, he bent his head, touched his lips to hers.

Her own lips softened, clung—she reacted, kissed him, offered her lips, took his, before she'd even thought.

He drew away. Their eyes met, held.

"We were meant for each other, *mignonne*—can you not sense it? You will be my salvation—and I will be yours."

A sound from the gallery beyond the closed door had them both turning. Sebastian swore beneath his breath. "We've run out of time tonight. Come." Taking her elbow, he steered her to the door leading to the next room.

"I wish to leave this house." She glanced at his hard face as he opened the door and ushered her through. She waited until he shut it, then stated, "I have not agreed to marry you."

He met her gaze, studied her eyes, then nodded. "You have not agreed—yet."

Helena growled as he urged her on.

"You are too wise to cut off your nose to spite your face—no matter how much your temper would like to."

She *hated* it that he could read her so well. "*Bien*, then I will visit your house and *consider* your proposal."

He ignored her waspish, decidedly haughty tone.

He opened another door, one leading into a minor corridor, avoiding the gallery altogether. "I will escort you downstairs to the front hall, then we'll send for the Thierrys." He glanced at her. "I fear you will need to guard your temper, *mignonne*. No one will believe you haven't accepted me."

She shot him another narrow-eyed look, but he was right—again. No one did. No one even thought to ask the question.

The Thierrys, summoned by a footman, joined them in the front hall. One glance at their faces was enough to confirm that the news was out and that they'd already heard.

"*Ma petite!* Such wonderful tidings!" Eyes wide, Marjorie hugged her delightedly. "*Vraiment!* It is a coup!" she whispered, then stepped back to let Thierry have his turn.

He, too, was openly thrilled. After congratulating her, he shook hands with Sebastian.

Who smiled easily, the very picture of a proud groom-to-be. Helena gritted her teeth, pressed her lips tightly together as Sebastian's blue gaze came to rest on her face.

"I read your letter just this evening," Thierry explained. "*Mille pardons*—I was from town. I came here *immédiatement* to tell madame and mademoiselle."

Sebastian nodded, waving aside the apology. "It seems our secret is out." He shrugged lightly. "It matters not at this juncture. I will be leaving London early tomorrow. If it's convenient, I will send my traveling coach to Green Street with instructions to leave at eleven. That will allow you an easy drive into Cambridgeshire. You will arrive in the late afternoon." He bowed. "And I will be there to greet you."

"It is all most amiable," Marjorie enthused. She gave him her hand. "We will be most thrilled to visit at such a grand house. I have heard it is magnificent."

Sebastian inclined his head; his lips quirked as he turned to Helena. "And you, *mignonne*, will you, too, be thrilled?" He murmured the words, deliberately suggestive, as he brushed his lips to her fingers.

Helena raised her brows. "As to that, Your Grace, we shall see."

Chapter Eight

Had he truly been thinking of marrying her all along? Swaying as St. Ives's traveling coach rumbled through the countryside, Helena considered the possibility. She would rate it no higher than that—he was the type of man she understood; regardless of his reputation, he would always adhere to honor's dictates. Especially over a woman such as she.

Unwritten rules had plagued her all her life; she comprehended them instinctively. Regardless of whether marrying her had always been his intention, on being discovered in a compromising situation, he would have reacted precisely as he had, giving her the protection of his name. And then insisting, making her believe, that he'd wanted to marry her from the first. Honor would have dictated the first action, his eccentric kindness the second.

She stifled a sniff. Glanced across the carriage at Louis, slumped, unhandsomely asleep, mouth agape. Louis had been drinking; he'd stumbled down the stairs this morning looking like death, his skin pasty, his eyes heavily shadowed. He'd barely acknowledged

the Thierrys' concerned inquiries, waving aside all of-
fers of breakfast, tight-lipped and trembly.

Which was altogether unlike Louis. He usually
craved attention, grabbed all that was offered.

If she had to guess, she would say something had occurred to shake him badly. She couldn't imagine what.

Marjorie sat beside her, thrilled, happy, and relieved.
Thierry sat opposite his wife, relaxed, less worried
than he'd appeared in recent days. Marjorie's maid,
Thierry's valet, and Louis's man Villard were following in another carriage with the baggage; the maid who
had been tending Helena had come down with a cold
and been left behind.

The St. Ives traveling coach had appeared precisely
on time—there had, of course, been no question that
they would accept St. Ives's invitation and journey into
Cambridgeshire. For her, it was an unexpected challenge, a sudden and unanticipated change in direction.

Secure, safe, and warm—the coach was the epitome
of luxury, all velvet and leather, the doors and windows fitted so well that not a single draft could get in—
yet she was not of a mind to allow herself to be lulled
into complaisance. Marrying a man like Sebastian Cynster had never been part of her plans. Nevertheless,
here she was, all but formally affianced to a man as
powerful as any she'd ever known. That fact alone
spoke volumes. Between Fabien and Sebastian there
was, she judged, little to choose—not in the matter of
real power, the ability to make things happen.

Fabien was a master. Sebastian was a past master.
Even worse.

With the usual contrariness of fate, that point was now a very strong argument urging her to accept him.

If she did, she'd be safe from Fabien.

But at what cost?

That, she told herself as she glimpsed a pair of imposing gateposts ahead, was what she had to learn.

Her first sight of Somersham Place, principal residence of the Dukes of St. Ives, distracted her. The coach rumbled through the open gates, then bowled along a well-tended drive bordered by trees, short stretches of lawn, and shrubs. Then they rounded a curve and left the trees behind—and the house stood before them, pale in the weak light of the winter's day.

Immense, imposing, impressive, yet not cold. Helena studied it, trying to find the right words. Built of sand-colored stone, the façade and all the walls she could see had stood for many years; they were solid, established, and had mellowed, settling into the landscape that had been created around them. The wide lawns, the size of the trees that dotted them, the way the lake she glimpsed beyond the lawns sat so perfectly within the vista, testified that both house and gardens had matured and reached a certain harmony.

Accustomed to the heavily structured, geometrically exact surrounds of French noble houses, Helena was intrigued by the lack of all such formality here. Despite that lack, the result was magnificent, palatial—unquestionably the home of a wealthy and powerful man. Yet there was more, something else. Something unexpected.

The house was welcoming. Alive. Oddly warm—as

if the stone façade were a benevolent defense protecting some gentler existence within.

A bemusing observation, yet as the coach halted before the sweep of steps leading up to the front door, she couldn't shake the conviction.

Thierry descended first, then handed her down. Moving past him, she fought at least to mask the eagerness that seized her—to hide it from Sebastian, who had come out of the door as the carriage rolled up and was now descending the steps with his usual languid grace.

She offered her hand; he took it and bowed, then straightened and drew her to him. Turning with her, he let his gaze travel along the handsome façade, then glanced at her, arching a brow. "Dare I hope my home meets with your approval, *mignonne*?"

The curve of his long lips, the light in his eye, suggested he knew that it did.

Helena lifted her chin. "I have yet to see beyond its façade, Your Grace. It's common knowledge façades can be deceiving."

Their gazes met, held, then, his smile deepening, he inclined his head. "Indeed."

Turning, he greeted Thierry and Marjorie, exchanged a nod with Louis, then led them indoors.

In the front hall Sebastian introduced her to his butler, Webster, and the housekeeper, a Mrs. Swithins. The latter was an unflappable, matronly woman; on learning of Helena's lack of a maid, she promised to send a girl up. "I'll have your bags taken up and unpacked the instant they arrive."

"Until then," Sebastian said, "we'll repair to the drawing room."

"Indeed, Your Grace." Mrs. Swithins bobbed a curtsy. "Tea will be ready—you need only ring."

Sebastian inclined his head, apparently unperturbed by the woman's familiarity; Helena inwardly shook her head. The English were different in many ways. She found their easier manners relaxing.

As Sebastian ushered them across the hall, she struggled not to look this way and that, to stare about her. Despite the fact that it was still weeks to Christmas, the scent of evergreens hung in the air. A holly wreath sporting bright red berries was mounted over the huge hearth at the end of the hall.

She'd fully expected that odd promise of warmth to be merely a feature of the façade. Instead . . . it wasn't warmth, real warmth, but rather a lingering sense of peace, of harmony, of happiness past, present, and anticipated that radiated from the walls, enfolding her in its welcome.

Fabien's fortress, Le Roc, was cold and barren; she'd never sensed any warmth there. Her own home, Cameralle, was . . . cool. It might, she thought, dredging her memories of the time her parents had been alive, once have held a similar sense of peace, but that had faded, dissipated; the long halls were now filled with a quiet sense of waiting.

Here there was a sense of waiting, too, but it was different—expectant, confident, as if happiness and joy were assured.

A footman opened a door; Sebastian ushered her

through. She put aside her fanciful thoughts as a short, plump lady with brown hair and soft brown eyes rose from the chaise, laying aside the book she'd been reading.

"Allow me to present my aunt, Lady Clara."

Clara smiled warmly and clasped her hand. "Welcome, my dear. I'm delighted to meet you."

Helena smiled back. She would have curtsied, but Clara stopped her, tightening her grip on her hand.

"I'm not at all clear, dear, who has precedence. Let's not confuse the issue—I won't curtsy if you won't."

Helena laughed and inclined her head. "It will be as you wish."

"Good! And you will call me Clara, won't you?" Patting her hand, Clara turned to greet Marjorie with the same rather vague benevolence, then waved them to seats.

"Do ring, Sebastian, and ask for tea." Subsiding onto the chaise, Clara waved him to the bellpull, then stopped, considering Thierry and Louis. "But perhaps the gentlemen would like something stronger?"

Thierry smiled and shook his head, assuring her that tea would suit him admirably.

Louis had blanched at the mention of sustenance. He waved his hands. "No—I thank you. Nothing for me." He retreated to a chair a little way from the group, summoning a weak smile as he sat.

Sebastian obeyed and, when Webster arrived, ordered the tea to be brought in; he seemed unperturbed at being the recipient of Clara's orders. His aunt was clearly another who did not go in awe of him.

They sat down to conversation and tea served in exquisite bone china; Helena was tempted to check—she suspected the set was de Sèvres's. Marjorie and Clara had settled into an easy patter. The china tweaked Helena's curiosity; she glanced around the room with newly opened eyes.

It was as she'd guessed; every single item her eye alighted on attested to its owner's wealth. But not only that; most pieces were not new. They spoke of the family's long-standing prominence, of the luxury and affluence Sebastian and Clara doubtless took for granted. Indeed, it was the same state of worldly grace into which Helena herself had been born, in which she felt most at home. It occurred to her that in the space of an hour she already felt comfortable here.

Her gaze slid to Sebastian. He sat elegantly relaxed in an armchair, apparently listening to Thierry satisfying Clara's request to be told of the masquerade, yet his eyes, under their hooded lids, rested on her.

She looked away, sipped her tea, then set down the cup. Looked again at its delicacy. Felt the padded softness of the velvet cushions at her back, the thickness of the Aubusson carpet beneath her shoes.

Seduction took many forms. Sebastian, she was sure, knew them all.

Shortly after, he took pity on Thierry and Louis and offered to show them around the house. The instant the door closed behind them, Clara turned to her. "Now, I daresay you'd like to hear about the Place."

Helena blinked, then nodded. "Please."

Within minutes she realized she had a firm supporter in Clara, that the older woman had, apparently on sight, decided she was the perfect wife for Sebastian, on whom, it quickly became apparent, she doted. She was his paternal aunt; she'd married young and been widowed early. Having spent most of her life at Somersham Place, she was acquainted with every aspect of running the great house.

It all poured from her; Helena listened and found herself pulled in, asking questions, drawing on Clara's knowledge. Managing a house this size—and the estate was formidable, too—was precisely the challenge she'd been raised and trained to meet, the challenge that, until now, Fabien had denied her. She might own vast estates and a château as well, but, unmarried, she'd lived under her guardian's auspices, for the most part under his roof. Cameralle was open but barely staffed—just enough to keep the house functioning for Ariele, who often retired there.

She'd never been a hostess, never had the chance to test herself in that arena, never tasted the joy of social triumph. As she listened to Clara paint a glowing picture of the purview of the Duchess of St. Ives, Helena hungered for the opportunity, thirsted for the position. Even knowing that Sebastian's machinations had probably extended to foreseeing such an outcome didn't dim her desire.

She was who she was—she'd long ago stopped imagining she could change that. She'd reluctantly accepted the fact that that meant she would always be, as Sebastian had labeled her, a prize for powerful men.

Sitting on the chaise listening to Clara's words, full re-alization struck. If she accepted all that, there was no reason she couldn't embrace the rest—the chance to claim her birthright as the wife of a powerful man.

Years of dealing with Fabien stopped her thoughts at that point, gave her the strength to pull back, out of the grip of the dream.

But the dream lingered in her mind as they finished the tea cakes, then Clara offered to show them their rooms.

"Helena."

They were crossing the gallery when Sebastian called. Helena turned to see him standing by one of the long windows.

"Hates to be kept waiting—forever impatient!" Clara spoke softly, then squeezed her arm, easing her in Sebastian's direction. "I'll take Marjorie on, then re-turn for you. I won't be long."

Nodding, Helena turned and walked down the gallery. Sebastian watched her approach. Fabien had the same ability to project a predatory stillness, yet with Fabien she'd never felt it personally, never felt any physical threat.

Never felt the slightest wish to embrace that threat. To encourage it.

Halting before Sebastian, she smiled and arched a brow. "Yes, Your Grace?"

Sebastian met her gaze. "*Mignonne*, do you think you could possibly use my name when we are private?"

Her lips twitched. "If you wish." She looked down,

hiding the smile he'd wanted to see. Without thinking, he raised a hand and tipped up her face.

He studied her wide eyes, took a certain satisfaction in their arrested expression. "I suspect it would be wise for me to write to your guardian informing him of my interest." He paused, then added, "I do not wish to dally over the formalities of our wedding."

An understatement; he wanted her to be his—now, today, this minute. The strength of that desire was strong enough to shake even him.

She lifted her chin from his fingers but continued to meet his gaze. "That will not be necessary."

Her expression was one of considerable satisfaction. It was his turn to arch a brow.

She smiled. "I do not trust my guardian, so when he suggested I come to England and look for a suitable husband, I asked for his permission to marry a suitably eligible *parti* in writing."

"From your smug expression, I take it he complied?"

"*Oui.* And there is a friend of my family, an old friend of my father's who remains attached to me—he is a judge and much experienced in such matters. I showed him the letter on our way through Paris—he confirmed that, as I had hoped, that document is all the permission I need."

"Provided the gentleman is suitable in terms of title, estate, and income, as I recall. Were there any other stipulations?"

She shook her head. "Just those three."

Sebastian read her self-congratulation in her eyes

and smiled. "Very good. In that case I see no reason to disturb your guardian just yet."

Once he'd declared his hand to Geoffre Daurent, it was more than likely the man would prove difficult over the settlements, try to wring concessions from him and generally drag his feet. Helena's route had a great deal to recommend it.

"My commendations, *mignonne*. Such foresight is enviable."

She smiled; her lids veiled her eyes as she turned as Clara reappeared. "You are not the only one who can scheme, Your Grace."

Clara escorted Helena to a large bedchamber halfway along one wing.

"The Thierrys are at the end, so you may be comfortable." Clara glanced about, noting the brushes and bottles on the dressing table, the trunks already emptied and set in one corner. "Now I can summon your maid and introduce you, if you wish."

"No, no." Helena turned from her own survey. The huge four-poster bed, hung with silk tapestries, draped in satin, had captured her attention. "I believe I will rest for an hour or so. I have time, have I not?"

"Indeed you have, dear. We keep town hours, more or less, so we'll dine at eight. Shall I tell the maid to wake you? Her name is Heather."

"I'll ring." The idea of an hour of blissful peace sounded wonderful.

"Then I'll leave you." Clara turned to the door, then

stopped and glanced back. Her eyes, Helena noted, had turned misty.

"I never thought Sebastian would marry, and that would have been a very big mistake." Clara paused, then added, "Words can't express how pleased I am you're here."

With that she departed, gently closing the door, leaving Helena pondering the wooden panels. She had never looked to be here, in this position, yet . . . there was much to be said for being a duchess.

Sebastian's duchess.

She drifted to the window. It looked out over a rose garden to the lake. Dusk was rapidly falling. The gardens seemed extensive; tomorrow she'd investigate. Returning to the dressing table, she lit a lamp, then sat and started to pluck pins from her hair.

The mass tumbled down around her shoulders as a knock fell on the door.

Sebastian? That first thought was immediately superseded by the reflection that it was unlikely. Ignoring the sudden thrill that had flashed through her, and its subsequent fading, she called, "Come."

The door opened; she turned and saw Louis standing in the doorway. She rose. "What is it?" He really did not look well.

"These are for you."

He held out two letters. Crossing to the door, Helena took them.

Louis shifted as she glanced at them. "I'll leave you to read them. Once you have"—he gestured vaguely—"we'll talk."

He turned and shambled off. Helena watched him go, then, frowning, closed the door and returned to the dressing table.

One packet was addressed to her in Fabien's distinctive hand. The other was from Ariele. Dropping Fabien's letter on the table, Helena sat and broke the seal on her sister's missive.

As she read the first words, she relaxed, very conscious of relief. The way Louis had behaved, she'd already tensed, worrying . . . but no. Ariele was well. The daily round at Cameralle went on much as usual.

Helena smiled again and again as she read the first sheet—read of their ponies and the exploits of the geese. Halfway down the second sheet, Ariele broke off, then continued.

Phillipe has arrived (how odd!). He says monsieur le comte wishes me to come to Le Roc and we must leave tomorrow. Bother! I do not like Le Roc, but I suppose I will have to go.

Helena paused, looked up, frowned. Fabien had claimed Ariele's guardianship as well as her own. Phillipe was Louis's younger brother; she had not met him in recent years. He'd always been quieter than Louis, but from Ariele's words, it seemed Phillipe, like Louis, was now engaged in Fabien's service.

Ignoring the ripple of unease the knowledge brought, Helena read on. After two paragraphs bemoaning the necessity of obeying Fabien, Ariele broke off again.

This time, when she resumed, it was clearly some days later.

> *I am now at Le Roc. Fabien says if I finish this letter he will send it with one of his. I am well, but alas this place is gloomy. Marie is ill and confined to her bed— Fabien said I should mention it. How I envy you in England, rainy and cold though it may be. It is rainy and cold here—I should have come with you. Still, if you were to find a useful Englishman and marry him, Fabien would be bound to let me come to be your bridesmaid. I most sincerely wish you luck in your search, dearest sister.*
>
> *I remain, as ever, your loving little sister,*
> *Ariele*

Helena's thumbs were pricking. Why? Fabien never did anything without good reason. What could he want with Ariele? And why did he wish her to know that Marie, his wife, a meek and sickly soul he had married for her connections, was ailing?

Laying aside Ariele's letter, she reached for Fabien's. As always, he was direct and succinct.

As she read his words, Helena's world—one that had started to glow with rosy hope—shattered, then re-formed into a dark landscape of despair.

> *As you will see from your sister's letter, she is now at Le Roc. She is currently well, as happy as might be ex-*

pected, and intact. There is a price, my dear Helena, for her continued well-being.

The gentleman in whose house you are now residing has something of mine. It is a family heirloom, and I wish it back. I have been unsuccessful over the years in convincing him to part with it, so you will now please me by retrieving it and returning it to me.

The heirloom in question is a dagger in its sheath. It is eight inches long, curved, with a large ruby set in the hilt. It was given to one of my ancestors by the Sultan of Arabia. There is no other like it—you will know it the instant you see it.

One thing—do not seek to discharge this duty by enlisting the aid of St. Ives. He will not part with the dagger, not for any reason. Do not think to appeal to his good nature—it will avail you naught and cost your sister dearly.

I expect you to obey me to the letter in this, and with all reasonable speed.

If you fail to bring me the dagger by Christmas, in recompense I will take Ariele as my mistress. Should she fail to please me, there are houses in Paris always ready to pay highly for tender chickens such as she.

The choice is yours, but I know you will not fail your sister.

I will expect you by midnight on Christmas Eve.

Yours, etc.
Fabien

How long she sat and stared at the letter Helena had no idea. She felt ill; she had to sit unmoving until the nausea passed.

She couldn't think, couldn't imagine . . .

Then she did, and that was worse.

"Ariele!" With a muffled cry, she bent forward, covering her face with her hands. The thought of what awaited her precious little sister if she failed swamped her mind, made her wits seize.

Her heart, her whole chest, hurt; a metallic taste filled her mouth.

The lesson was abundantly clear.

She had never been free of Fabien—he'd been pulling her strings all along. The letter she'd felt so clever about obtaining was worthless. She would never get an opportunity to use it.

Fabien had played her for a fool.

She would never be free.

She would never have a chance to live. To have a life that was hers and not his.

"Mignonne, are you well?"

Helena forced her lips to curve, glanced up briefly as she gave Sebastian her hand. She still couldn't think, could barely function. Until that moment she'd thought she was covering her state well; no one else seemed to have noticed. But Sebastian had just joined them in the small drawing room and had come straight to her side. "It is nothing," she managed, breathless, her lungs tight. "It's just the traveling, I think."

He was silent for a moment; she didn't dare meet his

eyes. Then he murmured, "We will have to trust that dinner will revive you. Come, let us see."

Collecting the others with a gesture, he led her to the family dining room, an elegant apartment that was considerably more intimate than the huge dining room she'd glimpsed from the front hall. As he sat her on his right, Helena could almost wish that he had chosen the larger room—she would have been farther from him and his too-sharp gaze.

Time had not been on her side. Before she'd had a chance to relieve her despair, give vent to her fury—to rail, to weep, to wail, then, perhaps, to calm and think—a maid had come scratching at her door, reminding her it was already late. She'd thrust the letters under her jewel box, then had to rush to get gowned, to show the maid how to dress her hair.

Rage, despair, and fear were a potent mix. She had to keep the roiling emotions bottled up, find strength, dredge deep, and put on a good show—had to manufacture smiles and small laughs, force her mind to follow the conversations rather than succumb to her feelings. Her performance was made more difficult by Sebastian, a shrewd observer. He sat relaxed in his huge chair, fingers lightly curled about the stem of his wineglass, and watched her from beneath his hooded lids.

The thing she remembered most of that hour was the sapphire he wore on his right hand, how it winked in the candlelight as his fingers languidly caressed the glass. The jewel was the same color as his eyes. Equally mesmerizing.

Then dinner was over. She could remember nothing of what had been said. They all rose, and she realized that the gentlemen would remain to pass the port. Relief swamped her. The smile she gave Sebastian as he released her hand came more easily.

She retired with Clara and Marjorie to the drawing room. By the time Sebastian entered with Thierry and Louis twenty minutes later, she had herself under control. She made herself wait until the tea trolley was brought in, until they'd all sipped and chatted. She increasingly fell silent.

When Sebastian came to relieve her of her empty cup, she smiled weakly—at him, at them all.

"I fear I have a headache, too." Louis had already retired, claiming the same ailment.

Thierry, Marjorie, and Clara all murmured in sympathy. Sebastian merely watched her. Clara offered to get her a powder.

"If I retire now and get a good night's sleep," she replied, still smiling faintly but reassuringly, "I am sure I will be recovered by morning."

"Well, if you're sure, dear."

She nodded, then looked up at Sebastian. He took her hand, helped her to her feet. She curtsied to the others, murmuring her good nights, then turned to the door. Her hand still in his, Sebastian turned with her, walked with her.

He paused before they reached the door. She halted, glanced up at him. Met his blue eyes, felt them search hers. Then he raised his other hand, smoothed a fingertip across her brow.

"Sleep well, *mignonne*. You will not be disturbed."

There was something in his tone, in his gaze, as if he would tell her, reassure her . . . She was too drained, too exhausted to fathom his meaning.

Then he lifted her hand, turned it, pressed his lips to the point where her pulse fluttered at her wrist. Let his lips linger until she felt the heat flow. Raising his head, he released her. "Sweet dreams, *mignonne*."

She nodded, bobbed a curtsy, then walked to the door. A footman opened it; she sailed through. The door shut softly behind her; only then was she free of Sebastian's gaze.

Wanting nothing more than a pillow on which to lay her aching head and the privacy to ease her heavy heart, to release her pent-up feelings, she climbed the stairs, crossed the gallery, and headed down the corridor to her room. Just before she reached her door, a shadow shifted; Louis stepped out to intercept her.

"What is it?" She made no effort to hide her anger.

"I . . . wanted to know. Will you do it?"

She stared at him blankly. "Of course." Then she realized. Fabien, as usual, was playing his cards close to his chest. Louis did not know with what his uncle had threatened her. If he had known, not even he would have asked such a stupid question.

"Uncle insists *you* fetch the item—not me."

Louis's surly tone nearly made her laugh. Hysterically. He was sulking because Fabien was using her talents, not his.

But why? Her mind fixed on the point, turned it over—then she saw. Because she was a woman—a woman Sebastian wanted. He'd apparently been too strong for Fabien's persuasions, so Fabien, with his usual vindictive touch, had chosen as his thief one who would not only succeed in retrieving the dagger but who, in doing so, would also dent Sebastian's pride.

Fabien would do what he could to hurt Sebastian; that it would hurt her, too, would neither occur to him nor perturb him if it did. Indeed, he would probably view any hurt she suffered as due punishment for her temerity in forcing that letter from him.

Louis scowled at her. "If you require any assistance, I'm to help you. But I would strongly suggest that until we leave, you keep St. Ives at arm's length—*if you take my meaning*."

Helena stared at him. How did he know? She tipped up her chin and looked down her nose at him. "I will retrieve your uncle's property as I see fit—you need not let my methods concern you."

With a dismissive nod, she swept past him to her door, opened it, and went in.

Louis stood still, staring after her. When the door clicked shut, he turned and headed for his room.

Villard was waiting. "Well?"

Louis shut his room door, ran his hands through his hair. "She says she will do it."

"*Bon!* Then all is progressing, and there is no reason you cannot write and tell monsieur le comte—"

"No!" Agitated, Louis paced before the hearth. Then he flung up his hands. "*Marriage!* Whoever would have *imagined*? Fabien said St. Ives had publicly decreed he would not wed, and that was years ago! Now suddenly the talk is of a wedding!"

By the bed folding shirts, Villard looked down. After a moment he murmured, "From what you said, it seems unlikely marriage was on monsieur le duc's mind, not until you directed those others into the library . . ."

Louis missed the malicious glance Villard slanted his way. "Precisely!" He continued to pace. "But what could I do? He would have had her there and then— and then what? Retired merrily to his estate for Christmas, without her. No. I had to stop him—and better those others than me. He would have been alerted had I gone in."

Villard's lip curled; he looked down at the shirts.

"I tell you, I had palpitations when I heard what everyone was whispering. No one cared about the masquerade anymore—all the talk was of St. Ives marrying!"

"I believe it is something of a coup, which is why, perhaps, a word to monsieur le comte—"

"No, I tell you! *No!* Things are back on track now. Helena knows what she must do—and she is not a fool, that one. She will not risk monsieur le comte's displeasure. She will not give herself to St. Ives."

"From your description, I thought she had."

"No. I am sure . . . He must have overwhelmed her. His reputation is *formidable*. Although I would have thought . . ." Louis frowned, then waved his tangled thoughts aside. "No matter. It is settled. She will not fail, nor will she give in to St. Ives—not now."

Villard studied the neat pile of shirts and let the silence

grow. Then he said, "What if—purely a supposition—what if she accepts him?"

"She hasn't. I would have heard of it. But even if she needs to do so, to lead him to believe all is progressing as it should, then weddings for such as they are take months to arrange. And they'd have to get Fabien's permission. *Huh!*"

The thought cheered Louis. He actually smiled.

Villard drew breath, lifted his head. "Do you not think it might be wise to warn monsieur le comte?"

Louis shook his head. "No need to start hares. All is proceeding as Fabien wished. The matter of this marriage is incidental." Louis gestured contemptuously. "There is no need to fuss, and Fabien won't care. As long as he gets his dagger back—that is all he cares about."

Villard silently exhaled, picked up the pile of shirts, and carried them to the wardrobe.

Helena sat at Sebastian's right at the breakfast table the next morning. As she buttered a piece of toast, she mentally recited what she had to do.

She had to hold Sebastian off, keep him at arm's length; Louis had been right about that. She had to find and take Fabien's dagger. And then she had to flee. Fast. Because nothing was surer than that Sebastian would come after her.

There would be no point taking the dagger, then trying to brazen it out. A dagger he'd taken from a French nobleman goes missing while a French noblewoman was visiting? Half a second, she estimated, would be all it would take for him to figure that out.

She would have to leave him and run.

He would be furious. He would see her act as a betrayal.

He'd assume she'd been part of Fabien's plot all along . . .

The realization had her raising her head, then she blocked off her thoughts—reached for the jam. Set her jaw.

Nothing else mattered but saving Ariele. She had no choice; she couldn't afford to let any other consideration sway her.

The Thierrys and Clara were discussing a walk in the gardens; Louis had yet to appear.

She nearly jumped when Sebastian ran a finger along the back of her hand. Eyes wide, she met his gaze.

His lips lifted lightly, but his gaze was sharp. "I wondered, *mignonne*, if you were sufficiently recovered to risk a ride. You might find the fresh air more invigorating than a slow stroll around the gardens."

Her heart leaped at the thought of a ride. And on horseback they wouldn't be that close—she wouldn't be risking any contact that might give her away, that might test the walls she was trying to erect around her heart.

Letting her lips curve, letting her eagerness show, she nodded. "I would like that very much."

He waved negligently. "As soon as you're ready."

They met in the hall half an hour later, she in her riding habit, he in long boots and a riding jacket. With a wave he ushered her on. They left the house by a side door and crossed the lawns, strolling under the bare branches of towering oaks to a stable block beyond.

He'd sent word ahead; their mounts stood waiting. A huge gray hunter for him, a frisky bay mare for her. He lifted her to the mare's saddle, then gathered the gray's reins and mounted. The beast shifted, snorted, eager to be away; the mare danced.

"Shall we?" Sebastian raised a brow.

Helena laughed—her first spontaneous reaction since reading Fabien's letter—and wheeled the mare.

They left the stable yard side by side, stride for stride. Sebastian held the gray in. The horse shook his head once, then settled, accepting the edict, accepting the masterful hand on his reins. Inwardly smiling, Helena looked ahead.

Despite the month, it was clear, but the morning chill had yet to leave the air. Soft clouds filled the skies, blocking out the weak sun, yet it was pleasant riding through the quiet fields, empty and brown, already touched by winter's hand. There was peace here, too. Helena felt it touch her, soothe her.

She'd ridden since she could stand, the stocky ponies of the Camargue her steeds. The activity required no conscious effort, leaving her free to look around, to appreciate, to enjoy. The mare was responsive, easy to manage; they rode without any need for words, she wheeling as Sebastian did, following him across his lands.

They topped a rise. To her surprise, the land beyond

lay flat, rolling before them to the horizon. She'd never seen such a sight before, but Sebastian didn't pause; he led her down the gentle slope into that seemingly infinite expanse.

A raised path led between two fields. They followed it, then Sebastian angled down into the pasture and set the gray to a canter. Helena followed—and suddenly realized the pasture was wet, waterlogged, yet not marshy. Sebastian let the gray stretch his legs; she matched him, fearlessly keeping pace, feeling the wind rush to meet them, then racing away through her hair.

Despite all, she felt the heavy cloud that lay over her heart lift, ease. Blow away.

They rode on through the morning, stride for stride, the sky wide and windswept above. The call of larks and waterbirds was the only sound to counterpoint the rhythm of the horses' hooves.

Then another path—a dike—appeared. The horses took the slope easily, then Sebastian wheeled and reined in. He glanced at her.

She met his gaze, a smile on her lips, a laugh bubbling up. "Oh!" She dragged in a breath. "It's just like home!"

"Home?"

"Cameralle is in the Camargue. It's"—she looked around—"not the same but similar." Gazing up, she lifted her arms to the sky. "Like here, the sky is wide and open." Lowering her arms, she stretched them to either side. "And the marsh runs forever."

She grinned and set the mare ambling beside the gray. "Many think it too wild a place."

From the corner of her eye, she saw him smile.

"And the occupants too wild for decency?"

She laughed and didn't answer.

It wasn't hard to keep her worries in check for the rest of that magical morning. In the wilds of the Camargue she had always been free; she felt the same sense of freedom, of being unfettered, here. Of being allowed to be free.

Even after, when, tired but refreshed, they cantered back to the stable, she managed, by dint of will, to keep her mind free of Fabien's contagion. She was still smiling when they reached the house. Sebastian led her to a side door, held it open, and ushered her in.

She entered, then stopped. The door gave directly into a small parlor, not a corridor as she'd supposed. The door clicked shut as she turned. Then Sebastian was there, and she was in his arms.

Lightly held, not seized. Cradled like something precious, something he wished to own.

She looked into his face, into those blue eyes, and saw that truth etched in the blue.

His hand was beneath her chin, tipping up her face.

Her lids fell as he lowered his head.

Practice made perfect. A self-evident fact, at least in this case. Their lips seemed to know each other's— touched, brushed, then fused with the confidence of familiarity.

The pressure increased. She hesitated, for one instant held back—realized in the same moment that she couldn't, couldn't hide from him in this, for he would know and grow suspicious. Realized she couldn't bear to let Fabien triumph in denying her even this.

Just this was all he'd left her—whatever experience she was brave enough to grasp, to seize. To take for herself—now.

Deliberately, she parted her lips, lured Sebastian in, tasted him and gloried—deliberately seized.

Just a kiss. Neither pushed for more, yet there was a flagrant promise in the melding of their mouths, in the hot tangle of their tongues. In the way their bodies came together, soft to hard, hips to thighs, breast to chest.

She took and he gave; he made demands and she met them gladly. Passion awakened, rose, stretched; desire watched from the wings. Heat, deep pleasure, and that sweet, aching yearning—they were there, hovering, yet held back by a knowing hand. A tantalizing promise.

How powerful could a kiss be?

Enough to leave them both panting, both urgently wanting more, yet conscious through the pounding that filled their ears of the luncheon gong echoing through the house.

Their eyes met, glances touching in sure recognition, then sliding away. Breaths merged, then they kissed again, came together again, a last caress before easing apart.

He held her until she nodded, once more sure on her feet. He released her but reluctantly, sliding his hands down her arms as she turned to the door. His fingers tangled with hers, twined, then slid away.

"Until later, *mignonne*."

She heard the deep murmur as she reached the door. Heard the promise in the words. She hesitated but could think of nothing to say. Opening the door, she led the way through. Sebastian followed.

Chapter Nine

❦

If Fabien was to deny her all chance of a life—the life that should by rights have been hers—then she would take what she could, experience all she could along the way.

Along the way to perdition.

Despite her defiant stance, Helena felt plagued by doubts, racked by guilt. By the sense that, while plotting to thieve from Sebastian, in taking pleasure from him, no matter how much she gave back, she was committing some heinous sin.

She should find the dagger quickly. Then go.

The house lay silent about her even though it was only just eleven. She'd heard a clock somewhere strike the hour as she'd slipped from her room. She'd considered waiting until after twelve, but by then she was sure all the lamps would be extinguished. Most had already been put out, but enough were still burning for her to see her way.

The house was too huge and as yet too unfamiliar for her to risk blundering about in the full dark. And she felt certain that Sebastian, the only one she feared meeting, would keep late hours. He was probably in his study, looking over some papers. So she devoutly hoped.

An ornate dagger of not-inconsiderable worth— where would he keep it?

Not in any of the rooms she'd thus far seen. A whispered conference had elicited the information that Louis, likewise, hadn't spotted it. Neither he nor that weasely man of his had any idea where it was. So much for Louis's help.

Reaching the gallery, she turned in the direction she'd seen Sebastian take when heading to change for dinner. She doubted he would keep such an object in his bedchamber, but his suite would doubtless include a private room—a room in which he kept his most precious things, the things that meant something to him.

Whether the dagger featured in that category, she didn't know, but . . . given the propensities of powerful men, she suspected it might. Fabien had not mentioned how Sebastian had come to possess a de Mordaunt family heirloom. Louis hadn't known that either. Helena wished she did—aside from anything else, knowing how Sebastian viewed the dagger would aid her in searching for it and in knowing how hard she would need to run once she found it.

Locating Sebastian's apartments wasn't difficult. The opulence of the hangings, furniture, and vases told her she had the right corridor; the coat of arms carved into the solid oak of the double doors at the end confirmed it.

No light showed below the double doors or beneath

the single door along the corridor to the right. Ladies to the left, gentlemen to the right—she prayed the English followed the same convention. Holding her breath, she eased open the single door. It opened noiselessly. She peeked in.

Moonlight poured through uncurtained windows, illuminating a large sitting room luxuriously furnished yet distinctly masculine.

The room was empty.

Helena whisked through the door, then carefully shut it. She scanned the room again and saw what she'd hoped to see. A trophy case. She crossed to it, stood before it, and examined all the items. A whip with a silver handle. An engraved cup. A gold plate with some inscription. Various other items, ribbons, decorations, but no dagger.

She looked around, then started circling the room, checking the tops of the small tables and sideboards, investigating all drawers. Reaching the desk, she glanced over the top, hesitated, then tried the drawers. None was locked; none contained any dagger.

"*Peste!*" Straightening, she glanced around one last time—and noticed that what she'd taken for a domed clock standing on a pedestal by one window now seen from this more revealing angle was not a clock at all.

She crossed quickly to the pedestal, slowing as she neared. The object that lay beneath the glass dome was not a dagger. It was . . .

Curious, she drew close, peered.

The silvery light lay like gilding on the slim leaves of a dried sprig of mistletoe.

She'd seen that sprig before. Knew the tree on which it had grown.

Remembered—too well—the night it had been taken, snapped off, placed in Sebastian's pocket.

One part of her mind scoffed—how could she be sure it was the same sprig? How nonsensical . . . and yet . . .

I had never forgotten you.

His words to her two nights ago. If she was to believe the evidence of her eyes, he'd been speaking the truth.

Which meant . . . he might well have been intending to marry her all along. Just as he'd claimed.

Fingertips touching the cold glass, Helena stared at the slim leaves, the slender twigs, while inside something swelled, welled, poured over . . .

While the veils shifted, lifted, and she saw the truth, tasted its aching sweetness.

And recognized, fully and finally, all she would lose in saving Ariele.

The deep bong of a clock made her start. It was echoed by others throughout the house. She blinked, stepped back. She was tempting fate.

With one last, lingering look at the sprig of mistletoe lying preserved forever under the glass, she turned to the door.

She reached her bedchamber without incident, but her heart was pounding. Slipping inside, she closed the door, then paused with one palm on the panels, giving her pulse a chance to slow.

Drawing in a tight breath, she turned into the room—

Sebastian was sitting in the armchair by the hearth. Watching her.

She halted, froze—her wits seized.

He rose, languidly graceful, and crossed the thick carpet toward her. "I've been waiting, *mignonne*. For you."

She felt her eyes widen as he halted before her. She clung to her surprise. "I . . . didn't expect you."

An understatement. She fought not to glance at the letters she'd left folded on the dressing table.

He raised one hand; long fingers framed her face. "I did warn you."

Until later. She remembered his words, remembered their tone. "Later," it appeared, had arrived. "But . . ."

He said nothing, simply studied her face, watched . . . waited. She swallowed, gestured weakly to the door. "I went for a walk." Her voice wavered; she forced a smile, let her nervousness show. Disguised the cause. "Your house is so large and in the dark . . . a little unnerving." She shrugged lightly; her heart was racing. She let her gaze fall to his lips. Remembered the mistletoe. "I couldn't sleep."

His lips curved, yet his features remained hard, unyielding. "Sleep?" The deep murmur reached her as he released her face. She felt his hands slide about her waist. "I have to admit, *mignonne*"—he drew her to him, bent his head—"that sleep is the furthest thing from my mind."

Her head tipped back of its own accord; her lips met his—and she couldn't have stopped, didn't try to stop herself from sinking into his embrace.

Desire flared, and she clung. Held to him as if he were her only salvation.

Knew it wasn't so, knew that for her there could be no savior, no release. No happy ending.

But she couldn't pull back, couldn't deny him what he wanted. Couldn't deny herself her only chance for this.

If she tried, he would suspect, but it wasn't any fear of revealing Fabien's scheme that drove her to agree. To slide her fingers into his hair and hold him to her. She met his demands, pressed her own—their tongues tangled, caressed, hinted boldly at what was to come, what they both sought, desired. It wasn't thoughts of Ariele that warmed her, that supported her through the moment when their lips parted and she felt his fingers on her laces.

She caught her breath on a hiccup. His lips brushed her temple in a soothing caress, but his fingers never paused.

The force that swept through her, that swamped her mind and directed her movements, that gave her the strength to follow his murmured directions, to stand, albeit swaying slightly, as he stripped first her bodice, then her skirts, petticoats, and lastly her chemise from her—that wasn't even desire. Not hers, not his.

Something more.

When she stood naked before him, her skin pearlescent in the moonlight, it was that transcendent power that opened her eyes, that had her glorying in the naked desire in his face, in the passion that burned in his eyes. She could feel his gaze like a flame as it swept from her face to her toes, then returned.

His eyes burned, held hers, and then he took her

hands, held them wide, then raised one, then the other, to his lips.

"Come, *mignonne*—be mine."

His tone—dark, gravelly, dangerous—sent a shiver racing through her. He drew her hands to his shoulders, released them, reached for her. She drew breath, felt her chest swell, felt her heart lift. She went to him, into his arms, eagerly, gladly.

She'd been made for this; she felt it in her bones, in her marrow, in her soul. He drew her close, kissed her deeply, then set his hands to her bare skin.

An innocent, she didn't know the ways, but she knew he did, trusted implicitly in what he would do, how he would treat her, take her, how he would make her his. She couldn't fight the power that drove her— never thought to do so—it was simply too powerful, too overwhelmingly sure. She gave herself up to it, surrendered completely to the moment, to all that she was, that he was, to all that would be.

His touch was exquisite; his hands moved on her so slowly, so languidly, yet there was heat in every caress, a blatant sensuality that burned. Passion and desire were twin flames, his to command, yet possessiveness was his rule, his guide, his driving need.

She could see it in the hard planes of his face; she touched them wonderingly, traced the edges, so harsh, so unyielding. Could sense it in the tension thrumming through his body, in the steely sinews caging her, in the reined strength in his hands as they held her. Could feel it in the rampant hardness of his erection, pressed to her soft stomach. Saw it flare in his eyes.

His gaze touched hers, swept her face, then he bent his head and took her mouth, ravaged, ravished her senses. His hands closed about her breasts, his fingers briefly tightened about the pebbled peaks, then he released them, released her lips, swept her up in his arms.

He carried her to the bed, knelt on it, laid her down on the silk coverlet. Shrugged off his coat, kicked off his shoes. She expected him to undress, but he didn't. In his fine linen shirt and lace, in his silk breeches, he sprawled beside her, half atop her, and took her mouth again. Set her wits whirling as he shifted her, arranged her, settled her half beneath him, then set his wicked fingers to her naked skin to strip all resistance away.

She didn't resist, had no intention of wasting that much effort, yet she was dimly conscious of his purpose, very aware of how she reacted to each sensual tactile taunt, each caress, each teasing glide. His lips played on hers; his long fingers played on her skin, played her nerves, her very senses, tracing her breasts until they ached, sliding away to outline her ribs, her waist, then gliding over her stomach until it contracted. Then he pressed. Knowingly.

He released her lips, listened to her gasp; she did, too. Her hips tilted; he kneaded gently, then his lips returned to hers and his fingers drifted away, trailing down her thighs. Up and down; down the outer faces, up the sensitive inner faces until she stirred and restlessly parted them, invited him to touch her there, where she throbbed. He didn't, not immediately, distracted by the soft curls at the base of her stomach, threading his fingers through them, touching her delicately, until she sank her fingers into his arm, kissed him madly, and moved her thighs farther apart.

The air touched her, cool against her fevered flesh, then his hand cupped her. Desire, illicit pleasure, jolted through her. Her spine tensed. She waited, tight with expectation, with sensual anticipation . . .

His hand shifted; his fingers traced. Over each and every fold, over and over again, until at last he parted them, opened her. Touched the entrance to her body.

She tensed again, but he didn't press further. Instead, that questing fingertip slid away, settled to tracing, caressing her softness. Teasing her nerves. Tantalizing her senses. He played, but deliberately, focused on her gasps, attuned to every quiver, every restless shift. He stripped away every last vestige of modesty with a ruthlessly gentle touch, until she was panting, wanting, aching—desperate for more.

She heard it in her breathing, felt need expand inside until she was awash with it, driven by it. She reached for him with her hands, with her body, with her lips. He kissed her—deeply, commandingly. He shifted over her, his body pressing her back into the bed.

She tried to tug him down to her, but he didn't move, propped on one elbow above her, his other hand still tracing the wet flesh between her thighs. His hips lay below hers, between her spread thighs; she tangled her legs with his, her skin sliding over the satin of his breeches as she clamped her calves to his flanks. She tried to tempt him to her—he kissed her again, so deeply she couldn't think, couldn't plan, could do nothing but lie back and let him have his way.

A sigh shivered above her; she realized it was hers. His lips had left hers to trail over her jaw, over the sensitive skin of her throat to that spot at its base where her pulse raced. He tasted her there, long, slow. His fingers resumed their play between her thighs. Then his lips moved lower, tracing the upper swell of one breast. To its tip. To the tightly contracted bud that throbbed, then ached fiercely as he kissed it. Exploded with sensation when he drew it deep into the hot wetness of his mouth. And suckled.

She arched beneath him, helpless in the grip of his expertise. He released her nipple, pressed hot kisses to her heated flesh, soothing, letting her ease back, before drawing her to him again.

So it went. She lost all touch with time, captured by the wicked pleasure of his mouth, of his lips, the hot sweep of his tongue, the light abrasion, the heated wetness, that tantalizing touch between her thighs. She'd come to crave them all; her breasts were aching and throbbing, full and firm when he shifted and set his tongue to her navel.

She jerked, but he held her firmly, one hand locked on her waist. No one had ever touched her as he had, his mouth on her stomach, his fingers caressing her below.

Then his lips pressed to her curls, his tongue touched between—she cried out.

"Sshhhhh." Sebastian whispered the injunction against the black curls that so fascinated him, lured the beast on. "Much as I would prefer to hear your screams, *mignonne*, tonight that cannot be." He raised his head just enough to see the glint of her eyes beneath her heavy lids. Her lips were swollen, bruised by his kisses. The ivory perfection of her breasts bore the marks of his possession; he didn't feel repentant in the least.

Lips parted, she breathed quickly, shallowly—she would soon not be able to breathe at all. As if she read his intention in his eyes, he saw hers widen, felt her reach for him.

He glanced down, breathed in; the scent of her sank to his bones as he shifted fractionally lower, used his shoulders to wedge her thighs even farther apart, then let his fingers, drenched with her desire, slide slowly, one last time over her swollen flesh, then away. He bent his head and replaced them with his lips. With his mouth, with his tongue. Clamped his hands about her hips and held her fast as he feasted.

She bucked, had to smother a scream as he searched and found the tight bud of her desire, erect, just waiting for his lips. He paid it due homage, and she writhed, panting, one hand pressed to her lips, the other groping blindly, then falling to grip the sheets convulsively.

He saw no need to rush, to deny either himself or her any of the pleasures to be had. There were many of those; he knew every one. He settled to teach her more.

Helena gasped, panted, fought to smother another shriek. Her senses were overloaded, swamped by the intimacy, the caress of his lips there, the skillful, artful probing of his tongue.

He'd brought her to the breaking point—the threshold beyond which the world fell away and nothing existed bar sensation—before, with his fingers. Now he did the same with his mouth, his lips, his wicked tongue. She knew what was coming, the shattering of her senses and the plunge into the white heat of the void, yet she clenched her fist tight in the sheet and tried to hold it back—tried to ride the tide. The intensity, this time, was frightening.

Yet she was helpless—helpless to stave it off, to deny him.

The rush of heat broke through her walls, caught her, swept her up, high onto a sensual plane of excruciating delight. She sensed his satisfaction, felt his hands tighten, felt the soft brush of his hair on the inside of her thighs as he bent once more to her.

Felt the probe of his tongue as he parted her, the slow glide as he entered her.

Then he thrust.

She shattered. Lost herself. Fell headlong, twisting and turning, into a well of pleasure so deep, so hot, it melted every bone.

She couldn't move, she couldn't think.

She could feel more intensely than ever in her life before, feel the heat spread under her skin, feel the ripples of delight spreading through her body.

Feel the broken sigh that fell from her lips as every last muscle gave, relaxed.

With one last, languid lick, he raised his head and surged over her. She could feel, see, take it in, know, even understand, but she couldn't react. Her muscles were passive. Her body had surrendered.

No resistance.

None as he released his staff from his breeches and set himself to her. As he pressed, tested, then thrust in—just a little. Her eyes had widened at the single glimpse she'd had of him, of his size. Had she been capable of voicing any opinion, she might have said no. But she couldn't summon even that much will; she could only lie there and experience, feel the pressure build as he pushed in a fraction farther. She sucked in a breath and let her lids drift down, but not before she'd seen him glance at her face. As she concentrated, shifted a little as the next rock of his hips brought pain, she was aware he was watching her reactions, gauging all she felt.

He eased back, not leaving her, but retreating to her entrance. He shifted and drew her knees up, pressed them high. Then he lifted her hips slightly, stuffed a pillow beneath them, then his weight returned, his arms trapping her knees high as he held her.

Held her steady as he pushed into her.

She gasped, arched; his weight held her down. He thrust again, and she cried out, turned her head away. He raised himself over her; the movement pressed him deeper into her, a brand searing into her body. Her next gasp was more a sob.

"No, *mignonne*—look at me." He came down on his elbows, framed her face with his hands; gentle but insistent, he turned her face to his. "Open your eyes, sweetheart. Look at me—I need to see."

There was a note in his voice she'd never thought to hear, a plea, guttural and commanding, yet still a plea.

She forced herself to do it—to lift her heavy lids, to blink, look into his blue eyes. Felt herself drawn in, felt herself drown in their darkness.

Releasing her face, bracing his arms, he held himself over her. "Stay with me, *mignonne*."

His eyes locked with hers, he pressed deeper, deeper. She felt her body give, open, surrender to his assault, even though she wanted to resist; she was still incapable of fighting as he pressed yet deeper into her. She fought to hold his gaze as discomfort turned to pain, and built, built—

Her lids fell, and she gasped, arched hard beneath him.

He drew back and thrust powerfully.

She screamed, the sound muted by his hand clamping over her lips. She pushed it aside and gasped, drew air deep, struggled to comprehend—to make sense of what her senses were relaying.

He couldn't be that deep inside her.

Eyes wide, she stared into his; the pain faded, and she realized . . . he could.

She shivered, caught her breath, gradually eased back to the bed. It felt . . . very strange.

"Sshhh—it's done." He bent his head; his lips cruised her forehead.

Instinctively, she tipped her head back. His lips found hers. He kissed her—and it tasted different—different now that he was inside her as well.

The angle was difficult. He drew away. "My apologies, sweetheart, but that was never going to be easy."

There was a hint of masculine pride in his voice; she

wasn't sure how to take it. Raising one hand, she absentmindedly brushed back the lock of hair that had fallen across his face. The rest of her mind was fully absorbed with the strange sensation of having him inside her.

He seemed to sense it, to read it in her face. He withdrew a little, not even half his length, then eased back in, as if testing her. She tensed, expecting pain, but . . .

She realized he was watching her face.

"Does that hurt?"

He repeated the movement, still slow, controlled.

She blinked, drew breath, shook her head. "No. It feels . . ." She couldn't find a word.

His smile flashed, but he said nothing, simply settled on his elbows over her and did it again. And again.

Then he bent his head, angled it, covered her lips. They kissed, and it was different again—more enthralling. Her head started spinning pleasurably. Then she tested her muscles and discovered she could, once again, command them.

She started moving with him, seeking to match the repetitive undulation. He gripped one hip, guided her, then, once she'd caught his rhythm, released her and raised that hand to her breast.

He moved over her, on her, within her; she was suddenly breathing faster, felt the heat rise within her once more, felt her body reaching for his, searching, wanting . . .

He slowed, stopped. "Wait." He withdrew from her, lifted away, and left the bed.

She felt empty, suddenly cold—bereft. She turned, arms reaching, easing her knees down, straightening her legs—then she realized he hadn't gone far.

His gaze on her, he was stripping off his shirt—he hauled it over his head, then dropped it on the floor. His breeches followed a second later, then he returned to her.

She smiled, opened her arms, welcomed him back. Ran her hands over his bare shoulders, over the warm skin of his back. Spread her fingers and held him to her as he settled her beneath him, then joined with her again.

This time he slid in without pain, although she felt every hard inch that speared her. Her body arched, took him in, eased about him of its own accord. She sighed—with anticipation, with an eagerness he heard.

He looked into her face, caught her gaze. "Put your legs around me."

She did, and the dance started again. Different again. Skin to skin, his hardness against her softness with no muting fabric between. If anyone had told her sensation came more intense than what he'd already shown her, she'd have laughed the idea to scorn. But now, as the heat flared and swirled, then sucked them into its flame, she found there was more, still more.

More to be experienced as his body plunged into hers to a steady, relentless rhythm. More to feel, to sense, to glory in. The heat swept in waves through her, then pooled deep inside, deep where he filled her, pressed in, and touched her heart.

The hair on his chest rasped her breasts as he moved over her, until she could stand it no more. She grasped and tugged—tried to pull him down to her. He glanced at her, then obliged, let his weight sink fully upon her, his chest to her aching breasts.

She sighed, tipped her head back—he had to angle his head, but he found her lips. Sank into her mouth.

And the dance changed again.

To two bodies fused by one aim.

To a whirlpool of sensation and feeling, of emotions that had no name, of urgent needs and desires, primitive wants and passions, of a glory that was never the same.

They all built and built, until she was writhing, his name on her lips, her body all his. Then the kaleidoscope fractured, and she was spinning through rapture, shards of bright sensation flying down her veins to melt, in heat, in glory, as she sighed and let go.

Let the last hold on reality slip from her grasp, let the glory claim her soul. Aware, at the last, of him thrusting deep within her, of his muted groan, of the pleasure that washed through her as his seed spilled deep, of the joy that suffused her as his hard body collapsed, spent, upon her.

She reached a hand to his hair, twined her fingers through it, held him close. Listened to his heart thunder, then slow.

Sensed, in that last precious minute of heightened lucidity, an unexpected vulnerability.

She smiled, wrapped her arms about him, and held him tight.

Before she recalled how dangerous that was, she slipped over the threshold into sleep.

The clocks throughout the house chimed three o'clock. Sebastian was already awake, but the sound drew him to full consciousness, out of the deep, soul-satisfying warmth that had held him.

He eased onto his back in the bed, glanced down. Helena lay sleeping, curled against him, pressing close, her small hands holding him as if she feared he would leave her. He considered her face, and wondered.

Mignonne, what are you hiding?

He didn't voice the thought, but he wished he had the answer. Something had happened, yet he was damned if he knew what. She'd arrived, and all had been well, then . . .

He'd checked with his staff; they knew nothing, had seen nothing. He hadn't asked specifically, but Webster would have mentioned if any letters had arrived and been waiting for her. Yet there were two letters on her dressing table; his sharp eyes had detected flecks of wax on the floor. She'd opened the letters here—he would swear that first night, before she'd come down for dinner.

That was when things had changed. When she had changed.

Yet precisely how she had changed—given the events of the last few hours—he was at a loss to understand.

Something had upset her, upset her deeply. A mere irritation and she would have let her temper show. But this was something so deeply troubling she'd sought to hide it, and not just from him.

She didn't yet realize, but matters between them had already—even before the last hours—progressed to a point where she couldn't hide her feelings, her emotions, not completely, from him. He could see them in her eyes, not clearly, but like some shadow clouding the peridot depths.

Her behavior had only reinforced his suspicion; when she'd come to his arms, she'd been controlled on the surface, and so fragile, so defenseless—so yearning—beneath. He'd sensed it in her kiss, a kind of desperation, as if what passed between them, what they'd shared in the last hours, was achingly precious, yet transitory. Doomed. That no matter how much she wanted it, yearned for it, regardless of his wishes, his strength, it would not last.

He hadn't liked that—not any of it. He'd reacted to it, to her, to her need.

He grimaced as he recalled all that had passed. Knew she wouldn't fully understand.

He'd seen her need for protection, her need to be possessed and cherished, and had responded and made her his in the only way that truly mattered to him. Or, in truth, to her.

His.

She wouldn't see what that meant, not immediately. Ultimately, of course, she would. She could hardly go through life without realizing that from this moment she was, and always would be, his.

A difficulty, that, for them both.

Inwardly sighing, he glanced down at her dark head, then brushed a kiss across her forehead, closed his eyes—and left fate to do her worst.

Helena was not proud of herself the next morning. She woke to find herself alone, yet the bed bore eloquent testimony to all that had transpired. The tangled sheets were still warm with Sebastian's heat. Without him, she felt chilled to the marrow.

Clutching a pillow, she stared across the room. What was she doing, allying herself so intimately with such a powerful man? It had been madness to have let it happen. Yet it seemed pointless now to pretend regret.

A regret that, despite all, she didn't feel.

Her one real regret was that she couldn't tell him everything, couldn't lean on his strength, draw on his undeniable power. After last night it would be such a relief to throw herself on his mercy, beg for his help. But she couldn't. Her gaze fell on the letters, folded on the dressing table.

Fabien had made sure she and Sebastian were on opposing sides.

Before she could sink deeper into the mire of her fears and wallow in despair, she rose and tugged the bell for her maid.

Sebastian was sitting at the head of the breakfast table, sipping his coffee and glancing over a news sheet when Helena walked into the room.

He looked up; their gazes met. Then she turned

away, exchanged an easy smile with Clara, and headed for the sideboard. His gaze remained on her, delectable in a silk print gown, while his mind rolled back through the night past, through the passion and fulfillment, both so intense, to the question—questions—to which he yet lacked answers.

Helena turned; he continued watching, waiting . . .

Plate in hand, she approached the table. She traded mild comments with Marjorie and Clara, then continued on to the chair at his right.

Just as well.

He waited until she sat and settled her skirts, then drew breath.

She looked up at that moment. He glimpsed the shadows swirling in her eyes, dulling the peridot depths. He started to reach for her hand—stopped as she looked down.

"I wondered . . ." With her fork, she toyed with a portion of kedgeree. "Do you think we might go for another ride—like yesterday?" She glanced at the window, at the day outside. "It's still clear, and who knows how long that will last."

There was a wistfulness in her voice, evoking the memory of how relaxed and, if not carefree, then at least temporarily relieved of her dark burden she had seemed the previous morning, when they'd flown across his fields before the wind. She glanced up again, brows gently arched.

Again he glimpsed her eyes.

Shackling his impatience, he inclined his head. "If you wish. There's a long ride north we could try."

She smiled, a fleeting gesture that too quickly faded from her lips. "That would be . . . pleasant."

Why she didn't simply say "a relief," Sebastian didn't know. That their ride together was that—a relief, a distraction from her troubles—was transparently obvious to him. And while she was in that state, relieved of that inner burden, he couldn't bring himself to shatter the mood and press her for details.

Thus, when they returned to the house three hours later, he was no nearer to answering either of his questions. One he would have to wait for her to tell him of her own accord; trust could not be forced, only earned. At least between them. From others he might command it, but not from Helena.

That left the more obvious question he had to ask her. There was no longer any reason he could not put that before her, on the table between them.

It might even help with the other, by encouraging the trust he sought to gain.

When they rose with the others from the luncheon table, he took her hand and drew her aside. "If you would grant me a few minutes of your time, *mignonne*, there are a few details I believe we should address."

He couldn't read her eyes as she studied his face. Then she glanced at the windows, to the prospect dimmed by the sheeting rain. No escape there. Marjorie and Clara passed them, going ahead as if they hadn't noticed. Thierry and Louis had already left for the billiard room. She drew in a breath as if girding her loins, then glanced at him and inclined her head. "If you wish."

He wished . . . a great many things, but he took her hand in his and led her to his study.

Helena struggled to mask her tension, her trepidation— not of him but of what he might tempt her to say, to do. To confess. He ushered her through the door a footman threw open, into what she perceived to be his study. The wide desk, obviously in use by the stacks of papers and ledgers on its top, the large leather chair behind it and the plethora of document boxes and ledgers packed into shelves around the room confirmed that. The room was, however, unexpectedly comfortable, even cozy. Wide windows looked over the lawns; although the light outside had dimmed, lamps had been lit, their golden glow falling softly on well-polished wood, on velvet and leather.

She crossed to where a fire burned brightly in the hearth, dispelling the chill creeping through the glass. On the way, she glanced about, surreptitiously searching for a case or a display cabinet—somewhere Fabien's dagger might reside. She felt driven to look, yet despaired at having to do so. For having to repay Sebastian in such a deceitful way.

Halting before the hearth, she held her hands to the fire, then straightened as he joined her.

He stopped before her, took her hands in his. Looked into her face, into her eyes. She couldn't read his, felt confident he couldn't read hers. As if acknowledging their mutual defenses, the ends of his lips lifted in a wry, self-deprecatory smile.

"*Mignonne*, after the events of last night, you know, and I know, that we've already taken the first steps down our joint path. In terms of making decisions, we've already made ours—you yours, me mine. Nevertheless, between such people as we are, there is a need for a formal yes or no, a simple, clear answer to a simple, clear question."

He hesitated; searched her eyes again. She didn't glance away, try to avoid the scrutiny—she was too busy searching herself, trying to sense his direction. Wondering if the uncertainty she sensed came from him—or her.

Then his lips twisted. He looked down, simultaneously raising her hands to kiss one, then the other.

"Be that as it may"—his voice had deepened, taken on that tone she now associated with intimacy—"I do not wish to press you. I will ask you my simple question when you are ready to give me a simple answer." He glanced up, met her eyes again. "Until then, know that I am here, waiting"—again his lips quirked—"albeit not patiently. But for you, *mignonne* . . . rest assured I will wait."

That last sounded like a vow. Her surprise must have shown in her face, in her eyes—in his a markedly self-deprecatory light glowed, as if he were shaking his head at himself over how lenient he was being with her.

And he was. More than most she understood that— that his natural impulse would be to press her to accept his offer, to declare herself won. To admit she was his, his to rule, to command.

She'd expected a demand to surrender formally; she'd steeled herself to vacillate, to prevaricate if need be, to use every feminine wile she possessed to delay any such declaration. If she gave in and allowed him to assume he'd triumphed and to crow, presumably publicly, over it, then when she fled, the damage would only be worse.

The rage her defection provoked would be only more intense.

She'd come into the room prepared to do whatever violence to her feelings was necessary to accomplish all she wished—to save Ariele while minimizing harm to him. "I . . ." What could she say in the face of such empathy? He knew nothing of her problem, yet he'd sensed her difficulty and drawn back from exacerbating her situation, even though he didn't understand.

"Thank you." The words left her lips in a soft sigh. Lifting her head, she held his gaze, smiled, let her relief and gratitude show in her eyes, in her expression. She drew breath—and it came easier. Gently tugging her hands from his, she clasped them before her. "I will . . . I promise I will tell you when I can answer your simple question."

She would never be able to do so, but there was nothing she could do to change that.

His gaze, piercing blue, searched her eyes again, but there was nothing more she was willing to show him. She kept her sadness at that last thought well hidden; for Ariele's sake, she had to remember that they were, in effect, adversaries now.

Already hard, his features hardened further. His expression a stony mask, he inclined his head. "Until then."

The strength of his reined temper reached her; she instinctively lifted her chin. He considered her for a moment, then said, his tone even, controlled, almost distant, "Clara will be in the back parlor. It would be wise if you were to join her there."

The warning could not have been more blunt. She held his gaze for one moment, then inclined her head. "I will leave you, then."

Gracefully, she swept around, her gaze taking in the room in one comprehensive glance. There were four large chests, set against the walls at various points, all shut, all with keyholes.

She crossed to the door, opened it, and went out, drawing it closed behind her. Only then losing the tell-tale warmth of Sebastian's gaze.

She would have to search his study.

Sometime.

Chapter Ten

❧

*N*o suitable time presented itself. In truth, as the days passed, Helena made little effort to further Fabien's goal, too focused on Sebastian, on his finer qualities, on all she would have gained by his side—all she would forgo when the time came and she had to act, steal the dagger, and run.

She knew how many days she had left, exactly how many hours; she was determined to make the most of every one.

If the morning was fine, they would ride—indeed, he seemed to take it for granted they would, unless rain intervened. She was too grateful for the moments of unalloyed peace to complain at his somewhat cavalier expectation that she would accompany him as a matter of course.

However, despite the fact that she did not, as he had so perspicaciously noted, like being taken for granted, she felt disappointed when he didn't appear at her door the next night. Or the next.

The following morning, as they returned from the stables and took their habitual shortcut through the small parlor, she slowed, then halted and faced him.

He stopped, studied her face, arched a brow.

"I . . . You . . ." She lifted her chin. "You have not again come to me."

Had once been enough? A disturbing thought—as disturbing as the notion that he'd found the experience less than satisfactory.

She could read nothing in his face or his eyes. After a moment he replied, "Not because I don't wish to."

"Why, then?"

He seemed to consider—to take note of the tone of her voice, the puzzlement she allowed to show—then he sighed. "*Mignonne,* I am rather more experienced in such matters than you. That experience suggests—no, *guarantees*—that the more we . . . indulge, the more I shall . . . require. Come to expect to have."

She folded her arms, fixed her gaze on his eyes. "And that is bad?"

He held her gaze. "It is if in the . . . having, I remove—take from you—all choice over the question of being my duchess." His tone hardened. "Once you're carrying my child, there will be no question, no choice for you to make. You know that as well as I."

She did, and she accepted it. But . . . She tilted her head, considered all she could see in his face. "Are you sure this . . . attitude of yours is not perhaps equally motivated by a hope that I will"—she gestured—"grow impatient and agree to answer your question quickly, and as you wish?"

He laughed, the sound cynical, not humorous. "*Mignonne,* if I wanted a lever to pressure you into marriage, you may be assured that particular tack is not one I would choose." He met her eyes. "The degree of impatience you feel is nothing to the . . . torment that racks me."

She glimpsed it in his eyes—a prowling need—sensed its force before his shields slid back and he shut her out once more. She frowned. "I do not like the idea that you are tormented over me. There must be some way . . ."

With one hand he framed her face, tipped it up to his. Captured her gaze. "Before you follow that thought too far, consider the fact that if there were, I would know of it and would certainly have employed it. But to ease my particular torment . . . no, there is only one remedy for that. And before you ask, I did not tell you how much I desire you, because that, too, is just another form of coercion." He searched her eyes. "*Mignonne*, I wish you to marry me because you desire to be my wife—not for any other reason. As far as I am able, I will not pressure you in making that decision, will not manipulate your feelings in any way. I will even engage to shield you from any pressure others might seek to bring to bear."

"Why? Why, when you want me as your duchess, why be so forbearing?" Given his nature, that was a highly pertinent point.

His lips curved, wryly cynical. "Yes, there is something I wish in return. But for my forbearance, I ask only one thing." His eyes were very blue as he gazed into hers. "The simple answer you eventually give me, *mignonne*, I wish it to be *yours*. Not one logically derived after due consideration of the facts, but the real truth of what you desire." He paused, then added, "Look into your heart, *mignonne*—the answer I want will be written there."

His last words echoed in her mind. All about was silent and still. Their gazes held, then fell away. He bent his head.

"*That* is what I want, what I will give a great deal to have." His words feathered her lips. "I want you to answer truly, to be true to yourself—and to me."

Sebastian kissed her, even though he knew it was unwise, that he would pay dearly for the indulgence. For giving in to the urge to reassure her, to wipe from her mind any notion he did not want her. He would pay, and she was too innocent to know the price—the effort it would take to stop at just a kiss and let her go.

Her lips parted beneath his; without hesitation, he took her mouth, captured her senses. Held them with a knowing hand.

Held her within his arms, soft, warm and vibrantly alive, the promise in her kiss echoed in the lushness of her firm flesh, the sensual tension in her spine. Held himself back from taking further advantage, from capitalizing on the fact that they'd come in half an hour early so no one would yet expect them, that the parlor was private and secluded. On the fact that she would be his if he wished, here and now.

Torment indeed—unslaked desire was not a demon he had any great experience in conquering. In this case, with her, conquering desire was out of the question— he'd settled for suppression, for caging the beast. For the moment. Promising himself that eventually, this way, she'd be his forever. All his.

His as he wished her to be.

To the depths of her sensual soul.

He was a connoisseur; he recognized the pinnacle of womanly perfection when he had her beneath him. Understood, too, enough of the possibilities to want them all. To want all of her.

Her passion. Her devotion. Her love.

All.

He wanted to seize, to simply take. Yet what he wanted could not be seized, taken.

It had to be given.

The clash of will and desire left his temper, never an amenable one, straining, tight, taut, ready to break.

On a gasp, he pulled back, drew back. Waiting for the drumming in his veins to subside, he watched her face as her senses, her wits, now that he'd freed them, returned.

Her lashes fluttered, then rose. She regarded him evenly through crystal-clear eyes. Puzzlement, and the fact that she was not yet sure of him, were easy to read.

Then she blinked; her gaze lowered.

His hand still lay beneath her chin; he tipped her face back up so he could see it.

Her eyes had dimmed. Even though she met his gaze calmly, the clouds had returned. With a gentle smile, she lifted her chin from his hand, then brushed a kiss across his fingers.

"Come." She drew back from his embrace. "We had better join the others."

He let her go. She turned to the door—he swallowed an urge to call her back—to ask outright what was troubling her. After an instant's hesitation he followed her.

He wanted her trust, wanted her to confide in him; he couldn't force either. And when all was said and done, while she might not yet be sure of him, he was even less sure of her.

In many ways Helena's visit was proceeding better than he'd hoped. Thierry and Louis were both keen shooters; at this season his coverts were teeming—there was plenty to keep them amused and out of his way. Marjorie and Clara had struck up a friendship; happily distracted by their own entertainments, they were very ready to leave Helena's entertainment up to him.

All of which should have been perfect. Unfortunately, the one person not falling in with his plans was Helena herself.

He wasn't sure she was going to accept him—and he was at a loss to understand why.

But it had something to do with those damn letters.

"Do you spend most of your days here, then?"

He lifted his gaze from the page he'd supposedly been deciphering, looked at her as she idly wandered the room. The "here" was his study; she'd eschewed joining Marjorie and Clara in a comfortable coze by the drawing room fire in favor of distracting him while he tried to work. "Usually. It's big enough, comfortable enough—and anything I'd want is generally to hand."

"Indeed?" She glanced at the ledger he was holding.

Surrendering, he shut it, pushed it aside. It was nothing crucial. Not compared with her.

She smiled and glided around the desk, leaned back against it as he eased his chair back.

"You asked me why I was in the garden at the convent all those years ago, yet you never told me what you were doing there."

"Falling from the wall."

"After leaving Collette Marchand's chamber."

"Ah, yes—the inestimable Collette." He smiled in reminiscence.

One black brow haughtily rose. "Well?"

"It was a wager, *mignonne*."

"A wager?"

"You will remember that in the days I haunted Paris, I was much younger, and rather wilder."

"The younger I will allow, but what was the subject of this wager that you needed to brave the convent's walls?"

"I had to procure a particular earring, one of some uniqueness, from Mlle Marchand by the end of that week."

"But she was due to leave two days later—in fact, she left the next day itself, after your visit."

"Indeed—that was part of the challenge."

"So you won?"

"Of course."

"And what did you gain by winning?"

He smiled. "What else but a triumph? And, even better, one over a French noble."

She humphed dismissively, yet her gaze was strangely distant. "Did you spend many years haunting Paris?"

"Eight, nine—all while you still wore pigtails."

Hmm. She didn't say it, but she thought it—he could see it in her face, could see the clouds gathering, darkening her eyes.

Did the letters have something to do with his past exploits in France? He couldn't remember crossing swords with any of the Daurents.

He watched her for a moment longer, watched her struggle with her demon. She'd grown so used to being in his presence that when she wasn't focused on him, aware of him, her mask slipped and he saw more. Saw enough to make him reach for her hand. *"Mignonne—"*

She started; she'd forgotten he was there. For a fleeting instant he glimpsed . . . horror, terror, but hanging over all a profound and pervasive sadness. Before he could react, she reassembled her mask and smiled—too brightly, too brittlely.

He tightened his grip on her hand, expecting her to rise and try to flee.

With barely a pause for thought, she trumped his ace. Pushing away from the desk, she slid onto his lap. *"Eh, bien*—if you have finished your work . . ."

His body reacted instantly; the soft, warm, distinctly feminine weight settling so trustingly, so confidently, had his demons slavering. While he struggled to rein them in, she freed her hand, turned his face to hers.

Set her lips to his.

She kissed him longingly, lingeringly—with a deep

yearning that he knew was unfeigned because he felt it, too.

He'd given his word he would not manipulate her; as she drew him deeper into the kiss, into the pleasure of her mouth, he realized he would have been wise to demand a corresponding reassurance.

His arms closed around her; moments later his hand sought her breast.

He could reassure her, pleasure her, let her distract him. But he knew what he had seen and he wouldn't forget.

Bittersweet. For Helena the days that followed were the definition of that. Bitter whenever she thought of Ariele, of Fabien, of the dagger she had to steal. Of the betrayal she had to practice. Sweet in the hours she spent with Sebastian; in his arms, for those fleeting moments, she felt safe, secure, free of Fabien's black spell.

But as soon as she left Sebastian's embrace, reality closed darkly about her. It took an ever-increasing effort to mask her leaden heart.

Sebastian had invited them for a week, but the week passed and no one cared or spoke of a departure. Winter tightened its grip on the fields and lanes, but at Somersham there were roaring fires and cozy rooms, and distractions aplenty to keep them amused.

Outside, the year died; inside, the great house seemed to stretch and come alive. Even though she wasn't directly involved, Helena could not miss the building excitement, that anticipation of joy that flowed from the myriad preparations for the Yuletide celebrations and the consequent family gathering.

Clara rarely stopped smiling, eager to point out this custom or that, to explain where the boughs and holly decorating the rooms were grown, what the secret ingredients of her Christmas punch were.

Again and again Helena found herself outwardly expressing an expectation of joy while inwardly experiencing the certainty of despair.

To her surprise, after that unnerving moment in his study when she'd become so engrossed in wondering how and when he'd met Fabien and won the dagger—considering them both, that was the most likely avenue by which Sebastian had come to possess it—that he'd startled her to the point she'd nearly told him all, since that time Sebastian had set himself to entertain her with stories of his ancestors, of his family, of his childhood—of his personal life.

Tales she knew he had told no one else.

Like the time he'd got stuck in the huge oak by the stables and had had to fall to get down. How frightened he'd been. Like how much he'd loved his first pony, how distraught he'd been when it died.

Not that he'd told her of that last, not in words. Instead, he'd stopped and abruptly changed the subject.

If he hadn't been trying so transparently hard to be transparent, she might have wondered if, despite his vow and even his intention not to manipulate her feelings, he simply couldn't help himself. Instead, all he said he said directly, even sometimes reluctantly, as if he were laying all that he was, all his past and by inference his future, at her feet. The less-than-complimentary as well as the laudable, exposing all without restriction, trusting her to understand and judge him kindly.

As indeed she did.

The days rolled quietly past, and she fell ever more deeply under his spell, came to yearn even more desperately that all he was offering her she could claim.

Knowing she couldn't.

She wished, beyond desperately, that she could tell him of Fabien's plan, but gentle tales did not in any way disguise the sort of man he was. Ruthless, hard, and at some time he and Fabien must have been rivals—nothing was more likely. If she told him her story, showed him the letters . . . he would not be human if he didn't wonder if all along she had been Fabien's pawn but now, with the splendor of the life of his duchess spread before her, she'd chosen to change her allegiance.

He'd made it clear what level of commitment he sought from her, made it clear he did not want her agreeing because of all the material gains she would enjoy. After the trust he'd shown her, she couldn't now accept his proposal, show him the letters, claim his protection, and leave him forever suspecting her motives.

And what if he declined to help her? What if she told him and he refused all aid? What if the nature of his relationship with Fabien was such that he rejected her utterly?

She would never get the dagger, and Ariele . . .

Telling him was a risk she could not take.

Instead, she watched each day fade, watched the

time for taking the dagger inexorably approach. Stubbornly, she clung to her last gasp of defiance, refusing to deny herself her last precious moments in the warmth of Sebastian's company, in the security of his embrace.

Her last hours of happiness.

Once she fled Somersham, betrayed him and left, one part of her life would be over. No other could ever mean as much to her as he now did; no other could take his place.

In her heart—he'd been right about that. The answer to his question was already engraved there—she knew what it was.

Knew she would never get a chance to tell him.

Guilt and a looming sense of incipient loss weighed on her spirits even through the hours she spent riding, laughing, talking, strolling the huge house by his side. She held the darkness at bay, shut it into a small corner of her mind, but it was still there.

Her one regret was that they would not love again. His stance was all that was noble, and she was not so unkind as to press him—she didn't have that right. To take from him that which she only rightly could if she was intending to be his wife. No, his way was better, certainly wiser.

But she still mourned the loss of the closeness they'd shared. Only now did she truly understand the word "intimacy"; the act had affected her more deeply than she'd expected, bonded them in some way, on some other plane. Having experienced the joy once, she would always long to experience it again.

She knew she never would.

But she had no choice. Ariele was her sister, and her responsibility.

Sebastian watched her, undeceived by her laughs, by her smiles. Behind them she was increasingly fragile; the light in her eyes was growing dimmer by the day. He'd tried by all means he knew to encourage her to trust him; on all logical levels he knew she did. Emotionally . . .

Despite all, he couldn't bring himself to press her, not any longer through any lack of self-assurance but simply because he—he who had never before drawn back from a necessary act because of another's feelings—couldn't bring himself to torture hers.

Any more than she already was.

He doubted she knew he knew, doubted she had any idea how much he saw every time her gaze grew distant, pensive—before she realized he was watching, put up her mask and put on her smile.

It was the letters, he was sure. They still sat on her dressing table tucked behind her jewel case; he'd entered her room and checked on a number of occasions while she was safely downstairs. Both letters showed evidence of being read and refolded countless times. He'd been tempted, sorely tempted, but he hadn't read them.

Yet.

If she didn't confide in him soon, he would.

He'd wanted her to trust him enough to tell him of her own accord, but she hadn't. He now suspected she wouldn't. Which left him wondering what—or who—was so powerful, had such a strong grip on her heart, that they could command such absolute obedience.

Such unswerving devotion.

"Villard says it is not in his chamber."

Helena kept her gaze fixed on the winter landscape beyond the library windows. Shades of brown showed through the hoarfrost that had laid siege to the land. Louis had found her here, alone; she'd retreated here to allow Sebastian to finish in peace some business that he'd admitted was urgent.

Louis closed his hand about her upper arm, almost shook her. "I tell you, you *must* do it soon." When she said nothing, he thrust his face close to hers. "Do you hear me?"

She'd stilled; now she turned her head and looked Louis in the eye. "Unhand me."

Her voice was low, even, uninflected. Centuries of command lay behind it.

Louis shifted, then released her. "We are running out of time." He glanced around, confirming they were still alone. "We have already been here longer than a week. I have heard there are family members expected in a few days. Who knows when St. Ives will run out of patience and decide we should go?"

"He will not."

Louis humphed. "So you say. But once his family is here . . ." He glanced at Helena. "There is talk of a wedding, as one might expect, but I do not like it. It is tempting fate to dally. You must get the dagger soon—tonight."

"I told you, it must be in his study." Helena turned

her head and regarded him coolly. "Why don't you get it?"

"I would, but Uncle has declared it must be you, and"—he shrugged—"I can see his point."

"His point?"

"If you steal it, St. Ives will not bruit the matter abroad. He will not make any public accusations or seek to take any public revenge, because he will not want it known he was bested by a female."

"I see." Helena turned once more to her contemplation of the lawns. "So it must be me."

"*Oui*—and it must be soon."

Helena felt the net draw tight, felt its bite. She sighed. "I will look tonight."

She waited until after the clocks had chimed midnight before she set out. Even then she wasn't sure that Sebastian would have quit his study, but she could look over the banisters halfway down the stairs and see if light shone from beneath the study door. Determined, she stepped out—she wasn't fool enough to skulk but walked briskly, confidently, along the corridor, keeping to the runner so her footsteps were muffled.

The corridor led to the long gallery. She reached its end and turned into the foyer at the top of the stairs—

And walked into a wall of muscle and bone.

She gasped. Sebastian caught her before she staggered back.

"What . . ." In the weak light from the uncurtained windows, she took in the fact that he was dressed in a silk robe and, she suspected, little else. She felt her eyes widen; undirected, her hands spread over his chest as he drew her to him. She looked up and met his gaze.

Saw one brown brow arch. *"Mignonne."*

Where are you going? He didn't ask, but the words were there nonetheless, implicit in his quiet watchfulness.

She dragged in a breath, felt her breasts swell against his chest. "What are you doing here?"

He studied her face. "I was coming to see you."

And you? his ensuing silence prompted.

The fact that, on one point at least, his patience had reached its limits was easy to read in the set of his features, the granite planes of his face. Limned by the pale light, they were etched with brutally reined desire. Beneath her hands, his body told the same tale; the wide, warm muscles were tense with need.

"I was . . ." *Coming to see you?* A lie. She moistened her lips, looked at his. "I wanted to see you."

The words had barely passed her lips before he sealed them with his. The kiss was savage in its intensity, fair warning of what was to come.

She pushed her arms up, wrapped them about his neck, welcomed that kiss, kissed him back with equal fervor.

Damned Fabien's scheme to one last night of delay.

Gladly gave herself—for one last night of passion—into Sebastian's arms.

She *had* wanted to see him, exactly like this, precisely for this reason. She wanted one last chance to show him all he meant to her, even if she could never tell him, never give him the words he wanted to hear. She could tell him in other ways.

Sebastian broke from the kiss; it had already raged beyond his control. Control—what a joke. He'd thought, despite all, despite the roiling need that had him in its grip, that the accumulated years of experience would see him still master of his desire.

Two minutes and she'd cindered every rein he possessed. Deliberately.

Held fast in his arms, she pressed against him, her supple curves, her lush lips, the trailing taunt of her fingers on his cheek, the rise and fall of her breasts against his chest—all a flagrant siren's call as old as time.

Her eyes glinted up at him from beneath her heavy lids.

So be it.

"Your room." His tone was gravelly with desire. "Come."

He released her, locked his hand about hers, and strode for her chamber. He didn't dare make more contact, had to move fast if he wanted to reach the privacy of her room. She hurried beside him without protest, committed, equally focused.

They reached her door, and he set it swinging wide. She went through, and he followed her.

Pushed the door closed behind him, never taking his eyes from her. He heard the latch click; in the same instant she turned to him and smiled her madonna's smile.

Held out her arms. "Come. Let us love."

A lamp was turned low on her dressing table. Even

in the weak illumination, the light that shone in her face, in her eyes, was impossible to mistake. He crossed to her without thought, drawn by all he could read, all she let him see. He took her hands, raised them to his shoulders, released them, slid his hands about her waist, and drew her to him.

Bent his head to hers. "*Mignonne*, you must tell me if I hurt you."

Her fingers slid into his hair. "You will not."

Their lips met, fused—all pretense at rationality, at control, slid away. She pressed herself to him, drew him deep into the heated cavern of her mouth, teased him with her tongue, wantonly invited him to ravish, to ravage, to plunder. She was with him every step of the way—every step further into the maelstrom of desire, into the whirlpool of physical and emotional energies that sparked about them. It drew them in, drew them down.

Into a world where passion ruled and desire reigned triumphant.

He was ravenous; she flagrantly encouraged him to devour. He wanted—she tempted him to take. He wanted to possess her so utterly she would never doubt she was his—she dared him, challenged him, urged him on—wanted him to do it.

Head reeling, he broke from the kiss to feel his robe slide from his shoulders. Desire burned beneath his skin, a sensual flame. She spread her hands over his flesh as if she could sense it, as if she sought to conjure it, to feed the fire. Chest heaving, he watched her face, watched the womanly wonder as she realized how

much power she held over him—watched fascination
dawn as it occurred to her just how she could wield it.

Her lips curved. She looked down. Let one hand
slide from his chest, slowly down to his groin. He gritted his teeth at the feather-light touch, bit back a groan
as she stroked, then closed her hand about him.

Saw her smile deepen.

Thought he would die when she brushed her thumb
over his throbbing head.

He reached for her—and suddenly realized she was
still fully dressed. Knew he would never be satisfied
until she lay naked beneath him. He backed her to the
bed. She clasped his side, her other hand cradling him.
Looked up when he pinned her against the side of the
bed. He kissed her deeply, letting his demons plunder,
and set his fingers to her laces.

Stripping her bodice, panniers, skirts, and petticoats
from her took mere minutes; with another woman he
might have dallied, stretched the moments. With her
he couldn't wait, refused to wait.

Then she was naked but for her fine chemise—the
last barrier between his skin and hers.

He paused. She'd stood naked before him before;
later she would lie naked beneath him again. But for
now . . .

Shackling his demons, he glanced around, assessing
the possibilities—then saw what he wanted. What they
both needed.

He glanced down at her as she closed her hand about
him again; he shut his eyes, let his head fall back.
Groaned.

Helena took that as an assent to further her attentions. Last time she hadn't had a chance to explore—this time she seized it, held him gently, stroked, fondled.

Sensed the tension in his spine increase with every touch. Felt the rampant strength beneath her hand grow ever harder.

Realized how much pleasure her touch gave him. Set herself to pleasure him more.

"Enough." He closed his hand about her wrist, drew her hand from him. His gaze, darkly burning, met hers. "Come. It's my turn to pay homage."

To her surprise he stepped back, turned, and led her across the room, to where one tall window stood uncurtained. It was freezing outside, the sky crystal clear. Moonlight, pale and silvery, poured in, creating a wide puddle on the dark carpet.

He halted in the shaft of light, drew her so it fell full upon her. His gaze was not on her face but on her body, veiled by the filmy silk of her chemise. He looked—and his long lips curved with sensual satisfaction.

"Perfect."

He went down on his knees before her. Because of the difference in height, his head was level with her breasts.

She looked down on him, one hand rising to spear through his hair. He settled lower on his knees before her, lifted both hands, and closed them about her breasts. Her lids fell as her body arched, wantonly inviting his caresses.

He caressed, gently at first, but as her breasts swelled and firmed, his touch turned possessive. Then his fingers closed on her nipples, and she gasped. He squeezed, then rolled the tight buds before releasing them.

Before leaning closer, lifting his face, inviting her kiss.

She kissed him, sank into his mouth, drowned in his heat, felt her senses drawn down, into the flood tide of need. Wrapping her arms about his head, she held him to her. He kneaded her breasts, then again his fingers searched, found, tightened, tightened—until her knees turned weak and she sagged.

Releasing his lips, she let her head fall back, heard her own gasp.

He raised up; hands locked about her waist, he held her steady as his lips, his mouth, hot and wet, trailed open-mouthed kisses over her jaw, down the column of her throat, then fastened over the spot where her pulse raced. He sucked, licked, then he shifted and his mouth trailed lower.

Over the tight swell of one breast.

His lips were like a brand, burning through the thin silk. She gasped again, tightened her hand about his skull, urged him on. Wickedly knowing, his lips skated, pressed, skated again. Tantalized. Teased.

Just before she gathered her wits to protest, he pressed closer still and licked. Over and around the peak of one breast. He laved until the silk clung, damp against her heated flesh. Then, slowly, he closed his mouth over the aching peak, curled his tongue about the tortured bud, and rasped it.

She sucked in a violent breath, let it slowly out, felt

the tension rising through her heighten further. He released that breast, repeated the subtle torture on the other neglected peak until both her breasts burned, heavy and full and tight.

Silk shifted, shushed in the night; she looked down, watched as, his large hands clasped about her sides, he stretched her chemise tight over her midriff, anchored it there. Settled lower on his knees and set his lips there. Sucked lightly, licked, tasted through the silk.

Traced her ribs, her waist, her navel, as if he were mapping his domain. Her breasts still ached, but the heat was spreading, lower, lower. Following his intimate attentions. Pooling deep.

One hard hand came to rest at the back of her waist as he pressed his mouth to her stomach. Then he shifted again, sinking onto his ankles, gripping her hips and stretching her chemise taut so he could nuzzle her freely, provocatively probe the indentation of her navel. The intimacy—hot, wet, and rough, yet veiled in silk—made her shudder.

His hands eased from her hips, drifted around, down, then rose under the chemise, lightly caressing the backs of her thighs before closing possessively about the globes of her bottom.

While he pressed his mouth to her stomach, probed increasingly explicitly with his tongue, his fingers flexed, kneaded, held her captive. His to savor as he pleased.

That last was evident, even more so when he shifted lower still and nuzzled into the hollow between her thighs. She caught her breath on a shattered gasp, clutched his head with both hands, fingers sifting, tense, through his hair. He lifted his head from her, pulled back just enough to rearrange his knees, insinuating both between her feet, forcing her legs wider.

Wider. She looked down, watched his face as he looked at her, at the triangle of black curls veiled by silk at the apex of her thighs. Then he leaned closer, set his hot mouth to the spot. She clutched his head, closed her eyes. Clenched her fingers in his hair when his tongue touched her. Felt his fingers flex possessively, then he tilted her, held her steady—and settled to feast.

All through the silk. The shifting fabric added an extra level of sensation—another source of light abrasion to her already sensitive flesh. He lapped, sucked, probed; her flesh turned swollen, damp, quickly wet. She clung, eyes closed, her breathing fractured. Then she cracked open her lids, watched his head move against her as he worshiped her.

Spiraling tension coiled through her, sharp and bright, but it seemed to have nothing to hold to, not yet. He pressed pleasure on her and she drank it in, felt it sink to her bones. Sensed the pleasure he took in pleasuring her, in paying homage as he'd said.

She glanced up as he pressed deeper, probed further. Before her lids fell, she glimpsed shadows on the glass. She looked—after a moment she realized she was looking at herself, reflected in the glass but weakly, the scene in the moonlight lit from a distance by the lamp behind them. She was neither side on nor full face to the window but halfway in between. The moonlight washed through the reflection—it was as if she were seeing through the same silk veil that screened her body from his sight. Yet she could see enough—enough to make out her body, arched in his hands, the slim columns of her legs, pressed wide, her feet only just touching the floor.

See him before her, naked, the powerful muscles of his shoulders sheened by the moonlight, his chestnut hair dark against the paleness of her body, shifting as he loved her. Pleasured her.

She was still watching when he drew back, laying his cheek against her thigh, juggling her weight so he could retrieve one hand. Her breath tangled in her throat, she glanced down; moving his free hand into the dark cleft between her spread thighs, he glanced up, caught her gaze. Held it as he shifted his hand, then pressed one silk-clad finger into her, slowly at first, then more definitely, then deeper still until, through the bunched fabric, his hand met her swollen flesh. He pressed, just a little; she dragged in a shattered breath.

Glanced at the window.

Saw him look once again at her mons pubis, then she felt his long fingers uncurl, spreading the fabric, separating her folds, parting them to reveal the throbbing bud of her desire, delicately screened by wet silk.

His finger pressed deep inside her again. Then he bent his head.

Set his mouth to her most sensitive flesh.

Suckled.

Pleasure rushed and rose through her like a tide. It swept her up, caught her, spun her, then flung her high.

She shattered in his hands, felt his mouth hot on her as she melted, felt his finger hard inside her. Felt it work within her while he licked, then suckled anew. The second rush reared like a tidal wave—and raced through her with devastating force.

From a distance she heard a muted scream. Dimly realized it was hers.

Through the whirling wonder, through the diminishing heat, through the slowly fading pleasure, she was aware of him disengaging. His head rose, his finger withdrew from the heated clasp of her body. He gently tugged her chemise free from between her legs, then, still supporting her, drew her to him so her body slid down his until her spread thighs rested on his.

His hand rose to cup her face. He held her steady and kissed her.

Voraciously. His message was explicit—that had been only the first course

Desire stirred, reawakening; she kissed him back—tasted her own essence on his lips. Kissed him harder.

Tried to reach between them to where his shaft thrust so blatantly, so promisingly, against her stomach.

He caught her hand before she reached her goal.

She drew her lips from his, sighed. "I want to pleasure you."

He met her gaze. "You will. But not like that."

His eyes were so dark, ringed with burning blue—the focused intent therein sent a shiver of anticipation down her spine. "How?"

He studied her as if weighing what he would tell her. Eventually he asked, "Can you stand?"

She blinked, then pushed away, tried it. She wobbled as she gained her feet, but he steadied her. Then he rose, held her hand, reached down and tugged a small footstool closer. She watched as he judged its position, then with his foot he nudged it nearer the window, until it was about two feet from the wall.

He drew her to him, then past him, turning her so she faced the window with him behind her. "Kneel on the stool."

She did. The stool was an ornamental one with a needlework top, about a foot long—just wide enough for her to be both comfortable and secure.

He knelt behind her, settled himself around her, her calves between his thighs, his knees wide on the carpet on either side of the footstool. He slid one hand around her, splaying his fingers over her waist.

"Can you reach the sill?"

She could if she tipped forward. The wide wooden ledge was about eighteen inches off the floor. "Yes." Puzzled, she added, "Why?"

He hesitated, then murmured, "You'll see."

The arm about her waist tightened, locking her back against him. She felt the hard ridge of his erection low against her spine. She didn't know what to do with her hands; in the end she wrapped her arms over his arm at her waist, gripped his hand and forearm.

He shifted behind her, and she sensed what he would do.

"If you need to brace yourself, reach for the sill."

Brace herself. She wasn't going to ask, but her mind was streaking in any number of promising directions when he lifted the back of her chemise and pressed himself, skin to scalding skin, against her.

She let her head fall back against his shoulder, murmured her encouragement, shifted her hips against him.

He laughed briefly, raggedly, then bent his head and set his lips to the point where her shoulder and throat met. She tipped her head farther back, spine bowing, her breasts thrust forward.

His free hand closed on them, first one, then the other, possessively kneading until she gasped, then he squeezed her nipples until she squirmed. Panted. His hand slid lower, over her stomach, kneaded evocatively. Wordlessly, she begged.

He bent her forward, over the arm at her waist. The columns of his thighs rested outside hers; they felt like steel, his hair-dusted skin rasping lightly. With her hips and thighs held against him and his arm around her, she felt caged by his strength. Trapped. Captured. Soon to be taken. She held tight to his arm, fingers sinking deep in intense anticipation as, behind her, he touched her, opened her, set himself to her. Then, slowly, he penetrated her, sinking inch by inch into her softness.

Sebastian couldn't breathe. His lungs locked tight as he watched his throbbing staff slide between the pale globes of her bottom, deeper, deeper, felt the scalding heat of her welcome him, felt her blossom and open for him, felt her body give, her sheath stretch and ease, then lovingly clasp him. At the last he exhaled, eyes shutting, senses reeling as he finally sank fully home deep inside her. The smooth silk of her bottom and thighs caressed him. Her nails sunk deep in his arm, she squirmed just a little, experimentally, not in pain.

Inwardly he smiled; outwardly he was incapable of expression, his features too set in passion's grip. He flexed his hips, withdrew just a little, and thrust— enough to show her how it would work.

Her interest was immediately evident.

She tried to wriggle, to shift upon him. He tightened his hold, held her still, withdrew and thrust again.

And again.

Until she was beyond doing anything other than holding tight to his arm and letting her body receive him. Over and over again. The erotic friction built, and she sobbed and let herself open even more deeply, let her body surrender even more completely to his possession.

And he took. Like a conqueror, he claimed her and prayed the act would be as deeply imprinted on her senses as it was on his. He closed his eyes, and sensation heightened; deprived of sight, his other senses expanded—to revel in the slick heat of her, the wet, wanton clasp of her body about him.

Lifting his lids, he let his gaze dwell on her silk-clad back, on the hemispheres of her bottom meeting his flat stomach again and again.

The rhythm strengthened. He reached around her and filled his hand with her breast, heard her sob. He kneaded, then found her nipple and squeezed, heard her moan.

He let his hand roam over the curves he now considered his, lifted the back of her chemise to her waist, caressed her bare bottom, lightly traced the cleft. Felt her shudder. Grasping the front of her chemise with the hand at her waist, he raised it. Reached around her to stroke her curls.

Thrust more deeply as he parted them.

Sensed the tension coiling inside her, thrust into it, and felt it tighten more. He caressed her lightly, not touching the tight button but tracing around it. Then he filled her deeply, held still, and carefully exposed it.

Oh-so-gently laid one fingertip upon it.

Then he picked up his driving rhythm again.

Her nails sank into his arm as she fought to hold on to her senses. She lasted less than a minute.

As she fractured, he pressed more firmly, thrust even deeper, then stopped, held still, savoring the powerful ripples of her release as they swept through her.

He waited, holding her curved over his arm, limp in the aftermath. Waited until he felt her stir, felt strength returning to her shaky muscles. He withdrew from her, rose, lifting her with him, then juggled her and swept her up in his arms.

Helena lifted her lids enough to see the bed rapidly approaching. She relaxed, set aside the protest she'd been about to make. She didn't want him leaving her—didn't want him leaving until she'd had the indescribable pleasure of knowing she'd pleasured him fully.

He stopped by the bed, dragged the coverlets down, then placed her in the middle of the soft mattress. He stripped off her chemise, then straightened, his gaze roaming her body, desire etched in his face. Then he reached for the covers and joined her in a crawling sprawl, his body caging hers as he wrestled the bed-clothes into a cocoon about them, close, almost tight. Then he looked down at her, lowered his body to lie upon her, gripped her thighs and parted them, settled between. Joined with her in a single powerful thrust. Then he settled himself fully upon her and thrust again.

Letting go of all restraint, Helena lay back, put her arms around him, let her body ease beneath him, shifted her legs to clasp him more definitely as he rocked deeply into her.

The cocoon of the covers transformed to a cave, a place of primitive needs, primal wants—unquestioned desire. Driven, he loved her; captured, she loved him back.

Broken breaths, sobs, moans, guttural groans became their language, the powerful, insistent merging of their bodies their only reality. He wanted, demanded, took; unstintingly, she gave, opened her heart and gave him the key, gave him her body as the heat whirled and fused them. Gave him her soul as rapture caught them and lifted them from this world.

Chapter Eleven

𝒯he creak of a floorboard pierced the deep slumber
that had enfolded Helena in its warmth. She blinked
into darkness. Realized from the deep silence that it
was nowhere near dawn. Realized that she was not at
Cameralle, that Ariele was not in the next room.

Realized that the warmth that surrounded her emanated from Sebastian, slumped heavily asleep by her
side.

Another creak, nearer and too tentative to be natural,
reached her. Sebastian had drawn the bed curtains.
Easing from his side, sliding from under the heavy arm
he'd draped over her, she searched for the gap in the
curtains, carefully parted them, and peeked out.

For one instant she thought it was Louis creeping
into her room. She nearly panicked, then her eyes adjusted, and the man, his hand on the latch of the open
door, glanced around the room. The weak light revealed the truth.

Phillipe. Louis's younger brother. He who had
fetched Ariele from Cameralle and taken her to Fabien.

Panic was the least of the emotions that rocked Helena. Phillipe entered, then eased the door closed. He glanced around the room again; his gaze came to rest on the curtained bed. He took a step toward it.

Helena clamped her hand to her lips, smothering her instinctive *"No!"* She glanced at Sebastian; he was still fast asleep, the deep rhythm of his breathing undisturbed.

But she was naked. Casting around, she spied her robe draped over the bottom corner of the bed, pushed back by the violence of their mating and now jumbled with the covers. Beyond the curtains, she could hear Phillipe cautiously approaching.

She stretched—and just managed to snag the edge of the robe and drag it to her. Frantically, she shrugged into it, fervently praying that Sebastian wouldn't wake, that Phillipe wouldn't draw back the curtains— that he'd realize the rings would rattle. Reminded herself of the same fact.

With the robe covering the top half of her, she held it closed, then, with an even more fervent prayer, eased from the bed.

She heard a whispered curse from Phillipe—he'd seen the curtains shift. As carefully as she could, she slipped from the bed, wriggling the robe down, then slid through the gap in the curtains.

The instant she emerged and saw Phillipe—face pale, eyes wide—she waved him back, then put a finger to her lips. With her other hand she held the robe closed, tugging it free of the covers until, at last, she stood barefoot on the floor, the robe falling to conceal her limbs, the curtains falling almost fully shut behind her.

She noticed the gap, glanced up at the rings, wondered if she dared risk closing the curtains fully. Sebastian hadn't stirred—yet . . . She couldn't reach the curtain rod to ease the rings along.

Leaving the gap, she turned to Phillipe, to the source of her most urgent worry. Her heart thudded painfully as she padded across the floor, waving him back, all the way back to where the shadows hung heaviest by the door. It was as far from the bed as they could get. She glanced briefly back at the sliver of darkness that was the gap in the curtains. She had to weigh her options carefully—for Ariele's sake, she didn't dare do otherwise. Outside in the corridor would be safer on the one hand, but how much trust could she place in Phillipe, knowing him to be one of Fabien's creatures?

"What are you doing here?" She kept the hiss barely above a whisper, yet her panic, and her accusation and distrust, rang clearly.

To her surprise, Phillipe flinched. "It's not what you think."

Even though he'd whispered, she frowned and waved at him to lower his voice. "I do not know *what* to think! Tell me of Ariele."

Phillipe paled even more; Helena's heart lurched.

"She is . . . well. For the moment."

"What do you mean?" Helena seized his arm, shook it. "Has Fabien changed his mind?"

Phillipe frowned. "Changed? No. He still intends . . ."

The disgust and heartache in his face were too familiar for Helena to mistake them. "But he hasn't changed his mind about Christmas—about me having until Christmas Eve to bring the dagger to him?"

Phillipe blinked. "Dagger? Is that what you have to get?"

Helena gritted her teeth. "*Yes!* But for pity's sake, *tell* me—has he changed his schedule?" She shook Phillipe's arm again. "Is that why you're here?"

Phillipe focused, seemed finally to grasp her question. He shook his dark head. "No—no. It's still to be Christmas, the blackguard."

Helena released him, watched his face closely. "Blackguard?" When Phillipe looked away, jaw setting, she prompted, "He's your uncle."

"He's no uncle of mine!" Phillipe spat the words, drenched with an equal mixture of fury and revulsion. He looked at her; even in the poor light she could see the anger burn in his dark eyes. "He's a *monster*—an unfeeling tyrant who would take a young girl and"—he gestured violently—"use her to force you to steal for him."

"On that we're agreed," Helena murmured. "But what has brought you here?"

"I came to help." Through the shadows Phillipe met her gaze. Desperation colored his voice. "I want to save Ariele. I didn't know, when he sent me to fetch her, what he wanted her for. I thought he was just concerned for her safety, alone with only the servants at Cameralle." He laughed bitterly. "More fool me. But my eyes have been opened—I've seen what he's truly like, I learned of his real plans."

Phillipe caught Helena's hand, holding it beseechingly between his. "You are Ariele's only hope. If there were any other way"—again he gestured, searching for the word—"of *freeing* her from his hold, anything I could do to draw her safely away, I would do it. But there is nothing. The law is the law—she is in his power. And she's currently at grave risk."

Another horror rose in Helena's mind; she clutched his hand. "Does she know?"

To her relief, Phillipe shook his head. "No. I do not believe she even imagines . . . She is such a sweet soul, so pure and untouched."

If she hadn't already realized what emotion was driving Phillipe, the look on his face as he spoke of Ariele would have confirmed the matter beyond doubt. One thing Fabien in his coldly calculating cleverness had not foreseen and could not control. The irony did not escape Helena. "Then things are as they were before. I must steal this dagger and take it to him by Christmas Eve."

"I only knew he had set you some task, and that if you failed . . ." Phillipe frowned at her. "Fabien thought the likelihood of your succeeding was slight."

Helena frowned back. "I do not think the thing impossible." She couldn't believe it—wouldn't believe it.

"Then why have you not brought this thing—this dagger—to him? When you didn't return soon . . . That is why I came. I thought there must be some problem."

"As to that . . ." Helena grimaced. There was a problem, but she would do it anyway. Had to, for Ariele. "Fabien says the dagger is here, somewhere in this great house, and in that I think him correct. But neither

Louis nor Villard has found it—between us, we've searched all the obvious places bar one. It must be there. I was going to search there tonight, but . . ."

Phillipe seized her hand. "Come—let us go there now. We can look while the house is asleep, find it, take it, and flee before any wake. I have a horse—"

"No." Helena tried to tug her hand free, but Phillipe clung. "We need more of a start than that, or monsieur le duc will catch us—and Ariele will not be saved."

Puzzled, Phillipe stared into her face, then said, "You are frightened of this duke. I had not thought it of you." Straightening, he looked censoriously down his nose at her. "But that is no matter. Now I am here, you can tell me where this dagger is and I will seize it, take it back, and free Ariele."

Only his patent sincerity saved him from her temper. "*No!* You don't understand." She bit her tongue against the urge to tell him he was yet a boy—a naive boy trying to influence the games of powerful men. "Do you not think Louis would have taken the dagger and gone long since to claim kudos from your uncle if it were *that* simple? Fabien has decreed *I* must be the one to take it. Me and no one else."

"Why? If he wants it, what matter the courier?"

Helena sighed. "He will have his reasons. Some I can see, others I can but guess at." The thought that hurting—wounding—Sebastian was almost certainly high on Fabien's list weighed on her heart.

Her deep reluctance must have reached Phillipe; he caught her hand again. "But you will take this dagger soon, yes?" He stared into her face, his whole expression one of earnest entreaty, then he relaxed, smiled, the gesture heartbreaking in its simplicity. "But yes, of course you will. You are good and loyal, brave and generous—you will not leave your sister to suffer at my uncle's hands." He pressed her hand, then released it, his smile gaining in confidence. "So you will take the dagger this coming night—you will, won't you?"

Helena took in the calm, solid confidence with which Phillipe regarded her and was distantly grateful that Ariele had found such a steadfast cavalier. Would that she herself had one similiar, who would come to rescue her. Patiently, Phillipe waited for her answer; she knew what it had to be.

Yet still she hesitated. Tried not to remember the warmth, the sharing, the glory—the powerful love of the hours just past. Tried to shut her mind to its beauty. Failed. Tried to oust Sebastian from her mind, from her heart—knew she never could. She felt as if her heart were slowly tearing in two.

Feeling tears gathering, she stiffened her spine, parted her lips, started to nod.

A deep sigh rolled across the room.

"*Mignonne,* you should have told me."

Helena gasped, whirled—hand to her lips, she stared at the bed. One white, long-fingered hand grasped the curtain. The scrape as it was pulled back echoed through the room.

Sebastian lay in her bed, propped on one elbow. The covers had fallen to his waist, exposing the heavy musculature of his chest. His gaze rested on her for a moment, then shifted to Phillipe. "You are related to the comte de Vichesse?"

His tone was even; a subtle menace growled beneath.

Phillipe swallowed, then, head high, stepped forward and bowed stiffly. "He is my uncle. Louis—who I believe is staying here—is my brother. To my shame. I am Phillipe de Sèvres."

Helena heard the words but didn't glance at Phillipe—wasn't sure she could meet his eyes. What must he be thinking, finding Sebastian, patently naked, in her bed?

The least of her worries. Her gaze was fixed on Sebastian—she could barely get her mind to function. His sigh, his words . . . what did they mean? He had found her out. She knew better than to hope he hadn't heard all. They'd spoken in French, but he was fluent in the language. He knew everything now. He would think the worst of her, yet . . . he'd still called her *"mignonne."*

His eyes had left Phillipe to return to her. Seconds ticked past. She could feel his gaze, sensed he was waiting, but for what she couldn't guess. Sensed he was willing her to understand, to read his mind—as if she could.

When she simply remained, literally struck speechless, rooted to the spot, he sighed again, then threw back the covers and rolled from the bed.

Rounding it, he crossed the room toward her.

Helena felt her eyes grow wide, then wider. She opened her mouth to protest. Couldn't find words. Her breath caught and stuck in her throat.

He was naked! And . . .

Did the man have no shame?

Transparently not. He walked toward her as if he were gowned in purple and gold—as if he were in truth the emperor he'd once pretended to be.

He ignored Phillipe completely.

When he was close enough for her to see his eyes, she opened her mouth to explain, to say something . . .

Nothing came.

She raised her hands to ward him off, weakly let them fall.

He halted directly before her. As always, his face remained inscrutable; his eyes were too shadowed for her to read.

Defeated, her heart in her throat, she flung up her hands and turned away. She could never explain.

He lifted one hand, turned her face back to him. He studied her face, briefly searched her eyes.

Then he bent his head and touched his lips to hers.

Made her lips cling with the gentlest caress. Lingered just long enough to reassure.

Then he lifted his head. Looked into her face. "Get back into bed, *mignonne,* before you take a chill."

She stared at him.

After a moment he lifted his head, looked at her dressing table, at the two letters wedged between the mirror and her jewel case. He looked back at her. Arched a brow. "With your permission?"

She hesitated, searched his face, then inclined her head. How did he know? What was he thinking?

Sebastian left her and walked to the dressing table.

Her wits were whirling; her head was reeling. She'd

stopped breathing too long ago. The bed wasn't such a bad idea. Without looking at Phillipe, she recrossed the room. Hugging the robe to her, she climbed into the bed, still warm with Sebastian's heat.

A sudden shiver racked her; dispensing with all pretense, she gathered the covers close about her. Felt a little of the paralyzing ice that had frozen her start to melt.

She watched Sebastian pick up the letters.

"You had better sit down, de Sèvres." Without looking up, Sebastian gestured with the first of the letters he'd opened, the obviously less-read of the two, to a chair by the wall. "This matter is clearly going to require more than two minutes to sort through."

He was aware of Phillipe's hesitation, of the quick glance the boy shot at Helena, but then Phillipe moved to the chair and sank down. One glance at Phillipe's face as he looked again at Helena confirmed that the boy was utterly at sea. He didn't know what to think, much less what to do. In gross features he was like his older brother—dark-haired, handsome enough, a younger version by two or so years—yet there was something much more open, honest, and straightforward about Phillipe.

Having heard his story, Sebastian saw no reason not to trust him. In setting himself to overturn Fabien's scheme, Phillipe had declared his hand with somewhat touching, if impulsive, naïveté.

The letter in Sebastian's hand was inscribed with a fine girlish script. He laid it down, lit the lamp, turned the wick high, then picked up the second letter.

He recognized Fabien's heavy hand even though it had been years since he'd last seen it—since the last offer for the ceremonial dagger. From memory, that had been the tenth such offer, each grudgingly increased over the years. Each had made him smile. He'd taken great delight in exceedingly politely refusing them all.

So Fabien had devised another scheme to make him pay for his temerity. He supposed he should have expected it.

He hadn't expected the guise, yet perhaps he should have anticipated that, too.

Fabien had a nice feel for irony, as did he.

He set down Fabien's letter and picked up the other. "You received these letters after you arrived here." It wasn't a question. "From whom?"

Helena hesitated, then replied, "Louis."

The confusion in her tone made him smile, even though he knew she couldn't see. She still didn't believe, still did not understand.

No matter—eventually she would.

He read through the letter from her sister—read every word. It was important he glean every bit of information; anything could be important in what was to come.

Finishing the first letter, he opened the second. The threat from Fabien. Even knowing what it would contain, even having guessed from the note Ariele had added at Fabien's request what the nature of the threat would be, he still saw red. His hands shook. He had to look away—stare into the lamp flame until he had his rage under control again. Fabien wasn't here for him to take apart with his bare hands. That could come later.

When he'd regained control, regained the ability to deal with his reaction to what Helena had been put through—all for a ridiculous dagger!—he finished the letter, then laid it down.

Paused for an instant to get all the facts straight in his mind. To see the whys behind her reactions, to draw comfort, reassurance, from her internal strife—from the fact that she'd dragged her heels, put off the moment of betrayal, clung to him for as long as she could. Even though it had been her sister, the one person she held most dear in her life, whose well-being had been set so deliberately on the other half of the scale.

Helena had guarded Ariele for many years; her reaction to any threat to her sister was instinctive, deeply ingrained. Fabien, as always, had chosen well.

Unfortunately for him, a higher power had been dealt into the hand.

Quickly, with the facility that had been his from birth, honed to excellence by the world in which he'd played for so many years, he assembled the basics of a plan. Noted the important facts, the essential elements.

Absentmindedly refolding the letters, he put them back by Helena's jewel case, then turned and walked to the bed. Picked up his robe from the floor beside it and shrugged into it.

Met Helena's gaze.

After a moment she asked, "Will you give me the dagger?"

He hesitated, wondered how much to tell her. If he

declared that Ariele was safe, that Fabien's threat was all bluff, designed and executed with an exquisite touch purely to force Helena to do his bidding, would either Helena or Phillipe believe him? He hadn't met Fabien for over half a decade, but he doubted men changed—not in that regard. He and Fabien had always shared the same tastes, which was in large part the cause of their rivalry.

It was also the reason Fabien had sent Helena—he'd known how to bait his trap. Unfortunately, in this case, the prey was going to bite the trapper; Sebastian did not feel the least bit sad.

However, quite aside from triumphing yet again over his old adversary, there was another, much more important, issue to consider. Unless Helena believed he could defeat Fabien, she would never, ever, feel totally sure, completely and absolutely free.

She might even remain, in the future, a prey for Fabien—and that he would not, could not, allow.

"No." He belted his robe, cinched it tight. "I will not give you the dagger. That is not the way the game will be played." He saw Helena's face fall, sensed the dimming of her gaze. "We will go to Le Roc and rescue Ariele."

The sudden reversal of her expression, the hope that flooded her face, made him smile.

"Vraiment?" She leaned forward, eagerly scanning his face, his eyes.

"You are in earnest?" Phillipe had started up at his refusal; now he stared at him with a painful intensity Sebastian didn't like to see. Didn't like to be reminded existed. Would he have looked the same if it had been Helena at Le Roc?

"Indeed." Turning back to Helena, he continued, "If I give you the dagger and you take it back to Fabien, what will you gain?"

She frowned at him. "Ariele."

He sat on the bed, leaned back against the corner post. Watched her. "But you would still be under Fabien's rule—both of you." He glanced at Phillipe. "All of you. Still his puppets, dancing to his tune."

Phillipe frowned, sat down, then nodded. "What you say is true, yet . . ." He looked up. "What is the alternative? You do not know Fabien."

Sebastian smiled his predator's smile. "Actually, I do—in fact, I know him rather better than either of you. I know how he thinks, I know how he'll react." He looked at Helena. "As you so elegantly phrased it, *mignonne*, I know well the games powerful men play."

She studied him, cocked her head. Waited.

Sebastian smiled again, this time indulgently. "Gather around, *mes enfants*. You are about to have an education in the games of powerful men."

He glanced at Phillipe, confirmed he had his attention. "First rule: He who seizes the initiative has the advantage. We're about to take it. Fabien believes Helena will return on Christmas Eve with the dagger. He won't look for her before that." He glanced at Helena. "Regardless of any feelings you may or may not have developed for me, he'll expect you to defy him that much and dally to the last day. As Louis is with you, Fabien will feel certain that nothing unexpected will occur without his being informed of it—in good time to take any necessary measures."

Sebastian glanced at Phillipe, wondered if he should tell him he'd been manipulated by a master, that his presence here was simply another of Fabien's little touches—decided against it. He looked back at Helena. "So, at present, monsieur le comte is feeling rather smug, fully expecting that his plans are proceeding exactly as predicted and all will fall out as he wishes."

She was watching him intently. He smiled. "Instead . . . let's see. It's the seventeenth today. We can be in France by tomorrow morning if the wind blows fair. Le Roc is—correct me if I err—less than a day's fast travel from the coast, say, from Saint-Malo. We will arrive on Fabien's doorstep long before he expects us. Who knows? He might not even be in residence."

"What then?" Helena asked.

"Then we'll discover some means of removing Ariele from the fortress—you really cannot expect me to give you a detailed plan before I see the fortifications—and then we leave at an even faster pace than that at which we arrived."

Helena stared at him, then asked, "Do you truly think it's possible?"

Looking into her eyes, he knew she wasn't referring simply to the rescue of Ariele. Reaching out, he clasped her hand, gently squeezed. "Believe me, *mignonne*, it is."

He would free her, and her sister, and Phillipe as well, from Fabien's coils. He could understand that after all these years she would find that hard to imagine.

She eased back a little but left her hand in his.

The chiming of clocks throughout the house distracted them all. Three chimes—three o'clock. Sebastian stirred. "*Bien*, there is much we have to do if we wish to be in France by tomorrow morning."

They both looked to him. Quickly, concisely, he outlined the specific points they needed to know. His tone was patient—blatantly paternalistic; for once Helena did not take umbrage. Along with Phillipe, she hung on his every word, followed where his mind led, saw the victory he painted.

"With Louis thus kept in ignorance, Phillipe and I will leave and drive to Newhaven—"

Helena jerked upright. "I am coming, too!"

Sebastian met her outraged gaze. "*Mignonne*, it will be better if you remain here." Safe.

"No! Ariele is *my* responsibility—and you do not know Le Roc as I do."

"Phillipe, however, does . . ." Sebastian glanced at Phillipe to find the young man shaking his head.

"*Non*. I do not know the fortress well. Louis has spent years there, but I've only recently joined my uncle's service."

Sebastian grimaced.

"And," Phillipe tentatively added, "there is a further problem. Ariele. She does not know what we know. I do not think, were I to appear to her in the dead of night, or any other time, that she would come with me. But Helena—she will always do exactly as Helena says."

Helena pounced on the point. "*Vraiment*. He speaks

the truth. Ariele is sweet but not stupid—she won't leave the safety of Le Roc except for good reason. And she knows nothing of Fabien's schemes."

She considered Sebastian's hard face, read his opposition very clearly. She leaned closer, curling her fingers, gripping his. "And it's likely you will wish to leave without any fuss, any noise—and without too much baggage, *n'est-ce pas?*"

His lips twisted briefly. He returned the pressure of her fingers. "You play hard, *mignonne.*" Then he sighed, "Very well. You will come, too. I'll have to think how to ensure that Louis is delayed."

Sebastian added that item to the list in his head. When he'd thought of Helena's witnessing his defeat of Fabien, he had been thinking figuratively. His instincts argued she should be left behind in safety, but ... perhaps, in the long run, it would be better if she accompanied them. This way she would share in Fabien's defeat; looking to the future, for one of her temperament that might be important.

The clocks chimed the half hour. He stirred, rose. "There is much to do and not much time to do it." Crossing the room, he tugged at the bellpull. He glanced at Phillipe. "I will have you shown to a bedchamber—ask for whatever you need." He looked across at Helena. "You will both oblige me by remaining in your chambers until I send for you. Dress for traveling—we'll leave at nine o'clock." His gaze rested on Helena. "You will be able to pack only a small bag, nothing more."

She nodded.

A tap sounded on the door. Sebastian crossed to it, opened it just a little way, blocking the doorway with his body. He instructed the sleepy footman to send Webster up, then shut the door.

He turned to Phillipe. "My butler, Webster, is entirely trustworthy. He'll put you in a bedchamber and tend to you himself. The fewer who know of your presence here, the less likely Louis and his man are to learn of it."

Phillipe nodded.

Sebastian paced before the dying fire until Webster arrived, then handed Phillipe into his care. Webster accepted the charge placed on him with his customary imperturbability; he led Phillipe away.

Helena watched the door close, watched Sebastian turn and pace back to the bed. Her mind was in turmoil; she couldn't focus her thoughts. Her emotions held sway—immense relief, puzzlement, uncertainty. Guilt. Excitement. Disbelief.

He slowed, absentminded as he planned; his gaze was distant when he glanced at her, then he focused. "That declaration you extracted from your so-dear guardian, *mignonne*. May I see it?"

She blinked, surprised by the tack. She pointed to her trunk, sitting empty in the corner. "It's behind the lining on the left side of the lid."

He went to the trunk, opened it, felt in the lining. She heard the rip as he tore it free, the crackle as he extracted the parchment. Rising, he returned to the dressing table, unfolded the document, smoothed it out, then read it in the light of the lamp.

Watching his face in the mirror, she saw his lips quirk. Then he smiled and shook his head.

"What is it?"

He glanced at her, then waved the parchment. "Fabien—he never ceases to amaze me. You say he simply sat down when you asked and wrote this?"

She thought back, then nodded. "*Oui*. He considered for but a moment . . ." She frowned. "Why?"

"Because, *mignonne*, in writing this and giving it into your hands, he was risking very little." He studied the document again, then glanced at her. "You did not tell me he'd used the words 'more extensive than your own.'"

"So?"

"So . . . your estates are in the Camargue, a wide, flat land. Of what size are your holdings?"

She named a figure; he smiled.

"*Bon*. We are free, then."

"Why?"

"Because my estates are 'more extensive than' yours."

She frowned, shook her head. "I still don't see."

He set down the document, reached for the lamp, "Consider this—England is a much smaller country than France."

She watched the light dim, watched him turn to the bed. Thought furiously. "There are not many English lords whose estates are more extensive than mine?"

"Other than myself—and Fabien knew I'd declared I would not wed—the only possibilities I can think of would be the royal dukes, none of whom would meet with your approval, and two others, both of whom are already married and old enough to be your father."

"Fabien would know this?"

"Assuredly. It's the sort of information he keeps at his fingertips."

"And you?"

He shook his head, intuitively answering the question she'd truly asked. "No, *mignonne*—I gave up playing the games Fabien indulges in years ago." He stopped by the side of the bed, studied her face. "I still know the rules and can engage with the best of them but . . ." He shrugged. "Truth to tell, the activity palled. I found better things to do with my time."

Seducing women—helping women. Helena watched as he unbelted his robe, let it slide to the floor. She sank back into the pillows as he lifted the covers and slid in beside her.

She remained still, wondering—hardly daring to do even that . . .

He reached for her. Dragged her down into the depths of the feather mattress, settling her half beneath him. She sucked in a breath, felt his fingers searching for the opening of her robe. Then he pushed the robe wide, lifted over her and lowered his body to hers—skin to skin, heat to heat.

The rush of warmth was a shock. Giddy, she found enough air to say, "So the document—you are saying it's worthless?"

He looked into her face as he set his hands to her body. "Not in the least. To us it's a prize." He considered her eyes, then smiled, bent his head, and brushed his lips across her furrowed forehead. "Your document is an ace, *mignonne*, and we're going to use it to trump Fabien in a most . . . satisfying way."

That he still meant to marry her—even now, after learning all about her deception—could not have been clearer. Yet guilt still lay heavy on her heart.

His hands were roaming, seducing her senses, stealing her wits. It would be so easy to sink under his spell, to give herself to him and let the matter slide.

She couldn't.

She caught his face, framed it in both hands, held it so that even in the dimness she could see every nuance. "You will really help me—you will help me rescue Ariele." No question; she didn't doubt he would. "Why?"

He met her gaze. "*Mignonne*, I have told you—often—that you are mine. *Mine*." On the word, he nudged her thighs apart, settled between. "Of all the women in the world, there is none I'm more devoted to helping, to protecting, than you."

She could see it in the blue of his eyes, see the fire and the feeling that supported it. "But me . . . I put another higher than you."

His gaze didn't waver. "If you'd acted as you did for Fabien, or any other man . . . yes, I would have felt betrayed. But you did as you did for your sister—out of love, out of responsibility. Out of caring. Of all men in the world, can you not see that *I* would understand?"

She looked into his eyes and did see. At last, let herself believe. "I should have trusted you—told you."

"You were afraid for your sister."

He bent his head and kissed her—long and deep. Making it patently clear that, to him, the matter was closed.

It was minutes later before she caught her breath enough to murmur, "You forgive me?"

Above her he paused, then touched a gentle hand to her cheek. "*Mignonne*, there is nothing to forgive."

In that moment she knew, not only that she loved him but why. Reaching up, she drew his head down, kissed him—delicately, tantalizingly, holding at bay the fire that was already raging between them. "I will be yours." She whispered the words against his lips. "Always."

No matter what was to come.

"*Bon.*" He took control of the kiss, plundered her mouth, then tilted her hips and entered her. Drank her gasp as the hot steel of him pressed inexorably in. All the way in.

Then he withdrew, and the dance began.

Helena gave herself up to it, up to him—surrendered completely. Opened her body to him, opened her heart. Offered him her soul.

In the dark cocoon of the bed, in their mingled breaths, the shattered sobs and low groans, as their heated bodies moved together, as the pace increased and the depth of his passion and need broke over her, buffeted her, pleasured her, a deeper understanding dawned.

While surrender was her gift to him, the most coveted element she brought to his bed, possession, in turn, was his gift to her. Yet as she sensed his control slip and his desire break free, take hold, and drive him relentlessly, while she sobbed and held him to her as he plundered her body, she had to wonder who was the possessed, who the posssessor.

Neither, she concluded as the wave broke and took them. Left them gasping. As they drifted, buoyed on fading glory, she recalled what he'd stated long before. They were made for this. For each other—him for her, her for him.

Two halves of the same coin, bonded by a power not even a powerful man could break.

Sebastian slipped from Helena's side two hours later. Shrugging into his robe, belting it, he crossed to the dressing table, picked up Fabien's declaration, read it again. He glanced at Helena; she remained sound asleep. He hesitated, then folded the document. Taking it with him, he quietly left the room.

Regaining his apartments, he summoned Webster, gave orders as he washed, shaved, and dressed. Leaving his valet, Gros, rushing hither and yon, packing the small bag he'd declared was all he would take, he quit the room and headed for his study.

There he started on the task of setting in place the foundations of his plan.

The first letter he wrote was a personal request to the Bishop of Lincoln, an old friend of his father's. Once he and Helena returned from France with Ariele, he was not of a mind to delay their wedding further. Finishing his letter, he sanded it, then set it aside, together with

Fabien's declaration. Helena had secured that prize—he fully intended to use it.

He rang for a footman, dispatched him to find Webster. With his customary magisterial calm, Webster led the senior staff into the study. They sat. In swift order Sebastian outlined his requirements, then they discussed, suggested, and eventually decided on various ploys to delay both Louis and Villard.

"I would expect the valet to be the comte's creature. Take care that while watching the larger fish you do not let the minnow slip through your net."

"Indeed not, Your Grace. You may rely on us."

"I will be. I reiterate—I do not wish you to do anything overt to delay de Sèvres and his man. I wish them to be mystified as to where mademoiselle la comtesse and I might be. If they realize they're being deliberately delayed, they'll guess where we've gone and follow swiftly." Sebastian paused, then added, "The longer they remain uncertain, the safer I, your future mistress, her sister, and the gentleman who brought us word last night will be."

He was rewarded by the sight of a slight curve in Webster's lips, a gleam of triumph in the butler's gray eyes. The man had been quietly prodding him for years—ever since Arthur had married—to do his duty and save them all.

Barely able to contain his pleasure while maintaining his imperturbable mask, Webster bowed deeply. "Might we extend our congratulations, Your Grace?"

"You may." After an instant Sebastian added, "But only to me."

Delighted, they all did so, then departed. Sebastian returned to his mental list of tasks.

After clearing his desk of all urgent business, he spoke briefly with his steward, then gave orders to have the Thierrys brought to him.

They appeared, confused, a little hopeful. Sebastian considered them as they sat in the chairs before his desk, then he leaned forward and told them all they needed to know—enough for them to realize their situation—that they had unwittingly been accessories to a plot to steal from him. They were as aghast as he'd expected; he cut short their horrified protestations to reassure them that he recognized their innocence.

He then gave them a choice. England or France.

England with his support; France as accessories in Fabien's soon-to-be failure.

Given that they'd been genuine émigrés before Fabien had recruited them, it took them no time at all to opt for England.

He suggested they remain at Somersham until he and Helena returned and they could discuss arrangements for their future. Although at that point in ignorance of his plans, Gaston Thierry, to his credit, suggested that he and Marjorie could act to delay Louis.

Sebastian offered Thierry his hand and sent them to confer with Webster.

The last person with whom he needed to speak fluttered into the room five minutes later.

"You wished to speak with me, dear boy?"

Sebastian rose, smiled, and waved Clara to the chairs before the fire. She sat in an armchair; he stood by the hearth, one arm resting on the mantelshelf, and told her much more than he'd told the Thierrys.

"*Well!* I knew it all long, of course." Eyes agleam, a smile of joy lighting her face, she rose and kissed his cheek. "She's perfect—quite perfect. I'm *so* glad. And I can state without fear of contradiction that the family will be delighted. Positively delighted!"

"Indeed, but you understand that I wish just the usual Christmas crowd and those others I'll list in my letter for Augusta—not the entire clan—here when we return?"

"Oh, indeed, indeed. Just a small crowd. We can invite all the others later, when the weather improves." Clara patted his arm. "Now, you'd best be on your way if you're to make Newhaven tonight. I'll be here when you get back, and so will Augusta and the others. We'll hold the fort here."

With another pat and an admonition to take care, Clara swept out, still beaming.

Sebastian rang for Webster. "Louis de Sèvres?" he asked when that worthy arrived.

"In the breakfast parlor, Your Grace."

"And his man?"

"In the servants' hall."

"Very well—fetch mademoiselle la comtesse to me here and have a footman take her bag to the coach. Send another footman to take Monsieur Phillipe to the stables by way of the side door."

"At once, Your Grace."

Sebastian was seated at his desk when Webster ushered Helena in, then retreated and shut the door.

"Mignonne." Rising, Sebastian came out from behind the desk.

Dressed in a traveling gown with a heavy cloak over her arm, Helena came to him, her gaze alert and watchful. "Is it time to go?"

Halting before the desk, he smiled and took her hand. "Almost." He kissed her gloved fingers, then turned to the two letters still lying open on his desk. "I took the declaration—I didn't want to wake you."

"I assumed you had." Head tilted, she looked up at him, and waited.

"In this country, for us to marry, the fastest way is to procure a special license—a dispensation, if you will. I've written to a well-disposed bishop, but in support of my request, given you're French and not your own mistress, I'll need to enclose Fabien's declaration." He paused, then asked, "Have I your permission to do so?"

She smiled, slowly, glowingly. *"Oui.* Yes. Of course."

He smiled. *"Bon."* Releasing her, he reached for the candle and sealing wax. As she watched, he set his seal to the letter.

"It's done." He laid the letter on top of his missive for Augusta and another letter addressed to the Court of St. James. "Webster will send it by rider."

He considered the second letter, wondered if he should mention it. He turned and met Helena's peridot eyes—clear, free of clouds, although not yet of lingering worry.

"Come." He took her hand. "Let's be on our way."

Chapter Twelve

❧

The coach was pulled by four powerful horses. It raced south through the countryside silent and still, frozen in winter's icy grip.

Cushioned in the comfort of leather upholstery, cocooned in the warmth of soft furs and silk wraps with hot, flannel-wrapped bricks beneath her feet, Helena watched the chill world flash by. She tried, initially, to sit upright, to keep her spine erect and eschew the temptation to lean against Sebastian, solid and immovable beside her. But the hours passed and she nodded, then dozed as the carriage rocketed along; she woke to find her cheek cushioned on Sebastian's chest, his arm heavy and reassuring around her, keeping her from falling to the floor.

Cracking open her lids, she glanced across the coach. Phillipe, sitting opposite, was asleep in one corner.

Letting her lids fall once more, she sank against Sebastian and slipped back into sleep.

And dreamed. A confusion of images that made no sense but were pervaded by desperation, by burgeoning hope, by a sense of fate and a nebulous fear.

She woke to the clatter of hooves on cobbles. Straightening, she glanced out the window, saw a jumble of shops and houses.

"London."

She turned to meet Sebastian's gaze. Phillipe, she noted, was peering interestedly at the streets. "We have to go through it?"

"Unfortunately. Newhaven's near Brighton, which lies directly south."

Her lips forming an "Oh," she looked at the houses and tried to suppress her impatience.

Tried to push aside the belief that now they'd set out on this journey, they had to hurry, hurry, or else they'd fail. That speed was of the essence.

Sebastian's hand closed about hers, tightened reassuringly. "There's no way Louis will be able to warn Fabien in time."

She glanced at him, searched his eyes, then nodded. She looked back at the houses.

A few minutes later Sebastian spoke to Phillipe, inquiring about a certain French noble family. From there the conversation expanded to the foibles of the French court. Phillipe appealed to Helena. Soon they were embroiled in an animated, far-from-felicitous dissection of the current political climate and the shortcomings of those supposedly at the country's helm. Only when she noticed the houses thinning and glimpsed open country again did Helena remember the passage of time.

She glanced at Sebastian, saw his blue eyes glint from under his heavy lids. Returning to the scenery, letting the conversation taper off of its own accord, she inwardly shook her head. He might no longer play the games Fabien did, but of his skill she entertained little doubt.

Or that, now that she was his, now that he deemed her to be so, she would have to grow accustomed to such nudges of manipulation—to the gentle tensing of her strings—all for her own good, of course.

It was a price she'd never believed she would be willing to pay, yet for freedom, for him . . .

To be his—safe, secure, and allowed to be free. Allowed to live her own life as she wished. To fulfill her destiny as a lady of position, as the wife of a powerful man.

What price such a dream?

She dozed again as the coach raced on. It was evening, the shadows fading to night, when the coach drew up outside an inn facing a quay. Sebastian stirred, then descended; Helena watched him speak with a sailor who'd hurried up. The steady splash of waves and the smell of brine carried clearly on the evening air. The sailor appeared to be in Sebastian's employ; having received his orders, he tugged his forelock and departed.

Sebastian returned to the coach. Opening the door, he beckoned. "Come, we have time to dine before the tide turns."

He handed her down; Phillipe followed. They crossed the cobbled yard to the inn door. Inside, all was cozy. The innkeeper beamed and bowed them into a private parlor. The table was set for three. The instant they sat, two maids arrived with steaming platters.

Helena glanced at Sebastian.

He caught her gaze, then flicked out his napkin. "I sent a rider down at dawn. Everything's in readiness. We can sail in good time."

Despite her relief, despite his planning, she could summon little appetite, a prey to unnameable worries. Sebastian insisted she consume at least the soup and a morsel or two of chicken. While she complied, he and Phillipe demolished everything else.

Then they were done, and Sebastian led her across the inn yard and onto the quay. His yacht, a sleek sloop that looked ready to slice through the water, stood bobbing, waiting, ropes straining as if it were a horse longing to race. All was in readiness, or so the captain informed him as he helped her down from the gangplank.

Sebastian gave the order to sail, then led her below.

She'd just stepped off the short ladder into the narrow corridor when the boat lifted on the swell, then surged. The sense of power, of being propelled forward— toward France, toward Ariele—was inexpressibly comforting. For one instant she paused, felt hope flare, let it grip her.

Realizing that Sebastian had stopped and was looking back at her, that Phillipe was still waiting to descend, she smiled and stepped forward, let Sebastian lead her to the stateroom at the corridor's end.

The cabin was small yet spacious, uncluttered. It bore the stamp of his wealth in the luxury of its fittings, in the wide bed anchored against the wall, in the sheen of the oak paneling, the quality of the linens.

He'd stepped back into the corridor; she heard him directing Phillipe to another cabin. Heard them discussing the likely time of arrival. Sometime in the morning, Sebastian said. Phillipe was impressed; he asked about the boat, about its design. Helena stopped listening.

She put back the deep hood of her cloak, set her fingers to the strings at her throat. There was only one bed. That Sebastian would expect her to share it she doubted not at all. Yet how she would manage to sleep . . .

In her mind the gray walls of Le Roc rose, cold and forbidding. Not even the orchards and park surrounding it could soften its harsh, despotic lines.

What was Ariele doing, thinking? Was she sleeping, soundly with a small smile curving her lips? The sleep of the innocent—trusting, naive . . .

A noise in the corridor jerked her to attention. She glanced down, tugging at her laces as the door behind her opened, then closed. She heard a clunk, realized Sebastian had set the sword belt and sword he'd worn on a chair. Then she sensed his presence behind her, felt her pulse leap as it always did when he drew close. He hesitated, then closed the gap so that his chest met her shoulders, his thighs her bottom. So that the ridge of his erection nudged into the small of her back.

She hadn't thought. "I'm . . . worried."

"I know."

His hands closed about her waist. He bent his head, ran the tip of his tongue about the rim of one ear; when she shuddered and tipped her head back, he trailed his lips to the pulse point at the base of her throat.

Laved as his hands shifted, rising to close possessively about her breasts. Sucking as he languidly kneaded, then lazily squeezed the ruched peaks.

She struggled to hold back the tide but couldn't. Her breasts swelled, firmed, heated . . . her thoughts splintered.

"It's too cold for you to be naked."

His deep purr told her he preferred her that way.

She managed to draw breath but couldn't break free of the drugging sensuality in his voice, in his touch. Couldn't pull free of his spell. "What, then?"

"Lift the front of your skirts and petticoats. To above your knees."

She summoned sufficient wit to comply. His hands fell to her waist, gripped. She gasped when he lifted her, then set her on her knees on the edge of the bed.

"Sssh." His lips returned to her throat, to the sensitive spot beneath her ear. "Phillipe's in the next room."

One of his hands had returned to pleasure her breasts. She could feel the other behind her, sifting through their clothes. Then she felt his staff press more definitely against her. Felt him start to raise the back of her skirts.

"I don't know if I can . . ."

His hand made contact with her bare bottom, caressed; she moaned.

Knew she could.

Knew she would.

He lifted her skirts and slid into her softness—and

the world fell away. His rhythm was slow, easy; desire rose like a gentle tide and swept her up to a place that existed only in the here and now, in the moment of heat and passion. A sensation-filled plane where pleasure built, stage by stage, step by step, inexorably, until at the end the towering wave broke and washed through her, leaving her shattered, exhausted . . . too exhausted to think.

She was only dimly aware of him drawing her dress from her, then laying her in the bed. He stripped and joined her; she curled instinctively into his warmth, into his strength.

His arm came around her; he held her close.

She sighed and drifted into sleep.

A sudden jerk woke her.

Helena looked about, remembered where she was—realized she was alone and that faint light tinged the circle of sky visible through the porthole.

France!

She went to throw back the covers—and couldn't.

The next second the yacht listed dramatically, held motionless for a second, then, with a slap, slammed back into the sea.

That was what had woken her. Pulling at the blanket, she realized that Sebastian had tucked her in securely so she wouldn't roll out of the bed. The yacht pitched again as she struggled free—she had to grab the side of the bed to stop herself from being hurled across the cabin.

Wrestling her way into her dress, then relacing it—

by herself while teetering about the cabin fighting to keep her feet—had her swearing. Under her breath. In French.

But when she left the cabin and climbed the short ladder and looked out at the sky and sea, words failed her.

Dark gray, nearly black, the sky churned; beneath it the waves ran in long, white-plumed rolls, breaking over the prow of the yacht before raging past. Through the spume thrown up by the boiling waves, whipped high by the tearing wind, she could see low cliffs; she squinted and could just make out a cluster of buildings at the head of an inlet some way across the water.

"*Sacre dieu*," she eventually managed. She would have crossed herself if she'd dared to risk releasing the rail she was clinging to.

She was facing the prow; the bridge and wheel were aft. Gradually, the buffeting of the waves subsided, eased to just a rocking. Dragging in a breath, she stepped up onto the deck. Shakily, she walked past the hatch housing, started to turn—and glimpsed the sea beyond the prow.

Saw the next set of roiling waves rush in.

The first hit; the deck tilted. She clutched a bollard and clung.

The deck was wet; the second wave hit, and her feet slipped, slid.

Frightened, she glanced around—and saw she was small enough to slip easily under the deck railing. She clung to the wet bollard for dear life.

The third wave hit, and she lost her footing. She

shrieked—felt her fingers slip on the smooth, wet surface. Heard a shout, then an oath.

Seconds later, just as the next wave hit and her fingers lost their grip, she was plucked up, snatched up against Sebastian's hard chest. His arm tightened about her waist, locking her to him, her back to his chest as he held tight to a rope while the yacht rode out the wave.

The instant it did, he lunged for the hatch, reached the ladder, and bundled her down it.

She didn't understand that many English swear words, but his tone left little doubt that he was cursing her.

"I'm sorry." She turned to him as he set her on her feet in the narrow corridor.

His eyes were burning blue, his lips thin, set, as he stood halfway down the ladder, blocking it. "You will henceforth bear one point firmly in mind. I agreed to rescue your sister, and I will. I agreed to let you accompany me, against my better judgment. If you do not have a care to yourself and your safety, I'm liable to change my mind."

She read the truth of that in his eyes, in the granite determination in his face. Placatingly, she held out her hands, palms up. "I have said I am sorry, and I am—I didn't realize . . ." Her gesture encompassed the tempest outside. "But can we not put into the harbor?"

He hesitated, then his features eased. He started to step down—the wind gusted a spray of water through the hatch onto his head. He growled, turned, climbed back up the ladder, and slammed the hatch shut, then came down again. He shook his head; droplets flew. He gestured her back. "In the cabin."

She retreated. He followed. She crossed to a small dresser bolted to the wall, pulled a towel from a rail, and walked back to hand it to him.

He took it—the next wave hit and pitched her into him. He caught her, held her to him. And she felt the rigid tension, the reined temper that gripped him. Then he sighed. The tension seeped, then flowed away. He bent his head, set his face to her curls. Breathed deeply. "Don't do anything that foolish again."

She lifted her head. Met his gaze. Saw, clearly, because he allowed her to see, the vulnerability behind the words. Raising a hand, wonderingly, she touched his lean cheek. "I won't."

Stretching up, she touched her lips to his—invited the kiss, gave it back.

For one instant that sweet power welled between them, then he lifted his head. They parted; he handed her to the bed, and she wriggled up to sit. He went past the bed to the porthole and looked out, toweling his hair dry.

She didn't repeat her question, just waited.

"We can't put in, not with the seas running like this. Not against the wind."

She'd guessed as much. Her heart sank, just a little, but she was determined. "Can we not run with the wind and put in somewhere else?"

"Not easily. The wind will more likely blow us onto the rocks." He glanced at her. "Besides"—he nodded to the porthole—"that's Saint-Malo. It's the closest, most convenient port to Le Roc. Once we land, it'll take a day, perhaps a little more, to reach Montsurs." He glanced at her. "Le Roc is close to there, I understand?"

"Half an hour, no more."

"So . . . these storms never last long. It's nearly midday—"

"Midday?" She stared at him. "I thought it was just dawn."

He shook his head. "We were still north of the islands at dawn and sailing free. This blew up only after we'd entered the gulf." He dropped the towel on the bed, then came to sit beside her. "So we have to weigh our chances. To get free of this wind, we'd have to either run north and pray the wind dies farther up the coast— which it may not—or go west and potentially have to round Brittany entirely to lay in to Saint-Nazaire. Either option leaves us farther from Le Roc than Saint-Malo."

She considered, drew in a breath, felt the tightness in her chest. "So you're saying it would be best to stay and wait for the storm to pass."

He nodded. After a moment, he added, "I know you're worried, but we have to weigh each hour carefully."

"Because of Louis?"

He nodded again, this time more curtly. "Once he realizes we've gone and he leaves Somersham, his route will be clear. He'll go to Dover and cross to Calais. It's unlikely this storm will affect him."

She slid her hand into his. "But then he'll have to drive down to Le Roc—that will slow him."

"Yes, and that's why I think we should sit tight

through today. Louis could have left Somersham only this morning—a few hours ago at best. He won't have succeeded in leaving before that, not with so many set on delaying him."

She thought, considered, then sighed. Nodded. "So we have time." She glanced at Sebastian. "You are right—we should wait."

He caught her gaze, searched her eyes, then raised a hand to frame her face. Bent his head to brush her lips with his. "Trust me, *mignonne*. Ariele will be safe."

She did trust him—completely. And, deep in her heart, she felt that Ariele would indeed be safe. With him and her acting together, determined on that outcome, she couldn't imagine that the rescue wouldn't come to pass.

Yet while they waited and the hours rolled by, another worry surfaced. Here Sebastian was, an Englishman preparing to slip into the heart of France and steal a young French noblewoman away from beneath her legal guardian's nose—all for her. What if he were caught?

Would his rank protect him?

Could anything protect him from Fabien, were he to fall into his hands?

The discussion on what guise they would adopt to travel through the countryside to Le Roc did nothing to quiet such nascent fears.

Phillipe had joined them for lunch at the table in the stateroom. The cabin boy served them; at a signal from Sebastian, he left and closed the door.

"I think it would be best if, once we leave the yacht,

we have some overt reason for our journey. I suggest that you"—with his head, Sebastian indicated Phillipe—"should be the youthful scion of a noble house."

Phillipe was listening intently. "Which house?"

"I would suggest the de Villandrys. If any should ask, you are Hubert de Villandry. Your parents' estate lies in—"

"The Garonne." Phillipe grinned. "I have visited there."

"*Bon.* Then you can be convincing should the need arise." Glancing at Helena, Sebastian waved languidly. "Not that I expect any difficulties. I'm merely making contingency plans."

She held his gaze, then nodded. "And who am I to be?"

"You're Hubert's sister, of course." Sebastian tilted his head, studied her, then pronounced, "Adèle. Yes, that will pass. You're Adèle de Villandry, and the reason you're traveling with us is that, after traveling briefly in England over these past months, Phillipe and I passed through London, where, having spent some months with relatives in the English capital, you joined us so we could escort you back to . . ." He trailed off, considering.

"To the convent at Montsurs." Helena took up their fictitious tale. "I've decided to take the veil and was sent to London in a last effort to get me to change my mind."

Sebastian grinned; reaching out, he squeezed her hand. "*Bon.* That will do very nicely."

"But who are you?" she asked.

"Me?" A devilish light danced in his eyes as he laid his hand over his heart and mock-bowed. "I'm Sylvester Ffoliott, an English scholar, the scion of a noble but sadly impoverished family reduced to having to make my way in the world. I was hired to conduct Monsieur Hubert on his travels through England and see him back to the de Villandry estate in the Garonne. That is where we—Hubert and I—are heading after we deposit you with the good sisters at Montsurs."

Both Helena and Phillipe fell silent, imagining, then Helena nodded. "It is possible. It will serve."

"Indeed. Furthermore, it will explain our hiring of a fast carriage to convey you to Montsurs and then the subsequent return of the carriage while we—Hubert and I—hire horses, the better to see the country as we travel south."

Phillipe frowned. "Why let the carriage go and switch to horses?"

"Because," Sebastian replied, "horses will be faster and more useful in fleeing." He considered Phillipe. "I presume you do ride."

"*Naturellement.*"

"Good. Because I don't expect your uncle to let Ariele—and Helena—slip from his clutches without trying to snatch them back."

None of them had expected Fabien to let them go gracefully, yet hearing the fact stated so bluntly established the likelihood more firmly in Helena's mind.

How would Fabien react—and how would Sebastian defeat him?

Later she stood at the railing looking toward the coast and watched the westering sun edge the storm clouds with fire. As the captain had predicted, the storm had blown itself out, leaving tattered remnants of clouds streaming across the sky. The wind whistled shrilly in the rigging. The sun sank and, with one last fiery flare, drowned in the sea.

The whistling gradually faded as the shadows closed in. Then, with one last, soft exhalation, the wind died.

Helena heard a footstep. Sebastian neared, drew closer to stand just behind her, to one side.

"Soon, *mignonne*, soon. As soon as the wind picks up again."

"Perhaps it won't —not tonight."

She didn't see his smile—even if she looked, his face would probably not show it—but she heard it in his voice, in his indulgent tone. "It will. Trust me. These waters are rarely calm."

He stepped closer; without looking, she leaned back, into his strength, into his warmth. Let herself feel his support and the hope it brought. He reached around her to lock his hands on the railing, caging her before him. Comfortably, securely.

For long moments they simply stood, thoughts and worries both abandoned to the silent beauty of the encroaching night.

"If we do get in this night, what then?"

"We'll hire rooms at a good inn and arrange for a carriage. We'll leave as early as possible in the morning."

She felt his chest expand as he drew in a breath. "Why not leave tonight?"

"Too much risk for too little gain."

She frowned.

She felt him glance down at her face. Then he continued, "Driving fast over country roads at night is too dangerous, and not just because of the state of the roads. It'll draw attention to us, and that may not be helpful. As for the gain—if we leave here tonight, we'll arrive there by midday tomorrow. That's dangerous, too. Arriving so close to Le Roc in daylight, we run the risk of someone's recognizing you and mentioning your presence to Fabien. I need hardly point out that that will not do."

Helena grimaced. Leaned more heavily back against him. "Very well, monsieur le duc. We will rest tonight."

Again she sensed his indulgent smile. *"Bon, mignonne."* He bent his head and pressed a kiss to her temple. "We'll be away at first light."

As if some celestial being had heard his decree and felt moved to comply, the rigging creaked, gently at first, then increasingly loudly, and then a puff of wind came from nowhere.

Sebastian lifted his head. Immediately shouts and calls erupted as the crew sprang to action. The heavy anchor chain rattled and clunked as the anchor was hauled up. Ropes rushed through pulleys; the sails rose, eagerly snapping in the freshening breeze.

Helena stood at the railing as the sails filled and the sleek yacht tacked and set course for Saint-Malo. With

Sebastian at her back, she watched the coast of France draw near.

Everything went as Sebastian had predicted. The yacht slid in to a berth on the quay at Saint-Malo, unremarkable amid the many sloops and boats of all kinds that crowded the stone quays. They left the yacht as if they'd merely been passengers, consigning their bags to a porter who followed behind as they walked the short distance to the Pigeon, one of the better, yet not the best, of the many inns the busy port boasted. There they found comfortable rooms.

Despite the quality of the bed, Helena slept little. She hadn't missed the fact that Sebastian had once again donned his sword. In common with every other gentleman, he frequently wore such a weapon, but it was usually an ornate one, more decoration than serious armory. The sword he had with him now was not like that. It was old, well worn, not overly ornate. It looked comfortable—if swords could ever be that—as if it was something he'd used often, a favorite. She hadn't missed the way his hand dropped unconsciously to the hilt, resting there, long fingers absentmindedly curling about the worked metal.

That sword seemed almost a part of him—an extension of him. It was not a toy but a tool, one he knew how to use. The fact he'd chosen to wear it . . . it was impossible not to realize the implications.

Inwardly sighing, she admitted the folly of thinking she could protect him—he who was here protecting her. There was even less point worrying . . . yet she did.

Every time she shut her eyes, her mind raced away, envisioning all manner of difficulties, hurdles that would spring up in their path and engage them, deflect them, somehow prevent them from reaching Ariele until the day after Christmas . . .

Helena woke with a start, her pulse racing, her stomach tense and tight—then she slumped back into the pillows. Shut her eyes, tried to sleep.

She was dressed and waiting when Phillipe tapped on her door in the chill of predawn. A cup of chocolate—only at Sebastian's insistence—and then they were away before the sun had even begun to rise.

When they'd left the inn yard, Sebastian had waved Helena and Phillipe into the coach, murmuring to Phillipe to sit beside her. He had taken the seat opposite, but once they'd left the town behind and were bowling along the open roads, he signaled to Phillipe to change places.

Settling beside Helena, Sebastian noted the dark circles under her eyes, the pallor of her face. He lifted an arm, placed it about her, juggling her so she fitted snugly against his side. She frowned at him; he smiled, touched his lips to her hair. "Rest, *mignonne*. You will be no use to your sister tonight if you are not wide awake and alert."

The mention of saving her sister and the part she would need to play gave her pause—gave her the excuse to yield to her tiredness and rest her head on his chest. Close her eyes.

Soon she was asleep. He held her safe against him, a warm, soft womanly weight, and watched the countryside flash past. He'd spent half the night searching out the best driver; the man was worth the price he'd paid. They rattled on throughout the day, stopping only for a half hour in the early afternoon.

Dusk was falling when the walls of the old town of Montsurs rose before them. Trading places once more with Phillipe, Sebastian directed the coachman to take them to a livery stable. When the coach rocked to a halt beside a not-too-prosperous-looking establishment, Sebastian grinned. "Perfect." He glanced at Helena and Phillipe. "Wait here and make sure no locals see you."

They nodded, and he left. The minutes ticked by, but they remained silent, watchful . . . increasingly fearful. But then they heard the clop of hooves—Sebastian returned leading four mounts, all saddled. The stable's owner trotted alongside, a huge smile wreathing his face.

Sebastian led the horses to the rear of the coach. Helena and Phillipe strained to hear. The stable master was giving directions, embellished with description. Helena recognized the way to the convent; she had to smile. Sebastian had thought of even that; if any asked after the unknowns who had bought horses that night, the trail would lead only to the convent.

He reappeared at that moment, thanking the garrulous stablemaster, then opening the door and entering, shutting it swiftly behind him.

Helena had shrunk back into the shadows; the stable master would very likely recognize her. But as he waved them off, the beaming man's gaze remained on Sebastian—in the gloom, he didn't see her.

"Where now?" she whispered once they were away.

Sebastian arched a brow at her. "The convent, of course."

It wasn't far, but at that hour the gates were shut and no one was around to see the coach pull up, see them climb down with their bags and untie the horses, see Sebastian pay off the coachman while she and Phillipe waited, reins in their hands. The man took the coins with a grin, turned his horses, and left them. They stood in the lane and watched the coach disappear, waited until they could no longer hear the clop of hooves on the packed earth.

As one, they turned and scanned the convent wall; then Sebastian walked to the stout gate and looked through the grate.

He turned to them, smiling. "No one." Returning, he took the reins Helena held. "Let's go."

He lifted her to her saddle, held the horse while she settled her feet. Then he mounted; with Phillipe leading the fourth horse, they rode down the lane and turned for Le Roc.

Half an hour later they rounded a hill, and the fortress of Le Roc came into view. Rising above a small valley, Fabien's fortress sat atop a finger of upthrust rock, like an extension of that intruding presence, a foreign overlord brooding over the fertile fields.

"Stop." Sebastian drew rein, glanced at Helena as she halted beside him. With his head he indicated the fortress. "That's it?"

She nodded. "From this side it's impregnable, but on

the other face there are paths leading up through the gardens."

"Just as well." He studied the building, the way it had been set into the stone. As fortresses went, it was impressive. "If we go much farther along this road, we'll risk being seen."

Helena nodded. "Because of the strife, there are guards, even at night."

He glanced at her; she felt his gaze and looked up, through the gloom searched his face. "I know the guards' routine—it never varies."

Phillipe snorted. "That's true. There are guards, but they don't really expect to be challenged."

"All the better if they're overconfident." Sebastian scanned the surrounding fields. "Is there some way we can circle and approach from the other side?"

"Yes." Helena nudged her mount into a walk. "There's a lane that joins this one just a little way along—it's the one the carts use to carry the apples away from the orchards."

With Phillipe bringing up the rear, Sebastian followed her. One hundred yards farther, she turned down a narrow lane just wide enough for a cart, deeply furrowed but overgrown. Unless you knew it was there, you'd never suspect; following Helena in single file, Sebastian didn't, however, doubt that Fabien knew. If they had to leave fast . . .

He was deep in plans for all manner of contingencies when Helena drew rein and glanced back. "We should leave the horses here. There are gates farther on, but if we take the horses into the orchards"—with her head she indicated the land that rose above them—"the guards might hear them."

Squinting through the shifting shadows, Sebastian studied the terraces that sloped ever upward, eventually meeting what appeared to be a garden wall. While well protected from the road and any force that arrived from that direction, the fortress was much more vulnerable from this angle.

"Très bien," he murmured, eyes searching the night. "We'll leave the nags here and go on on foot."

The orchard wall was eight feet high but roughly built of stone blocks. It was easy to climb, even for Helena in her skirts. Tucking the hems into her boots, she scaled the wall under Sebastian's watchful eye, then sat atop it while with a few quick steps he joined her. Swinging his legs over, he dropped to the ground. She looked down, then sniffed, turned, and descended more carefully.

Sebastian plucked her from the wall when she was only halfway down and set her on her feet. With a regal nod in thanks, she dusted her hands, gestured up the sloping orchard, then set off.

He prowled by her side as they ducked from deep shade, through open spaces into the skeletal shadows thrown by the next tree. The moon had yet to rise; they only had the faint light of the stars to hide from.

They reached the top of the orchard and slipped into the dense shadows in the lee of the next wall. This one was more of a deterrent; it stood over eight feet high, and its construction was excellent, each block flush with the next, leaving the surface smooth, free of hand- or footholds. Sebastian studied it, then looked at Helena. She waved him to wait while she and Phillipe conferred in low whispers, then she gestured to their left. She pushed past him and led the way along the wall.

Sebastian followed. She scurried along, hugging the wall's shadow until he estimated they must be almost directly opposite the main gates. She stopped, glanced back at him, held a finger to her lips, then turned and went on— a few steps more took her to the other side of a wrought-iron gate.

He stopped, as did she, and looked up at the gate. It was as high as the wall and topped with very long spikes. There was no way to climb over it. He glanced at Helena and saw her beckoning. He joined her beyond the gate; she reached up and pulled his head down so she could whisper.

"It's locked, but there's a key. It hangs on a peg on the other side of the wall from here." Releasing him, she pointed to a spot on the wall about a foot from the base, nearly two feet from the frame of the gate. Then she pressed close again. "Can you reach it?"

Sebastian looked at her, looked at the spot she'd indicated. "Keep your hand there." He turned to the gate. Kneeling by its side, he put his right arm through the last gap, rested the side of his head against the iron rail, then, his gaze on Helena's hand, directed his fingers to the opposing spot. If he didn't lift the key cleanly but dropped it . . .

His fingertips touched metal, and he stopped. Froze. Then, very delicately, he reached farther, tracing the outline of the key, following the cord up to the nail from which it hung. He stretched and slipped his fingers through the cord, crooked them, lifted.

Withdrew his arm and looked down at the heavy key in his palm.

Before he could react, Helena swiped it up. He caught her as she moved past him to the lock and hauled her down.

"The guards?"

She turned her face to him, whispered back, "These are the kitchen gardens—they check here only once early, then once again close to dawn."

He nodded, released her. Stood and dusted his knee while she carefully slid the cumbersome key into the old lock, then turned. Phillipe helped her; together they wrestled the tumblers over. Tentatively, clearly worried about the possibility of squeaks, Phillipe eased the gate open. The hinges grated, but the sound was low and wouldn't carry.

Visibly sagging with relief, Helena followed Phillipe into the garden, onto the beaten path leading to the house. Sebastian followed, paused, watched his two collaborators sneak quietly and eagerly up the path. Then he sighed, shook his head, carefully closed the gate, locked it, and removed the key.

Helena glanced back and saw him tuck the key into his coat pocket. They'd all worn dull colors. Under her dark cloak, her gown was dark brown, plain and unadorned now she'd removed all the braid; Phillipe had worn black. Sebastian was wearing a coat and breeches of a brownish gray with soft, thigh-high boots of a similar hue. The color suited him in daylight, but in night's faint light he appeared a phantom of the shadows, unreal—surely a figment of a young woman's imagination as he walked softly toward her, his prowling gait never more pronounced, the grace that invested his large body a symphony to her senses.

He joined her, and she had to force herself to breathe. She nodded to the archway where Phillipe waited. "We must avoid the servants' quarters. We can reach the rose garden through there. Only Marie, Fabien's wife, has rooms in that wing. As she is ill"—she shrugged—"it will most likely be the safest place to get in."

They saw no guards as they circled the stone house with three floors and more of windows looking out on them. Despite the fact that it was long after midnight, Sebastian's nape prickled. He could see the distant wing Helena was making for; while following in her wake, he scanned the nearer ground-floor rooms.

They were flitting past a stand of rhododendrons when he reached out and caught her arm. "What's through there?"

He pointed at a pair of narrow doors opening to a small paved area. Helena leaned back to whisper, "A small parlor."

Sebastian slid his fingers to her hand and gripped, then signaled with his head to Phillipe. Drawing Helena with him, he cut through the intervening garden and slid into the shadows close by the house.

She'd followed without protest, but now she asked, "Why this?"

Sebastian studied the narrow doors. "Watch." He bent his knees, set his shoulder to the place where the two halves came together at the lock, braced his upper arm along the join. Then he gave a sharp shove.

With a click, the lock popped. The doors swung ajar.

Helena stared. "How . . . simple."

Sebastian pushed the door wide, bowed her in, then followed. Phillipe joined them; Sebastian shut the door, then looked around. The room was small, neat, and quietly elegant. He joined Helena by the main door, put a hand on her wrist to stop her from opening it. "How far to your sister's chamber?"

"Not as far as it would have been—the chamber she usually has is in the central wing."

He considered, then looked at Phillipe. "You go first, but go slowly. We'll follow. Stroll along; don't skulk. If any servants should appear, they'll think you've just returned."

Phillipe nodded. Sebastian let Helena open the door. Phillipe led the way as directed; they flitted in his wake like ghosts.

They had to climb the main stairs; Helena breathed easier when they reached the top and entered the long gallery. The moon had at last risen. Silver light poured through the many long windows, mercilously illuminating the long room. She and Sebastian hugged the inner wall as they followed Phillipe, who at Sebastian's wave hurried through the gallery.

They slowed again as they entered the maze of corridors beyond. Helena's tension eased as panic left her and eagerness and anticipation took hold. In minutes she would see Ariele again, know she was safe. See that she was.

Sebastian tugged on her hand, then lowered his head to whisper, "Where are Fabien's apartments?"

"That way." She waved back. "At the end of the gallery, he goes the other way."

Ahead, Phillipe stopped before a door. He looked back and waited until they joined him. "Is this it?"

Helena nodded.

Sebastian closed his hand on her arm. "You go in. We'll wait here until you're sure she won't take fright." He tightened his grip briefly, then released her. "Make sure she understands the need for silence."

Helena nodded. She held his gaze, then closed her hand briefly over his. Turning to the door, she eased up the latch and slipped in.

Chapter Thirteen

*H*elena forced herself to pause inside the door until
her eyes adjusted. Then she rounded the curtained bed,
knowing Ariele would be sleeping facing away from
the door. Quietly parting the curtains, she looked in,
saw the mound under the covers, saw the sheen of
Ariele's honey-brown hair splayed across the pillows,
saw the pale sliver of one white cheek.

Smiling, tears threatening, Helena stepped closer.

"Ariele? Ariele—wake up, *mon petit chou*."

Brown lashes flickered, lifted; eyes greener than Helena's peeked out, then Ariele smiled sleepily. Her lids
fell again.

Helena reached out and shook her gently.

Ariele's eyes opened fully. She stared at Helena, surprised wonder in her face. Then, with a cry of joy, she
threw herself into Helena's arms. "It *is* you! *Mon Dieu!*
I thought you were a dream."

"Sssh." Helena hugged her fiercely, closed her eyes
for one rapturous moment, and gave thanks. Then she
pushed Ariele away, held her at arm's length. "We have
to leave. *Vite*. Phillipe and another—the Englishman I

am to marry—are waiting beyond the door. But we must hurry. You must dress—dark clothes."

Ariele had never been slow-witted. She'd scurried from the bed even before Helena had finished speaking. She ran to her armoire, searched, pulled out a brown gown, showed it to Helena.

"Yes—that's perfect."

"Where are we going?" Ariele scrambled into the gown.

"To England. Fabien . . . he is mad."

"Mad?" Ariele cocked her head. "Disgustingly arrogant, true, but . . ." She shrugged. "So he does not know we are leaving?"

"No." Helena came to help with her laces. "We must be very quiet. And we can take only a small bag—just your brushes and important things."

"I didn't bring much with me from Cameralle. I'd hoped to go home for Christmas."

Helena tied off the laces, then hugged her. "*Ma petite*, we won't see home for some time—"

"Yes, but think of the adventure!"

Reassured, Helena left Ariele brushing out her long hair while she hunted and found a small bag in the armoire, then piled all the little items from the dressing table into it, then hurried to the prie-dieu to collect prayer book and crucifix.

A tap on the door had them both looking up; Phillipe peered in. He saw Ariele and slipped in, crossed to her. Sebastian followed him into the room. Helena stared at him, drank in his strength, calmed her tense nerves. All would be well.

Sebastian returned Helena's regard, then, satisfied that all was as she'd expected, switched his gaze to Phillipe and the young girl he assumed was Ariele. Phillipe was whispering earnestly, explaining his part in things. The girl was listening politely.

Ariele was taller than Helena, larger overall, yet not above average. Her hair lay like a curtain of old gold down her back. He could see her profile, as perfect as Helena's. See her hands gesture, swift and delicate, reassuring Phillipe and hushing his apologies.

Then she sensed his presence and turned. Smiled shyly.

He walked forward, held out his hand.

She reacted instinctively and laid her fingers in his. He bowed over them. Ariele shook off her surprise and curtsied prettily.

Sebastian raised her. "I'm honored to meet you, my dear, but I think we should leave further pleasantries until later. We must leave immediately." He looked into eyes that were darker than Helena's, a different shade of green. "If all goes as we plan, we'll have years to get to know each other better."

Ariele tilted her head at that, looked at him almost challengingly. The same fire that burned so brightly in Helena had not missed Ariele.

Sebastian laughed softly; leaning closer, he dropped a light kiss on Ariele's forehead. "Do not fence with me, *ma petite*. You are not—yet—in your sister's league."

Ariele made a sound that could only be described as a chortle. She shot a quick glance at Helena, her face alight with innocent query. No mystery why Phillipe had been smitten.

Releasing her hand, Sebastian stepped back. "Come. We dare not dally."

Helena had remained rooted to the spot watching the interplay between her sister and him; now she bustled up, took the brush from Ariele's hand, dropped it in the bag, and cinched the drawstring tight. She looked at him. "We are ready."

He took her hand, kissed her tense fingers. "Good. This is what we'll do."

They left the room, four silent shadows slipping through the slumbering house. As before, Phillipe led the way; Ariele, in her cloak with the hood already up, followed at his heels, much as if he'd been sent to summon her and she was grumpily complying. They walked swiftly but quietly down the corridors. A few yards behind, Helena, also fully cloaked, followed with Sebastian, keeping to the shadows as much as they could.

Helena's heart thumped. As she hurried along, she felt giddy. They were nearly free—all of them. And Ariele liked Sebastian. The two people she loved the most would get on. Relief mingled with anxiety; lingering trepidation weighed against her burgeoning joy.

They reached the gallery and started along it.

A single, confident footstep was all the warning they had before Fabien swung into the gallery from the other end. He'd taken three long strides before he halted, staring. The moonlight sheened his fair hair. Booted and spurred, dressed as always in unrelieved black, he was carrying his riding gloves in one hand. His rapier was at his side.

For one instant they all stood transfixed in the light of the moon.

Then Helena heard a soft curse, and Sebastian stepped past her. The sibilant hiss as his rapier left its scabbard shimmered, menacing in the tense quiet.

It was immediately answered by a similar hiss as Fabien's rapier flashed into the night.

What followed, Helena later understood, took but a few minutes, yet in her mind each action was ponderous, laden with meanings, subtle hints, and portents.

Like the smile that curved Fabien's lips as he recognized Sebastian, the unholy light that flared in his dark eyes.

The fact that Fabien was considered a master swordsman flashed into her mind. She felt ill for one instant, then rallied. Remembered Sebastian's confidence over younger men challenging him—remembered that indeed they didn't.

The memory allowed her to grab back her wits, to hold panic at bay—to think. Phillipe had stepped back, shrinking against the windows. He'd pulled Ariele with him.

In the center of the gallery, bathed in moonlight, Sebastian and Fabien slowly circled, each waiting for the other to make the first move.

With a sudden rush, Fabien did—the clash of steel made Helena flinch, but she kept her eyes open, fixed on the scene, and saw Sebastian parry the attack without apparent effort.

Fabien was shorter by a few inches and slighter—faster on his feet. Sebastian was almost certainly the stronger and had a longer reach.

Again Fabien lunged; again Sebastian deflected his blade with ease.

Helena heard thumping, looked down at their feet. Realized . . .

Dragging in a breath, she eased along the wall, then slipped past them and fled to the gallery's end. There she dragged the doors shut, turned the key. Swung around and looked back to see Phillipe and Ariele doing the same at the gallery's other end. If the servants heard the thumps and came to investigate, the doors would buy them precious time.

Sebastian was aware of the problem—he saw the ends of Fabien's lips lift mockingly and knew his old foe had seen it, too. The longer he and Fabien danced in the moonlight, the less likely they were to escape, regardless of the outcome of their play.

And play it was. Neither would kill; it was not in their natures. To triumph, yes, but what was the point of winning if one didn't get to gloat over the vanquished? Besides, they were both noble born. Either one's dying could prove difficult for the other to explain, especially as one was on foreign soil. Killing was not worth the effort. So they'd aim to disarm, to wound, to win.

But in the larger game—the more important game—the advantage was now Fabien's. Sebastian flicked aside a probing thrust and set his mind to the task of wresting it from him.

Confident that, regardless, he was risking nothing more than his arm, Fabien was eager to engage. They were both past masters; for Fabien this meeting was long overdue. The Frenchman had speed, but Sebastian had strength and an agility he consistently disguised. He pushed Fabien back, turning parry into thrust, declining to follow Fabien's answering feint in favor of another riposte that had his opponent quickly retreating.

Feinting, trying to lure him into opening his guard, relying on his quickness to keep him safe—that was Fabien's style. Sebastian held back from any feints, projected his own style as straightforward, direct—undisguised. He needed to finish this quickly; against that, the only sure way past Fabien's skill was to fool him, and that meant time.

Meant minutes of skirmishing, enough to establish his assumed style in Fabien's mind. Meant backing Fabien toward one corner of the gallery—near where Helena watched, her back to the doors. He wished her elsewhere but couldn't shift his attention from Fabien long enough to send her away.

The instant he had Fabien positioned where he wanted him, he launched a textbook series of thrust-counter-thrust, backing the Frenchman so he suddenly realized that being stuck in a corner with a stronger and larger opponent before him wasn't the wisest place to be.

Fabien started looking for a way out.

Sebastian gave it to him.

Feinted to his left.

Fabien saw the opening, stepped left, lunged—

Sebastian heard a strangled scream. Already committed, he dropped, turned his wrist and sent his point flashing upward—in the same instant saw an explosion of brown coming in from his left.

With his weight behind his blade, his body extending into the lunge, he couldn't stop her.

Could only watch in horror as she appeared between them, screening the space where his left chest had been, where she'd thought Fabien was aiming.

He glanced at Fabien—saw his own horror reflected in his face.

Too late—there was nothing Fabien could do to stop his lunge. His rapier took Helena in the shoulder.

Sebastian heard her cry as his own blade covered the last inches, couldn't stop his guttural roar, couldn't prevent his wrist rolling, deflecting the point three inches inward.

Fabien tried to spin away but couldn't avoid the deadly thrust. The point pierced his coat, bit, and sank into flesh, slid along a rib—

Sebastian pulled back, released the rapier before he completed the killing stroke. Let the weapon clatter to the floor as he caught Helena.

Fabien staggered, then collapsed against the wall and slid down, one hand pressed to his side, his face paler than death. As he lowered Helena to the floor, then pulled Fabien's blade free, Sebastian was aware of the Frenchman's burning gaze. Knew he hadn't meant to harm Helena.

Ariele and Phillipe reached them in a rush. Sebastian

steeled himself to deal with hysterics—instead, Ariele checked the wound, then set about ripping the flounce from her petticoat, instructing Phillipe to fetch Fabien's cravat.

Phillipe approached cautiously, but Fabien, moving weakly, gave up the cravat of his own accord, without comment.

Sebastian's opinion of Helena's sister increased by leaps and bounds. Cradling Helena, he watched as Ariele efficiently formed a pad, then bound it over the narrow wound. She looked into his face, a question in her eyes. He nodded. "She'll live."

As long as she was properly cared for.

She'd swooned from the shock and pain; she was still unconscious, but not deeply. Relinquishing his position to Ariele, Sebastian stood and walked to Fabien. He bent and picked up his rapier, flicked out a handkerchief and wiped the blade.

Fabien's gaze had remained on Helena. Now he glanced up at Sebastian. "You will tell her I never meant that?"

Sebastian met his gaze. "If she doesn't already know."

Fabien closed his eyes and shuddered. "*Sacre dieu!* Women! What they do . . ." He grimaced with pain but continued, his voice weakening, "She was ever unpredictable."

Sebastian hesitated, then murmured, "She's too much like us—didn't that ever occur to you?"

"*Mais, oui*—of course. She schemes and plots and thinks quickly, yet she is hardly up to our weight."

Sebastian humphed. He looked down on his old foe, knew the wound he'd delivered would cause serious discomfort for weeks. Counseled himself that that, together with all that would come, was fair payment for all Helena had suffered—that he couldn't, no matter what he wished, exact further physical retribution. "You and your games—I gave them up years ago. Why do you still play them?"

Fabien opened his eyes, looked up, then shrugged— grimaced again. "Ennui, I suppose. What else is there to do?"

Sebastian considered him, shook his head. "You're a fool."

"Fool? *Me?*" Fabien tried to laugh, but pain cut off the sound. His eyes closed again, tight, but still he inclined his head to where Helena lay. "It is not I who has, it appears, been caught in the oldest trap of all."

Sebastian looked down at Fabien's white face and wondered if he should mention that he knew Fabien had been caught in the same trap many long years before. But in Fabien's case there'd been no happy ending, only a prolonged, slowly deepening sorrow. His Marie had proved too weak to bear children, and now she was dying. At the thought, Sebastian's lingering anger faded. Declining to touch on the matter or mention that he knew Fabien's closely guarded truth, he slid his rapier back into its sheath. Looked at Helena. "Blood will tell, I suppose."

Fabien frowned, then glanced up at him.

Sebastian didn't deign to explain.

Fabien looked again at the others. "One thing I must know. Whose estates are larger—hers or yours?"

Sebastian grinned grimly. "Mine."

Fabien sighed. "Well, you have won this round, *mon ami*." His voice faded; he closed his eyes. "But you have yet to win free."

Sebastian saw Fabien's muscles relax, saw him slip into unconsciousness. Hunkering down, he briefly checked Fabien's wound—confirmed it was serious but not immediately life threatening. Standing, Sebastian beckoned Phillipe, pointed to a door off the gallery. "What's through there?"

It was the library; they left Fabien laid out on the chaise before the cold hearth, hands and feet bound with curtain cords, gagged with his handkerchief. He'd be found soon enough.

They returned to Ariele and Helena, who was now conscious but clearly in pain. White-faced, Phillipe considered her, then turned to Sebastian. "How will we manage now?"

He told them, quickly, succinctly. From the silence beyond the doors, they assumed that no servants had heard the thuds and muffled screams. "But if they have, we can use it to strengthen our hand."

"You"—he pointed at Phillipe—"and Helena have just arrived with Fabien. He summoned you posthaste and met you at Montsurs, but you were delayed, and so you have only just arrived. He has ordered you both to take Ariele to Paris. He's retired, leaving you to it— but he wants her gone immediately. He said he is not to be disturbed, he has a headache."

"A migraine." Helena's voice floated up, weak but distinct. "He is prey to migraines—the staff know it is worth their heads to disturb him at such times."

"Perfect. He has a migraine and has left you with specific orders to take Ariele and leave now. The 'now,' for reasons unknown to you, is vital—Fabien has made that clear." Sebastian looked at Ariele. "You are not happy at being roused from your bed and marched off to Paris." He looked down at her feet, at the pattens she'd put on. "You're going to clump down the stairs and be difficult and scowl. Wail if you need to cover any sound. Helena will appear to be holding you—in reality you will be holding her."

He looked down at Helena. "Can you walk, *mignonne*?"

Lips tightly set, she nodded.

He paused, looking down at her, but accepted her word. He couldn't think of any other way to get her safely out of the house. "*Bon.*" He looked at Phillipe. "So it's time for you to summon the carriage. Clatter down the stairs in a rush and set everyone in a panic. Do *not* answer any questions as to how you arrived here—brush them aside. You must be totally focused on getting Ariele away at once as your uncle has ordered. If the staff balk, tell them Fabien is lying down in his chamber with a migraine—and suggest they check with him." He paused, considered the young man. "When they question you, behave as Fabien would—or as I would. You've been helping get Ariele moving, but now Helena is bringing her along, and you want the carriage there *now*, so there'll be no further delay . . ."

Phillipe was nodding. "Yes, I see."

Sebastian continued, outlining the last phase of his plan. Finally he clapped Phillipe on the shoulder. "Go, then—we'll listen from here and come down as the carriage arrives. We don't want Helena on her feet any longer than necessary."

Phillipe nodded, opened the gallery doors, looked out—then looked back, nodded again, and went.

They listened to his footsteps, confident and definite as he strode along, fade. Sebastian hunkered down beside Helena. She gripped his sleeve, looked into his face. "And you? How will you join us?"

He caught her hand, raised it to his lips. "I don't propose to let you out of my sight, *mignonne*. Once you're in the coach, I'll join you."

Helena accepted his word, marshaled her strength for the battle to come. Although her wound had bled copiously and the blood had seeped into her thick cloak, the wool was dark enough to hide the stain.

They heard the furor as Phillipe sent up a shout and roused the servants. The butler balked at taking his orders, but Phillipe dealt with him with a high-handed arrogance that would have done Fabien proud.

He got the coach ordered. From the shadows of the upstairs foyer, Sebastian and Ariele, with Helena supported between them, watched Phillipe pace agitatedly— for all the world as if he expected Fabien to appear and quietly inquire why he was still there.

His apprehension was contagious. Ten minutes after a footman had been sent flying to the stables, the stamp of hooves heralded the coach. Sebastian pressed his lips to Helena's temple, held her for an instant longer, then stepped back. "Go!"

Ariele glanced back at him. Then she scowled and muttered, scuffed her feet as if she were being dragged, all the time holding Helena, who clung to her.

From the hall below, Phillipe glanced up. "Where are they?" he inquired of no one in particular. "Come on— come *on*!" With quick strides he started up the stairs, then Helena and Ariele appeared at the top. "There you are!" Phillipe continued up. He came to Ariele's side but reached around her to surreptitiously help Helena.

"Into the coach, now. Don't be difficult. You don't want Uncle to come down, do you?"

Stepping down on the stairs, Helena gasped, swayed.

Ariele clutched and grouched louder. A trifle breathlessly.

Watching from the shadows above, Sebastian prayed. Saw Helena lift her head, nod all but imperceptibly. They continued on.

The butler was still fretting. He looked to Helena— she waved imperiously. "We must leave at once!"

Her voice was sharp, tight with pain, but they heard it as irritation.

It was enough. Everyone scurried out of their way, solicitously holding the door wide, then piling onto the steps to watch as the trio, clinging together, descended.

The clang of iron-shod hooves on the cobbles of the forecourt covered Sebastian's footsteps. He descended the stairs quickly, then slid into the shadows alongside the staircase. Everyone was on the front porch. Craning his neck, he could just see the coach. The timing was going to be critical.

Helena entered the coach first; Ariele quickly followed. Phillipe put his foot on the step, then paused, turned to the groom clinging to his perch at the coach's back, called him down, at the same time waving the footman to put up the steps and close the coach door. Mystified, the footman did as he was bid while Phillipe walked to the back of the coach to meet the groom.

Sebastian drew in a breath and started for the front door, striding confidently, his boot heels ringing on the marble floor. Startled, the butler and his minions, all still in their nightshirts, swung around, ready to bow and scrape to their master . . .

Their eyes widened. Jaws slackened.

Sebastian looked down his nose at them and walked straight through. They fell back, not daring to inconvenience him.

He strode on, descending the steps, his long stride effortless, eating the distance across the forecourt to the coach. He passed the befuddled footman returning to the house. Was conscious that the man turned and slowed, watching him. All the others were gathered on the porch, doing the same, totally bewildered as to what was going on, what they should do.

Sebastian glimpsed Helena's white face at the coach window. Raised a hand in salute. They'd done it—they were away.

His stride unfaltering, he shot a glance at Phillipe— nodded. Phillipe turned back to the groom.

Sebastian reached the coach. In one fluid movement he climbed to the box seat. Surprised, the coachman turned to him. Sebastian grabbed the reins, dropped them, grabbed the man and tossed him onto the patch of lawn on the other side of the coach.

Seizing the reins, Sebastian yelled, slapped the horses' rumps, then sat as the coach rocketed off. He glanced briefly back, saw the groom sprawled in the dust, saw Phillipe hanging on grimly in the groom's place.

Facing forward, Sebastian whipped up the horses. There were shouts, confused jabbering from behind, but the sounds quickly faded as he took the curve toward the fortress gates at speed.

The gates stood open.

Another carriage was driving in.

A gig, its horse in a lather.

The moon sailed forth. Sebastian's lips curved as he recognized the gig's driver and the passenger clinging to the rail, pointing at the coach bearing down upon them.

The gig cleared the gates. The drive was wide enough for only one carriage. Beside the drive lay a duck pond.

Sebastian urged the coach's four horses on. He drove the coach directly at the gig.

Louis yelled and hauled on the reins.

The gig slewed and careered down the bank into the pond.

Villard flew out and splashed down in the pond's center.

The coach swept on, straight for the gates.

Inside the coach, Helena heard the shouts, forced her eyes open, ignored the waves of pain.

She looked through the window—saw Louis, white-faced, cursing as he jumped from the gig, only to land in the mud.

Then the gates of Le Roc flashed past—and she knew she was free. She and Ariele. Totally free.

Relief was like a drug, spreading through her veins.

Her lids sank, fell.

The coach hit a rut.

Pain lanced through her. Blackness rose like a wave and dragged her down.

She woke to warmth, to softness and comfort, to the distant smell of baking. Mince pies. Sweet pastries. Rich baked fruit.

The aromas wafted her back to childhood, to memories of Christmases long past. To the time when her parents had been alive and the long corridors of Cam-cralle had been filled with boundless joy, with laughter, good cheer, and a pervasive, golden peace.

For minutes she hung, suspended in time, a ghostly visitor returning to savor past joys, past loves. Then the visions slowly faded.

The peace remained.

Inexorably, the present drew her back, the smells reminding her she was ravenously hungry. She remembered what had happened, felt the ache in her shoulder, the stiffness and the restriction of bandages.

Opening her eyes, she saw a window. There was snow on the sill, snow between the panes, ice patterns on the glass. Her eyes adjusting to the gray light, she looked farther, into the shadows beyond the window—and saw Sebastian sitting on a chair.

He was watching her. When she said nothing, he asked, "How do you feel?"

She blinked, drew in a deep breath, let it slowly out, easing past the pain. "Better."

"Your shoulder still hurts."

Not a question. "Yes, but . . ." She eased onto her back. "Not as badly. It's manageable, I think." Then she frowned. "Where are we?" She lifted her head. "Ariele?"

His lips curved briefly. "She's belowstairs with Phillipe. She's well and safe." He drew his chair closer to the bed.

Helena reached out a hand; he took it, clasped it between his. "So . . ." She was still puzzled but inexpressibly comforted by the warmth of his hands closing about hers. "We are still in France?"

"*Oui*. We couldn't travel far, so I rejiggered our plans."

"But . . ." She frowned at him. "You should have driven straight to Saint-Malo."

The look he bent on her told her not to be stupid. "You were injured and unconscious. I sent a message to the yacht and came here."

"But Fabien will follow."

"He'll undoubtedly try to, but he'll send to Saint-Malo or Calais. He'll search to the north, expecting us to run that way. Instead, we came south and away from the coast."

"But . . . how will we return to England?" She wriggled higher against the pillows, ignored the stabbing pain. "You must get back for Christmas—for your family gathering. And if Fabien is searching, we cannot stay here. We must—"

"*Mignonne,* be quiet."

When she fell silent, unsure, he continued, "All is arranged. My yacht will be waiting at Saint-Nazaire when we're ready to depart. We'll be home in good time for Christmas." His eyes, very blue, held hers. "There is nothing for you to do but recuperate. Once you're well enough to travel, we'll leave. Is there anything more you need to know?"

She looked at him, considered the asperity coloring his tone. Treasured it. She sighed and squeezed his hand. "I am a sad trial, am I not?"

He snorted. "You took years off my life. And Fabien's."

She frowned, recalling. "He did not wish to injure me, did he?"

"No—he was horrified. As was I." Sebastian considered her, then added, "He never intended to harm you. Or Ariele."

"Ariele? But—" She broke off, searching his face, then her eyes cleared. "It was a *ruse*?"

"A heartless one perhaps, but yes—it was the surest way to get you to do as he wished."

He could see her thinking back, remembering, reassessing. She shook her head. "He is a strange man."

"He's an unfulfilled man." Looking down at her lying in the bed, Sebastian knew that was true. Understood what it took for men like him and Fabien to be fulfilled. Accepted it.

Helena stirred, glanced at him. "There is one thing I do not yet know—tell me how you got this dagger of his."

He smiled. Looked down at her hand lying between his. Twining his fingers with hers, he lifted them to his lips, brushed a lingering kiss across them. "I won the dagger"—he lifted his gaze to her eyes—"on the night we first met."

Her eyes widened. "*Vraiment?* That was the reason you were after Collette's earring?"

"*Oui.* I won a large amount from Fabien's younger brother, so Fabien sought me out, to put me in my place. We English were widely known for our wild wagers. Fabien manipulated the scene so I could not refuse— not without losing face. He didn't, however, expect me to turn the tables and ask for the dagger to balance the scales. He'd brought half the glory of France with him—before them, he had to agree."

"But he sent word to the convent."

"Naturally. I knew he would. I pretended I was drunk and rolled off to my hotel—and from there straight to the convent." He looked into her eyes. "To meet you in the moonlight."

She smiled, not just with her lips but with her peridot eyes, now clear of all clouds and worries. There was more color in her cheeks than there had been when she woke. He squeezed her hand, then released it and stood. "*Bon.* So if you are now awake and reassured, I'll fetch Ariele and tell the innkeeper's wife you're ready to eat."

Her smile was all he'd hoped for. "Please." She eased up to sit; he helped her. "I will eat, and then we can leave."

"Tomorrow."

She looked at him, looked at the window. "But—"

"You will eat and rest and gather your strength, and *if* you're well in the morning, we'll leave."

She met his gaze, read his determination, then sighed and sank back on her pillows. "As you will, Your Grace."

"Indeed, *mignonne*—it will be precisely as I will."

Naturally, it was. Helena wondered if she would ever get used to the sensation of being swept up and along by a will more powerful than hers.

The rest of that day passed peacefully. In the afternoon she left her bed and dressed and ventured downstairs to view the tiny, family-run inn Sebastian had found tucked away in the valley of the Sarthe. There was no main road near; the family was truly grateful for their custom. She was sure they had no idea they were playing host to an English duke and a French comtesse.

They had the inn to themselves; a fresh snowfall had reduced all outdoor activities to the strictly necessary. The inn parlor was warm and cozy; it was pleasant to sit by the fire beside Sebastian and watch as he played chess with Phillipe.

There were only a few days remaining before *la nuit*

de Noël; the inn was already filled with a sense of calm, of peace—the expectation of joy. As she sat beside Sebastian, safe and warm, Helena found her heart free of worries, free of cares—for the first time in all the years since her parents had died, free to relax, to enjoy, free to let the calm, the peace, and the anticipation of joy assured flow in and fill her soul.

Closing her eyes, she felt the promise of the season pour in, overflow.

The next day she insisted she was well enough to travel. Sebastian viewed her critically but agreed. After a large breakfast they set out through the melting snow and found the way clearer the farther south they went. They reached Saint-Nazaire as evening approached. Sebastian's yacht lay bobbing by the quay—they spotted it from the cliffs above the town, Helena with some relief.

Then they were aboard. The sails were set; they filled with the freshening breeze, and the sleek vessel turned and headed home.

It was an uneventful passage, much of which she spent in the main cabin with Sebastian. Whether it was some ploy of his to keep her resting or, as she increasingly suspected, a delayed reaction to her injury, the danger he'd seen her in, those hours were filled with a heated passion more possessive and undisguised than all that had gone before.

Her murmurs that Ariele was in the next cabin had little effect; when she met her sister on the deck, strolling in the calm of the evening, Ariele only smiled shyly, a little too knowingly, and hugged her.

That her sister went in no fear of Sebastian was apparent; he treated her with fraternal indulgence while she laughed and teased. Helena watched them and felt her heart fill until she thought it might burst.

After a day and another night, the yacht laid into Newhaven with the morning tide. The coach was waiting; after breakfast, with her and Ariele tucked up in furs and silk wraps, they set out on the last leg of their journey home.

Home.

As the miles vanished beneath the heavy hooves of Sebastian's powerful horses, Helena considered that. Cameralle—in truth, she'd left her childhood home long ago. Le Roc? The fortress had never been home, not in the sense of a place of comfort, somewhere to return at journey's end. A place of contentment.

Somersham?

Her heart said yes even though her mind still questioned, still hesitated. Not over him, but, as the houses of London rose and engulfed them, she could not ignore the fact that both he and she held positions that embodied, and affected, more than their individual selves.

Family. Society. Politics.

Power.

His world, and hers. She'd been wrong to imagine she could ever walk away; it was in her blood as well as in his.

The horses checked, turned. She glanced out as the coach clattered into a fashionable square. The horses slowed even more, then halted before the steps leading up to an imposing mansion.

She glanced at Sebastian.

He met her gaze. "St. Ives House. This is Grosvenor Square."

She looked at the house. "Your town residence?"

"Ours. We'll stop here for half an hour. There are matters I need to check into, then we'll go on."

Ariele had been sleeping; now she stretched and shook out her gown—grimaced at its state.

"No matter." Sebastian laid his hand on her wrist briefly as he moved past her and descended to the pavement. He held out a commanding hand—helped Helena down, then Ariele. "My aunt Clara's at Somersham, and my sister, Augusta, too—they'll be thrilled to help organize gowns for you. But there's no one here at present, so you needn't worry."

Helena was relieved on the same score; she felt just a little bedraggled. Sebastian led her up the steps. The day was dark and gloomy; lights burned in the hall and lit the fanlight.

A very correct butler opened the door; seeing them, he struggled to suppress a delighted smile. He bowed low. "Welcome home, Your Grace."

Sebastian, leading Helena into the warmth and welcoming ambience of elegant luxury, raised a brow, directing a sharp glance his butler's way. "Why, Doyle?"

"We've been entertaining guests, Your Grace." With unimpaired calm, Doyle switched his gaze to Helena.

Sebastian sighed. "This is the comtesse d'Lisle—soon to be your mistress. Her sister, Mlle de Stansion, and M. de Sèvres." He glanced around as the butler took his cloak, then moved to take Helena's. "Where the devil are the footmen?"

"I regret that they're currently required in the library, my lord."

Sebastian turned to fix his gaze on the man. "Doyle—"

The door to their left opened. "*Really*, Doyle, what do you mean by it? Why haven't you shown whoever it is in? . . ."

Lady Almira Cynster froze on the threshold of the drawing room and stared—stunned—at Sebastian. Then she colored. "Sebastian! Well! I thought you were in the country or . . ." Her words trailed off as she took in their party. She dismissed Phillipe and Ariele with a cursory glance; her gaze darkened as it fixed on Helena. Her face set in uncompromising lines.

"What are you doing here, Almira?"

Sebastian's soft, almost menacing tones brought Almira's gaze back to his face. Helena quelled a shiver; it had been weeks since she'd last heard such tones from him.

"I . . . ah, well . . ." Almira gestured vaguely, coloring even more.

After a brief, uncomfortable pause, Sebastian murmured, "Doyle, please show mademoiselle and M. de Sèvres to the library . . . ah, no, I forget—perhaps the parlor will be more to their taste—and serve them suitable refreshments. Mademoiselle la comtesse and I will join them shortly. We will be leaving within the hour for Somersham."

"Indeed, Your Grace." Doyle bowed, then ushered

Ariele and Phillipe down the long hall and away.

"Now, Almira, perhaps we might continue in my drawing room, rather than the hall."

She turned with a humph and flounced ungracefully back to plump down in the middle of a silk-covered sofa. Accepting that if she was to become Sebastian's wife she would have to deal with the woman, Helena suppressed the urge to slink cravenly away with Ariele and Phillipe; instead she let Sebastian lead her into the drawing room.

A footman materialized and shut the door behind them. If it had been any other lady, Helena would have felt dismayed to be seen in her brown gown, washed and with the hole at the shoulder repaired by Ariele, but still crumpled and stained. Almira, however . . . she simply couldn't consider the woman as one whose opinion should worry her.

As they neared the sofa, she saw that the table before it supported teapot, cups and saucers, and two plates with biscuits and cakes. There were four cups set out, all with tea in them, three untouched.

Sebastian regarded the display and faintly raised one brow. "I repeat—what are you doing here, Almira?"

His tone was softer, less frightening.

Almira humphed. "I'm practicing, aren't I? I'll have to do it someday—indeed, we should be living here now. Scandalous to have such a great house with no lady to run it."

"I agree—at least with your last statement. So you'll be pleased to hear that Mlle d'Lisle has consented to become my wife. My duchess."

Reaching for her teacup, Almira stilled, then looked up. "Don't be daft!" Her face filled with dismissive contempt. "They all said you were going to marry her, but you've just spent the better part of a week gadding about alone with her." She snorted and picked up her cup. "You won't catch me with that. You can't marry her—not now. Think of the scandal."

The thought of the scandal clearly heartened Almira; she smiled gloatingly as she lowered her cup.

Sebastian regarded her, then sighed. "Almira, I don't know why you fail to perceive it, but as I've told you before, there's a vast difference between the unwritten laws that govern the conduct of one such as I, or Mlle d'Lisle, and those that apply to the bourgeoisie." His tone left little doubt as to the difference. "Hence, you will most definitely be required to attend our wedding, and that in the not overly distant future."

The delicate cup cradled between her hands, Almira stared blankly at him. Then she suddenly set down the cup. "Charles! You must see him."

She surged to her feet. Sebastian stayed her with an upraised hand. "You will bring him to Somersham as usual—I'll see him there."

Almira pouted. "There'll be others there. He's your heir—you must spend more time with him. Besides, he's here."

"*Here?*" The single word was loaded with foreboding. "Where? No—silly question. I take it he's in the library?"

"Well, what of it? It'll be his one day . . ."

Sebastian whirled and strode for the door.

"Well, it *will*!" Almira hurried after him.

Towed along, her hand locked in Sebastian's, Helena heard him mutter as he hauled open the drawing room door, "Not if I have anything to say about it."

The library was two doors along; a footman saw them coming and flung the door wide. The scene they came upon would have been farcical if it hadn't been so strange. Three footmen stood in a wide ring around a toddler, who was sitting on a rug some way before the hearth. The little boy simply sat, face glum, and stared woodenly at the dark shelves lining the long room.

The child was instantly recognizable as Almira's—the same round face and receding chin, the same ruddy complexion.

She rushed past them and swept the boy up in her arms. To Helena's surprise, the child showed no reaction, but simply turned his wooden gaze on Sebastian and her.

"*See!*" Almira all but thrust the boy at Sebastian. "You don't have to marry her—there's no need! You already have an heir—"

"*Almira!*"

The single word cracked; shocked, Almira blinked, shut her mouth.

Helena glanced at Sebastian, sensed him rein in his temper, cast quickly about for the best direction to take.

Then he released her hand; stepping between Almira and her, he took Almira by the elbow. "Come. It's time you went home." He led her up the long room toward the door. "Mlle d'Lisle and I will be married at Somersham; you will bring Charles there, and you will both attend the wedding. Helena will then be my duchess. After that it will not be appropriate for you to call here while we are not in residence. Do you understand?"

Almira paused; even across the width of the room, Helena could sense her frustrated puzzlement. "She will be your duchess."

"Yes." Sebastian paused, then added, "And her son will be my heir."

Almira looked back at him; her face slowly leached to its previous wooden state. "Well, then." Hoisting Charles in her arms, she turned to the door that a footman held open. "Of course, if she's to be your duchess, then there's no need for me to come and take charge of things here."

"Indeed."

"Well, good-bye, then." Without a backward glance, Almira went out.

Sebastian gestured, and the footmen—all, Helena noticed, looking hugely relieved—quickly left. They shut the door behind them; his expression distant, Sebastian walked back to her. Then he shook his head, looked up, and met her gaze. "I regret that that is what you'll have to deal with. But there's no one more difficult, that I can promise."

She smiled, wondering . . .

He looked at her, into her eyes, then sighed and took her hands. "*Mignonne*, we will get along a great deal better if you will simply tell me your thoughts, rather than leaving me to guess them."

She frowned at him, uncertain.

His next sigh was less patient. "You're worrying again—about what?"

She blinked, suppressed a smile, considered, then, drawing her hands from his, walked to the nearby window, a wide bay looking over a lawn. The shrubs surrounding the lawn were wet and gleaming, bejeweled by the misty rain.

She owed him so much—her freedom, Ariele's as well. She was more than willing to give him the rest of her life in recompense—to put up with his dictatorial ways, to bow to the possessiveness that was so much a part of him. That would be the least of a fair exchange.

Yet . . . perhaps she owed him still more.

Something that only she could grant him.

Perhaps she owed him his freedom, too.

"You said—before, at Somersham—that you had a question you were waiting to ask me, once I was ready to give you an answer." She lifted her head, drew in a breath, surprised to discover how tight her chest felt. "I wish you to know that I will understand if you no longer, truly, in your heart, wish to ask me that question."

She held up a hand to stop him from speaking. "I realize you must marry, but there are many others who could be your duchess. Others to whom you would not be . . . bound, as you are to me. As I am to you."

Looking across the garden, she forced herself to say, her voice quiet, clear, "You never wished to marry, perhaps because you never wished to be bound, as you will be if we wed. If we marry, you will never be free— the chains will always be there, holding us, linking us."

"And what of you?" His voice was deep, low. "Will you not be equally bound, equally snared?"

Her lips curved fractionally. "You know the answer." She glanced at him, met his blue gaze. "Regardless of whether we marry or not, I will always be yours. I will never be free of you." After an instant she added, "And I do not wish to be."

The declaration—and her offer of freedom—hung between them. She slowly drew breath and looked back at the lawns, at the glistening shrubs.

He watched her, unmoving; a long moment passed, then she sensed him draw near. His arms came around her, closed, then locked tight. He bent his head, held her close, leaned his chin against her temple.

Then he spoke, his voice low.

"No power on earth could make me give you up. The power that rules the heavens would never let me live without you. And that doesn't mean as duke and mistress, but as day-to-day lovers—husband and wife." Easing his hold, he turned her, met her gaze. "You are the only woman I have ever thought of marrying, the only woman I can imagine as my duchess. And yes, I feel chained, and no, I do not appreciate the sensation, but for you—for the prize of having you as my wife—I will bear those chains gladly."

She studied his eyes; his emotions were for once unmasked, etched clearly in the burning blue. She read them, acknowledged their truth, accepted it. Still . . . "Almira mentioned scandal. Tell me truly—is she correct?"

His lips curved, his smile a trifle wry. "No scandal. In

France it may be different, but here—it's not actually considered possible to create a scandal through traveling with one's betrothed."

"But we're not . . ." She tilted her head, considered his eyes. "What aren't you telling me?"

"I wasn't sure how long we'd be away, so . . . I sent an announcement to the Clerk of the Court for inclusion in the Court Circular."

She felt her eyes widen as realization dawned. "*Before* we left Somersham?"

"Before you take umbrage, pray consider this point." Capturing her hands, he raised them to his lips, captured her gaze with his eyes. "If you now refuse me, you'll expose me to the ridicule of the entire ton. I've laid my heart and my honor at your feet, publicly— they're yours to trample if you choose."

He was manipulating her again—she knew it. Trample his heart? All she wanted was to cherish it. "Humph!" It was hard to frown when her heart was soaring. Lifting her chin, she nodded. "Very well—you may ask me your question now."

He smiled, not triumphant but wistfully grateful, and her heart turned over.

"*Mignonne*, will you be mine? Will you marry me and be my duchess—my partner in all my enterprises . . . my wife for the rest of my days?"

Yes seemed far too simple. "You already know my answer."

He shook his head, his smile deepening. "I would never be so foolish as to take you for granted. You must tell me."

She couldn't not laugh. "Yes."

He arched a brow. "Just yes?"

She smiled gloriously, reached up and twined her arms about his neck. "Yes with all my heart. Yes with all my soul."

There was nothing more to say.

In perfect accord they traveled on to Somersham as Sebastian had decreed, but when they arrived, he discovered that, powerful though he might be, there were yet some things beyond his control.

The huge house was full, filled to the rafters with family and friends, all waiting to hear their news.

"I *said* just the usual crowd." He bent a narrow-eyed look on Augusta as, beaming and bright, she kissed his cheek. "You've assembled half the ton!"

Augusta pulled a face at him. "It wasn't me who sent a notice to the Clerk. After that, what would you do? You can hardly expect the ton *not* to be interested in your nuptials."

"Indeed, dear boy." Clara was in alt. "Such a *momentous* occasion! Of course everyone wanted to be here. We could hardly turn them away."

Augusta embraced Helena warmly. "I'm so pleased, as is everyone here! And I hope you won't think us too busy, but Clara and I knew how it would be—my brother would never let a little thing like a wedding gown stand in his way—so we've had a gown, my mother's old gown, remade. It should fit—we used the gowns you left here to match, and Marjorie's been so helpful. I do hope you like it."

"I'm sure . . ." Helena's head was whirling, but she couldn't keep the smile from her face. She introduced Ariele, who Augusta greeted with glee.

"Sixteen? Oh, my dear, you'll do wonderfully well!"

Phillipe, understandably, frowned when he was introduced, but Augusta didn't notice. Ariele flashed him a quick smile, and he brightened. Before Helena could pay more attention herself, Augusta gathered her and Ariele and waved her fingers at her brother. "You'll have to fend for yourself, Your Grace. The ladies have been waiting to meet Helena, and she'll want to change first." She glanced over her shoulder as she urged Helena and Ariele to the stairs. "You might want to check in the library. Last time I looked in, they'd broached your best brandy. You know, that French stuff you had brought in by water . . ."

Sebastian cursed beneath his breath. He frowned at his sister, who paid not the slightest heed. With a muttered imprecation, he set off for the library.

The front hall and all the major rooms were bedecked with holly wreaths and evergreens, the bustle and cheer of the season augmented and heightened by the excitement of their wedding. Huge logs burned in every grate; the smell of yuletide baking and mulled wine spiced the air.

Christmas was upon them; a time to trust, a time to give. A time to share.

Everyone gathered in the great house felt the inexorable rise of the tide, experienced the welling joy.

So it was on the morning of Christmas Eve, with snow covering the grass, crisped by a hard frost and scattered with diamonds, a gift from the sun that shone in the clear sky, Helena stood in the chapel in the grounds of Somersham Place and took the vows that would bind her to Sebastian, to his home, to his family, for all time. Heard him take the corresponding vows to protect and cherish her, now and forever.

In the atmosphere of blessed peace, of joy in love, in the time of the year when those emotions held sway and touched every heart, they were married.

She turned to him, set back the delicate veil that had been his mother's, noting the jeweled lights playing over them as the sun shone in benediction through the rose window. She went into his arms, felt them close around her. Knew she was safe.

Knew she was free—free to live her life under the protection of a loving tyrant.

She lifted her face, and they kissed.

And the bells rang out, joyously pealing in salute to the day, in salute to the season—in salute to the love that bound their hearts.

Frost etched the glass in myriad patterns in the window beside which Sebastian sat writing. It was the next morning, and the huge house lay still, slumbering lazily, the guests too worn out by the revelry of the day before to bestir themselves so soon.

In the large, luxuriously appointed ducal bedchamber with its massive four-poster bed, the only sounds to break the silence were the scritch-scratch of his pen, crossing and recrossing the parchment, and an occasional crackle from the fire. Despite the freeze that had laid siege beyond the glass, the temperature in the room was comfortable enough for him to sit and write in just his robe.

On the desk, beside his hand, lay a dagger, old and worn, sheathed in leather. The hilt was gold, ornate, supporting a large, pigeon's-egg-size star ruby. Although worth a small fortune by weight alone, the dagger's true value could not be measured in any scale.

Reaching the end of his missive, Sebastian laid down his pen, then glanced at the bed. Helena hadn't stirred; he could see the tangle of her black curls lying on his pillow, just as he'd left them when he'd slipped from her side half an hour before.

She'd been welcomed into the Cynster clan with a joy that had transcended even the joy of the season. During their wedding breakfast, which had lasted all day, he'd seen her blossom—shackling Martin and George with her eyes, with her laughter and her smiles, making them forever her slaves, exchanging glances with Augusta, conspirator and companion, already firm friends. He'd seen her deal calmly and graciously with Almira, with an understanding he lacked. Watched her charm Arthur, the most reserved of them all.

As for the rest—the wider family, friends, and connections gathered to witness and pass judgment—as Therese Osbaldestone had baldly informed him, they all thought him a lucky dog.

Little did they know—much less did they see, except perhaps for Therese. Helena, after all, was too much like him.

He'd never be able to take her love for granted, to expect her love as his due. Powerful he might be, noble and wealthy, yet there remained one thing he could not command. So he would always be there, watching, always ready to protect her, to ensure that she remained forever his.

Such was the vulnerability of a conqueror.

Therese would doubtless say he'd got all he deserved.

Lips curving, he looked back at his letter. Read it through.

I am returning with this an item to which I believe you are entitled. You will recall the circumstances in which it came into my hands, seven years ago. What you never knew was that in sending me to the Convent des Jardinières de Marie, you set me in the path of your ward, then staying there.

That, my friend, was the one piece of information you lacked. We had met before you sent her to retrieve your item, met and exchanged a promise. In sending her to me to secure that item, you gave us the chance to revisit that earlier promise, to explore it as we had not had a chance to do before.

We have now explored the potential fully and have reached our own agreement. I am now in possession of something worth inexpressibly more than your item— and for that I must thank you. Our future, hers and mine, we owe to you.

Pray accept the enclosed item—yours once again— as a token of our thanks.

You will be interested to know that your ward was

*not seriously inconvenienced by the accident that un-
fortunately marred our recent visit. Her energy and
inventiveness are undimmed—to that I can personally
attest.*

And yes, mon ami, *she is now the Duchess of St.
Ives.*

Bonne chance—until next we cross swords.

Sebastian smiled, imagining Fabien reading it. He
signed the letter, then sanded it; as he replaced the
shaker, a rustling had him turning to the bed.

Brushing back her mane of hair, Helena smiled, languid and sultry, and sank back on the pillows. "What
are you doing?"

Sebastian grinned. "Writing to your guardian."

"Ah." She nodded, then lifted one hand and beckoned. The gold band he'd placed on her finger the day
before glinted. "I think now that it is I you should deal
with first, Your Grace."

His title on her lips, the Rs heavily rolled, was a blatant invitation.

Sebastian left the letter and rose, returned to the bed.

To her.

To the warmth of her arms.

To the promise in her kiss.

Afterword

Regretably, neither Sebastian, fifth Duke of St. Ives, nor Helena, his duchess, kept diaries. The following, however, was extracted from the diaries of the Reverend Julius Smedley, who filled the position of chaplain to the Duke of St. Ives from 1767 to 1794. Reverend Smedley officiated at the marriage of Sebastian and Helena and was a faithful recorder of all that took place in his circumscribed world. From him we learn that:

Ariele de Stansion and Phillipe de Sèvres remained at Somersham Place for some years, Phillipe assisting with the management of the estate and Ariele spending much time with her sister. She assisted at the difficult birth of Helena's only child, Sylvester. Phillipe remained devoted to Ariele through the years, and for her part, Ariele never looked at another, although there were gentlemen aplenty who sought to attract her notice. Consequently, with Sebastian's assistance, Phillipe bought a sizable holding north of Lincoln. He and Ariele married and moved north, and thus beyond the Reverend Smedley's purview.

The only other note of interest over those early years

of the duke's marriage was an oblique reference to the death of one Marie de Mordaunt, Comtesse de Vichesse, the wife of the duchess's and her sister's erstwhile guardian, also Phillipe's uncle.

Shortly after, the Terror came to France. Sebastian, working with Phillipe and his own extensive contacts in that country, had already acted to liquidate and remove to England much of Helena's and Ariele's inherited wealth, as well as a number of their loyal servants.

Phillipe's brother, Louis, disappeared during this time, and no more was heard of him.

The St. Iveses, after considerable searching, learned that the comte de Vichesse, called back from Paris to his fortress in the Loire, found Le Roc besieged. The tale that reached London was that the comte, at considerable risk to himself, gained access to the fortress, where he dismissed all his loyal retainers, instructing them to save themselves. Thereafter the comte disappeared. No further mention of the comte appears, either in the Reverend's diaries or indeed in any account of those times.

However, there is a fascinating mention of a French gentleman who arrived at Somersham a month after the fall of Le Roc. He is described as tall, lean, fair of face and hair, and indeed of address. He commonly wore all black and was observed to be a close comrade of the duke's; the pair were often to be seen fencing on the terrace.

In a departure from his usual love for detail, Reverend Smedley coyly leaves this French gentleman unnamed.

The Frenchman remained at Somersham for some months, but then, to the duke and duchess's clear sorrow, determined to leave England. He left Somersham for Southampton, there to take ship for the Americas.

What's next from *New York Times* bestselling author
Stephanie Laurens?

You'll see Simon (Amanda and Amelia Cynster's
brother!) meet his match as the Cynster men
continue their escapades in Stephanie's
newest romance,

The Perfect Lover

Coming February 2003 from William Morrow!

$\mathcal{R}$eaching the crest of the rise, she continued over and on—and only then realized he was following her. The glance she threw him was black, then she stopped and waited, swinging to face him as he halted before her.

She glared at him, her eyes like shards of dark flint. "You are *not* going to follow me all the way back to the Hall."

Portia didn't bother asking what Simon thought he was doing—they both knew the answer to that. They'd last seen each other at Christmas, seven months before, and then only distantly, surrounded by the combined hordes of their families. He hadn't had a chance then to get on her nerves, something that, ever since she'd turned fourteen, he'd seemed absolutely devoted to doing—if possible, every time they met.

He briefly studied her. Something—temper? decision?—flashed behind the deceptively soft blue of his eyes. Then his lips firmed; he stepped around her with his usual fluid grace, oddly unnerving in a man so large, and continued down the path.

She whirled and watched. He didn't go far but stopped a step beyond the point where the footpath to the village led down to the lane below.

Turning, he stared at her. "You're right. I'm not." With a wave, he indicated the path leading down.

Looking in that direction, she saw a curricle—his curricle—waiting in the lane.

"Your carriage awaits."

Lifting her gaze, she met his. Directly. He was blocking the path to the Hall—quite deliberately.

"I was intending to walk back."

He didn't waver. "Change your mind."

His tone—sheer male arrogance laced with a challenge she hadn't previously encountered and couldn't quite place—sent a peculiar shiver through her.

She let her glance flick over him; there was no overt aggression in his stance, yet she didn't for a moment doubt he could, and would, stop her if she tried to get past him.

Temper, wild willfulness—her customary response to such tactics, especially from him—flooded her, yet this time there were other, equally powerful, certainly more distracting, emotions in the mix. She stood perfectly still, her eyes level and locked in silent combat with his, the old struggle for supremacy yet . . . something had changed.

In him.

And in her.

Was it simply age? How long had it been since they'd last crossed wills like this—three years or more? Regardless, the field had altered, the battle was no longer the same. Something was fundamentally different, and she had no real idea what it was.

Her vow echoed in her head. She mentally shook aside the distraction, yet still she heard . . .

Head rising, she walked forward, every bit as deliberate as he.

She saw the watchfulness in his eyes condense, until his attention was focused exclusively on her. Halting before him, she held his gaze while another tingle of sensation slithered down her spine.

What did he see? Now she was looking, trying to see past his guard only to discover she could not. Odd surely, for they'd never before sought to hide their mutual dismissiveness, had they? What was he hiding? What was the reason for the subtle threat she sensed emanating from him?

She had no answers, but to her surprise, she wanted to know.

Drawing a deliberate breath, she evenly stated, "Very well."

Surprise flashed through his eyes, swiftly superceded by suspicion; she pivoted and looked down, stepping onto the path to the village, hiding her smile. Just so he wouldn't imagine he'd won, she added, "As it happens, one of my shoes is pinching."

She'd taken no more than three steps when she sensed him draw near, moving too swiftly, sweeping down on her.

Her senses leapt—she hesitated.

He didn't halt but bent and swept her up in his arms. Without breaking his stride, he juggled her—ignoring her strangled gasp—until he had her cradled, carrying her as if she weighed no more than a child.

"What do you think you're *doing?*"

Total incomprehension invested every word; she couldn't imagine . . . never before had he shown the slightest sign of reacting to her jibes in any physical way.

She was . . . what? Shocked? Or . . . ?

Thrusting aside the thought, she focused on his face as he briefly looked her way.

"Your shoe's pinching—we wouldn't want your delicate little foot to suffer unnecessary damage."

His tone was bland, his expression equally so—the look in his eyes would even pass for innocence.

Portia blinked. They both looked ahead. She considered protesting—and discarded the notion in the next thought. He was perfectly capable of arguing until they reached the curricle; she'd only make herself appear ridiculous, which was doubtless his aim.

As for struggling she was intensely aware—far more aware than she liked to be—that she was physically much weaker than he. The arms that were supporting her were doing so effortlessly; his stride never faltered, easy and assured. The hand clasping her thigh just above her knee—decently protected by her full skirts— grasped firmly; the width of his chest and its muscled hardness locked her in. If arguing was ridiculous, struggling would be ludicrous and equally futile. Normally, she never regarded his strength as anything she needed to consider or weigh; for the first time in their acquaintance, she realized that if he was going to bring physical contact into their equation, she would need to think again.

And not just purely on the basis of strength.

Being this close to him, in his arms, made her feel quite strange . . .

Distrust of that strangeness, wondering what it meant, distracted her, then he slowed and she refocused. With a flourish, he set her on the curricle's seat.

Startled, she grasped the railings, righting herself, out of habit drawing her skirts close so he could sit beside her, noting the equally startled face of Wilks, Simon's groom.

"Ah . . . afternoon, Miss Portia." Wide-eyed, Wilks bobbed as he handed the reins to Simon.

Wilks had to have witnessed the entire performance; he was waiting for her to explode, or at least say something cutting.

And he wasn't the only one.

She smiled and nodded with perfect equanimity. "Good afternoon, Wilks."

Wilks blinked but nodded respectfully, then hurried back to his place.

Simon glanced at her as he climbed up beside her, as if expecting her to bite, or at the very least snarl.

He wouldn't have believed a sweet smile so she faced forward, perfectly composed, for all the world as if her joining him in the curricle had been her idea. His wariness was worth every tithe of the effort such sunny compliance cost her.

The curricle jerked, then rolled forward as he set the bays trotting. The instant he had them bowling along, she asked, "How are your parents?"

A pause greeted her inquiry, but then he replied.

She nodded and launched into an account of her own family, all of whom he knew—their health, their whereabouts, their latest interests. As if he'd asked, she continued, "I came down with Lady O." For years, that had been their shorthand for Lady Osbaldestone, a connection of the Cynsters and an old friend of her family's, an ancient beldame who terrorized quite half the *ton*. "She spent the last weeks at the Chase, and then had to travel down here. She's an old friend of Lord Netherfield, did you know?" Viscount Netherfield was Lord Glossup's father and was presently visiting at Glossup Hall.

Simon was frowning. "No."

Portia smiled quite genuinely; she was fond of Lady O but Simon, in company with most young gentlemen of his ilk, found her perspicaciousness somewhat scarifying. "Luc insisted she shouldn't cross half the country alone, so I offered to come, too. The others who've arrived so far . . ." She rattled on, acquainting him with those present and those yet to arrive, precisely as any friendly, well-bred young lady might.

The suspicion in his eyes grew more and more pronounced.

By the time he swung the bays into the circular forecourt of Glossup Hall, Simon was thoroughly disconcerted. Not a common feeling for him; there wasn't much in *ton*nish life that could throw him off balance.

Except Portia.

If she'd railed at him, used her sharp tongue to its usual effect, all would have been normal. He wouldn't have enjoyed the encounter, but neither would he have felt this sudden disorientation.

Rack his brains though he might, he couldn't recall her ever behaving toward him with such . . . feminine softness was the description that sprang to mind. She was usually well armored and prickly; today, she'd apparently left her shield and spears behind.

The result was . . .

He reined in the bays, pulled on the brake, tossed the ribbons to Wilks, and stepped down.

Portia waited for him to come around the carriage and hand her down; he watched, expecting her to leap down in her usual, independent, don't-need-you way. Instead, when he offered his hand, she placed her slim fingers across it and let him assist her to alight with quite stunning grace.

She looked up and smiled when he released her. "Thank you." Her smile deepened; her eyes held his. "You were right. My foot is in an unquestionably better state than it otherwise would have been."

Her expression one of ineffable sweetness, she inclined her head and turned away; her eyes were so dark he hadn't been able to tell if the twinkle he'd thought he'd seen in them was merely a trick of the light.

He stood in the forecourt, grooms and footmen darting around him, and watched her slender figure glide into the house. Without a single backward glance, she disappeared into the shadows beyond the open front door.

The sound of gravel crunching as his curricle and pair were led away jerked him out of his abstraction. Outwardly impassive, inwardly a trifle grim, he strode to the door of Glossup Hall and followed her in.